Sturgeon's peers have this to say about THE STARS ARE THE STYX:

"If the stars are the Styx, then Sturgeon is Charon. You pay your money and get on his boat and—hang tight!—you're off on a journey you'll never forget. You'll see both Hell and the Elysian Fields."

—PHILIP JOSE FARMER

and this to say about Sturgeon the writer:

"Theodore Sturgeon is one of the finest writers alive, by any standards whatsoever. His knowledge of people and their world is profound, his gift of language incomparable. Reissue of his work is a genuine public service and should be an occasion of joy to all literate folk."

—POUL ANDERSON

"The most accomplished technician this field has produced, bar nobody."

—DAMON KNIGHT

"A writer of legendary skills and irresistible power . . . His work explores and illuminates the entire spectrum of emotion, human and otherwise, from beyond the infrared into the deep ultraviolet. . . ."

—ROBERT SILVERBERG

"Theodore Sturgeon has made himself the finest conscious artist science fiction ever had."

—JAMES BLISH

"Perhaps the best way I can tell you what I think of a Theodore Sturgeon story is to explain with what diligent interest, in the year 1940, I split every Sturgeon tale down the middle and fetched out its innards to see what made it function. I looked upon Sturgeon with a secret and gnawing jealousy."

—RAY BRADBURY

THE STARS
ARE
THE STYX

THEODORE STURGEON

A DELL BOOK

Published by
Dell Publishing Co., Inc.
1 Dag Hammarskjold Plaza
New York, New York 10017

Cover painting based on photographs by Jay K. Klein

"Tandy's Story" first published in *Galaxy*, April 1961
"Dazed" first published in *Galaxy*, September 1971
"Occam's Scalpel" first published in *If*, August 1971
"The Stars are the Styx" first published in *Galaxy*, October 1950
"The Other Man" first published in *Galaxy*, September 1956
"The Claustrophile" first published in *Galaxy*, August 1956
"When You're Smiling" first published in *Galaxy*, January 1955
"Granny Won't Knit" first published in *Galaxy*, May 1954
"The Education of Drusilla Strange" first published in *Galaxy*, March 1954
"Rule of Three" first published in *Galaxy*, January 1951

Reprinted with permission of *Galaxy* Magazine
(UPD Publishing Corporation).
Copyright © by UPD Publishing Corporation under
International, Universal and Pan-American
Copyright Conventions

To the one who has made
all of the worst of it,
all of the waiting,
worthwhile:

LADY JAYNE STURGEON

CONTENTS

TANDY'S STORY / 11

RULE OF THREE / 37

THE EDUCATION OF
DRUSILLA STRANGE / 75

GRANNY WON'T KNIT / 111

WHEN YOU'RE SMILING / 171

THE CLAUSTROPHILE / 201

THE OTHER MAN / 235

THE STARS ARE THE STYX / 289

OCCAM'S SCALPEL / 333

DAZED / 357

INTRODUCTION

These stories are all from *Galaxy* (except for the one which was in *If*, which really is the same thing). The birth and growth of *Galaxy* was the most important single element in my science fiction career except, of course, for my meeting in the late '30s with John Campbell.

Galaxy was Horace L. Gold's creation and for a time, I think, his life. When word went out that he had a new magazine, he was flooded, deluged, swamped, with manuscripts. He gave half of them to the late Groff Conklin and half to me. Groff and I read them and wrote comments, and then swapped our piles of paper. They then went back to Horace, who read them all and did the final selections. I don't know how he did it. I don't know how he did anything in those days; he wasn't well, and he was carrying burdens and undergoing stresses the like of which have foundered many a well man. Yet in all the years he ran *Galaxy,* he met his deadlines, he paid his writers, and he consistently refused to buy inferior work from his closest friends. What more could anyone want of an editor?

(I hear a voice from the fog crying, "I damn well want an editor who will keep his blue pencil the hell off my story!" and it is true that from time to time he made changes, and among these, there were alterations that drove certain writers and a reader or two straight up the wall. I learned, however, that if I had a certain turn of phrase or a sequence that I didn't want him to mess with, I would write "stet" in the margin—a printer's term which means "run it as it stands." And he never failed to respect it.)

Horace was an editor-in-depth, by which I mean that his concern went a good deal further than the black marks on white paper. He considered the source—considerately. Just one example:

A writer, from time to time, trips up on the convolutions of his own literary intestines and falls flat; can't move, can't write. That happened to me because of the machinations of a maverick senator. His hi-jinks struck me in a special way. Think of Asimov's dictum that there are three kinds of science fiction: What If—, If Only—, and If This Goes On. My preoccupation has always been the latter, and applied to what I saw was happening in the country, I was terrified, not so much by the actual, but by the potential, all of which became very real to me. Where it stalled my writing machine was my feeling that though I had a large-caliber typewriter, I was using it only to entertain, and I couldn't think of a way to use it where it might do some real good.

Horace called me one day, concerned, and I spilled the whole thing to him. He said, "Well, I'll tell you what to do. Write me a story about a guy who goes to the bus station to pick up his wife; she's been away for the weekend. And the bus comes in and the place is suddenly full of people. And across the crowd he sees his wife, talking avidly to a young man. She sees her husband coming and says a word to the young man, who hands her her suitcase, tips his hat, and disappears into the crowd. She walks across, meets her husband, gives him a kiss hello.

"Write me that, Sturgeon, *and everybody in the country will know how you feel about that meathead senator!*"

Well, for the moment I was as perplexed as, possibly, you are. But gradually it dawned on me what the man was saying. It was this: that if you have real convictions, if you really believe in something, it's going to come through, no matter what you're writing about.

I never did write the bus station story. Instead I wrote a story that, judging from the mail I got (some of it hate mail), was right on target. And since then I have been able to write what I please, secure in the knowledge that my convictions will come through *as long as I am a convinced human being.* Take care of that, and that quality called Message, or Meaning, will take care of itself.

I think you'll find this special **Horace Gold** imprint throughout this book. I hope so.

I would like to extend my warmest thanks and appreciation to Don Bensen and Jim Frenkel, editors extraordinary as well as generous and patient people; to Paul Williams, whose yeoman efforts helped bring this collection to the light of day; to Rowena Morrell for her extraordinarily beautiful and sensitive paintbrush; and most and always, to my incomparable Lady Jayne.

—THEODORE STURGEON
June 1979

TANDY'S STORY

One is conditioned to be austere and objective—I don't know why, or who started it; somehow it's not supposed to be "appropriate" (a word I hate a lot) to bring oneself and one's bloodstream into public view.

Well, I say the hell with it. Most of what I write is written by the simple process of opening a vein and dripping it (all too slowly) into the typewriter. My research has always been people, and more often than not, it's the people closest to me that I can research most conveniently. And the process of compiling such a collection as this must of necessity bring a sharp focus on the environment in which they are written.

Tandy's Story was designed to be the first in a series, ultimately to be collected as a book, of short stories and novelettes, to be called The Family. There would be this, and Noël's, and Timothy's (he's the baby mentioned in these pages) and Robin's, and then The Mother's Story and finally The Father's Story.

But then one of those great winds that sweep across our biographies arose, and I was separated from these people by some thousands of miles and days, and here I am a week away from having watched Noël graduate from college and "the baby" Timothy whack his head against a six-foot door lintel. Robin has been celebrated elsewhere in my work, and Noël's turn is coming some day soon, I'm sure, as is something special for Tim, but these can't happen in the same matrix as this one. Nostalgia is often tinged with regret; mine is not. But at the same time I am poignantly aware that in a contiguous universe there is a volume called The Family which will not and cannot be written. I'd like to read it.

This is Tandy's story. But first, take a recipe: the Canaveral sneeze; the crinkled getter; the Condition adrift; the analogy of the Sahara smash; Hawaii and the missing moon; and the analogy of the profit-sharing plan. There is no discontinuity here, nor is the chain more remarkable than any other. They are all remarkable.

If this were your story, it might compound from the recipe of a letter that never got mailed, a broken galosh clip, a wistful memory of violet eyes, the Malthusian theory and a cheese strudel. However, it is Tandy's.

We begin then with the Canaveral sneeze, delivered by a white-gowned, sterile-gloved man in a germ-free lab, as gently he lifted a gold-plated twenty-three-inch sphere into its ultimate package. Not having a third hand at the time, he was unable to cover his mouth in time. *Gesundheit.*

And now to Tandy's story.

Tandy's brother Robin was an only child for the first two years of his life and he would never get over it. Noël, her sister, was born when Tandy was crossing that high step into consciousness called Three Years Old. (Timothy, the other brother, wasn't until later. Anyway, this isn't his story. This is Tandy's story.)

When Tandy was five, then, it was clear to her that while the older Robin was bigger, stronger, more knowledgeable and smarter (he wasn't, but she hadn't been around long enough to learn that yet) and could push her around at will until she yelled for help—while, to put it another way, she was attacked from above—the sister below was excavating the ground under her feet. Noël unaccountably delighted everyone else, even Robin, for she was a blithe little bundle. But her advent necessarily drained off a good deal of parental attention from Tandy, who lost the household position of The Baby without gaining Robin's altitude as The Firstborn. It didn't seem fair. So she did what she could about it. She yelled for help.

It wasn't any ordinary yell, if an ordinary yell is a kind of punctuation or explosion or communicative change-of-pace. There were times when it wasn't, except for its purpose and figuratively, a yell at all. It was at times a whine —a highly specialized one, not very loud but strident, that could creep in and out of her voice twice in a sentence. Or it might be merely a way of asking for something, and asking and *asking*, so that she couldn't even hear a "yes" and was not aware of the point at which it furiously turned to a "no." Or perhaps an instantaneous approach to tears, complete with filling eyes and twisting mouth, where anyone else might use the mildest emphasis: "It *was* Tuesday I wore the blue dress, not Monday," and the equally instantaneous disappearance of the tears (which, somehow, was the annoying part). Or utter, total, complete, unmoving non-response to an order through the third, the fourth, the fifth repetition, and then a sudden shattering screech: "I *heard* you!"

Tandy had, in short, a talent approaching genius for getting under one's skin and prickling.

This established, it is mere justice to all concerned to report also that Tandy was loved and lovable as well. Her parents took the matter of child-rearing seriously. The reasons (over and above innate talent) for Tandy's more irritating proclivities were quite known to them. And Tandy, long-lashed, supple, with hair the color of buckwheat honey and golden freckles spattered across her straight perfect nose, was an affectionate child, and her parents loved her and showed it very often.

And this did not alter one whit her position as No. Two Child, her distaste for the rôle, her yelling for help and therefore, for all the love, the concurrent war of abrasion.

There were times when she and Robin got along as contemporaries and splendidly. And of course almost anyone could get along with the biddable Noël. But these times were more wished-for than often. When they occurred, they were so welcome that one is reminded of the lady with the perennially battling children who called out into an unwonted silence one mid-morning: "What are you kids doing?" From under the porch a young voice replied,

"Burning the wrappers off these razorblades with matches, Mommy." "That's nice," she replied, "Don't fight . . ."

At such times, in short, they could get away with practically anything, and Tandy's usual occupations were staged alone and away from people.

Yet never completely away.

Perhaps as a result of her crowded loneliness, she liked to be on the outside looking in or on the inside looking on, but not *of* the group. When the neighborhood gathered on the lawn for hide-and-seek or kickball, and the game was well started, Tandy would be seen forty paces off, squatting by the driveway, making a cake-sized cake of earth, perhaps, and decorating it with pebbles and twigs; or acting out some elaborate dialogue with her doll Luby (whether or not Luby was with her), bowing and mugging and murmuring the while in a number of voices. Tandy spoke beautifully. She had since the beginning, and her command of idiom and tone was too expert to be cute. There were times when it was downright embarrassing, as when the father overheard her demanding of a peonybush, with precisely his own emphasis, *"What the hell are you, hypnotized?"* There were times when these performances at the edge of the activity of others attracted considerable attention. She was surprisingly deft for a five-year-old, being one of these kids who from birth, apparently, can with a single movement draw a closed figure so that you are unable to see where the ends of the line join, and whose structures with blocks never seem jumbled, but quite functional (as indeed, to the fantasy of the moment, they are). Once in a while she drew quite a gallery of the curious with, say, six careful rows of red Japanese maple leaves and deep pink trumpet-vine blossoms alternating on the lawn, before which she would posture severely, murmuring under her breath and pointing to one and another with a stick. At such times she seemed quite oblivious to six or eight children magnetically drawn round her, who watched mystified. Sometimes she would answer and sometimes she would not. Sometimes it would take drastic measures, as for example Robin's shuffling through the careful arrangement of leaves and petals, before it could be learned (the hard way, in this case) that she was teaching school, that the leaves were boys and the trumpets girls, and that she was now going to tell Mama to throw Robin's Erector set into the garbage, and a good deal more—precisely what more, no one knew, for by then the screech would have destroyed intelligibility.

The crinkled getter was placed near the base and inside the metal envelope of an RF amplifier tube in the telemetry circuit of the big rocket's second stage. The getter's function was to absorb the residual gases in the tube and harden the vacuum therein. Its crinkle was an impurity, but so slight as to cause no trouble until the twelfth hour of countdown. Then rarefied gas began to ionize and *foop!* discharge and ionize and *foop!* discharge again.

To replace the tube required that they go back to twenty-four hours and start the countdown again. The extra twelve hours delay enabled sneeze-mist to dry on the sphere, and certain bacilli to die, and others to encyst, and a smear of virus, sub-microscopically, to turn to a leathery, almost crystalline jelly.

Tandy lived in a house in the woods which in turn were in, or nearly in, the very middle of the upstate village, a pleasant accident derived from the land-grabbing, land-holding traditions of three neighbors' fathers, and grandfathers, and great-grandfathers. The three acres on which Tandy's house stood were surrounded by perhaps twenty acres of other people's woods and a small swamp; yet the house was barely ten minutes on foot away from the village green.

Somewhere, then, in house or garden, lawn, swamp or wood, the brownie came to Tandy.

It had that stuffed-toy, left-out-in-the-rain aspect possible only to stuffed toys which have been left out in the rain. It was about nine inches high. Its clothing, or skin (properly, the outside layer was both), was variously khaki-colored and mottled green. The appellation "brownie" derived from what appeared to be a tapered hat, though once the father was heard to remark that it was the damn thing's head that was pointed. The arms and legs were taut and jointless, and looked like sausages on which lived lichens. For hands there were limp yellow-pink leaves of felt, and for feet, what might have been the model for a radical cartoonist's rendering of the knotted moneybags of Old Moneybags. As for a face—well, it was a face. That's all. Black disks for eyes, so faded you couldn't tell whether they were supposed to be open or closed, a ditto-mark for a nose and a

streak below which may have been some clumsy whimsy—
a smile up on the right scowling downward to the left—or
a streak of dirt.

In the light of all that happened, one would think there
would be a day of discovery, an hour of revelation, an
open-the-package kind of Event. But there wasn't.

The brownie was kicking around the place for weeks,
months maybe; they had all seen it, kicked it aside, used it
as a peg for that parental sigh, "Got to clean out all this
junk sometime . . ." Robin dug a grave for a dead cat once
and then couldn't find the cat, so buried the brownie instead. Noël had taken it to bed with her once, and the
mother had thrown it out the window during the night. It
was one of those things, along with the bent but not quite
broken doll carriage, the toy electric motor with the broken
brush and Noël's wind-up giraffe, which needed new ears.
So the brownie wove its indistinct thread into the tapestry
of days, in and out of the margin between toys and trash.

The exact beginnings of Tandy's preoccupation with the
brownie were also vague, and even when first her interest
was total, it made little impression, because Tandy was . . .
well, for example, the caterpillar. Once when she was four
she caught a tent caterpillar and kept him in a coffee can
for two days and named him Freddy and fed and watered
him and even covered him at night with a doll blanket.
During the second night she awoke crying, agonizing after
Freddy, inconsolable until the can was found and brought
and shown to her. Her grandmother, who was around at
the time, said sagely, "*That* child needs a pet!" and everybody nodded and conversed about pets. The next morning
Tandy put Freddy on the flagstones out front "so he could
go for a walk." He went for a walk. Altogether.

For half a day people tiptoed around Tandy as if she
were full of fulminate and had dined on dynamite.

But not only did she not ask about Freddy, she never
even mentioned him. She stumbled over the can and almost
fell and kicked it away and did not even glance at it. Thereafter Tandy's preoccupations were beyond judgment or
prediction; they might be blood-sistership, like the affair
with her doll Luby Cindy, or they might be passing passions like Freddy. The brownie . . . well, people became
aware not that Tandy had a new one, but that for some
indeterminate time she had been orbiting around this arti-

fact. And when Tandy orbited, so did the cosmos or it—all of it—would be accountable to Tandy.

Mention of orbit brings up the Condition adrift. No other name for it will do, and even that is inaccurate. It was . . . well, matter; but matter in such a curlicue, so self-involved in stress, that Condition is a better word than Thing. It had been made where it was useful to its makers, and one might say it had a life of its own though it had not used it in some millions of megayears. By a concidence as unlikely as the existence of the reader of this history or a world to read it on, but as true, the Condition adrift found itself matching course and speed with the golden ball in space. It contacted, interpenetrated, an area of the golden surface four by eight microns, and happily found itself a part of organic material—a dried and frozen virus and two encysted bacteria. The latter it dissected and used. The former it activated, but in a wild reorganizing way so radical its mammy amino wouldn't have recognized it. The Condition became then a Thing (without losing its conditional character) and it scored itself across and divided. And divided again. And that was the end of that, for it had used up its store of a certain substance too technical to mention, but as necessary as number. Such was the nature of this organism that once alive it must grow, but if it could not grow it must cease dividing, and if it ceased dividing it must undergo an elaborate, eons-long cycle before it could come round to being again a mere Condition adrift. But unless it could begin that cycle it must die.

By means known to it, it flowed through the lattices of the sputtered gold, quartered the sphere, searched and probed, and at last stopped.

It turned its attention to the great globe underneath.

Some time or other—it was in the early spring, though Tandy herself could never remember just when—she got the brownie a house. Actually it was an old basketwork fishing creel she had found behind the garage, but the one thing one learned most quickly about Tandy was that things were what she said they were. Anything else was only your opinion, to which you were not entitled. And there was a certain justice in her attitude, for it did not take long for such an object to lose its creelship and become what she said it was.

She set it against the back wall of the garage, in the

tangled ground between the wall and the old stone fence, under the shelter of the adjoining carport—for a wall-less shelter had been hung to the side of the garage to accommodate the second car they hoped for some day. It was a nice sort of outdoors-indoors place. She drove a row of stakes in front of the creel and on it placed a rectangle of discarded plywood—a miniature of the carport—but as time went on she added walls. First they were cardboard. The creel was the bedroom and the rest of it was the living room.

At Easter she saved her basket and it was a bed. She got the brownie up every morning and put him to bed every night, and on weekends he took his nap too.

She fed him.

She had a small table—not a cream cheese box, a table! —for him, and on the table were clamshell plates and an acorn cup, and a pill-bottle—strike that; a flower vase— which, from the time spring first started to show her colors, she kept supplied. But before that she was feeding him snow ice cream, sawdust cereal, mushroom steaks, and wooden bread. She talked to him constantly, sometimes severely. And in that unannounced way of hers, she spent all her free time with him.

No one noticed it especially, in March and almost through April, except perhaps to be grateful for the quiet. A minute spent with the brownie was a minute without Tandy's moaning, whining, sobbing, screeching or otherwise yelling for help. Of course, there had to be minutes spent away from the brownie. Most of them were at school.

School was kindergarten, of course, and it may have been that there was just too much of it for Tandy. Due to factors of distance and necessities of school buses, the kindergarten was not, as is usual for such establishments, a nine-to-noon affair, but instead lasted for the whole school day, ending at three. In spite of a long rest period after lunch, it was the opinion of many that this was asking too much of five-year-olds. It may have been the teacher's opinion as well. It was certainly Tandy's opinion. Her first report card was not resoundingly good, and her second one was somewhat worse. Neither was bad enough to cause concern, but the parents were jolted by the specific items on which she scored worst. Beside the item *Speak clearly and distinctly* the teacher had marked the symbols which meant

"Hardly ever," and beside *Knows right from left* was the mark for "Seldom." The parents looked at one another in amazement, and then the father said, "That can't be right!" and the mother said, "That can't even be Tandy. She's given her the wrong report card!"

But she had not, as the mother found out by visiting the teacher at school one afternoon.

The mother, going in like a lion, came out numb with awe for the teacher's forbearance, and for the second time (Robin had done this to her once, on another matter) suffering that partly amused but nonetheless painful experience of learning how little one knows of one's own. Or as the bemused father put it, "It's a wise father who knows his own child." For, fully documented and with inescapable accuracy, the teacher had described a Tandy they never saw around the house—a Tandy recalcitrant, stubborn, inactive, disobedient and, most incredible of all, talking incessant baby talk. The teacher's ability to see below the surface, to know that the child wasn't *really* as bad as all that, helped the overall picture not at all, because it became manifest that Tandy did not know right from left on purpose; that she spoke baby-talk by choice; that she fell from grace in matters of handkerchiefs and handwashing not because she forgot, but because she remembered.

Above and beyond everything else was that the degree of this behavior was by no means excessive. She had never once been subjected to the routine punishment of being made to stand out in the hall. She could always stop just short of outright delinquency. She was the foot that drags, the pressure which is not quite toothache, the discomfort which is not yet heartburn.

The parents conferred unhappily with each other and then with Tandy, who answered every *"Why?"* with "I just—" and an infuriating shrug, rolling upward of the eyes, flinging the hands out and down to flap helplessly against the thighs. It was the mother's exact gesture, which of course is precisely why it was infuriating.

So the father, his anger at last arriving, drew a bead on Tandy with his long forefinger and declared, "This is a *rule*. No more brownie."

The analogy of the Sahara smash is the anecdote of one of the desert crashes of a B-17 in Africa. Unlike tragic others, this one had a happy ending, and this is why: the crew made no attempt to trek out of there in a body, but instead assigned one man to march out and get help. The significant thing is that he carried with him not only a compass, but almost their entire water supply. The rest of the crew rationed themselves down to three tablespoons a day and lay as still as possible buried in the sand under the broken fuselage. So it was that the organism on the golden satellite told one of itself to ooze patiently out to the tip of one of the whip antennae; then, by means known to it— for as related, it contained unheard-of stresses, neatly curled up and intertwined—it bent the whip double and released it, and out into the emptiness, in the opposite direction from orbital motion, was snapped this infinitesimal fleck of substance. It tracked along with the satellite for a long time, but separating always, until it was lost in the glittering emptiness. But with it it carried all but a fraction of the organic substance available to the whole. Three parts were left quiescent, waiting moveless to die or be saved. The fourth fell toward Earth, which took—as long as it took . . .

Now there is a school of control-by-giving (hits in the head or ice cream) and a school of taking away, and the father, when aroused, tended to the latter. In extreme cases a child can learn never to express preference or fondness for anything lest he qualify it for the disciplinary list. This was not that extreme. It would not be because of the mother, who despised this kind of thing and whose reactions were very fast. One glimpse of Tandy's stricken face at this "No more brownie!" dictum and she added. ". . . if you go on making people unhappy." And, ignoring the father's stifled cry of rage, she went on, "Now you run on out and talk it over with the brownie."

Tandy did as she was told, leaving her parents to instruct one another about child-rearing, and communed with the brownie: and perhaps this was the real beginning of it all.

For she had done a great deal for this brownie. Now, for the first time, she had made it clear that there were things that needed doing for her.

If things changed at school, it was naturally not immediately apparent at home. Things at home did not change. That is, the busy-ness with the brownie continued to use up the whining time, the screeching time, the opportunities for chance medley and battle royal with Noël and Robin.

One weekday morning the mother had hung out a line-full of clothes and, being face to face with the garage, was moved to go round and see how Tandy was coming along with Project Brownie. She hadn't seen it for some weeks. She recalled vaguely that the cardboard sides had been replaced, and she knew that the tiny flower-vase had borne violets, and baby's breath, and alyssum. And she recalled the time she had turned out her sewing basket and the kitchen gadget drawer and rearranged them, all in one morning, and had given the detritus to Tandy for her brownie. Time was when Tandy would have gathered up such a treasure-trove with a shrill shriek of joy, would have fought selfishly and jealously with the other children over the ownership of every ribbon-end, every old cork and worn-out baby-bottle nipple, only to leave bits and pieces exasperatingly all over the house and yard within the next couple of hours. But this time she had spread the whole clutter out on the living room table, darted her deft small hands in and out of the pile, and in a few seconds had selected the blunt end of a broken nutpick, the china handle of a Wedgewood pitcher, a small tangle of pale blue nylon-and-wool yarn, and a brass wing-nut. "He wants these," she said positively. "That's all?" the mother had asked, astonished. And Tandy had replied, precisely mimicking the father, "Now what would a brownie want with all that junk?" It wasn't so much the modesty of Tandy's wants that had surprised the mother. It was the absolute and unhesitating certainty with which she chose.

Thinking of this, the mother rounded the garage and saw the brownie's house.

The old creel was still the bedroom, but the rest of the structure had vastly altered. The cardboard walls had been replaced with wood—some ends of shiplap that used to lie under the sleeping porch—and since the mother had heard nothing of any carpentry by or for Tandy, she could see that the stony ground had been carefully and laboriously dug to various depths so that the little boards, buried upright, could present an even eaveline. On one side were two small square window-openings, glazed with cellophane; on the other was a longer opening like a picture-window. The roof, still the castoff piece of plywood, had been covered with a layer of earth, and smoothly, brilliantly, it was thatched with living star-moss.

The mother knelt to look inside. The floor of the house was covered with a blinding-white powder of some kind. She took a pinch of it and felt it and smelt it and even tasted it a little without recognizing it; she'd ask Tandy later. The table was covered with a cloth which had once been part of a dust-rag which had once been one of the mother's dresses; it was spotlessly clean—it seemed to have been ironed—and was so folded and placed that the torn edges were out of sight. On the table was the pill-bottle flower-vase, just half full of clean water, in which stood a single stem and blossom of bleeding-heart. The effect was simple, tasteful, sort of Japanese-y. And further inside was the creel bedroom, with an oval dresser (despite the neat cloth cover and skirt, she recognized the lines of an inverted sardine tin) over which was the mirror which had been in Tandy's birthday pocketbook, and before which was a handsome little round chair, made of a bit of cardboard glued to a large wooden thread-spool, also covered and skirted with a scrap of material matching the dresser. And in bed was the brownie.

The mother had to go down almost flat on her stomach to see what it was which covered his pillow so whitely, so clean and thick-textured. A luxury material indeed—dogwood petals. He was covered with a quilt (she couldn't bring herself to call it one of her old pot-holders) and he was sleeping.

She chuckled at herself. How were those round black painted eyes to look open or closed? . . . and she looked again and thought they were open. She almost said "Excuse me!" and she actually did blush at disturbing his nap. Wagging her head, she backed away and stood up.

Between her and the old stone fence was usually a carpet of weeds. There was no pretense of making lawn or garden out of the stony soil here. Actually, the front lawn had been grown on trucked-in topsoil. Yet—

Yet this area was not planted. A row of early marigolds between the brownie's house and the onetime weed-bed. And, from there to the fence, a dark-green plant, low, spidery, in rows. She did not recognize the plant except perhaps as just another weed.

Speechless, she returned to the house.

Trouble on the school bus that day; Robin came home bloody and triumphant.

Mother had meant to talk about brownie, but it was some time before events sort themselves out. It appeared that a "big kid" had started chanting the well-known chant about "I seen Tandy's underwear," and Robin had punched him and gotten clobbered for it. The bus monitor broke it up, and in spite of Robin's having gotten the worst of it, he came home bursting with pride and Tandy awash with admiration.

The mother felt both. It was the first time Robin had ever brought arms to bear in defense of his sister, and after the question and cross-question and verbal jigsaw-puzzling which is always necessary to get an anecdote out of a child, and the awkward telephone conversation with the parent of the party of the other part, she found herself alone not with Tandy, but with Robin, Tandy having escaped to her preoccupation behind the garage.

"Robin, I don't like fighting but I must say, I like the way you took up for Tandy."

"Aw, she's okay," said Robin, not noticing how the mother of what he usually called that little tattletale, that squeaky wheel, that pushfaced squint-eyed bow-legged stoop . . . how the mother of this repulsive sibling let drop her jaw, and slumped into a chair.

She was still sitting there, trying to recover her strength, while Robin pedalled away on his bicycle and while, a moment later, Tandy came in. She came totteringly, mounded down with clean laundry. The mother leapt up to help her get the screen door open and then had to sit down again. "Tandy!" she cried.

"Well, they was all dry, Mommy, so I brought them in."

"They *were*," said the mother weakly.

"Sure they were. Mommy . . ."

She was going to ask for something. If it was a diamond tiara, the mother thought, she'd get her one if she had to murder for it. "Yes, honey."

"Mommy, would you teach me how to set the table? I could do it every day while you get dinner."

So for the time being the mother utterly forgot to ask any questions about the brownie.

The mother thought about the brownie a good deal, although—perhaps it was a remnant of her comical embarrassment at having caught him in bed—she seldom went back there to look at the house. But one afternoon, thinking about the neatness of the little table, the dresser and chair and mirror, the shining white floor (what *was* that stuff, anyway?) it occurred to her that the three-year-old Noël would find that arrangement back there irresistible, and she shuddered at the mental picture of Noël bellying delightedly into the careful structure, churning up the white floor, leaning too hard on the cheese-box table, tumbling the mossy roof. "Noël . . ."

"?"

"Noël, we've all got to be specially careful of Tandy's brownie house. You wouldn't ever play with it unless she asked you to, would you?'

Noël gravely shook her helmet of tight curls. "I not allowed."

The mother tipped her head to one side and regarded the child. There were a number of things Noël was not allowed to do which she . . . "But all the same, you won't go back there by yourself."

"I not *allowed*," said Noël with great emphasis, and simultaneously the mother thought (a) that she'd like Tandy's formula for not allowing if it worked like this and (b) let's keep an eye on Noël all the same.

It was demonstrated, about ten days later, just how unnecessary it was to stand guard over the brownie's house. It was a Saturday. The father was home, Robin was off somewhere on his bicycle, and Tandy was slaving happily away behind the garage. The father, from the front of the house, called out, "Do you know what happened to the hand cultivator?"

The mother's photographic memory saw it lying beside a row of green. Oh, of course. "Noël, darling, run out behind the garage and get the cultivator. Tandy'll show you."

Pleadingly, "No, Mommy!"

"Noel!"

"I not *allowed* to!" said Noël, and incredibly, for she was a cheerful child, she began to cry.

The first impulse was to lay on some muscle and authority, the next a deep sympathy for the little one. "Oh . . . Noël . . ."

"I gon' *hide!*" shrieked Noël in something very like Tandy's special rasping shriek; and go she did, hide she did, ineffectively (the mother knew she was in the baby's blue chiffonier) but with great purpose. Apparently her "not allowed" was big enough to make it worth while defying the giants. Sighing, the mother went to the back door. "Tandy!"

"Yes, Mommy . . ."

"Bring Daddy's cultivator to him, he needs it!"

"The handle-fingers?"

"That's right, dear.'

She watched Tandy, in a yellow dress, bounding from behind the garage and heading for the front lawn. She waited until she saw the flash of yellow again and called her to the back steps.

"Tandy, you must have been terribly rough to Noël about not playing with your brownie. She's afraid to go back there because you said she's not allowed."

"No, I didn't, Mommy."

"Tandy!" (The explosion of the name alone was the mother's favorite curb.)

For the first time in many weeks Tandy began to pucker up, the eyes grew bright, the mouth trembled. "I reely, reely, reely . . ."

Moving on impulse, the mother stepped forward and took Tandy's wrist. "Shh, honey. Take me out and show me what you're doing."

Tandy immediately shut it all off and they went back of the garage, Tandy skipping. The mother was prepared to be complimentary as one normally is, multiplied by the wonder of what she had seen before; but she was not prepared for what she found.

One wall had been removed from the little house, the shiplap scraps unearthed and tossed aside. The roof was still supported by the other side and the top of the creel. A heap of flat stones lay near, and a small sack of ready-mixed concrete. A seed-flat was doing service as a miniature mortar-board, and a discarded pancake-turner as a trowel.

Tandy was composedly replacing the wooden wall with one of fieldstone.

"Tandy! Why, I never . . . who taught you to do this?"

"I asked Mr. Holmes-the-gym-teacher." (Tandy's teachers' names were all compounded like this.)

"But—but . . . where did you get the concrete?"

"I boughted it. I saved my 'lowance money and all my ice-cream money. That's all right, isn't it? I didn't go into town, Robin did on his bicycle." She slopped water from a toy sand-bucket and began to mix the concrete.

"Robin never told me," said the mother faintly.

"I guess you never asked him, Mommy."

"I guess I never." The mother wet her lips. "Tandy, how did you ever think of all this?"

"I didn't think of it. I just did it, that's all." She picked up a slather of cement and ladled it on to the top course of her new wall. "You wouldn't expect a brownie to go on living in a ol' wood house, now, would you?" she demanded in grandmotherly tones.

"No, I—I suppose not . . . Tandy, I saw the dresser and the little chair and the tablecloth. They're lovely. Tandy, did someone iron the tablecloth for you?"

"Oh, it irons itself," said Tandy. "You wash it an' rinse it and stick it on a window an' when it's dry it's ironed."

"What's that lovely white floor?"

Tandy selected and hefted a stone, then carefully laid it on the course. "Borax," she said.

"And you bought that with your ice-cream money too?"

"Sure. Brownies like borax and the little lumps off roots and that stuff there." She pointed to the rows of dark green weed.

"What is that?"

"The brownie's farm."

"I mean, the plant."

"I don't know what the real name is. I found it through the woods there, there's a whole patch. I call it brownie spinach. Look, over there's the lumps. It's like candy to a brownie." She pointed to a heap of roots, from some legume or other—the mother couldn't tell, for the leaves were gone; but the root-hairs had clusters of the typical nitrogenous nodules. "Tandy, how on earth do you know so much about brownies?"

Tandy gave her an impish glance. "I guess the same way you know about little girls."

The mother laughed. "Oh, but I had little girls of my own!"

Tandy just nodded: "Mm-hm."

The mother laughed again. When she left Tandy was fitting a whiskey-bottle—the three-sided "pinch" bottle—full of water, into the wall she was building, taking infinite pains to have it slant just so.

The mother wasn't laughing, though, later when she told her husband about it. As such things occasionally do, these developments had come about invisibly to him, having shown themselves mostly when he was away during the day. He listened, frowning thoughtfully, and when the children were glued to the television set the parents went out to look at the brownie house. All he said—all he could find to say, over and over, was: "Well, how about that."

When they left he snapped off a sprig of the dark green weed and put it in his pocket.

"And she sets the table every night," breathed the mother.

After she finished the fieldstone house (even the roof was stone, laid over the plywood from which the mossy earth had been swept away) Tandy seemed to abandon the brownie and his house altogether. She went back to one of her earlier passions, modelling clay, and spent her time studiously working it. But not ducks, not elephants. She would make thick rectangular slabs of it, and draw, or score, deeply into it. Some of the channels she cut were deeper than others, some curved, some straight but cut with her stylus at an acute angle, so that portions were undercut. "Looks like a three-dimensional Mondrian," said the father one night when the kids were asleep. He worked in a museum and knew a great many things, and had access to a great many more. That plant, for example. "It's *astralagus vetch*," he told his wife. "And I knew I'd read something about it somewhere, so I looked it up again. It's a pretty ordinary sort of vegetable except for some reason it has a fantastic appetite for selenium. So much so that proposals have been made to mine selenium—and you know, that's that light-sensitive element they use in TV tubes and photocells and the like—by planting the vetch where selenium is known to be in the soil, harvesting the whole plant, burning it and recovering selenium from the ash. All of which is beside the point—what on earth made the little fuzzhead pick the stuff up and plant it?"

"Brownies like it," the mother said, and smiled.

It was the very next morning that Tandy was missing from the breakfast table.

There was only a small flurry about it; the mother knew just where to look. The child was busily packing armloads of vetch and tangles of knobby roots into a hole in the solid front of the brownie house. The brownie himself sat against the garage, its face turned toward her, its not-closed, not-open eyes seeming to watch. "I'm sorry, Mommy," Tandy said brightly, "but I'm not late for school, am I?"

"No, dear, but your breakfast is ready. What on earth are you doing to the brownie's house?"

"It isn't a house any more," said Tandy, in the tones of one explaining the self-evident to one who should know better without asking, "it's a factory." She put both hands in the hole and pushed hard. Apparently the house was baled full of weeds and roots. She daubed mortar around the opening quickly.

"Come, dear."

"Just finished, Mommy." She took a flat stone and set it into the opening, which must have been prepared for it, for it seemed a perfect fit. Another slap of mortar and she was up smiling. "I'm sorry, Mommy, but this is the day I had to do that."

"For the brownie."

"For the brownie." They went back to the house.

In Hawaii, a specialist, who should have been but was not more than a sergeant at the missile tracking station, grunted and straightened away from the high definition screen. "Lost it." He pulled a tablet toward him, glanced at the clock, and started filling in the log.

Nobody saw the faint swift streak as the satellite died. But if there had been a witness to that death—placed not to see faint swift streaks, but right on the scene, with a high-speed stroboscopic viewing device, he would have had some remarkable pictures.

As the golden sphere surrendered to the ravening attack of fractional heat, in that all but immeasurable fragment of time wherein parts became malleable, plastic, useful—they were used. Selenium from the solar cells, nitrogen from the pressurized interior, borosilicates ripped from refractory parts, were gleaned and garnered and formed and conformed. For a brief time (but quite long enough) there existed a device of molten alloy bars and threads surrounding a throat, or gate, which was composed of a pulsing, brilliant blue non-substance.

Anything placed within this blue area would cease to

exist—not destroyed in any ordinary sense, but utterly eliminated. And the laws of the universe being what they are, such eliminated matter must reappear elsewhere. Exactly where, depends of course on circumstances.

That morning the mother was hanging clothes when a flash of light caught her eye. She put down her clothes-basket and went to the back of the garage.

The brownie sat with his back to the garage, staring glumly at the torn-up remnants of his "farm." The mid-morning sunlight, warm and bright in this clear dry day, struck down through a gap in the trees and poured itself on and over the pinch bottle, half in and half out of the near wall of the little house. The colors were, she found by screening her vision through her eyelashes, lovely and very bright—flame-orange and white—why, the bottle it-self seemed to be alight.

Or was it the inside of the little house?

There was a violent, sudden hiss as the bottle, full of water, popped its cork and sent a gout of water inside the little stone structure. Steam rolled up and then disappeared, and she took a pace back from the sudden wave of heat. Terrified, she began to think of hose, or extinguisher . . . the garage, all these trees, the house . . . and then she saw that the side of the brownie's house which adjoined the wooden garage was fieldstone too. The heat, whatever it was, was contained.

It seemed to diminish a little. Then the glass bottle wavered, softened, slumped and fell inside. Heat blasted out again and again diminished.

She stepped closer and peered down through the hole left by the bottle. She could clearly see, lying on the floor of the stone chamber, the clay slab Tandy had made, with its odd, geometrical system of ditches and scorings. But they seemed filled with some quivering liquid, which even as she watched turned from yellow to silver and then dulled to what could only be called a chalky pewter. The lines and ditches, filled with this almost-metal, made a sort of screen, but not exactly. It was too tangled for that. Say an irregular frame about an irregular opening in the center of the slab. And this center area began to turn blue and then purple, and then throb in some way she would never be able to describe. She had to turn her eyes away.

Looking away seemed to snap the thread of fascination

with which she had leashed fear. She fled to the house, dialed the telephone, got her husband. "Quick," she said, and stopped to pant, alarming him mightily. "Come home."

It was all she could manage. She hung up and sank into a couch. She was therefore unaware of Noël, who came trotting across the back of the house and straight and fearlessly behind the garage. She stood for a while with a red lollipop in her mouth and pink hands behind her, watching the heat-flickers over the stones, then circled them carefully to windward and squatted down where she could peer inside. Carefully then, and much more steadily than even a deft three-year-old might be expected to move, she reached down with her delicate lollipop and probed the molten slag.

"Oh, don't, don't!" the mother said later back of the garage, as the father stabbed angrily at the hot stones with a crowbar. "Tandy might ... she might ... oh, it's meant so much to her ..."

"I don't care, I don't care," he growled, stabbing and slashing and ruining. "I don't like it. Just say it's about fire, like playing with matches. We won't punish her or anything."

"No?" she said woefully, looking at the ruins.

"And this," he said, "damn devilish thing." He scooped up the brownie and thrust it among the scorching rocks. It flamed up easily. The last thing to go was the pair of dull eyes. The mother was at last sure they had been open the whole time. "Just tell her we almost had a fire," growled the father.

. . . which was the selfsame day Tandy brought back her report card, the absolutely perfect report card, and the note:

> ... truly the first absolutely perfect report card I have ever made out in my twenty-eight years of teaching school. The change in Tandy is quite beyond anything I have ever seen. She is an absolute delight, and I think it is safe to say that probably she always was; her previous behavior was, perhaps, a protest against something which she had now accepted. I shall never be able to express my gratitude to you for coming in for that talk, nor my admiration of you for your handling of the child (whatever that was!). It might be

gracious of you to say that perhaps I had something to do with this; I would like to forestall that compliment. I did nothing special, nothing extra. It is you who have wrought the most pleasant kind of miracle.

It was signed by her teacher, and it left them numb. Then the mother kissed Tandy and exclaimed, "Oh darling, whoever in the world magicked you?"

Exclamation or no, Tandy took it as a question and answered it directly: "The brownie."

There was a heavy silence, and then the mother took Tandy's hand. "You have to know about something," she said, and ungently to the father, "You come too."

They went out behind the garage, the woman touching Tandy's shoulders with ready mother hands. "There was a fire, honey. It all burned up. The brownie burned too."

The father, watching Tandy's face, which had not changed at the sight of the ruin (was this that un-seeing you read about, when people in shock deny to themselves what they see?) said suddenly and hoarsely, "It was an accident."

"No, it wasn't," Tandy said. She looked at her father and her mother but they were both looking at their feet. "And anyway *he* isn't burned up, he wasn't in that fire."

"He was," said the father, but she ignored him. "Anyway," the mother said, "I'm terribly sorry about your pretty little house, Tandy."

Tandy poked out her lips briefly. "It wasn't a house, it was a factory, I told you," she said. "And anyway it's all finished with anyway."

"You better understand," said the father doggedly, "that brownie did burn."

"You remember. You left him sitting right there," said the mother.

"Oh," said Tandy, "*that* wasn't a brownie! You can't see a brownie, silly. I've got the brownie. Don't you know that? Didn't you see the 'port card?"

"How did the . . ." She couldn't say it.

"It was easy. Any time I got to do something, I think about should I or not, and if I should, how I should do it; when I think of the right way, something inside here goes *bwoop-eee!*" (she made a startlingly electronic sound, the first syllable glissading upward and the second flat and unmusical, like a "pure" tone) "and I know that's what I should do. It's easy, And that's the brownie."

"Inside you."

"Mm-hm. That dirty old doll, that was just a way to get some fun out of all that hard work. I couldn't've done it without having some sort of fun. So I made it easy for brownies to live in this whole world and they make it easy for me."

The mother thought about a metallic twisted thing with a purple mystery atremble in it. It was like looking through a window into a—another place. Or a door.

"Tandy," she said, moved as she sometimes was by sheer impulse, "how many brownies came through the door?"

"Four," said Tandy blithely, and began to skip. "One for me, one for Robin, one for Noël and one for the baby. Could I have some juice?"

They walked back to the house. Robin was home. He was giving Noël back her lollipop and saying "Thank you" the way they always wished he would. Noël always was a generous child. She had already given the baby a lick.

The analogy of the profit-sharing plan appears as we imagine a self-satisfied tycoon at his desk and a bright-eyed junior exec sprinting in bearing mimeographed sheets. "Gosh, J. G., this is that first look I had at the new plan. You're doing a lot for your people here, J. G., a whole lot." And homiletically the great man inclines his head, accepting the tribute, and says "A happy worker is a loyal worker, my boy." And while bobbing his head, the junior executive is thinking. "Yeah, and what's good for the happy workers is good for management, how about that?"

Yet enlightened and cooperative self-interest is not always to be sneered at. Ask any symbiote. Whatever it was that bubbled up out of that blue orifice had been designed simply and solely to adapt a host fully to its environment, in order to induce that cardinal harmony called —joy.

Not satisfaction, not contentment, not pleasure. These can be had in other ways, and by using less than all of the environment. A surge of joy within the host created that special substance on which the symbiote fed, and it was as simple as that. Oh happy worker. Oh happy management . . .

"Well, thank God anyway she's back to normal," said the father. He came in from the porch where he and the mother had stood watching the neighborhood kids and Robin and Tandy playing on the lawn. The mother did not point out to him that Tandy, in and of the whole group now, may have been playing normally, but she wasn't back to it; she'd come to it. The mother stood watching, silent, happy, and frightened.

Inside, the father picked up his newspaper and threw it down again when he heard one of those special in-group code sounds which come to families like secret ciphers. This one was the click of heavy glass against hardwood, and meant that the baby, who had been put down in the crib in the master bedroom, had lashed out with a strong left hook in his random way and belted his bottle out of his mouth and up against the crib bars.

The father stopped just inside the bedroom. His jaw dropped, and all he could do was slowly to raise a hand to his chin and close it and hold it closed. For the baby, the six-months-old Timothy, who only yesterday could hopelessly lose a bottle five-eighths of an inch away from his hungry face, pulled himself to a sitting position by the bars, half-turned to the left and pulled the pillow on which the bottle had been perched away from the side of the crib and up to a formal position across the end of the mattress; half-turned to the right to grasp the bottle, then lay back.

He not only took the bottle firmly in his two hands; he not only got his mouth on it; he also elevated it so it would flow freely.

And for a long moment there was no sound but his suckings, his rhythmic murmurs of sheer joy, and the faint susurrus of tiny bubbles valving back into the bottle; for the father was holding his breath. At last the father inhaled and opened his mouth to call his wife witness to this miracle. He then thought better of it, closed his mouth, wagged his head and quietly left the room.

As he entered by one door, Robin, the firstborn, bounded in at the front. The screen door went to the stretch, and uncorked a curve that promised to tear out the moldings when it hit. The father squinched up his face and eyes in preparation for the crash, but Robin, for the first time in his life—a boy has to be at least eleven before he stops slamming screen-doors, and Robin was only eight—Robin reached behind him without looking and buffered the door with his fingertips, so it closed with a whisper and a click. He galloped past the unthunderstruck father and went into the kitchen; a moment later he was seen, all unbidden, lugging the garbage out.

The father fell weakly back into the big wicker chair.

"Daddy . . ."

He put down his paper. Noël came to him with a long cardboard box stretching her three-year-old arms out almost straight. She pleaded, "You wanna play chest with me?"

He looked at her for a long moment. Many times they had sat on the carpet and made soldier-parades with the chessmen. But now he—he . . .

He shuddered. He tried to control it but he couldn't. "No, Noël," he said. "I don't want to play chest with you . . ." But oh, that's Noël's story, not Tandy's.

RULE
OF
THREE

My preoccupation for some time has been with the nature of marriage, and whether or not we haven't gotten ourselves off on the wrong foot. Divorce statistics would seem to indicate that there is nothing more destructive of marriage than monogamy. "Let me not to the marriage of true minds admit impediment," wrote Elizabeth Barrett (a monogamist if there ever was one), but she had a point there. Although the person who wrote Rule of Three *clearly regarded the desirability of monogamy as axiomatic, the astute reader—another term for postgame quarterbacking—might find in it the seeds of later ideation. One tends to work out one's own convictions in writing fiction —especially in science fiction—and to test them against possibilities, however untimely or unformed or wishful or improbable. Anyway, in this story (1951) one may find what is possibly the first suggestion in science fiction that love may not after all be confined to gender or to monogamy. Here are the seeds of later work like* More Than Human, *and the growing concept that perhaps, after all, the greatest advance we can make is to accept what we are, and then to grok, to blesh, to meld, to join. Real science fiction talk, that, ain't it?*

They were a decontamination squad—three energy-entities (each triple)—on a routine check of a known matter-entity culture. What they traveled in was undoubtedly a ship, since it moved through space, except that it was not a physical structure of metal. It slowed down like a light wave that had suddenly grown tired.

"There it is," said RilRylRul.

The two other triads merged their light-perceptions and observed it. "Out at the edge," said KadKedKud, in satisfaction. "It should not be too difficult to handle out there. When infection spreads near the heart of a Galaxy, it can be troublesome."

MakMykMok cautioned, "Don't underestimate the job until it's surveyed."

"It's a very small sun," said Ril. "Which one of the planets is it? The fourth?"

"No, the greenish-blue one, the third."

"Very well."

In due time the ship—a bubble of binding energy and collapsed, rarefied gas molecules—entered the atmosphere. It reshaped itself gradually into a round-nosed, tapered transparency and dropped sharply, heading due west over the planet's equator.

"Busy little things, aren't they?"

As the world turned under them, they watched. They saw the ships, the cities. In the microscopic, intangible fluxes of force which were nerve and sinew and psyche to their triple structure, they stored their observations. They recorded the temperature of steel converters and ships' power plants, calculated the strength of materials of buildings and bridges by their flexture in a simply computed wind velocity, judged and compared the flow-shapes of air and ground vehicles.

"We could return right now," said Kad. "Any race which has progressed this far in such a brief time must be a healthy one. Otherwise how could—"

"Look!" Ril flashed.

They watched, appalled. "They are *killing* one another!"

"It must be a ritual," said Kad, "or perhaps a hunt. But we'd better investigate closer."

They dropped down, swiftly overtook a low-flying open-cockpit biplane with a black cross on the fuselage, and settled on the cowling behind the pilot's head. Mak interpenetrated the ship's wall and, treading and passing the air molecules which fled past, reached the pilot's leather helmet at the nape of the neck. Contact was made and broken almost in the same moment of time, and Mak hurtled back in horror to the skin of their ship.

"*Get clear!*" he ordered.

In three microseconds the invisible ship was in the upper atmosphere, with Mak still clinging to the outer skin.

"What was it?"

"Pa'ak, the most vicious, most contagious energy-virus known. That creature is crawling with them! Never have I *seen* such an infestation! Examine me. Irradiate me. Be careful, now—be sure."

It was strong medicine, but effective. Mak weakly permeated through the ship's wall and came inside. "Disgusting. Utterly demoralizing. How can the creature live in that condition?"

"Worse than Murktur III?"

"Infinitely worse. On Murktur I never saw a concentration higher than 14, and that was enough to reduce the natives to permanent bickering. These bipeds can apparently stand a concentration of over 120 on the same scale. Incredible."

"Perhaps that individual is quarantined."

"I doubt it. It was flying its own machine; it can apparently land at will anywhere. But we will check further. Mak, you were quite right," said Ril. "Don't underestimate the job, indeed. Why, with an infestation like that, and a drive like that . . . what couldn't they accomplish if they were clean?"

They swooped close to the land, barely touched the hair of a child on a hilltop, and soared again, shaken and frightened.

"From what we've seen, that one was no more than 15% of maximum size. How do you read the Pa'ak concentration?"

"Over 70. This place is a pesthole. These creatures must be stopped—and soon. You know how soon such a technology reaches for the stars."

"Shall we send for reinforcements?"

"Before investigating? Certainly not. And after all, there are three of us."

"We shall have to protect ourselves," Ril pointed out.

"You mean—dissociate? Divide our triple selves?"

"You know that's the only way we can remain undetected by the Pa'ak. Of course, once we know exactly how they have developed here, and have analyzed the psychic components of the natives, we can re-synthesize."

"I hate the thought of dividing myself. So weak, so impotent . . ."

"So safe. Don't forget that. Once we've encased ourselves in the minds of these creatures and analyzed them, we'll have to join ourselves again to fight the Pa'ak."

"Yes, indeed. And we'll be together again soon. Take care," added Mak, the cautious one. "The Pa'ak are mindless, but exceedingly dangerous."

"Hungry," Ked supplemented.

"Especially for our kind. Shall we begin?"

The ship disappeared, bursting like a bubble. The three dropped, sharing a wordless thought that was like a handclasp. Then each of them separated into three, and the nine particles drifted down through the atmosphere.

The news is apples for the unemployed . . . disarmament . . . the Model A Ford.

A young girl lay on her stomach under a tree, reading. She yawned widely, choked a little, swallowed, and went back to her book.

Two friends shook hands. Later, one absentmindedly palmed the back of his neck. Something was rubbed into his skin. The other young man scratched his wrist as he walked away.

Something was in the drinking water, though neither the nurse, as she filled the glass, nor the little girl, as she drank, knew of it.

Some dust settled on a toothbrush.

A small boy sank his teeth into his bread-and-jam. The rich, red preserve drooled to the table. The boy put his finger in it, thrust the finger into his mouth.

Another youngster ran through the dewy morning grass in his bare feet.

Somewhere, two dust motes were waiting their turn.

And a number of years went by.

The news is Korea and Tibet . . . protein synthesis . . . Aureomycin . . . leaf and grain hormone poisons . . . the McCarran Act.

There was a character at the party named Irving, and Jonathan Prince, Consulting Psychologist, didn't like him. This Irving played guitar and sang folk songs in a resonant baritone, which was fine; but after that he would put a lampshade on his head and be the "March of the Wooden Soldiers" or some such, and that was as funny, after the fourth viewing, as a rubber crutch. So Jonathan let his eyes wander.

When his gaze came to the dark girl sitting by the door, his breath hissed in suddenly.

Priscilla was sitting next to him. She said "Ouch," and he realized he had squeezed her hand painfully.

"What's the matter, Jon?"

"I just—nothing, Pris." He knew it was tactless, because he knew the sharpness of Priscilla's tilted eyes, but he couldn't help it; he stared back at the dark girl.

The girl's hair was blue-black and gleamed like metal, yet he knew how soft it would be. Her eyes were brown, wide apart, deep. He knew how they would crinkle on the outside ends when she smiled. He knew, as a matter of fact, that she had a small brown mole on the inside of her left thigh.

Irving was still singing. Of course it had to be "Black Is the Color of My True Love's Hair." Priscilla pressed Jon's hand, gently. He leaned toward her.

She whispered, "Who's the charmer? Someone you know?"

He hesitated. Then he nodded and said, without smiling, "My ex-wife."

Priscilla let his hand go.

Jonathan waited until Irving finished his song and, in the applause, rose. " 'Scuse . . ." he muttered. Priscilla didn't seem to be listening.

He crossed the room and stood in front of the dark girl until she looked up at him. He saw the little crinkle by her eyes before he saw the smile.

"Edie."

"Jon! How *are* you?" Then she said, in unison with him, "Can't complain." And she laughed at him.

He flushed, but it was not anger. He sat on the ottoman by her feet. "How've you been, Edie? You haven't changed."

"I haven't," she nodded seriously. There was an echo in his mind. *"We'll always be friends, Jon. Nothing can change that."* Was that what she meant? She said, "Still trying to find out how the human mind works?"

"Yes, on the occasions when I find one that does. Are you in town for long?"

"I've come back. They closed the Great Falls office. Jon . . ."

"Yes?"

"Jon, who's the redhead?"

"Priscilla. Priscilla Berg. My assistant."

"She's lovely, Jon. Really lovely. Is she . . . are you . . ."

At last he could smile. "You can ask, Edie," he said gently. "Here, I'll ask you first. Are you married?"

"No."

"I didn't think so. I don't know why, but I didn't think so. Neither am I."

He looked down at his hands because he knew she was smiling, and somehow he didn't want to look into her eyes and smile too. "I'll get us a drink."

She waited until he was on his feet and a pace away before she said what she used to say: "Come back quickly."

Someone jostled him at the bar.

"What's up, Doc?" said Irving, and nickered. "Hey, that assistant of yours, she drinks scotch, doesn't she?"

"Rye on the rocks," he said absently, and then realized that the scotch suggestion was Irving's shot in the dark, and that he'd given the idiot an opening gambit with Priscilla. He was mildly annoyed as he ordered two Irish-and-waters and went back to Edie.

* * *

Communication was dim and labored.

"We're trapped . . ."

"Don't give up. Ked is very close to me now."

"Yes, you and Ked can achieve proximity. But these creatures won't combine emotionally in threes!"

"They can—they must!"

"Do not force them. Remain encysted and work carefully. Did you know the Pa'ak got Mak?"

"*No!* How horrible! What about Myk and Mok, then?"

"They will be guardians, watchers, communicators. What else can they do?"

"Nothing . . . nothing. How terrible to be one-third dead! What happened to Mak?"

"The creature Mak occupied killed itself, walked in front of a speeding vehicle as Mak tried to synthesize. Mak could not get clear in time from the dead thing."

"We must hurry or these beasts will leap off into space before we join our strength again."

The club wouldn't be open for hours yet, but Derek knew which of the long row of herculite doors would be unlocked. He shouldered it open and sidled in, being careful not to let it swing shut on his bass viol.

Someone was playing the piano out back. Piano . . . hadn't Janie been knocking herself out looking for a piano man before he went away? He mumbled, "Hope she—" and then Jane was on, over, and all around him.

"Derek, you tall, short underdone yuk, you!" she crooned. She hugged him, and put a scarlet print of her full mouth on his cheek. "Why didn't you wire? God, man, I missed you. Here, put down that Steinway and smooch me once. Am I glad to see your ugly head . . . Look at the man," she demanded of the empty club as he leaned the big bass against the wall and stroked its rounded flank with the tips of his fingers. "Hey, this is me over here."

"How are you, Janie?" He delivered a hug. "What's been giving around here?"

"Me," she said. "Giving, but out. Ma-an . . . a hassel. For ten days I had a sore throat clear from neck to tonsil, carrying that piano man. Damn it, I got a way I sing, and a piano's got to walk around me when I do it. Chopsticks this square makes—*eggs—ack—ly—on—the—beat,*" she stressed flatly. "And then a bass player I had, a doghouse complete with dog, and tone-deaf to boot. I booted him. I worked the last three nights without a bass, and am I glad you're back!"

"Me too." He touched her hair. "We'll get you a piano player and everything'll riff like Miff."

"A piano I *got*," she said, and her voice was awed. "Little cat I heard in a joint after hours. Gives his left hand a push and forgets about it. Right hand is *crazy*. Real sad little character, Derek. Gets the by-himself blues and plays boogie about it. Worse he feels, the better he plays. Sing with him? Man! All his chords are vocal cords for little Janie. He's back there now. Listen at him!"

Derek listened. The piano back there was talking to itself about something rich and beautiful and lost. "That just one man?" he asked after a moment.

"Come on back and meet him," she said. "Oh, Derek, he's a sweetheart."

"Sweetheart?"

She thumped his chest and chuckled. "Wait till you see him. You don't need to lie awake nights over him. Come on."

He was a man with a hawk face and peaceful eyes. He huddled on the bench watching what his hands did on the keyboard as if he hadn't seen them before but didn't much care. His hands were extraordinarily eloquent. He didn't look up.

Derek said, "I'm going to go get my fiddle."

He did, and picked up the beat so quietly that the pianist didn't hear him for three bars. Then he looked up and smiled shyly at Derek and went on playing. It was very, very good. They volleyed an intro back and forth for a while and then, before Derek fully realized what they were playing, Janie was singing "Thunder and Roses":

> *"When you gave me your heart*
> *You gave me the world . . ."*

And, after, there was a chord with a tremendous emphasis on an added sixth, and then it was augmented—a hungry, hungry leading tone, which led, with a shocked sort of satisfaction, into silence.

Derek put by his bass, carefully, so it wouldn't make any sound.

Jane said, in a mouselike voice, "I can breathe now?"

The pianist got up. He was not tall. He said, "You're Derek Jax. Thanks for letting me play along with you. I always wanted to."

"Thanks, he says." Derek gestured. "You play a whole mess of piano. What's your name?"

"Henry. Henry Faulkner."

"I never heard of you."

"He was head of the Orchestration Department at the Institute for twelve years," said Jane.

"Hey? That's all right," said Derek. "Symphony stuff. What'd you leave for?"

"Squares," said Henry. To Derek, it was a complete explanation. "I'd like to work here."

Jane closed her eyes and clasped her hands. "Yummy."

Derek said, from a granite face, "No."

Jane stood frozen. Henry came out from behind the piano. He walked—he all but trotted up to Derek. "No? Oh, please! A—joke?"

"No joke. Just no."

Jane breathed, "Derek, what are you on? Goofballs?"

Derek threw up his hands. "No. It's a good word. Ain't 'no' better than a whole lot of yak? No, that's all."

"Derek—"

"Mr. Jax," said Derek.

"Mr. Jax, please think it over," Henry said. "I've been wanting to work with you ever since you recorded 'Slide Down.' You know how long ago that was. I don't just want to play piano someplace. I want to play here—with you. I don't care about the pay. Just let me back up that bass."

"He never talked like that to me," said Jane with a small smile. "You've made yourself a conquest, puddinhead. Now—"

"I don't want to hear that kind of talk," exploded Derek. "I don't want to hear any kind of talk. I said no!"

Jane came to him. She squeezed Henry's forearm and gave him a long look. "Walk around some," she said kindly. "Come back and see me later."

Derek stood looking at the piano. Jane watched Henry go. He walked slowly, holding himself in, his head forward. At the other side of the dance floor he turned and opened his mouth to speak, but Jane waved him on. He went out.

Jane whirled on Derek. "Now what the God—"

Derek interrupted her, rasping, "If you got any more to say about this, you can look for a new bass man too."

Pallas McCormick was fifty-three years old and knew what she was about. She strode briskly down Eleventh Street, a swift, narrow figure wtih pointed shoulders and sharp wattles at the turn of her thin jaw. It was late and the tea room would be closed before long.

Verna was there before her, her bright white hair and bright blue eyes standing out like beacons in the softly lit room.

"Good evening, Pallas." Verna's voice was soft and pillowy, like her pudgy face and figure.

"Evening," said Pallas. Without preliminaries she demanded, "How are yours?"

Verna sighed. "Not so well. Two are willing, one isn't. The little fool."

"They're all fools," said Pallas. "Two billion stupid fools. Never heard of such a place."

"They want to do everything by twos," said Verna. "They're all afraid they'll lose something if they don't pair off, pair off. They've been schooled and pushed and ordered and taught that that's the way it must be, so—" she sighed again— "that's the way it is."

"We haven't much more time. I wish we hadn't lost—" There followed a dim attempt to project "Mak," a mental designation for which there was no audible equivalent.

"Oh, dear, *stop* saying that! You're always saying that. Our first third is gone, all eaten up, and that's the way it is."

"We're two," said Pallas caustically, "and we don't want to be. Are you all right?"

"Thoroughly encysted, thank you. Pa'ak can't get to me. I'm so well encased I can barely get through to control this—" she lifted her arms and dropped them heavily on the table—"this bag of bones. And I can't telepath. I wish I could communicate with you and the others directly, instead of through this primitive creature and its endless idioms. I've even got to use that clumsy terrestrial name of yours—there's no vocalization for our real ones." Again there was an effort to identify the speaker as "Myk" and the other as "Mok," which failed.

"*I* wish I could get through to the others. Goodness! A

weak signal once in a while—a mere 'come close' or 'go away'—and in between, nothing, for weeks on end."

"Oh, but they've got to stay closed up so tight! You know how the Pa'ak infection works—increasing the neurotic potential so that the virus can feed on the released nervous energy. There are two groups of three people who must come together by their own free emotional merging, or Ril's three parts and Kad's three parts can never become one again. To allow them that emotional freedom is to allow the Pa'ak virus which infests them to remain active, since they tend to be attracted to one another for neurotic reasons. At least we don't have *that* much trouble. There was so little neurosis or anything else left in these minds when we took them over that they were poor feeding grounds for Pa'ak. And that's the—"

"Verna, can you spare me that everlasting—"

"—the way it is," finished Verna inexorably. "I'm sorry, Pallas, truly. There's a horrid little pushbutton in this mind that plays that phrase off every once in a while no matter what I do. I'm rebuilding the mind as fast as I can; I'll get to it soon. I hope."

"Verna . . ." said Pallas with an air of revelation. "We can speed this thing up. I'm sure we can. Look. These fools won't group in threes. And Ril and Kad can't complete themselves unless their three hosts are emotionally ready for it. Now then." She leaned forward over her teacup. "There's no important difference between *two* groups of *three* and *three* groups of *two*."

"You really think . . . why, Pallas, that's a *marvelous* idea. You're so clever, dear! Now, the first thing we'll have to—"

They both froze in an attitude of listening.

"My word," said Verna. "That's a bad one."

"I'll go," said Pallas. "That's one of the creatures I'm guarding. Ril is in it."

"Shall I come too?"

"You stay here. I'll take a taxi and keep in touch with you. When I'm far enough away I'll triangulate. Keep watch for that signal again. Goodness! What an urgent one!"

She trotted out. Verna looked across at Pallas' untouched teacup. "She left me with the check." A sigh. "Well, that's the way it is."

* * *

The news is the artificial satellite program and flying discs . . . three-stage rockets and guilt by association.

Dr. Jonathan Prince was saying, "The world's never been in such a state. Industrialization is something you can graph, and you find a geometric increase. You can graph the incidence of psychoneuroses the same way and find almost the same curve, but it's a much larger one. I tell you, Edie, it's as if something were cultivating our little traumas and anxieties like plowed fields to increase their yield, and then feeding off them."

"But so much is being done, Jon!" his ex-wife protested

Jon waved his empty glass. "There are 39,000 psychotherapists to how many millions of people who need their help? There's a crying need for some kind of simple, standardized therapy, and people refuse to behave either simply or according to standards. Somewhere, somehow, there's a new direction in therapy. So-called orthodox procedures as they now exist don't show enough promise. They take too long. If by some miracle of state support and streamlined education you could create therapists for everyone who needed them, you'd have what amounted to a nation or a world of full-time therapists. Someone's got to bake bread and drive buses, you know."

"What about these new therapies I've been reading about?" Edie wanted to know.

"Oh, they're a healthy sign to a certain extent; they indicate we know how sick we are. The most encouraging thing about them is their diversity. There are tools and schools and phoneys and fads. There's psychoanalysis, where the patient talks about his troubles to the therapist, and narcosynthesis, where the patient's troubles talk to the therapist, and hypnotherapy, where the therapist talks to the patient's troubles.

"There's insulin to jolt a man out of his traumas and electric shock to subconsciously frighten him out of them, and CO_2 to choke the traumas to death. And there's the pre-frontal lobotomy, the transorbital leukotomy, and the topectomy to cut the cables between a patient's expression of his aberrations and its power supply, with the bland idea that the generator will go away if you can't see it any more. And there's Reichianism which, roughly speaking, identifies Aunt Susan, who slapped you, with an aching kneecap which, when cured, cures you of Aunt Susan too.

"And there's—but why go on? The point is that the mushrooming schools of therapy show that we know we're sick; that we're anxious—but not yet anxious enough, *en masse*—to do something about it, and that we're willing to attack the problem on all salients and sectors."

"What kind of work have you been doing recently?" Edie asked.

"Electro-encephalographics, mostly. The size and shape of brain-wave graphs will show a great deal once we get enough of them. And—did you know there's a measureable change in volume of the fingertips that follows brain-wave incidence very closely in disturbed cases? Fascinating stuff. But sometimes I feel it's the merest dull nudging at the real problems involved. Sometimes I feel like a hard-working contour cartographer trying to record the height and grade of ocean waves. Every time you duplicate an observation to check it, there's a valley where there was a mountain a second ago.

"And sometimes I feel that if we could just turn and look in the right direction, we'd see what's doing it to us, plain as day. Here we sit with our psychological bottle of arnica and our therapeutic cold compresses, trying to cure up an attack of lumps on the headbone. And if we could only turn and look in the right place, there would be an invisible maniac with a stick, beating us over the head, whom we'd never detected before."

"You sound depressed."

"Oh, I'm not, really," he said. He stood up and stretched. "But I almost wish I'd get away from that recurrent thought of looking in a new direction; of correlating neurosis with a virus disorder. Find the virus and cure the disease. It's panacea; wishful thinking. I'm probably getting lazy."

"Not you, Jon." His ex-wife smiled at him. "Perhaps you have the answer, subconsciously, but what you've learned won't let it come out."

"Very astute. What made you say that?"

"It's a thing you used to say all the time."

He laughed and helped her up. "Edie, do you have to get up early tomorrow?"

"I'm unemployed. Didn't I tell you?"

"'I didn't ask," he said ruefully. "My God, I talk a lot. Would you like to see my new lab?"

"I'd love to! Oh, I'd love it. Will it be—all right?"

"All right? Of course it—oh. I see what you mean. Priscilla. Where is she, anyway?"

"She went out. I thought you noticed. With that man who plays the guitar. Irving." She nodded toward the discarded instrument.

"I hadn't noticed," he said. Over his features slipped the poker expression of the consulting psychologist. "Who did you come with?"

"The same one. Irving. Jon, I hope Priscilla can take care of herself."

"Let's go," he said.

Faintly, and with exasperation, Ril's thought came stumblingly through to Ryl and Rul:

"How can a thinking being be so stupid? Have you ever heard a more accurate description of the Pa'ak virus than that? 'Cultivating our little traumas and anxieties like plowed fields to increase their yield, and then feeding off them.' And 'a new direction.' Why haven't these people at least extrapolated the idea of energy life? They know that matter and energy are the same. An energy virus is such a logical thing for them to think of!"

And Rul's response: "They can no more isolate their experiments from their neuroses than they can isolate their measuring instruments from gravity. Have patience. When we are able to unite again, we will have the strength to inform them."

Ril sent: "Patience? How much more time do you think we have before they start to spread the virus through this whole sector of the cosmos? They are improving rockets, aren't they? We should have sent for reinforcements. But then—how could we know we'd be trapped like this in separate entities which refuse to merge?"

"We couldn't," Ril answered. "We still have so much to learn about these creatures. Sending for reinforcements would solve nothing."

"And we have so little time," Rul mourned. "Once they leave Earth, the Pa'ak pestilence will no longer be isolated."

Ril responded: "Unless they are cured of the disease before they leave."

"Or prevented from leaving," Ryl pointed out. "An atomic war would lower the level of culture. If there is no choice, we could force them to fight—we have the power—and thus reduce their technology to the point where space flight would be impossible."

It was a frightening idea. They broke contact in trembling silence.

They had a drink, and then coffee, and now Irving was leading her homeward. She hadn't wanted to go through the park, but it was late and he assured her that it was much shorter this way. "There are plenty of places through here where you can cut corners." It was easier not to argue. Irving commanded a flood of language at low pitch and high intensity that she could do without just now. She was tired and bored and extremely angry.

It was bad enough that Jon had deserted her for that bit of flotsam from his past. It was worse that she should have walked right past him with her hat on without his even looking up. What was worst of all was that she had let herself be so angry. She had no claims on Jonathan Prince. They were more than friends, certainly, but not any more than that.

"Who's the girl you came to the party with, Irving?" she asked.

"Oh, her. Someone trying to get a job at the plant. She's a real bright girl. Electronics engineer—can you imagine?"

"And—"

He glanced down at her. "And what? I found out she was a cold fish, that's all."

Oh, she thought. So you ditched her because you thought she was a cold fish, and scooped me up. And what does that make me? Aloud she said, "These paths wind around the park so. Are you sure it's going to take us out on the downtown side?"

"I know everything about these woods." He peered. "This way."

They turned off the blacktop walk and took a graveled path away to the right. The path was brilliantly lit by a street-lamp at the crossing of the walks, and the light followed the path in a straight band through the undergrowth. It seemed so safe . . . and then Irving turned off to still another path. She turned with him, unthinking, and blinked her eyes against a sudden, oppressive darkness.

It was a small cul de sac, completely surrounded by heavy undergrowth. As her eyes became accustomed to the dim light that filtered through the trees, she saw benches and two picnic tables. A wonderful, secluded, restful little spot, she thought—for a picnic.

"How do you like this?" whispered Irving hoarsely. He sounded as if he had been running.

"I don't," she said immediately. "It's late, Irving. This isn't getting either of us anywhere."

"Oh, I don't know," he said. He put his arms around her. She leaned away from him with her head averted, swung her handbag back and up at his face. He caught her wrist deftly and turned it behind her.

"Don't," she gasped. "Don't . . ."

"You've made your little protest like a real lady, honey, so it's on the record. Now save us some time and trouble. Let's get to it."

She kicked him. He gasped but stood solidly. There was a sharp click behind her. "Hear that?" he said. "That's my switch-blade. Push a button and zip!—seven inches of nice sharp steel. Now don't you move or make a sound, sweetheart, and this'll be fun for both of us."

Locking her against him with his left arm, he reached slowly up under the hem of her short jacket. She felt the knife against her back. It slipped coldly between her skin and the back of her low-cut dress. "Don't you move," he said again. The knife turned, sawed a little and the back strap of her brassiere parted. The knife was removed; she heard it click again. He dropped it into his jacket pocket.

"Now," he breathed, "doesn't that feel better, lamb-pie?"

She filled her lungs to scream, and instantly his hard hand was clamped over her mouth. It was a big hand, and the palm was artfully placed so that she couldn't get her mouth open wide enough to use her teeth on it.

"Let's not wrestle," he said, his voice really gentle, pleading. "It just doesn't make sense. I'd as soon kill you as not—you know that."

She stood trembling violently, her eyes rolled up almost out of sight. Her mouth sagged open when he kissed it. Then he screamed.

His arms whipped away from her and she fell. She lay looking dully up at him. He stood straight in the dim light, stretched, his face up and twisted with pain. He had both hands, apparently, on one of his back pockets. He whirled around and her eyes followed him.

There was someone else standing there . . . someone in black. Someone who looked like a high-school teacher Priscilla had once had. Gray hair, thin, wattled face.

Moving without haste but with great purpose, the spinsterish apparition stooped, raised her skirts daintily and kicked Irving accurately in the groin. He emitted a croaking sound and dropped to a crouch, and began a small series of agonizing grunts. The old lady stepped forward as if she were dancing a minuet, put out one sensible shoe and shoved. Irving went down on his knees and elbows, his head hanging.

"Get out," said the old lady crisply. *"Now."* She clapped her hands once. The sound stiffened Irving. With a long, breathy groan he staggered to his feet, turned stupidly to get to his bearings and hobbled rapidly away.

"Come on, dear." The woman got her hands under Priscilla's armpits and helped her up. She half-carried the girl over to one of the picnic tables and seated her on the bench. With an arm around Priscilla's shoulders, she held her upright while she put a large black handbag on the table. Out of it she rummaged a voluminous handkerchief which she thrust into Priscilla's hands. "Now, you sit there and cry a while."

Priscilla said, still trembling, "I can't," and burst into tears.

When it was over she blew her nose weakly. "I don't . . . know what to say to you. I—he would have killed me."

"No, he wouldn't. Not while I'm alive and carry a hatpin."

"Who are you?"

"A friend. If you'll believe that, child, that's good enough for me and it'll have to be good enough for you."

"I believe that," said Priscilla. She drew a long, shuddering breath. "How can I ever thank you?"

"By paying attention to what I tell you. But you must tell me some things first. How did you ever get yourself mixed up with such an animal? You surely have better sense than that."

"Please don't scold . . . I was silly, that's all."

"You were in a tizzy, you mean. You were, weren't you?"

"Well," sniffed Priscilla, "yes. You see, I work with this doctor, and he and I—it isn't anything formal, you understand, but we work so well together and laugh at the same things, and it's . . . nice. And then he—"

"Go on."

"He was married once. Years ago. And he saw her tonight. And he didn't look at me any more. I guess I'm foolish, but I got all upset."

"Why?"

"I told you. He just wanted to talk to her. He forgot I was alive."

"That isn't why. You were upset because you were afraid he'd get together with her again."

"I—I suppose so."

"Do you want to marry him?"

"Why, I—I don't . . . No, I wouldn't. It isn't that."

The old lady nodded. "You think if he married her again—or anyone else—that it would make a big difference in the work you do together, in the way he treats you?"

"I . . . don't suppose there would be any difference, no," Priscilla said thoughtfully. "I'd never thought it through."

"And," continued the old lady relentlessly, "have you thought through any other possible course of action he could have taken tonight? He was married to her for some time. He apparently hasn't seen her for years. It must have been a small shock to him to find her there. Now, what else might he have done? 'Goodness gracious, there's my old used-up wife. Priscilla, let's dance.' Is that what you expected?"

At last she giggled. "You're wonderful. And you're right, you are so absolutely right. I have been sil—Oh!"

"What is it?"

"You called me Priscilla. How did you know my name? Who are you?"

"A friend. Come along, girl; you can't sit here all night." She drew the startled girl to her feet. "Here, let me look at you. Your lipstick's smeared. Over here. That's better. Can you button that jacket? I think perhaps you should. Not that it should matter if your bust *does* show, the way you brazen things dress nowadays. There now, come along."

She hurried Priscilla through the park, and when they reached the street, turned north. Priscilla tugged at the black sleeve. "Please—wait. I live *that* way." She pointed.

"I know, I know. But you're not going home just yet. Come along, child!"

"Where are you—we—going?"

"You'll see. Now listen to me. Do you trust me?"

"Oh, my goodness, yes!"

"Very well. When we get where we're going, you'll go inside alone. Don't worry now, it's perfectly safe. Once you're inside you'll do something very stupid indeed."

"I will?"

"You will. You'll turn around and try to leave. Now, then, I want you to understand that you must *not* leave. I shall be standing outside to see that you don't."

"But I—But why? What am I supposed . . . where . . ."

"Hush, child! You do as you're told and you'll be all right."

Priscilla walked along in silence for a time. Then she said, "All right." The old lady turned to look into the softest-smiling, most trusting face she had ever seen. She put her arm around Priscilla's shoulders and squeezed.

"You'll do," she said.

Henry Faulkner sat in a booth, far from the belly-thumping juke box and the knot of people chattering away at the headend of the bar. Henry's elbows were on the table and his thumbs, fitted carefully into the bony arches over his eyelids, supported the weight of his head. The cafe went round and round like a Czerny etude, but with a horizontal axis. The walls moved upward in front of him and down behind him, and he felt very ill. Once he had forced down three beers, and that was his established capacity; it had bloated him horribly and he'd had a backache in the morning. Tonight he'd had four double ryes.

"There he shtood," he said to one of the blonde girls who sat opposite, "nex' to the conductor, watching the orch'stra, an' sometimes he'd beat time wiz arms. When the last movement ended, th' audience rozhe up as one man an' roared. An' there he shtood, nex' to the conductor—"

"You said that before," said the girls. They spoke in

unison, and the pair of them had only one voice, like the doubled leading tone in a major chord.

"There he shtood," Henry went on, "shtill beating time after the music stopped. An' the conductor, wi' *eyes* in his tears—wi' *tears* in his eyes—turned him around so he could *shee* the applause."

"What was the matter with him?" asked the girls.

"He was deaf."

"Who was?"

"Beethoven." Henry wept.

"My God. Is that what you're tying one on about?"

"You said to tell you the sad story," said Henry. "You didn't say tell you *my* sad story."

"Okay, okay. You got money, ain't you?"

Henry lifted his head and reared back to get perspective. It was then that the girl merged and became one; he realized that there had been one all along, in spite of what he had seen. That explained why they both had the same voice. He was extravagantly pleased. "Sure I got money."

"Well, come on up to my place. I'm tired uh sittin' around here."

"Very gracious," he intoned. "I shall now tell you the sad story of my laysted wife."

"What type wife?"

"I beg your pardon? I've never been married."

The girl looked perplexed. "Start over again."

"Da capo," he said with his finger beside his nose. "Very well. I repeat. I shall now tell you the story of my wasted life."

"Oh," said the girl.

"I have had the ultimate in rejections," said Henry solemnly. "I fell in love, deeply, deeply, deeply, dee—"

"Who with?" said the girl tiredly. "Get to the point and let's get out of here."

"With a string bass. A bull, as it were, fiddle." He nodded solemnly.

"Ah, fer Pete's sake," she said scornfully. She stood up. "Look, mister, I can't waste the whole night. Are you comin' or ain't you?"

Henry scowled up at her. He hadn't asked for her company. She'd just appeared there in the booth. She had niggled and nagged until he was about to tell her all the things he had come here to forget. And now she wanted to walk out. Suddenly he was furious. He, who had never raised his hand or his voice in his whole life, was suddenly so angry that he was, for a moment, blind. He growled like the open D on a bass clarinet and leaped at her. His clawed hand swept past her fluffy collar and got caught, tore the collar a little, high on the shoulder.

She squealed in routine fear. The bartender hopped up sitting on the bar and swung his thick legs over.

"What the hell's going on back there?" he demanded, pushing himself off onto the floor.

The blonde said, shrilly and indignantly, exactly what she thought Henry was trying to do.

"Right there in the booth?" said a bourbon up the row.

"That I got to see," replied a beer.

They started back, followed by the rest of the customers.

The bartender reached into the booth and lifted Henry bodily out of it. Henry, sick and in a state of extreme panic, wriggled free and ran—two steps. The side of his head met the bridge of the bourbon's nose. Henry was aware of a dull crunch. There were exploding lights and he went down, rolled, got to his feet again.

The girl was screaming in a scratchy monotone somewhere around high E flat. The bourbon was sitting on the floor with blood spouting from his nose.

"Get 'im!" somebody barked.

Powerful hands caught Henry's thin biceps. A heavy man stood in front of him, gigantic yellow mallets of fists raised.

"Hold him tight," said the heavy man. "I'm gonna let him have it."

And then a sort of puffball with bright blue eyes was between Henry and the heavy man. In a soft, severe voice it said, "Leave him alone, you—you bullies! You let that man go, this very minute!"

Henry shook his head. He regretted the movement, but among the other things it made him experience was clearing sight. He looked at the puffball, which became a sweet-faced lady in her fifties. She had gentleness about her mouth and sheer determination in her crackling blue eyes.

"You better stay out of this, Granny," said the bartender not unkindly. "This character's got it comin' to him."

"You'll let him go this instant!" said the lady, and stamped a small foot. "And that's the way it is."

"Al," said the heavy man to the bartender, "just lead this lady off to one side while I paste this bastard."

"Don't you put a hand on me."

"Watch your language, Sylvan," said the bartender to the heavy man. He put a hand on the lady's shoulder. "Come over her a sec—*uh!*"

The final syllable was his staccato response to the old lady's elbow in the pit of his stomach. That, however, was not the end of her—literally—chain reaction. She swung her crocus reticule around in a full-armed arc and brought it down on the heavy man's head. He sank to the floor without a whimper. In the same movement she put her other hand swiftly but firmly against Henry's jaw and pushed it violently. His head tipped back and smashed into the face of the man who stood behind him holding his arms. The man staggered backward, tripped, and fell, bouncing his skull off an unpadded bar stool.

"Come along, Henry," said the old lady cheerfully. She took him by the wrist as if he were a small boy whose face needed washing, and marched him out of the cafe.

On the street he gasped, "They'll chase us . . ."

"Naturally," said the lady. She put two fingers into her mouth and blew a piercing blast. A block and a half away, a parked taxicab slid away from the curb and came toward them. There was shouting from the cafe. The taxicab pulled up beside them. The lady whipped the door open and pushed Henry in. As four angry men shouldered out on the sidewalk, she reached deep into her reticule and snatched a dark object from it. She stood poised for a moment, and in the neon-shot half-light Henry saw what was in her hand—an old-fashioned, top-of-stove flat iron. He understood then why the heavy man had drowsed off so readily.

The lady hefted the iron and let it fly. It grazed the temple of one of the men and flew straight through a plate glass window. The man who was hit went to his knees, his hands holding his head. The other three fell all over each other trying to get back out of range. The lady skipped into the cab and said calmly, "Young man, take us away from here."

"Yes, *ma'am!*" said the driver in an awed tone, and let in his clutch.

They jounced along in silence for a moment, and then she leaned forward. "Driver, pull up by one of these warehouses. Henry's going to be sick."

"I'm all right," said Henry weakly. The cab stopped. The lady opened the door. "Come along!"

"No, really, I—"

The lady snapped her fingers. .

"Oh, all right," said Henry sheepishly. In the black shadows by the warehouse he protested faintly, "But I don't *want* to be sick!"

"I know what's best," she said solicitously. She took his hand, spread it, and presented him with his long middle finger, point first, as if it were a clinical thermometer. "Down your throat," she ordered.

"No!" he said loudly.

"Are you going to do as you're told?"

He looked at her. "Yes."

"I'll hold your head," she said. "Go on."

She held his head.

Afterward, in the cab, he asked her timidly if she would take him home now.

"No," she said. "You play the piano, don't you, Henry?"

He nodded.

"Well, you're going to play for me." She reached forcefully into her reticule again, and his protest died on his trembling lips. "Here," she said, and handed him an old-fashioned mint.

Priscilla mounted the stairs. She had a "walking-underwater" feeling, as if she were immersed in her own reluctance. She had trod these stairs many times at night—usually downward after a perplexing, intriguing series of experiments. She did not know why she should be returning to the laboratory now, except that she had been ordered to do so. She freely admitted that if it were not for the thin, straight figure in black who waited downstairs, she would certainly be in bed by now. But there was an air of command, of complete certainty about the old lady who had saved her that was utterly compelling.

She walked quietly down the carpeted hall. The outer door of the lab office was ajar. There was no light in the office, but a dim radiance filtered in from the lab itself, through the frosted panel of the inner door. She crossed to it and went in.

Someone gasped.

Someone said, "Priscilla!"

Priscilla said, "Excuse *me!*" and spun around. She shot through the office and out into the hall, her cheeks burning, her eyes stinging. "He—he—" she sobbed, but could not complete the thought, would not review the picture she had seen.

At the lower landing she raced to the street door, valiantly holding back the tears and the sobs that would accompany them. Her hand went out to the big brass doorknob, touched it—

As the cool metal greeted her hand she stopped.

Outside that door, standing on the walk by the iron railings, radiating strength and rectitude, would be the old lady. She would watch Priscilla come out of the building. She would probably nod her head in knowledgeable disappointment. She would doubtless say, "I told you you would want to leave, and that it would be foolish."

"But they were—" said Priscilla in audible protest.

Then came the thought of trustfulness: "Listen to me. Do you trust me?"

Priscilla took her hand away from the knob. She thought she heard the murmur of low voices upstairs.

She remembered the talk about Jon and his meeting with Edie at the party. She remembered herself saying, "I—just didn't think it through."

She turned and faced the stairs. "I can't, I can't possibly go back. Not now. Even if . . . even if it didn't make any difference to me, they'd . . . they'd hate me. It would be a terrible thing to do, to go back."

She turned until the big brass knob nudged her hip. Its touch projected a vivid picture into her mind—the old lady, straight and waiting in the lamplight.

She sighed and started slowly up the stairs again.

When she got to the office this time the light was on. She pushed the door open. Jon was leaning against the desk, watching it open. Edie, his ex-wife, stood by the laboratory door, her wide-spaced eyes soft and bright. For a moment no one moved. Then Edie went to Jon and stood beside him, and together they watched Priscilla with questions on their faces, and something like gentle sympathy. Or was it empathy?

Priscilla came in slowly. She went up to Edie and stopped. She said, "You're just what he needed."

The wide dark eyes filled with tears. Edie put her arms out and Priscilla was in them without quite knowing which of them had moved. When she could, Edie said, "You are so lovely, Priscilla. You're so very lovely." And Priscilla knew she was not talking about her red hair or her face.

Jon put a hand on each of their shoulders. "I don't understand what's happening here," he said, "but I have the feeling that it's good. Priscilla, why did you come back?"

She looked at him and said nothing.

"What made you come back?"

She shook her head.

"You know," he smiled, "but you're just not talking. You've never done a wiser thing than to come back. If you hadn't, Edie and I would have been driven apart just as surely as if you'd used a wedge. Am I right, Edie?"

Edie nodded. "You've made us very happy."

Priscilla felt embarrassed. "You are giving me an awful lot of credit," she said in a choked voice. "I didn't really do anything. I wish I had the—the bigness or wisdom you think I have." She raised her eyes to them. "I'll try to live up to it, though. I will . . ."

The phone rang.

"Now who could that—" Jon reached for it.

Priscilla took it out of his hand. "I'll take it."

Edie and Jon looked at each other. Priscilla said into the phone, "Yes . . . yes, it's me. How in the world did you . . . Tonight? But it's so late! Will you be there? Then so will I. Oh, you're wonderful . . . yes, right away."

She hung up.

Jon said, "Who was it?"

Priscilla laughed. "A friend."

Jon touched her jaw. "All right, Miss Mysterious. What's it all about?"

"Will you do something if I ask you? You, too, Edie?"

"Oh, yes."

Priscilla laughed again. "We do have something to celebrate, don't we?" When they nodded, she laughed again. "Well, come on!"

* * *

It was easier to carry the chopsticks piano-player with Derek to help, Jane concluded. She watched the rapt faces in the club. The house counted good, and it was going great, but she couldn't help thinking what it would be like if Derek hadn't been so pigheaded about little Henry. She finished her chorus and the piano took it up metronomically, nudged on the upbeats by the authoritative beat of Derek's bass. She looked at him. He was playing steadily, almost absently. His face was sullen. When he got absentminded he wasn't colossal any more; only terrific.

The piano moved through an obvious C-sharp seventh chord to change key to F-sharp, her key for the windup. She drifted into the bridge section with a long glissando, and disgust moved into her face and Derek's in perfect sychronization as they realized that the pianist was blindly going into another 32 bars from the beginning.

Derek doubled his beat and slapped the strings hard, and the sudden flurry of sound snapped the pianist out of it. Blushing, he recovered the fluff. Jane rolled her eyes up in despair and finished the number. To scattered applause she turned to the piano and said, "Tinkle some. Derek and I are going to take ten. And while you're tinkling," she aded viciously, "*practice,* huh?"

She smiled at the audience, crossed the stand and touched Derek's elbow. "I'm going behind that potted palm and flip my lid. Come catch it."

He put his bass out of harm's way and followed her into the office. She let him pass her and slump down on the desk. She banged the door.

"You—"

He looked at her sullenly. "I know what you're going to say. I threw out the best ten fingers in the business. I told you I don't want to talk about it. You don't believe that, do you?"

"I believe it," she said. Her eyes glittered. "Derek Jax, I love you."

"Cut it out."

"I'm not kidding. I'm not changing the subject, either. I love you this much. I'm going to call your hand, kid. I love you so much that I'm going to make you talk about what's with this business of Henry, or I'm going to see you walk out of here with, and into, your doghouse."

"That don't make a hell of a lot of sense, Janie," he said uncomfortably.

"No, huh? Listen, the guy I love talks to me. I understand him enough so he can talk to me. If he won't talk to me, it's because he thinks I won't understand. I think you see what I mean. I love the guy I think you are. If you won't talk about it, you're just not that guy. Maybe that doesn't mean anything to you."

"Could be," he growled. He rose and stretched. "Well, guess I'll be going. Nice working with you, Janie."

"So long," she said. She went and opened the door.

"By God," he said, "you really mean it."

She nodded.

He licked his lips, then bit them. He sat down. "Shut the door, Janie."

She shut the door and put her head against it. He flashed her a look. "What's the matter?"

She said hoarsely, "I got something in my eye. Wait." Presently she swung around and faced him. Her smile was brilliant, her face composed. The vein in the side of her neck was thick and throbbing.

"Jane . . ." he said with difficulty, "that Henry—did he ever make a pass at you?"

"Why, you egghead. No! To him I'm something that makes music, like a saxophone. It's you he's interested in. Hell, did you see his face when you came in with your bass this afternoon? He'd rather play to that bass than go over the falls in a barrel with me. If that's all that was on your mind, forget it."

"You make it tough for me," he said heavily. "I'll play it through for you a note at a time. Got a stick?"

She rummaged in the desk drawer and found him a cigarette. He lit it and dragged until he coughed. She had never seen him like this. She said nothing.

He seemed to appreciate that. He glanced at her and half his mouth flashed part of a smile. Then he said, "Did I ever tell you about Danny?"

"No."

"Kids together. Kids get close. He lived down the pike. I got caught in a root one time, swimming in a rock quarry. Danny seemed to know the instant I got tangled. He couldn't swim worth a damn, but in he came. Got me out, too."

He dragged on his cigarette, still hungry, hot and harsh. The words came out, smoking. "There was a lot of stuff . . . we played ball, we run away from home, we broke into an ol' house and pried loose a toilet and threw it out a fourth-floor window onto a concrete walk. We done a lot.

"We jived a lot. He had natural rhythm. We used to bang away on his ol' lady's piano. I played trumpet for a while, but what I wanted to do was play string bass. I wanted that real bad.

"We grew up and he moved away. Some lousy job trying to learn cabinet-making. Saw him a couple times. Half-starved, but real happy. I was playing bass by then, some. Had to borrow a fiddle. Wanted my own instrument *so* bad, never had the money. So one day he called me up long distance. Come over. I didn't have no trainfare, so I hitch-hiked. Met him at a barrelhouse joint in town. He was real excited, dragged me out to his place. A shack—practically a shanty. When we got in sight of it he started to run. It was on fire."

Derek closed his eyes and went on talking. "We got to it and it was pretty far gone. I got there first. One wall was gone. Inside everything was burning. Danny, he—he screamed like a stung kid. He tried to jump inside. I hung on to him. Was much bigger'n him. Then I saw it—a string bass. A full-size string bass, burning up. I sat on Danny and watched it burn. I knew why he'd moved out of town. I knew why he took up cabinet-making. I knew why he was so hungry an'—an' so happy. Made the box with his own two hands. We watched it burn and he tried to fight me because I would not let him save it. He cried. Well—*we* cried. Just two kids."

Jane said a single, unprintable word with a bookful of of feeling behind it.

"We got over it. We roomed together after that. We done everything together. Crowd we ran with used to kid us about it, and that just made it better. I guess we were about nineteen then."

He squeezed out a long breath and looked up at her with stretched, blind eyes. "We had something, see? Something clean and big that never happened before, and wasn't nothing wrong with it.

"Then I come home one night and he's at the back window staring into the yard. Said he was moving out.

Said we weren't doing each other any good. He was in bad shape. Somebody'd been talking to him, some lousy crumb with a sewer mouth and sewer ideas. I didn't know what it was all about. We were still just kids, see?

"Anyway, I couldn't talk him out of it. He left. He was half-crazy, all eaten up. Like the time we watched the bull-fiddle burn up. He wouldn't say what was the trouble. So after he went I milled around the joint trying to make sense out of it and I couldn't. Then I—"

Derek's voice seemed to desert him. He coughed hard and got it back. "—Then I went and looked out the window. Somebody'd wrote our names on the fence. Drew a heart around 'em.

"I never gave a damn what anyone thought, see? But Danny, he did. I guess you can't know how someone else feels, but you can get a pretty fair idea. First I was just mad, and then I pretended I was Danny looking at a thing like that, and I got an idea how bad it was. I ran out lookin' for him.

"Saw him after a time. Up by the highway, staggering a bit like he was half-soused. He wasn't, though. I ran after him. He was waiting for the light to change. There was a lot of traffic. Tried to get to him. Couldn't begin to. He sort of pitched off the curb right under oh my God I can still see it the big dual wheel it run right over his head . . ." he finished in a rapid monotone.

Jane put her hand on his shoulder. Derek said, "I didn't know then and I don't know now and I never will know if he was so tore up and sick he just fell, or if he done it on purpose. All I know is I've lived ever since with the idea I killed him just by being around him so much. Don't try to talk me out of it. I know it don't make sense. I know all the right answers. But knowing don't help.

"That's the whole story."

Jane waited a long time and then said gently, "No, Derek."

He started as if he had suddenly found himself in an utterly strange place. Gradually his sense of presence returned to him and he wiped his face.

"Yeah," he said. "Your boy Henry. Danny—he played piano, Janie. I started with him. Danny played piano like nothing that ever lived except this Henry. Everything I ever drug out of a string bass was put in there first by the way he played piano. He used to sit and play like that and every once in a while grin at me. Shy.

"So I walk in here on a guy playing that kind of piano and he grins shy like that when he plays, and besides, here's that *real close* stuff around him like a fog. That Henry's a genius, Janie. And he's a—he's the type of guy they ought to use for a mold to make *people* out of. And he just wants to be near my fiddle. And me. And you want me to keep him around here until he knocks hisself off.

"Janie," he said, with agony in his voice, *"I'm not goin' through that again!"*

Jane squeezed his shoulder. She looked back over the afternoon and evening and words flitted through her mind: "You wont have to lose any sleep over him" . . . "Looks like you've made a conquest" . . . "Did he ever make a pass at you?" Aloud she told him, "I've sure said all the right things . . . take a swing at me, pudd'nhead."

Derek pulled her hand close against his cheek and pressed it there so hard it hurt her. She let him do it as long as he wanted. "I love you, Janie," he whispered. "I shoulda told you all that about Danny a long time ago."

"How could you tell till you tried?" she asked huskily. "Let's go on out there before ol' Kitten on the Keys drives all the customers away."

"I can't go in there," said Henry Faulkner in genuine panic.

"You can and you will," said the old lady firmly.

"Listen, there's a man in there who'll throw me out on sight."

"Have I been wrong yet? This is your night to do as you're told, young man, and that's the way it is."

In spite of himself he grinned. They went in through the herculite doors. Janie was just finishing a number. The piano fluffed the last chorus badly. Henry and the old lady stood in the back of the club until Derek and Jane walked off the floor.

"Now," she said briskly, "go on up there and play for me. Play anything you want to."

"But they have a piano player!"

"He's in a pet. Just go up there."

"Wh-what'll I say to him?"

"Don't say anything, silly! Just stand there. He'll go away."

He hesitated, and the lady gave him a small shove. He shambled around the dance floor and diffidently approached the piano.

The pianist was playing a dingdong version of *Stardust*. He saw Henry coming. "You again."

Henry said nothing.

"I suppose you want to take my job again."

Henry still said nothing. The man went on playing. Presently, "You can have it. How anyone can work with a couple sourpusses like that . . ." He got off the stool in mid-chorus, leaving *Stardust's* garden gate musically ajar. Henry's right hand shot out and, catching the chord as if it had been syncopated instead of shut off, began molding it like a handful of soft clay. He sat down still playing.

Edie said, "I can't help feeling a little peculiar. This is wonderful, so wonderful—but there are still two of us and one of you."

"Three of us," corrected Priscilla.

"In some ways that's so," said Jon. He swallowed the rest of his drink and beckoned the waiter. "Pris is the best statistician and psychological steno I've ever run across. And you're a genius with the machines. Why, between us we will do research that'll make history."

"Of course we will. But—isn't three a crowd?"

Priscilla said, without malice, "From anyone but you I'd consider that a hint. Don't worry about me. I have the most wonderful feeling that the miracles aren't finished."

"Pris, are you ever going to tell us about the miracles?"

"I don't know, Jon. Perhaps." Her eyes searched the club. Suddenly they fixed on a distant corner table. "There she is!"

"Who?" Jon twisted around. "Well, I'll be damned!"

"What is it?" asked Edie.

"Excuse me," said Jon, and rose. "Someone I've got to see." He stalked over to the corner table and glowered down at its occupants. "May I ask what you're doing here?"

"Why, Dr. Prince!" said Pallas. "Imagine meeting you here!"

"What are you two doing here at this time of night?"

"We can go where we like," said Verna, smoothing her snowy hair, "and that's the way it is."

"We're not due to report to you until the day after tomorrow," said Pallas self-righteously.

"There's no law against a lady having a spot at bedtime," amended Verna.

"You two never cease to amaze me," Jon said, chuckling in spite of himself. "Just be careful. I'd hate to see my prize exhibits get hurt."

They smiled up at him. "We'll be all right. We'll talk to you again later, won't we, Verna?"

"Oh, yes," said Verna. "Definitely. That's the way it is."

Still chuckling, Jon went back to his table. "There sits the damnedest pair of human beings I've encountered yet," he said as he sat down. "Three years ago they were senile psychotics, the two of them. As far as I can determine they had no special therapy—they were in the County Home, and as mindless as a human being can get and stay alive. First thing you know they actually started feeding themselves—"

"Pallas and Verna!" said Priscilla. "You've mentioned— holy Pete! Are you sure?"

'Of course I'm sure. I'm on the Board out there. You know the case history. They have to report to me every sixty days."

"Well—I—will—be—damned," Priscilla intoned, awed.

"What is it, Pris? I didn't think you'd ever seen them. They've never been to the lab . . . Say, how did you recognize them just now?"

"Could . . . could you bring them over?"

"Oh, come now. This celebration is only for—"

"I've heard enough to be curious about them," said Edie. "Do invite them, Jon."

He shrugged and returned to the other table. In a moment he was back with the two spinsters. He drew out chairs for them in courtly fashion, and called a waiter. Pallas ordered a double rye, no chaser. Verna smiled like a kitten and ordered scotch on the rocks. "For our colds," she explained.

"How long have you had colds?" he demanded professionally.

"Oh, dear, we don't get colds," explained Verna sweetly. "That's because we drink our liquor straight."

Dr. Jonathan Prince felt it within him to lay down the law at this point. A patient was a patient. But there was something in the air that prevented it. He found himself laughing again. He thought he saw Pallas wink at Priscilla and shake her head slightly, but he wasn't sure. He introduced the girls. Without the slightest hesitation he introduced Edie as "my wife." She colored and looked pleased.

"Listen to that music," breathed Priscilla.

"Thought you'd notice it," said Pallas, and smiled at Verna.

They all listened. It was a modal, moody, rhythmic invention, built around a circle of chords in the bass which beat, and beat, and beat on a single sonorous tone. The treble progressed evenly, regularly, tripped up on itself and ran giggling around and through the steady structure of the bass modulations, then sobered and marched again, but always full of suppressed mirth.

Priscilla was craning her neck. "I can't see him!"

Verna said, "Why don't you go up there, dear? I'm sure he would not mind."

"Oh . . . really not?" She caught Pallas's eye. Pallas gave her one firm nod. Priscilla said, "Do you mind?" She slipped out of her chair and went up past the dance floor.

"Look at her," breathed Edie. "She's got that—that 'miracle' expression again . . . Oh, Jon, she's *so* lovely."

Jon said, looking at the spinsters, "What are you two hugging each other about?"

Henry looked up from the keyboard and smiled shyly. "Hello," Priscilla said.

"Hello." He looked at her face, her hair, her body, her eyes. His shyness was there, and no boldness was present; he looked at her the way she listened to his music. It was personal and not aggressive. He moved over on the bench. "Sit down."

Without hesitation she did. She looked at him, too—the hawk profile, the gentle gray-green eyes. "You play beautifully."

"Listen."

He played with his eyes on her face. His hands leaped joyfully like baby goats. Then they felt awe and hummed something. Henry stopped playing by ear. He began to sight-read.

Note followed note followed note for the line of her nose, and doubled and curved and turned back for her nostrils. The theme became higher and fuller and rounded and there was her forehead, and then there were colorful waves up and back for her hair. Here was a phrase for an ear-lobe, and one for the turn of the cheek, and now there were mysteries, two of them, long and subdued and agleam and end-tilted, and they were her eyes . . .

Derek came out of the office and stopped so abruptly that Jane ran into him. Before she could utter the first startled syllable, her breath was taken away in a great gasp.

Derek turned and gestured at the music. "You—"

She looked up at him, the furious eyes, the terrified trembling at the corners of his mouth. "No, Derek, so help me God, I didn't ask him to come back. I wouldn't do that, Derek. I *wouldn't*."

"You wouldn't," he agreed gently. "I know it, hon. I'm sorry. But out he goes." He strode out to the stand. Jane trotted behind him, and when they turned the corner she caught his arm so violently that her long fingernails sank into his flesh. *"Wait!"*

There was a girl on the bench with Henry, and as he played he stared at her face. His eyes moved over it, his own face moved closer. His hands made music like the almost visible current which flowed between them. Their lips touched.

There was a tinkling explosion of sound from the piano that built up in fullness and sonority until Jane and Derek all but blinked their eyes, as if it were a blaze of light. And then Henry's left hand picked up a theme, a thudding, joyous melody that brought the few late-owls in the club right to their feet. He no longer looked at the girl. His eyes were closed, and his hands spoke of himself and what he felt— a great honest hunger and new riches, a shy and willing experience with a hitherto undreamed-of spectrum of sensation.

Jane and Derek looked at each other with shining eyes. Jane said, deliberately, "Son, you got a rival," and Derek laughed in sheer relieved delight.

"I'm going to get my fiddle," he said.

When Derek started to play, four people left their table and came up to the piano as if cables drew them. Hand in hand, Jon and Edie stopped close by Priscilla and stood there, rapt as she, Pallas and Verna stood at the other end of the bench, their eyes glowing.

And out of the music, out of the bodies that fell into synchronization with the masterful pulse of the great viol, came a union, a blending of forces from each of six people. Each of the six had a part that was different from all of the others, but the shape of them all was a major chord, infinitely complete and completely satisfying.

"Ril!"

"Oh, make it formal, KadKedKud!"

"RilRylRul, then . . ."

"If only Mak were here."

"Myk is with us, and Muk. Poor partial things, and how hard they have worked, guarding and guiding with those pitifully inadequate human bodies as instruments. Come, Ril; we must decide. Now that we can operate fully, we can investigate these creatures."

Just as they had investigated, compared, computed and stored away observations on industrial techniques, strength of materials, stress and temperature and power and design, so now they took instant and total inventory of their hosts.

RilRylRul found classicism and inventiveness, tolerance and empathy in Henry. In Derek were loyalty and rugged strength and a powerful intepretive quality. In Jane was the full-blown beauty of sensualism and directive thought, and a unique stylization of the products of artistic creation.

KadKedKud separated and analyzed a splendid systematization in Priscilla, a superior grasp of applied theory in Edie, and in Jon that rarest of qualities, the associative mind—the mind that can bridge the specialties.

"A great race," said Ril, "but a sick one, badly infected with the Pa'ak pestilence."

"The wisest thing to do," reflected Kad, "would be to stimulate the virus to such an extent that humanity will impose its own quarantine—by reducing itself to savagery through atomic warfare. There is such a great chance of that, no matter what we do, that it would seem expedient to hasten the process. The object would be to force atomic warfare before space travel can begin. That at least would keep the virus out of the Galaxy, which is what we came here to effect."

"It's a temptation," conceded Ril. "And yet—what a tremendous species this human race could be! Let us stay, Kad. Let us see what we can do with them. Let us move on to other human groups, now that we know the techniques of entry and merging. With just the right pressure on exactly the right points, who knows? Perhaps we can cause them to discover how to cure themselves."

"It will be a close race," worried Kad. "We can do a great deal, but can we do it soon enough? We face three possibilities: Mankind may destroy itself through its own sick ingenuity; it may reach the stars to spread its infection; or it may find its true place as a healthy species in a healthy Cosmos. I would not predict which is more likely."

"Neither would I," Ril returned. "So if the forces are that closely balanced, I have hope for the one we join. Are you with me?"

"Agreed. Myk—Muk . . . will you join us?"

Faintly, faintly came the weak response of the two paltry parts of a once powerful triad: "Back in our sector we would be considered dead. Here we have a life, and work. Of course we will help."

So they considered, and, at length, decided.

And their meeting and consideration and decision took four microseconds.

The six people looked at one another, entranced, dazed.

"It's—gone," said Jon. He wondered, then, what he meant by that.

Henry's fingers slid off the keys, and the big bass was silent. Priscilla opened her tilted eyes wide and looked about her. Edie pressed close to Jonathan, bright-faced, composed. Jane stood with her head high, her nostrils arched.

They felt as if they were suddenly living on a new plane of existence, where colors were more vivid and the hues between them more recognizable. There was a new richness to the air, and a new strength in their bodies; but most of all it was as if a curtain had been lifted from their minds for the first time in their lives. They had all reached a high unity, a supreme harmony in the music a second before, but this was something different, infinitely more complete. "Cured" was the word that came to Jonathan.

He knew instinctively that what he now felt was a new norm, and that it was humanity's birthright.

"My goodness gracious!"

Verna and Pallas stood close together, like two frightened birds, darting glances about them and twittering.

"I can't think what I'm doing here," said Pallas blankly, yet aware. "I've had one of my spells . . ."

"We both have," Verna agreed. "And that's the way it is."

Jonathan looked at them, and knew them instantly as incomplete.

He raised his eyes to the rest of the people in the club, still stirring with the final rustle of applause from the magnificent burst of music they had heard, and he recognized them as sick. His mind worked with a new directiveness and brilliance to the causes of their sickness.

He turned to Edie. "We have work to do . . ."

She pressed his hand, and Priscilla looked up and smiled.

Derek and Jane looked into each other's eyes, into depths neither had dreamed of before. There would be music from that, they knew.

Henry said, with all his known gentleness and none of the frightened diffidence, "Hey, you with the red hair. I love you. What's your name?" And Priscilla laughed with a sound like wings and buried her face in his shoulder.

On earth there was a new kind of partnership of three. And . . .

The news is new aggression threatens unleashing of atomic weapons. . . . President calls for universal disarmament. . . . First flight to Moon possible now with sufficient funds. . . . Jonathan Prince announces virus cause of neurosis, promises possible cure of all mental diseases. . . .

Watch your local newspapers for latest developments.

THE
EDUCATION
OF
DRUSILLA
STRANGE

This is one of my very favorite stories, for a number of reasons.

Novelettes were for a long time "lost"; once they had appeared in a magazine, book publishers were chary of using them because of a conviction that the moron reader couldn't sustain his attention span for more than five thousand words, and that he would feel cheated if he didn't get a dozen or fourteen items in the Table of Contents. This is the chief reason that Drusilla has gotten so little exposure.

My dream for Drusilla is to see her education as a major motion picture, and then to spin off as a television series dealing with the educated Drusilla Strange. It isn't the glory (of which my readers have given me fulsomely) or the money (because I have found out that the line between owning money and being honestly broke is the line between owning money and being owned by it) but because it's a prime opportunity for a strong dramatic role to be given to a woman. I discount imitation bionic men and imitation male police officers, and of course sitcom pie-in-the-face, perennial teases, and Daddy-is-an-oaf so-called comedies. Drusilla is a super-woman, with super-empathy, super-compassion, super-libido (if you like), but also super-responsibility, so that, because she knows she will live for a thousand years, she knows that with ethical responsibility, she must always move on. The educated Drusilla Strange has a prime drive: her deeply convinced and passionate love for humanity, and her desire, with all her powers, to solve human problems.

Oh, well . . . when Hollywood is through with 1927 to 1935 science fiction, and is ready to look at inner space instead of outer space, perhaps it will do right by our Drusilla.

The prison ship, under full shields, slipped down toward the cove, and made no shadow on the moonlight water, and no splash as it slid beneath the surface. They put her out and she swam clear, and the ship nosed up and silently fled. Two wavelets clapped hands softly, once, and that was the total mark the ship made on the prison wall.

For killing the Preceptor, she had been sentenced to life imprisonment.

With torture.

She swam toward the beach until smooth fluid sand touched her knee. She stood up, flung her long hair back with a single swift motion, and waded up the steep shingle, one hand lightly touching the bulging shoulder of the rocks which held the cove in their arms.

Ahead she heard the slightest indrawn breath, then a cough. She stopped, tall in the moonlight. The man took a half-step forward, then turned his head sidewise and a little upward away from her, into the moon.

"I'm—I beg your—sorry," he floundered.

She sensed his turmoil, extracted its source, delved for alternative acts, and chose the one about which he showed the most curious conflict. She crouched back into the shadows by the rock.

I didn't see you there.

"I didn't see you until you . . . I'm sorry. Why am I standing here like this when you . . . I'll move on down the . . . I'm sorry."

She took and fanned out his impressions, sorted them, chose one. *My clothes—*

He started away from the rocks, looking about him, as if he might have been leaning against something hot, or something holy. "Where are they? Am I in the way? Shall I put them near the . . . I'll just move on down."

No . . . no clothes. Directly from him she took *Where are they?*

"I don't see any. Somebody must've—are you sure you put them—*where* did you put them?" He was floundering again.

She caught and used the phrase *Why, who would . . . what a lowdown trick!*

"Is your—do you have a car up there?" he asked peering up at the grassy rim of the beach. He added immediately, "But even if you got to the car . . ."

I have no car.

"My God!" he said indignantly. "Anybody that would . . . here, what am I standing here yapping for? You must be chilled to the bone."

He was wearing a battered trench coat. He whipped it off and approached her, three-quarters backward, the coat dangling from his blindly extended arm like a torn jib on a bowsprit. She took it, shook it out, turned it over curiously, then slipped into it so that it fell around her the way it had covered him.

Thank you.

She stepped out of the shadows, and the huge relief he felt, and the admixture of guilty regret that went with it made her smile.

"Well!" he said, rubbing his hands briskly. "That's better, now, isn't it?" He looked up the lonely beach, and down. "Live around here somewhere?"

No.

"Oh." He said it again, then, "Friends bring you down?" he asked diffidently.

She hesitated. *Yes.*

"Then they'll be back for you!"

She shook her head. He scratched his. Suddenly he stepped away from her and demanded, "Look, you don't think I had anything to do with stealing your clothes, do you?"

Oh, no!

"Well, all right, because I didn't, I mean I couldn't do a thing like that, even in fun. What I was going to say, I mean, now I don't want you to think anyth . . ." He ground to a stop, took a breath and tried again. "What I mean is, I have a little shack over the rise there. You'd be perfectly safe. I have no phone, but there's one a mile down the beach. I could go and call your friends. I mean I'm not one of those . . . well, look, you do just what you think is best."

She searched. She felt it emerged correctly: *I really mustn't put you to that trouble. But you're very kind.*

"I'm not kind. You'd do exactly the same thing for me, now wouldn't . . ."

He stopped because she was laughing silently, her eyes turned deep into the corners to look at him. She laughed because she had sensed his startled laughter at what he was saying even before it had uncurled.

"I—can't say you would at that," he faltered, and then his laughter surfaced. By the time it had run its course, she was striding lithely beside him.

They walked for a while in silence, until he said, "I do the same thing myself, go swimming in the—I mean without . . . at night. But generally not this late in the year."

She found this unremarkable and made no reply.

"Uh," he began, and then faltered and fell silent again.

She wondered why he felt it so necessary to talk. She probed, and discovered that it was because he was excited and frightened and guilty and happy all at once, full of little half-finished plans concerning cold odds and ends of food and the contents of a clothes closet, the breathless flash of a mental picture of her emerging from the water with certain details oddly highlighted, the quick blanking of the picture and the stern frown that did it, the timid hope that she did not suspect feelings that he could not control . . . Oh, yes, he must talk.

"You have a—do you mind if I say something personal?"

She looked up attentively.

"You have a funny sort of way of talking. I mean—" he leaned close—"you hardly move your lips when you talk."

She turned her head slightly and flexed her lips. She made the effort and said aloud, "Oh?"

"Maybe it's the moonlight," he informed himself. Inwardly he pictured her still face and said *Strange, strange, strange.* "What's your name?"

"Dru. Drusilla," she said carefully. It was not her name, but she had probed and discovered that he liked it. "Drusilla Strange."

"Beautiful," he breathed. "Say, that's a beautiful name, did you know that? Drusilla Strange. That's just . . . just exactly *right*." He looked about at the cool white blaze of the beach, at the black grass under the moon. "Oh!" he said abruptly, "I'm Chan. Chandler Behringer. It's a clumsy sort of name, hard to say, not like—"

"Chandler Behringer," she said. "It sounds like a little wind catching its tail around a—" she dipped into him swiftly—"palm frond."

"Huh!" he shouted. It was one syllable of a laugh, and it was sheer delight. Then he found the rest of the laugh.

He put his hand on her arm just above the elbow and steered her off the beach. The feel of her flesh under the flat close fabric caused a shock that ran up his arm and straight through his defenses.

"Here's my place," he said, with all the wind and none of the cordal vibration necessary to make a voice. He moved away from her and marched up the slope, frowning, leading the way. He ducked into a lean-to porch and fumbled too busily with a latch. "You'd better wait for a moment while I light the lamp. It's sort of cluttered."

She waited. The doorway swallowed him, and there was a fumbling, and a scratching, and suddenly the cabin had an interior. She moved inside.

"You needn't be afraid to look around," he said presently, watching her.

She did, immediately. She had been looking straight at him, following his critical inventory of the entire place, and she now knew it every bit as well as he. But, "Oh," she said, "this is—" she hesitated—"cosy."

"A small place," he said, "but it's dismal." He laughed, and explained apologetically, "I got that line from a movie."

She sorted out the remark, wondered detachedly why he had made it, half-heartedly probed for the reason, then dropped it as unessential effort.

"A nice soft blanket," he said, lifting it. Her hands went reflexively to the top button of the trench coat and fell away at his next words. "When I go out, you just wrap yourself up nice and snug. I won't be long. Now give me the number."

His mental code for "number" was so brief and so

puzzling—a disk with holes in it superimposed on ruled paper—that she was quite at a loss. "Number?"

"Your friends. I'll phone them. They can bring you some clothes, take you home." He laughed self-consciously. "I'll try to say it so that . . . I mean, make it sound . . . Do you know, I haven't the first idea of just what I'll tell them?"

"Oh," she said. "My friends . . . have no phone."

"No—oh. What, no phone?" He looked at her, around at the walls, and inevitably at the bed. It was a very small bed. He gestured weakly at the door. "A . . . telegram, maybe, but that would take a long time, and . . . Oh, I know. I have clothes, dungarees and things. A lumberjack shirt. Why didn't I think of it? Girls wear all that kind of —but shoes, I don't know . . . And then I'll get you a taxi!" he finished triumphantly, and the chaos within him was, to misuse the term, deafening.

She considered very, very carefully and then said, "No taxi could take me back. It's much too far for a taxi to travel."

"Isn't there anyone that—"

"There isn't anyone," she said firmly.

After a long, complicated pause, he asked gently, "What happened?"

She averted her face.

"It was something sad," he half-whispered, and although he was quite still, she could feel the tendrils of his sympathy reaching out toward her. "That's all right, don't worry. Don't," he said loudly, as if it were the first word of a very important pronouncement; but it would not form. He said at last, inanely, "I'll make coffee."

He crossed the room, raising his hand to pat her shoulder as he passed, checking it, not touching her at all, while the echo of that first shock bounded and rebounded within him. He bent over the stove, and in a moment the evil smell of the lamp, which had been pressing closer and closer upon her consciousness, was eclipsed completely by what was to her a completely overpowering, classic, catastrophic and symphonic stench. Her eyelids flickered and closed as she made a tremendous nervous effort and at last succeeded in the necessary realignment of her carbon-oxygen dynamic. And in a moment she could ignore the fumes and open her eyes again.

Chan was looking at her.

"You'll have to stay."

"Yes," she said. She looked at his eyes. "You don't want me to."

"I want you to," he said hurriedly, "I want . . ." He thought *She's in trouble and she's afraid I'm going to take advantage of it.*

"I'm in trouble," she said, "but I'm not afraid you'll take advantage of it."

He flashed a startling white grin. *She trusts me.* Then the grin faded and the internal frown clamped down. But it could not hide the thought: *She's . . . she expects . . . she's maybe the kind who . . .*

"I'm not the kind," she said levelly, "who—"

"Oh, I know I know I know!" he interrupted rapidly, and with it he thought *Why is she so damned sure of herself?*

"I just don't know *what* to do!" she said.

He smiled again. "You just leave everything to me. We'll make out fine, I mean you're quite safe, you know. And in the morning everything will look a lot brighter. Oh, that coat, that wet old coat. Here," he bustled, "here— here."

From curtained clothes-pole and paper-lined orange crate came blue denims, a spectral holocaust in woolen plaid, a pair of socks of a red that did not belong within four miles of any color in the shirt. She looked at the clothes and at him. He turned his back.

"I'll go on with the cook-cook-coffee and you know," he said nervously.

She took off the trench coat and while her fingers solved the logical problem called buttons and the topological one whereby a foot enters a sock, she pondered Chandler Behringer's extraordinary sensitivities. Either this species must overpopulate its planet in nine generations, she thought whimsically, or it must die from nervous exhaustion in four. The dungarees gouged and rasped her skin until she damped its sensitivity, but the feel of the heavy, washed wool of the shirt was delightful.

He set out plates and in a moment slid a handsome orange-and-white edible onto them. She looked at it with interest, and then her eyes traveled to the small table by the stove, and she saw the shells. *By the Fountain Itself,* she said silently, *ova! They eat EGGS!*

She forced her feelings into a desensitized compartment of her mind and corked it. Then she sat opposite Chandler and ate heartily. The coffee was bitter and, to her palate, gritty, but she drank her second cup with composure. *He's so very pleased that I eat with him,* she thought. *They probably do everything gregariously, even where cooperation is not involved.* She was conscious of no disgust, for that, too, was insulated—and so it must stay for the rest of her imprisonment, which is to say the rest of her life.

The food seemed to have relaxed him: a sphygmomanetic allocation, she deduced. And involuntary. How very confining. His chatter had eased and he was taking a silent pleasure in watching her. When she met his eyes finally, he leaped up nervously and scraped and washed the plates energetically. He thought, *I wonder if she liked it.* And: *She knows how to be a guest, and how to keep herself from plunging into the dish-washing, putting them back in the wrong place and all.* And: *I like doing things for her. I wish I could do everything for . . .* And then the frown.

Suddenly in a rush of embarrassment and self-accusation, he spun around and said, "I haven't even asked you, I mean told you, if you, I mean, well, this is just a shack and we haven't all the fixtures."

She looked at him blankly, then probed.

Oh. This is loaded, too. But not eating. Amazing.

She made it as easy for him as she could. She rose and gave him the quick nervous smile that was correct.

"It's outside," he said. "To your left. That little path."

She slipped outside, stalked directly down to the water's edge and with as little effort and even less distress than a polite cough might have cost her, she vomited up the eggs and the coffee. She had eaten, after all, only two days ago.

He had the bed made up when she came in, the pillow smooth, crisp sheets flat and diagonally folded at the head end.

"I bet you're as tired as I am," he said. "And that's a whole lot."

"Oh," she said, looking at the bed. For sleeping! What would she want sleep for? Because of a phylic habit unbroken in these savages since they were forced to spend the dark hours immobile in a rocky hole to save themselves from nocturnal carnivores? But she said, "Oh, how neat. But I can't take your bed. I'll sit up."

"You'll do no such thing," he said severely, and her eyes widened. He busied himself with a blanket roll and sleeping bag, which he put on the floor just as far—four feet or so—as it could possibly go from the bed. "I love this old bag. Look, nylon and down—the only expensive thing I own. Except my guitar."

She visualized "guitar" and immediately put it down as something to investigate. The flash she got in his coding was brief, but sufficient for her to recognize its size, shape and purpose, and to conclude that although its resonant volumes were gross and its vents inaccurately placed, it was closer to the engineering she knew and understood than most things she had glimpsed here so far.

"You didn't tell me you played the guitar," she said politely.

"I get paid for it," he said, yawning, and she knew that this yawn belonged to this remark and not to the circumstance of somnolence. "Ready for bed?"

Patiently she bowed to his formalities. "You're very kind."

He went to the lamp and turned it out. The low moon streamed in.

He hesitated, slid into his sleeping bag after removing only his shoes. There ensued a considerable amount of floundering, ducking, and thumping on the floor, and at last he brought his trousers out, folded as small as possible. He wadded them between the corner of the sleeping bag and the wall as if they were a secret. Then he sat up and took off his shirt. He hung it on the corner of the window sill, lay down, zipped the bag up to his neck, and ostentatiously turned on his side with his face to the wall. "Good night."

"Good night," she said. Resignedly she got between the sheets, as indicated by the folded-down corner, pulled up the blanket, porpoised out of her trousers, folded them, brought them out and hid them; removed her shirt, reached out a long arm and hung it on the other corner of the window sill. Did he still have his socks on? He did.

She wriggled her toes and slightly desensitized her ankles where the weave pressed them.

"You're perfectly safe. Don't worry about a thing."

"Thank you, Chan. I feel safe. I'm not worried. Good night."

"Good night. *Dru*," he said suddenly, lifting himself on one elbow.

"What is it?"

He lay down again. "Good night."

She watched with deep interest the downward spiralings of his thoughts into the uprising tides of sleep. It happened to him suddenly, and the "noise" factor of his conscious presence slumped away out of the room.

And the torture began.

She had known it was there, but Chandler Behringer was a fine foil for it. He alleviated nothing, but he set up a constant distraction purely by the bumbling, burrowing busyness of his mind. Now it had faded to a whisper, to an effective nothing, and her torture poured down on her. From the warp-shielded, indetectable satellites which guarded the prison planet and administered the punishment, agony poured down to her.

Thus it will be tonight, and the next and next nights, and every night for all of my own forever. Hushed in the day and hungry and sweet at night, it will rain down on me. And I can lie and relax, and I can harbor my anger and anchor my anguish, but the tide will rise, the currents will tug until they break me, if it takes two hundred years. And when I'm broken by it, the torture will go on and on—and on.

Most of the torture was music.

Some of the torture was singing.

And a little of the torture was a thing hardly describable in Earthly terms, which made pictures—not on a screen, not on the mind like memories, however poignant—but pictures so clear and true that the sudden whip of a pennant brought, a second later, spent wind to buffet the eyelids, pictures wherein one walked barefoot on turf and knew a mottling of heat and coolth in the arches with the moisture of the grass its broken green bleeding. These were pictures where to loose a sling was to know the draw of the pectorals and the particled bite of soil under the downdriven toenails, and to picture a leap was to kick away a very planet, to have that priceless quarter-second of absolute float, and to come back to a cushioning of one's own litheness.

This was music of an ancient planet peopled by a race far older. This was music with the softness and substance of weathered granite, and the unwinding intricacies of a fern. It was ferocious music with a thick-wristed control of its furies so sure that it could be used for laughter. And altogether it was music that rose and cycled and bubbled and built like the Fountain Itself.

This was the high singing of birds beauty-lost in altitude, and the heavier, upward voices expressed by the reaching of trees. It was the voice of the tendon burst for being less strong than the will, and the heart of the sea, and its base was the bass of pulsations of growth (for even a shouldering tree trunk has a note, if listened to for years enough) and altogether these were the voices that made and were made by the Fountain Itself.

And these were the pictures of the Fountain Itself . . .

And such were the tortures of those who were exiled, imprisoned and damned.

She lay there and hated the moonlight; the moon she regarded as ugly and vulgar and new. It seemed to her an added lash, as were all things similar and all things contrasting to the world she had lost. She turned eyes grown cold on the sleeping man, and curled her lip; the creature was a clever counterpart, a subtle caricature, of the worst of the men of her race, in no way perfect, in no way magnificent, but in no way so crude an artifact as to permit her to forget what was surely its original.

By comparison and by contrast, Earth, this muddy, uncouth ball of offal, pinioned her soul to her home. Earth had everything that could be found on her world—after a fashion—racecourses comparatively an armspan wide, racing dun rats ridden by newts in sleazy silks . . . men whose eyes sparkled in the sun not quite as much as her racial brother's might when he, with only his shaded hand to help him, sought and found a ghostly nebula.

Cell by interlocking cell, ion by osmotic particle, she belonged elsewhere. And Earth, which was her world falsified; and the endless music, which was her world in truth—these would never let her forget it.

So she cursed the moonbeams and the music sliding down them, and swore that she would not be broken. She could soak herself in this petty planet, zip it up to her neck to conceal anything of her real self in her pettiest acts; she could don the bearing and the thoughts themselves of Earth's too-fine, too-empty puppets—and still inwardly she would be herself, a citizen of her world, part of the Fountain Itself. As long as she was that, in any fiber, she could not be completely an exile. Excommunicated she might be; bodily removed, wingless and crawling, trembling under the dear constant breath of her home; but until she broke, her jailers had failed for all their might and righteousness.

The sun rose and turned her away from her bitterness, a little. Chan's sleeping consciousness came close and roared around her, fell back into blacknesses. She rose and went to the door. The sea was rose-gold and breathing and the sun was aloft, a shade too near, too yellow, and too small. She damned it heartily with a swift thought that spouted and spread and hung in the air like the mist from a fountain, and went and dressed, all but those stupid socks.

She glanced at the percolator, understood it, and deftly made coffee. At its first whisper in the tube, Chan sighed and his consciousness came upward with a rush. Drusilla slipped outside. Patience she had in full measure, but she felt it unworthy to tap it for such unwieldy formalities as she knew she must witness if she stayed in the room during the cracking of his nylon chrysalis.

There was a hoarse shout from inside, a violent floundering, and then Chandler Behringer appeared. He was tousled and frightened. His panic, she noted, had been sufficient to drive him outdoors without his shirt, but not without his trousers. He squeezed his eyelids so tight shut that his cheekbones seemed to rise; then opened them and saw her standing by the beach margin. The radiance that came from his face competed for a moment with the early tilting sunlight.

"I thought you'd gone."

She smiled. "No."

She came to him. His eyes devoured her. He raised both hands together and placed them, one on the other, on his left collarbone. She understood that he was concealing the vestigial nipples (which were absent in males of her race) with his wrists. She examined this reflex with some curiosity, and filed away for future puzzlement the fact that he did this because he wore trousers; had they been bathing trunks, the reflex would not have appeared. He took a deep breath so deep that she empathized his pain.

"You are the most beautiful woman I have ever seen," he said.

She did not doubt it, and had no comment.

"The most beautiful woman who ever lived," he murmured.

Abruptly she turned her back, and now it was her eyes which squeezed shut. "I am *not!*" she said in a tone so saturated with hatred and violence that he stepped back almost into the doorway.

Without another word she strode off, down the beach, her direction chosen solely by the way she happened to be facing at the time. In a moment she was conscious of his feet padding after her.

"Dru, Dru, don't go!" he panted. "I'm sorry, I didn't mean, *hah!* to do anything that *hah!* oh, I was only—"

She stopped and turned so abruptly that had he taken two more steps they would have collided. Far from taking steps, however, he had all he could do to stay upright.

She stood looking at him, unmoving. On her face was no particular expression; but there was that in the high-held head, the slightly distended nostrils, the splendid balance of her stance, and her gracefully held, powerful hands that made approach impossible. His eyes were quite round and his lips slightly parted. He extended one hand and moved his mouth silently, then let the hand fall. His knees began to tremble visibly.

She turned again and walked away. He stood there for a long time watching her go. When she was simply a brilliant fleck on the brightening dunes, the purposeless hand came forward again.

"Dru?" he said, in a voice softened to soprano inaudibility by all the cautions of awe. And she was gone, and he turned slowly, as if he had a tall and heavy weight on his rounded shoulders, and plodded back to the cabin.

She found a road which paralleled the beach and climbed to it. Fools cluster about the Universe, she thought, like bubbles about the fountain pool, shifting and pulsing at random, without design, purpose or function. She had left such a fool and she was such a fool. There was far more culpability in her folly than in that of the man. He had little control over what he might say, and less understanding, because of his nature and his limitations. Neither his faculties nor his conditioning could enable him to understand why she felt such fury.

She stabbed her heels into the sandy roadbed as she walked. She ground her teeth. *The most beautiful woman who ever lived . . .*

Her beauty!

Where, exile—where, criminal, has your beauty brought you?

She strode on, her mood so black it all but eclipsed the torture music.

Perhaps fifteen minutes later, she became conscious of a shrill ultrasonic, a rapidly pulsing, urgent, growing thing that would be a silence to all but her. She slowed, stopped finally. The sound came from behind her, but she would not confuse her analysis by looking back. She listened as an intervening wind carried the vibrations away and then let them come back again, nearer, stronger. She sensitized her bare feet; she raised an arm and took the vibrations on the back of her hand. She became conscious of synchronous sounds.

Something rotated at approximately thirty-eight hundred and forty rpm. Something was chaindriven and the chain was not a metal. Something pounded . . . no, paced —something rolled endless soft cleats on the earth. She heard the straining of coil springs, the labored slide of heavy transverse leaf-springs, the make-and-break in the meniscus of the oil guarding busy pistons.

The utter stupidity of so complex a thing as an automobile was, to her, more wondrous than a rainbow.

At last she turned to look, and in a moment she saw it climb a rise some two miles away. The piercing ultrasonic was beyond bearing, and she adjusted her hearing to eliminate everything between eighty-six and eighty-eight thousand cycles.

More comfortable now, she waited patiently. The car slid down a straight and gentle grade toward her, spitting sunlight through its chromium teeth, palming aside the morning air and pressing it back and down its sleek flanks, while underneath, where there was no hint of fairing, air shocked and roiled and shuddered and troubled what dust it could find in the sandy road. It was a very large and very new car. Drusilla watched it, wide-eyed. She came to wonder what conclusions one would have regarding these —these savages, if one knew nothing of them but such a vehicle. What manner of man streamlines only where he can see?

The lovely thought, then: *It's a world of clowns.*

She smiled; the driver saw it and his foot came down on the brake pedal. The car threw down its glittering baroque nose, slid a hand's breadth, and lowered itself sitzwise into its warm bath of springs.

The driver's eyes were long and flat and his nose and chin were sharp. Drusilla watched what he was doing, which was watching himself watch her.

Suddenly he said, "How far is it to—" and before the first word was spoken, she knew he was completely familiar with these roads.

She said, "Your—" and raised her hand to point accurately at the hood, while she searched him for the term. "Your rocker-arm's not getting oil. The third one from the front." Even while the motor idled, the soundless shriek of that dry friction would have been unbearable had she let it.

"Sounds all right to me," he shrugged. He looked—he journeyed, rather—down from her eyes, down until he saw that her feet were bare. He left his gaze where it was and said, "Let me give you a lift." He half turned then, reached one thin spidery arm back and across without looking, and the rear door swung open.

Drusilla took one step forward and only then saw that the man was not alone in the car. She stopped, amazed—not at the woman who sat there, but at the fact that perceptions such as hers had missed so much. She glanced at the man, and realized that it was his feeling, or lack of it, that had numbed and blinded her to everything about the woman who sat beside him. She was companion reduced to presence, minified to fixture, reduced to a very limbo of familiarity. Drusilla stared at her, and the woman stared back.

She was a small woman, compact, so coiffed and clad that she was only a blandness. What kept her from being featureless as an egg was a pair of achingly blue eyes large enough for a being half again her size, and a perfect mouth painted such a transcendental, pupil-shrinking red that surely it would melt fuse-wire. Her wide eyes were blank.

To Drusilla's horror, a growth like an iridescent liver sprang into being between the flaming lips, grew to the size of a fist and collapsed limply. The lips parted, a pink tongue deftly caught, cleared, and drew the limp matter back between an even flicker of paper-white teeth. And again the face was molded and smooth and motionless.

"My wife," said the man, "so you're chaperoned. My God, Lu, you got bubble gum again." The woman took her gaze away from Drusilla and placed it on the driver, but there was otherwise no change. "Get in."

Drusilla's mind played back a fleeting inner sensation she had taken from him when he had said "My wife." It was . . . pride? No. Admiration? Hardly! *Compliment;* that was it. This woman was a compliment he paid himself. He had no tiny fleck of doubt that he was admired for her careful finish.

The big blue eyes swung to her again and she probed.

For a ghastly micro-second, she had all the sensations of walking into a snakepit with chloroform on her scarf. She recoiled violently, moved far back to the low bank; and she shuddered.

"Come on, uh, hey, what's the matter?" the driver called.

Drusilla shook her head twice, not so much in refusal as in an attempt to escape from something that was laying clammy strands of silk on her face and hair. Without another word, she turned and walked away down the road, behind the car.

"Hey!"

Drusilla did not look back.

He started the car and drove off slowly. In a moment, the woman leaned forward and tugged hard on the wheel. The car heeled back on the road, and at last he took his eyes from the rear view mirror.

"Now what's with her?" he demanded of the windshield wiper.

Lu blew another bubble.

When the car was gone, Drusilla went slowly back and

past the place she had met it, and on toward the town. From her marrow she swore a mighty oath that never again would she be trapped into sending her probes into such a revolting mess. The driver hadn't been like that; Chan Behringer hadn't. Yet she knew with a terrible certainty that there must be thousands like that creature here on the prison planet.

So as she walked she devised something, a hair-triggered synaptic structure, a reaction pattern that could, even without her conscious knowledge, detect the faintest beginnings of a presence such as this; and it would snap down her shields, isolate her, protect her, keep her clean.

She was badly shaken. The presence of that woman had shaken her, but the most devastating thing of all was the knowledge that she could be shaken. It was a realization most difficult for her to absorb; it had little precedent in her cosmos.

Walking, she shuddered again.

Drusilla came to the town and wandered until she found a restaurant which needed a waitress. She borrowed the price of a pair of beach sandals from the weary cashier and went to work. She found a little room and at the end of the second day she had the price of a cotton dress.

In the second week she was a stenographer and, in the second month, secretary to the head of a firm which made boat-sails and awnings. She invested quietly, sold some poems, a song, two articles and a short story. In terms of her environment, she did very well indeed, very fast. In her own estimate, she did nothing but force her attention randomly away from her torture.

For the torture, of course, continued. She bore it with outward composure, shucked it off as casually as, from time to time, she changed her name, her job, her hairstyling and her accent. But like the lessons she learned, like the knowledge of the people she met and worked with, the torture accumulated. She could estimate her capacity for it. It was large, but not infinite. She could get rid of none of it, any more than she could get rid of knowledge. It could be compacted and stored. As long as she could do this with the torture, she was undefeated. But she was quite capable of calculating intake against capacity and she had not much time. A year and a half, two . . .

She would stand at the window, absorbing her punishment, staring up into the night sky with her bright wise eyes. She could not see the guardian ships, of course, but she knew they were there. She knew of their killer-boats which could, if necessary, slip down in moments and blast a potential escapee, or one about to violate the few simple rules of a prisoner's conduct.

Sometimes, objectively, she marveled at the cruel skill of the torture. Music alone, with its ineffable spectrum of sadness and longing and wild nostalgic joy, could have been enough and more than enough for a prisoner to bear; but the sensory pictures, the stimulative and restimulative flow and change of taste and motion and all the subtleties of the kinetic senses—these, mixed and mingled with music, charging in where music lulled, marching in the footprints of the music's rhythmic stride—these were the things which laughed at her barriers, sparred with her, giggling; met her fists with a breeze, her rapier with a gas, her advances with a disappearance.

There was no fighting attacks like these. Ignorance would have been a defense, but was of no use to her who was so nerve-alive to all the torture's sense and symbolism. All she could do was to absorb, compact, and hope that she could find a defense before she broke.

So she lived and outwardly prospered. She met some humans who amused her briefly, and others she avoided after one or two meetings because they reminded her so painfully of her own people—a smile, a stride, a matching of colors. If she met any others with the terrifying quality of the woman in the car, she was not aware of it; that part of her defense, at least, was secure.

But the torture still poured down upon her, and after half a year she knew she must take some steps to counteract it. At base, the solution was simple. If she did nothing, the torture would crush her, and there was no surcease in that, for having broken, she would go on suffering it. She could kill herself, but that in itself would fulfill the terms of her sentence—"life imprisonment—with torture." There was only one way—to be killed, and to be killed by the guardians. She was not under a death sentence. If she forced one, they would have to violate their own penalty, and she would be able to die unbroken, as befits a Citizen of the Fountain Itself.

More and more she studied the sky, knowing of the undetectable presence of the guardians and their killer-boats, knowing that if she could think of it, there must be a way to bring one of them careening silently down on her to snuff her out. She made sendings of many kinds—even of the kind she had used to extinguish the life-force of the Preceptor—without altering the quality or degree of torture in the slightest.

Perhaps the guardians sent, but did not receive; perhaps nothing could touch them. Geared to the pattern of a Citizen's mind and conditioning, they patiently produced that which must, in time, destroy it. The destruction would be because of the weakness of the attacked. Drusilla wanted to be destroyed through the strength of the attacker. The distinction was to her, clear and vital.

There had to be a way, if only she could think of it.

There was, and she did.

He came onstage grinning like a boy, swinging his guitar carelessly. The set was a living room. He plumped down on a one-armed easychair and hooked a brown-and-white hassock toward him with his heel. There was applause.

"Thank you, Mother," said Chan Behringer. He slipped the plectrum from under the first and second strings. Dru thought *Your D is one one hundred-twenty-eight tone sharp*.

Deftly, out of sight of the audience, he plugged in the pickup cable. Dru watched attentively. She had never seen a twelve-string guitar before.

He began to play. He played competently, with neither mistakes nor imagination. There was a five-stage amplifier built into his chair and a foot-pedal tone control and electronic vibrato in the hassock. A rough cutoff at twenty-seven thousand cycles, she realized, and then remembered that, to most humans, response flat to eight thousand is high fidelity.

She was immensely pleased with the electrical pickups; she had not noticed them at first, which was a compliment to him. One was magnetic, sunk into the fingerboard at the fourteenth fret. The other was a contact microphone, obviously inside the box, directly under the bridge. The either-or both switch was audible when he moved it, which she thought disgraceful.

He finished his number, drawled a few lines of patter, asked for and played a couple of requests and an encore, by which time Drusilla had left the theater and was talking to the stage doorman. He took the paper parcel she handed him and sent it to the dressing rooms via the call-boy.

In a matter of seconds, there was a wild whoop from backstage and Chan Behringer came bounding down the iron steps, clutching a wild flannel shirt, a pair of blue dungarees, and some tatters of paper and string.

"Dru! Dru!" he gasped. He ran to her, his arms out. Then he stopped, faltered, put his head very slightly to one side. "Dru," he said again, softly.

"Hello, Chan."

"I never thought I'd see you again."

"I had to return your things."

"Too good to be true," he murmured. "I—we—" Suddenly he turned to the goggling doorman and tossed the clothes to him. "Hang on to these for me, will you, George?" To Drusilla he said, "I should take 'em backstage, but I'm afraid to let you out of my sight."

"I won't run away again."

"Let's get out of here," he said. He took her arm, and again there was the old echo of a shock he had once felt at the touch of her flesh through fabric.

They went to a place, all soft lights and leather, and they talked about the beach and the city and show business and guitar music, but not about her strange fury with him the morning she had stalked out of his life.

"You've changed," he said at length.

"Have I?"

"You were like—like a queen before. Now you're like a princess."

"That's sweet."

"More . . . human."

She laughed. "I wasn't exactly human when you first met me. I'd had a bad time. I'm all right now, Chan. I—didn't want to see you until I was all right."

They talked until it was time for his next act, and after that they had dinner.

She saw him the next day, and the next.

The chubby man with a face like a cobbler and hands like a surgeon made the most beautiful guitars in the world. He sprang to his feet when the tall girl came in. It was the first time he had paid such a courtesy in fourteen years.

"Can you cut an F-slot that looks like this?" she demanded.

He looked at the drawing she laid on the counter, grunted, then said, "Sure, lady. But why?"

She launched into a discussion which, at first, he did not hear, for it was in his field and in his language and he was too astonished to think. But once into it, he very rapidly learned things about resonance, harmonic reinforcement, woods, varnishes and reverse-cantilever designs that were in no book he had ever heard about.

When she left a few minutes later, he hung gasping to the counter. In front of him was a check for work ordered. In his hand was a twenty-dollar bill for silence. In his mind was a flame and a great wonderment.

She spilled a bottle of nailpolish remover on Chan's guitar. He was kind and she was pathetically contrite. It was all right, he said; he knew a place that could retouch it before evening. They went there together. The little man with the cobbler's face handed over the new instrument, a guitar with startling slots, an ultra-precision bridge, a fingerboard that crept into his hand as if it were alive and loved him. He chorded it once, and at the tone he put it reverently down and stared. His eyes were wet.

"It's yours," Drusilla twinkled. "Look—your name, inlaid on the neck-back."

"I know your guitars," said Chan to the chubby man, "but I never heard of anything like this."

"Tricks to every trade," said the man, and winked.

Drusilla slipped him another twenty as they left.

The electronics engineer stared at the schematic diagram. "It won't work."

"Yes, it will," said Drusilla. "Can you build it?"

"Well, gosh, yes, but who ever heard of voltage control like this? Where's the juice supposed to go from . . ." He leaned closer. "Well, I'll be damned. Who designed this?"

"Build it," she said.

He did. It worked. Drusilla wired it into the prop armchair and Chan never knew anything had been changed.

He attributed everything to the new instrument as he became more familiar with it and began to exploit its possibilities. Suddenly there were no more layoffs. No more road trips, either. The clubs began to take important notice of the shy young man with the tear-your-heart-out guitar.

She stole his vitamin pills and replaced them with something else. She invited him to dinner at her apartment and he fainted in the middle of the fish course.

He came to seven hours later on the couch, long after the strange induction baker and the rack of impulse hypodermics had been hidden away. He remembered absolutely nothing. He was lying on his left arm and it ached.

Dru told him he had fallen asleep and she had just let him sleep it out.

"Poor dear, you've been working too hard."

He told her somewhat harshly that she must *never* let him sleep like that, cutting off the circulation in his fingering arm.

The next day, the arm was worse and he had to cancel a date. On the third day, it was back to normal, one hundred per cent, and on the fourth, fifth, and sixth days it continued to improve. And what it could do on the fingerboard was past description. Which was hardly surprising: there was not another arm on Earth like it, with its heavier nerve-fibers, the quadrupling of the relay-nodes on the medullary sheaths, the low-resistance, superreactive axones, and the isotopic potassium and sodium which drenched them.

"I don't play this damn thing any more," he said. "I just think the stuff and that left hand reads my mind."

He made three records in three months, and the income from them increased cubically each time. Then the record company decided to save money and put him under a long-term contract at a higher rate than anyone had ever been paid before.

Chan, without consulting Drusilla, bought one of a cluster of very exclusive houses just over the city line. The neighbors on the left were the Kerslers, whose grandfather had made their money in off-the-floor sanitary fixtures. The neighbors on the right were the Mullings—you know, Osprey Mullings, the writer, two books a year, year in and year out, three out of four of them making Hollywood.

Chan invited the Kerslers and the Mullings to his housewarming, and took Drusilla out there to surprise her.

She was surprised, all right. Kersler had a huge model railroad in his cellar and his mind likewise contained a great many precise minutiae, only one of which was permitted to operate at a time. Grace Kersler's mind was like an empty barn solidly lined with pink frosting. Osprey Mullings' head contained a set of baby's blocks of limited number, with which he constructed his novels by a ritualistic process of rearrangement. But Luellen Mullings was the bland-faced confection who secretly chewed bubble gum and who had so jolted Drusilla that day on the beach road.

It was a chatty and charming party, and it was the very first time that humans had been capable of irritating Drusilla so much that she had to absorb the annoyance rather than ignore it. She bore this attack on her waning capacities with extreme graciousness, and at parting, the Kerslers and the Mullings pressed Chan's hand and wished him luck with that *beautiful* Drusilla Strange, you lucky fellow you.

And late at night, full to bursting with success and security and a fine salting of ambition, Chan drove her back to town, and at her apartment he proposed to her.

She held both his hands and cried a little, and promised to work with him and to help him even more in the future —but, "Please, please, Chan, never ask me that again."

He was hurt and baffled, but he kept his promise.

Chan studied music seriously now—he never had before. He had to. He was giving concerts rather than performances, and he played every showcase piece ever composed by one virtuoso to madden and frustrate the others. He played all of the famous violin cadenzi on his guitar as well. He made arrangements of the arrangements. He did all this with the light contempt of a Rubinstein examining a two-dollar lesson in chord-vamping. So at length he had no recourse but to compose. Some of his stuff was pretty advanced. All of it took you by the throat and held you.

One Sunday afternoon, "Try this," said Drusilla. She hummed a tone or two, then burst into a cascade of notes that brought Chan up standing.

"*God*, Dru!"

"Try it," she said.

He got his guitar. His left hand ran over the fingerboard like a perplexed little animal, and he struck a note or two.

"No," she said, "this." She sang.

"Oh," he whispered. Watching her, he played. When she seemed not pleased, he stopped.

"No," she said. "Chan. I can only sing one note at a time. You have twelve strings." She paused, thoughtfully, *listening*. "Chan, if I asked you to play that theme, and then to—to paint pictures on it with your guitar, would that make sense?"

"You usually make sense."

She smiled at him. "All right. Play that theme, and with it, play the way a tree grows. Play the way the bud leads the twig and the twig cuts up into space to make a hole for the branch. No," she said quickly, as his eyes brightened and his right thumb and forefinger tightened on the plectrum, "not yet. There's more."

He waited.

She closed her eyes. Almost inaudibly, she hummed something. Then she said, "At the same time, put in all the detail of a tree that has already grown." She opened her eyes and looked straight at him. "That will consolidate," she said factually, "because a tree is only the graphic trajectory of its buds."

He looked at her strangely. "You're quite a girl."

"Never mind that," she said quickly. "Now put those three things together with a fountain. And that's all."

"What kind of a fountain?"

She paled, but her voice was easy. "Silly. The only kind of fountain that could *be* with that theme, the tree growing, and the tree grown."

He struck a chord. "I'll try."

She hummed for him, then brought one long finger down. He picked up the theme from her voice. He closed his eyes. The guitar of all instruments the most intimately expressive, given a magic sostenuto by its electronic graft, began to speak.

The theme, the tree growing, the tree grown.

Suddenly, the fountain, too.

What happened then left them both breathless. Music of this nature should never be heard in a cubic volume smaller than its subject.

When the pressured stridency of the music was quite gone, Chan looked at a cracked window pane and then turned to watch a talc-fine trickle of plaster dust stream down from the lintel of the french window.

"Where," he said, shaken, "did you get *that* little jangle?"

"Thin air, darling," said Drusilla blithely. "All the time, everywhere, whenever you like. Listen."

He cocked his head. There was an intense silence. His left hand crept up to the frets and spattered over them. In spite of the fact that he had not touched the strings with his right hand, a structure of sound hung in the room, reinforcing itself, holding, holding . . . finally dying.

"That it?" he asked, awed.

She held up a thumb and forefinger very close together. "About so much of it."

"How come I never heard it before?"

"You weren't ready."

His eyes suddenly filled with tears. "Damn it, Drusilla . . . you're—you've done . . . Oh, hell, I don't know, I love you so much."

She touched his face. "Shh. Play for me, Chan."

He breathed hard, thickly. "Not in here."

He put down his guitar and went to get the portable amplifier. They set it upon the rolling lawn and plugged in the guitar. Chan held the instrument for a silent moment, sliding his hand over its polished flank. He looked up suddenly and met Drusilla's eyes. Chan's face twisted, for her ecstasy and gaiety and triumph added up to something very like despair, and he did not understand.

He would have thrown down the guitar then, for his heart was full of her, but she backed away, shaking her head lightly, and bent to the amplifier to switch it on. Her fingers pulled at the rotary switch as she turned it, and only she knew the nature of the mighty little transmitter that began to warm up along with the audio. She moved back still further; she did not want to be close to him when it—happened.

He watched her for a moment, then looked down at the guitar. He watched his four enchanted left fingers hook and hover over the fingerboard; he looked at them with a vast puzzlement that slowly turned to raptness. He began to sway gently.

Drusilla stood tall and taut, looking past him to the trees, to the scudding clouds and beyond. She dropped her shields and let the music pour in. And from the guitar came a note, another, two together, a strange chord. *For this I shall be killed*, she thought. To bring to the mighty scorn her people had of Earth and all things Earthly, this molded savage who could commune like a Citizen . . . this was the greatest affront.

A foam of music fell and feathered and rushed inward to the Fountainhead Itself, and every voice of it smashed and hurtled upward. The paired sixth strings of the guitar flung up with them in a bullroar *glissando* that broke and spread glistening all over the keyboard, falling and falling away from a brittle high spatter of doubled first strings struck just barely below the bridge, metallic and needly; and if those taut strings were tied to a listener's teeth, they could not be more intimate and shocking.

The unique sound box found itself in sudden shrill resonance, and it woke the dark strings, the deep and mighty ones. They thrummed and sang without being touched; and Chan's inhuman fingers found a figure in the middle register, folded it in on itself, broke it in two, and the broken pieces danced . . . and still the untouched strings hummed and droned, first one loud and then another as the resonances altered and responded.

And all at once the air was filled with the sharp and dusty smell of ozone.

With it all, the music, hers and Chan's, settled itself down and down like some dark giant, pressing and sweeping and gathering in its drapes and folds as it descended to rest, to collect its roaring and crooning and tittering belongings all together that they may be pieced and piled and understood; until at last the monster was settled and neat, leaving a looming bulk of silence and an undertone of pumping life and multi-level quiet stripes of contemplation. The whole structure breathed, slowly and more slowly, held its breath, let a tension develop, rising, painful, agonizing, intolerable . . .

"Play Red River Valley, hey, Chan?"

Drusilla gasped, and the ozone rasped her throat. Chan's fingers faltered, stopped. He half-turned, with a small, interrogative whimper.

Standing on the other side of the far hedge, near her

house, was Luellen Mullings, her doll-figure foiled like a glass diamond by a negligible playsuit, her golden hair free, her perfect jaw busy on her sticky cud.

There was born in Drusilla a fury more feral, more concentrated, than any power of muscle or mind she had ever conceived of. Luellen Mullings, essence of all the degradation Earth was known for, all the cheapness, shallowness, ignorance and stupidity. She was the belch in the cathedral; she would befoul the Fountain Itself.

"Hi, Dru, honey. Didn't see you. Hey, I saw a feller at the Palace could play guitar holding it behind his back." She sniffed. "What's that funny smell? Like lightning or something."

"Get back in your house, you cheap little slut," Drusilla hissed.

"Hey, who you calling—" Luellen dipped down and picked up a smooth white stone twice the size of her fist. She raised it. Even Drusilla's advanced reflexes were not fast enough to anticipate what she did. The stone left her hand like a bullet. Drusilla braced herself—but the stone did not come to her. It struck Chan just behind the ear. He pivoted on his heel three-quarters of a revolution, and quietly collapsed on the grass, the guitar nestling down against him like a loving cat.

"Now look at what you made me do!" Luellen cried shrilly.

Drusilla uttered a harpy's scream and bounded across the lawn, her long hands spread out like talons. Luellen watched her come, round-eyed.

There is a force in steady eyes by which a tiger may be made to turn away. It can make a strong man turn and run. There is a way to gather this force into a deadly nubbin and hurl it like a grenade. Drusilla knew how to do this, for she had done it before; she had killed with it. But the force she hurled at Luellen Mullings now was ten times what she had dealt the Preceptor.

For a moment, the Universe went black, and then Drusilla became aware of a pressure on her face. There was another sensation, systemic, pervasive. Her legs, her arms, were weighted and tingly, and she seemed to have no torso at all.

She gradually understood the sensation on her face. Moist earth and grass. She was lying on her stomach on the lawn. She absorbed this knowledge as if it were a complicated matrix of ideas which, if comprehended, might lead to hitherto unheard-of information. At last she realized what was wrong with her body. Oxygen starvation. She began to breathe again, hard, painful gasps, inflations that threatened to burst the pulmonary capillaries, exhalations that brought her diaphragm upward until it crushed in panic against the pounding cardium.

She moved feebly, pulled a limp hand toward her, rested a moment with it flat on the grass near her shoulder. She began to press herself upward weakly, failed, rested a moment, and tried again. At last she raised herself to a sitting position.

Chan lay where he had fallen, still as death, guitar nearby.

Pop!

Drusilla looked up. Over the hedge, like an artificial flower, nodded Luellen's bright head. The quick deft tongue was retrieving the detritus of a broken bubble.

Drusilla snarled and formed another bolt, and as it left her something like a huge soft mallet seemed to descend on her shoulder-blades. Seated as she was, it folded her down until her chest struck the ground. Her hip joints crackled noisily. She writhed, straightened out, lay on her side gasping.

Pop!

Drusilla did not look up.

Presently she heard Luellen's light footsteps retreating down the gravel path. She gave herself over to a wave of weakness, and relaxed completely to let the strength flow back.

Shh . . . shh . . . approaching footsteps.

Drusilla rolled over and sat up again. Her head felt simultaneously pressured and fragile, as if any sudden move would make it burst like a faulty boiler. She turned pain-blinded eyes to the footsteps. When the jagged ache receded, she saw Luellen sauntering toward her on this side of the hedge, swinging her hips, humming tunelessly.

"Feeling better, honey?"

Drusilla glared at her. The killer-bolt began to form again. Luellen sank gracefully to the grass, near but not too near, and chose a grass-stem to pull up.

"I wouldn't if I were you, hon," she said pleasantly. "I

can keep this up all day. You're just knocking yourself
out."

She regarded the grass stem thoughtfully from her wide
vacant eyes, poked out a membrane of gum, hesitated a
moment, and drew it back in without blowing a bubble.
The gum clicked wetly twice as she worked it.

"*Damn* you," said Drusilla devoutly.

Luellen giggled. Drusilla struggled upward, leaned heavily on one arm, and glared. Luellen said, without looking
at her, "That's far enough, sweetie."

"Who are you?" Drusilla whispered.

"Home makuh," said Luellen, with a trace of Bronx
accent. "Leisure class type home makuh."

"You know what I mean," Drusilla growled.

"Whyn't you look and see?"

Drusilla curled her lip.

"Don't want to get your pretty probes dirty, huh? Know
what you are? You're a snob."

"A—a what?"

"Snob," said Luellen. She stretched prettily. "Just too
good for *anybody*. Too good for him." She pointed to
Chan with a gesture of her head. "Or me." She shrugged.
"*Any*body."

Drusilla glanced at Chan and probed anxiously.

"He's all right," said Luellen. "Just unplugged."

Drusilla swung her attention back to the other girl.
Reluctantly she dropped her automatic shield and reached
out with her mind. *What are you?*

Luellen put her hands out, palms forward. "Not that
way. I don't do that any more. Look if you want to, but
if you want to talk to me, talk out loud."

Drusilla probed. "A criminal!" she said finally, in profound disgust.

"Sisters under the skin," said Luellen. She popped her
gum. Drusilla shuddered. Luellen said, "Tell you what I
did."

"I'm not interested."

"Tell you anyway. Listen," Luellen said suddenly, "you
know if you try to do anything to me, you'll go flat on
your bustle. Well, the same thing applies if you don't
listen to me. Hear?"

Drusilla dropped her eyes and was furiously silent. Reluctantly she realized that this creature could do exactly as she said.

"I'm not asking you to like it," Luellen said more gently. "Just listen, that's all."

She waited a moment, and when Drusilla offered nothing, she said, "What I did, I climbed over the wall at school."

Drusilla gasped. "You went outside?"

Luellen rolled over onto her stomach and propped herself on her elbows. She pulled another blade of grass and broke it. "Something funny happened to me. You know the feeling-picture about jumping?"

Drusilla recognized it instantly, the sweet, strong, breathless sensation of being strong and leaping from soft grass, floating, landing lithely.

"You do," said Luellen, glancing at Drusilla's face. "Well, I was having that picture one fine morning when it—*stuck*. I mean like one of the phonograph records here when it gets stuck. There I was feeling a jump. Just off the ground, and it all froze.

She laughed a little. "I was real scared. After a while, it started again. I went and asked my tutor about it. She got all upset and went to the Preceptor. He called me in and there was no end of hassle about it." Again she laughed. "I'd have forgotten the whole thing if he hadn't made such a fuss. He wanted me to forget it in the *worst* way. Tried to make me think it happened because there was something wrong with me.

"So I got to thinking about it. When you do that, you start looking pretty carefully at *all* the pictures. And you know, they're full of scratches and flaws, if you look.

"But all the time they were teaching us that this was the world over the Wall—perfect green grass, beautiful men, the fountain and the falls and all the rest of it, that we were supposed to graduate to when the time came. I wondered so much that I wouldn't wait any more. So I went over the wall. They caught me and sent me here."

"I don't wonder," said Drusilla primly.

Luellen put pink fingers to her lips, hauled the gum out almost to arm's length, and chewed it back in as she talked. "And all you did was knock off the Preceptor!"

Drusilla winced and said nothing.

Luellen said, "You been here about two years, right? How many of us prisoners have you run into?"

"None!" said Drusilla, with something like indignation. "I wouldn't have anything to do with—" She clamped her lips tight and snorted through her nostrils. "Will you *stop* that giggling?"

"I can't help it," said Luellen. "It's part of the pattern for home makuhs. All home makuhs giggle."

". . . And that voice!"

"That's part of the pattern too, hon," said Luellen. "How do you think I'd go over at the canasta table if I weren't a-flutter and a-twitter, all coos and sighs and gentle breathings? My God, the girls'd be scared right out of their home permanents!" She tittered violently.

"Again!" Drusilla winced.

"You might as well get used to it, hon. I had to. You'll be doing something equally atrocious yourself, pretty soon. It goes under the head of camouflage . . . Look, I'll stop fooling around. There's a couple of hard truths you have to get next to. I know what you did. You set up a reflex to blank out any ex-Citizen you might meet. Right?"

"One must keep oneself decent," insisted Drusilla.

Luellen shook her head wonderingly. "You're just dumb, girl. I don't like you, but I have to be sorry for you."

"I don't need your pity!"

"Yes, you do. You've been asleep for a whole lot of years and you just have to snap out of it." Luellen knelt and sat back on her heels. "Tell me—up to the time they shipped you here, where did you go?"

"You know perfectly well. The Great Hall. My garden. My dormitory. That's all."

"Um-hmm. That's all. And every minute since you were born, you've been conditioned: a Citizen is the finest flower of creation. Be a good obedient girl and you'll gambol on the green for the rest of your life. Meanwhile there are criminals who get sent to prison, and the prison is the lowest cesspool in the Universe where you live out your life being reminded of the glory of the world you lost."

"Of course, but you make it sound—"

"Did you ever see any of those big muscular beautiful men the pictures told you about? Did you ever see that old-granite and new-grass landscape, or get warm under that nice big sun?"

"No, I was sent here before I had—"

Luellen demonstrated her ties to Earth by uttering a syllable which was, above all else, Earthy. "You're the dumbest blind kitten I ever saw. And tell me, when they took you to the ship, did you get a chance to look around?"

"I wasn't . . . worthy," said Drusilla miserably. "If a—a criminal was privileged to see outside the Wall—"

"They blindfolded you. Yes, and you never got a chance to look out of the ship when it left, either. Look, Citizen," she said scornfully, "if you hadn't had the good sense to get yourself sent here, you never would have gotten over the Wall!"

"I had only six more years before I—"

"Before you'd be quietly moved to another Walled Place with your age group. And maybe you'd have been bred, and maybe not, and by the time you realized there was no release for you, you'd be so old you wouldn't care any more. And they call that a world and this a prison!"

Drusilla suddenly put her hands over her ears. "I won't listen to this! I won't!"

Luellen grasped her wrist in a remarkably powerful little hand. "Yes, by God, you will," she said between her perfect teeth. "Our race is old and dying, rotten to the core. Know why you never saw any men? Because there are only a few hundred of them left. They lie in their cubicles and get fat and breed. And most of their children are girls, because that's the way it was arranged so long ago that we've forgotten how it was done or how to change it. You know what's over the Wall? Nothing! It's an ice-world, with a dying sun and thinning air, and a little cluster of Walled Places to breed women for the men to breed with, and a few old, old, worn transmitters for music and pictures to condition the blindworms who live and die there!"

Drusilla began to cry. Luellen sat back and watched her, a great softness coming into her eyes.

"Cry, that's good, sweetie," she said huskily. "Ah, you poor brat. You could've gotten straightened out the day you arrived. But no. Criminals were the lowest of the low, and you wouldn't associate with them. Earth and humans were insects and savages, because that's what you were taught. To be a Citizen was to be a god among gods, and to hear the music was your torture, for what you'd lost."

"What about the torture?"

"Transmitters in the guardian ships. You know about that."

"But the Citizens on board them—"

"What? Oh, for Pete's sake, hon! They're machines, that's all."

"They're not! The killer-boats are—"

"The killer-boats home on any human mind that begins to operate near the music bands. You had a close call, kitten."

"I wish one had come," Drusilla said miserably. "That's what I wanted."

"One did come, silly. But I don't get you. What did you want?"

"I wanted it to kill me. That's why I taught Chan to—"

Luellen clapped her hands to her face. "I thought that, but I couldn't really believe it! Sweetie, I got news for you. That boat wouldn't have killed you. It was after your boy-friend there."

Drusilla's face went almost as white as her teeth. She put her fist to her mouth and bit it, her eyes round, full of horror.

"It's all right," Luellen murmured. "It's gone. It was homing on him, and when he stopped radiating, it stopped coming. It's just a machine."

"You stopped it," Drusilla breathed. Slowly she sat up straight staring at the little blonde as if she had never seen her before.

"Pity if one of us couldn't outthink a machine," said Luellen deprecatingly. Then, "What is it, Dru? What's the matter?"

"He might have been . . . killed."

"You only just thought of that. Really thought of it."

Drusilla nodded.

"I'll bet this is the first time you ever thought of someone else. See what snobbery can do?"

"I feel awful."

Luellen laughed at her. "You feel fine. Or you will. What you've got is an attack of something called humility. It rushes in to fill the hole when the snobbery is snatched out. You'll be all right now."

"Will I?" She licked her lips. She tried to speak and

could not. She pointed a wavering finger at the unconscious man.

"Him?" Luellen answered the unspoken question. "Just you keep him asleep for a while. Give him more music, but keep him away from that." She pointed to the sky. "He won't know the difference."

"Humility," said Drusilla, thoughtfully. "That's when you feel . . . not good enough. Is that it?"

"Something like that."

"Then I don't . . . I don't think I understand. Lu, do you know why I killed the Preceptor?"

Luellen shook her head. "It was a good idea, whatever."

Drusilla said with difficulty. "My group went to be chosen for breeding. There's a—custom that the . . . ugliest girl must be sent back to her garden. H-he pointed me out. I was the ugliest one there. He said I was the ugliest woman in the world. I went . . . kind of . . . crazy, I guess. I killed him."

Suddenly she was in Luellen's strong small arms. "Oh, for God's sake," said Luellen with a roughness that made Drusilla cry again. "You're the sorriest most mixed-up little chicken ever. Don't you know that a perfect necklace has to have an ugliest diamond in it somewhere?" She thumped Drusilla's heaving shoulder. "We've been bred for beauty for more generations than this Earth has years, Dru. On Earth you're one of the most beautiful women alive."

"He told me that once, and I could have . . . killed him," Drusilla squeaked. She swallowed hard, moved back to peer piteously into Luellen's face. "Is that humility? To feel you're not good enough?"

"That's humiliation," said Luellen. She paused thoughtfully. "And here's the difference: Humility is knowing something is finer and better than you can ever be, so it's worth putting everything you have behind that something. Everything! Like . . ."

She laughed. "Like me and that ham novelist of mine. Bit by bit, year by year, he gets better. I give him exactly what he needs, in his own time. Right now what he wants is an irresponsible little piece of candy he can pick up or put down, and meantime get envied all over the neighborhood for. He's got it in him to do some really important work some day, and when he does he'll need something else from me, and I'll be here to give it to him. If, fifty years from now, he comes doddering up to me and tells me I've grown with him through the years, I'll know I did the thing right."

Drusilla worried at the statement, turning it over, shaking it. She parted her lips, closed them again.

Luellen said, "Go ahead. Ask me."

Drusilla looked at her timidly, dropped her eyes. "Is he really finer and better?"

"Snob!" said Luellen, and this time it was all kindliness. "Of course! He's an Earthman, Dru. Earth is young and crude and raw, but it's strong and it's good. Do you call an infant stupid because it can't talk, or is a child bad because it hasn't learned reason? We have nothing but decadence to bring to Earth. So instead we help Earth with the best it has. You keep your eyes open from now on, Dru. Nine women out of ten who truly help their men to realize themselves are what you've been calling criminals.

"You'll find them all over, up and down the social scale, through and through the history of this culture. Put up your shields again—for fun—and watch the women you meet. See how some seem to understand one another on sight—how they pass a glance that seems to be full of secrets. They're the hope of the world, Dru darling, and this world is the hope of the Galaxy." She followed Drusilla's gaze and smiled. "Now that you come to think of it, you love him, don't you?"

"Now that I come to think of it . . ."

She raised her head and looked at the sky. Gradually a smile was born on her trembling lips. She shook herself and took a deep breath of the warm evening air.

"Listen," she said. She laughed unevenly. "It *is* sort of scratchy, isn't it?"

GRANNY
WON'T
KNIT

This story had, for me, a most unusual nascence. Usually my stories emerge from hidden convolutions of my gut—my very own personal gut. In this case, a time arrived when Horace Gold, having saved space for me in an upcoming issue, called to ask, as politely as possible, "Where the hell is the novelette?" and I answered with perfect truth that although my gut was in perfect operation, it hadn't taken that certain turn just yet. So he put me on hold, and called another writer with whom he had discussed an idea, but who had later said he had decided to do nothing with it, and asked him if he would mind his passing the idea over to Sturgeon. The writer said go right ahead; he'd never do anything with it himself. The basic idea was this matter transmission thing. So I wrote Granny, *hardly getting up from the typewriter, at about the time the other writer changed his mind and wrote* The Stars My Destination. *I do indeed love Granny, but I wish I'd written the superb novel Alfred Bester did.*

I

For Roan, there was a flicker of blackness, almost too brief to notice, and he had arrived at his destination. He stepped down from the transplat and took three preoccupied steps before he realized, shockingly, that he had not materialized in the offices of J. & D. Walsh at all, but in a small plat-court hung with heavy and barbarous drapes. There was a fresh and disturbing odor in the air, which was too warm.

He cast about him worriedly, hunting for the dialpost that would send him to his father's office. It was not where it should be, at the corner of the court. Petals! He was late and lateness meant trouble.

"Well-l-l?" drawled a half singing, half whispering voice.

Roan spun, hitting the side of his foot painfully on the corner of the transplat. It made him hop. He had never felt so excruciatingly foolish in his entire thirty years.

"I'm sorry," he spluttered. "I must have dialed the wrong number." He located the source of the voice—a door across from him was open at its top panel and, in the small space, was framed a face . . .

The face!

If you dream about faces, you dream about them *after* you meet them, not before! The thought blazed at him, made him blink, and he blinked again at the cloud of golden hair and the laughing green eyes.

". . . the wrong, you see," he concluded lamely, "number."

"Maybe it was and maybe it wasn't," she said, in tones which could have been scored on a musical staff. Her hand appeared, to press back the side of the golden cloud.

A bare hand.

Tingling with shock at such wanton exposure, he looked

away quickly. "I'll have to—uh—may I use your transplat?"

"It's better than walking," she said and smiled. "It's over there." A long bare arm appeared, carrying a pointing finger. The arm was retracted and there was a small fumbling at the door-latch. "I'll show you."

"No!" How could this creature forget that—that she wasn't decently covered? "I'll find it." He floundered against the drapes, fumbled along them, at last threw one away from the dial pedestal. With his back firmly toward her, he said, "I have no tokens with me."

"Do you *have* to go?"

"Yes!"

She laughed. "Well, either way, be my guest."

"Thanks," he managed. "I'll—uh—send—" he began to dial busily and carefully, to avoid another wrong number— "send it to when I as soon as good of you three *five.*"

Averting his eyes, he stood on the transplat. She was still inside her cubicle, thank the powers. Then he remembered that he hadn't the slightest idea of the number he had mistakenly dialed; although it had stared him in the face on her dialpost, he had been too distraught to read it.

"Oh, I didn't get your number!" he said hoarsely, but the familiar flicker of total blackness had come and gone, and he was standing on the transplat inside the office of J. & D. Walsh, waving his hand stupidly at Corsonmay, the oldish receptionist with the youngish hair.

"My number?" Corsonmay echoed. Appallingly, she giggled. "Why, Roan *Walsh,* I never!" Under the privacy hood, her hands flickered. As he passed her desk, she pressed upon him a slip of paper. "It's really a very easy one to remember," she simpered.

He wordlessly stepped to his door. It slid back. He entered and, while it was closing behind him hurled the paper violently at the disposal slot. *"Blossom!"* he cursed and slumped into his chair.

"Roan, step in here a moment!" snarled the grille above him.

"Yes, Private!" Roan gasped out.

He sat for a moment, drawing deep breaths as if the extra oxygen would somehow give him the right words to say. Then he rose and approached a side panel, which slid open for him. His father sat glowering at him. His father was dressed exactly as he was, exactly as Hallmay and Corson-may and Walshmam and everyone else in the world was, except—but don't think about *her* now, whatever happens!

Private Walsh swung his glower, board and all, across Roan, then slipped his gloved hands under the privacy hood and studied them thoughtfully. Though Roan could not see them, he knew they were held with the fingers decently together, as unlike living things as possible.

"I am not pleased," said Private Walsh.

What now? Roan wondered hopelessly.

"There is more to a business than making profits," said the bearded man. "There is more to this business than moving goods. It is not a large business, but an arch's key is not necessarily a large stone. The transportation platform—" he droned, using the device's formal name as if the service wore a mitred hat—"is the keystone of our entire culture, and this firm is the keystone of the transplat industry. Our responsibilities are great. *Your* responsibilities are great. A position such as yours requires certain intangibles over and above your ability to make out manifests. Integrity, boy, reliability—respect for privacy. And, above all, personal honor and decency."

Roan, having heard this many times before, wrenched his features into an expression of penitence.

"One of the first indications of a gentleman—and to be a good businessman, one must be a good man, and the best of good men is a gentleman—one of the first ways of detecting the presence of a gentleman in our midst, I say, is to ask oneself this question: 'Is he punctual?'" Private Walsh leaned so far forward that his beard audibly brushed the privacy hood. The sound made Roan's flesh creep. "You were late this morning!"

Roan had a hysterical impulse to blurt, "Well, you see, I stopped off at a girl's place on the way and had a chat with her while she waved her bare arm . . ." But even hysteria yielded to his conditioning. And then his mind began to work again.

"Private," he said sorrowfully, "I *was* late. I can explain—" he heard the intake of breath and raised his voice slightly—"but I cannot excuse and will not try." The breath slid out again. Roan stepped backward one step. "With your permission, then, Byepry."

"Bye nothing. What is this explanation?"

This had better be good, Roan told himself. He put his hand behind him. He knew this, with face downcast, added to his penitent appearance.

"I awoke this morning caught up with a great idea," he said. "I think I have found an *economy*."

"If you have," rumbled the beard, "it's been hiding from *me*."

"Each load of freight we transplat carries a man with it. This man does nothing but hold the manifest in his hand and look up the receiver's clerk at the arrival point. My plan is to eliminate that man."

"You awoke with this in mind?"

"Yes, Private," Roan lied, still marveling at his mental resourcefulness.

"And thinking about it delayed you?"

"Yes, Private."

"Since you were apparently fated to be late in any case," the old man said acidly, "you'd have done better to stay asleep. You would have wasted less of your time—and mine."

Roan knew enough to keep his mouth shut.

"In the history of matter transmission," said his father, "nine shipments have gone astray. The consequences are appalling. I shall assign you to read the history of these nine cases and memorize the figures. In one such case—the arrival of one hundred and twelve cubic meters of pig-iron in a private house measuring eighty-four meters—the results were spectacularly expensive."

"But that can't happen now!"

"No, it can't," admitted Private Walsh. "Not since the capacity-lock, which prevents the shipment of any volume to a smaller one. But there is still room for some gruesome possibilities, as in the Fathers of Leander case, when two hundred female assembly workers were sent, in error, into the monastery of this silent order. The damages—first degree violation of privacy, you know—were quadrupled for the particular aggravation and multiplied by the number of Fathers and novitiates. Eight hundred and fourteen, if I remember correctly, and I do.

"Now, the employment of a properly trained operator would have reduced the presence of these females in that building to a matter of tenths of a second and the damages accordingly. The shipment would have been returned to its source almost before it had arrived. As long as such things can occur, the wages paid these operators are cheap insurance indeed." He paused ironically. "Is there anything else you want to suggest?"

"If you please, Private," Roan said formally, "I am acquainted with these matters. My suggestion was this—that phone contact be made with the receiving party when the shipment is ready—that our bonded transplat operator dial seven of the eight digits necessary—and that the final impulse be activated at the receiving point by audio or video, or even by a separate beamed radio, which we could supply to our regular customers or deliver by messenger a few minutes before the main shipment."

It got very quiet in the office. "You see," said Roan, pressing his advantage, "if the final shipping orders come from the receiver himself, it is difficult to imagine how anyone else could possibly receive the load."

This silence was longer, and was ended by a sound from the beard precisely as if the old man had bitten into an olive pit. "You mentioned a messenger for the impulse-device. Where's your saving?'"

"Most of our trade is with regular customers. Each of these could be given his own signal device."

Silence.

Roan all but whispered, "An exclusive service of J. & D. Walsh."

"Well!" said Private Walsh. It was the most unreadable syllable Roan had ever heard. "This is not a suggestion, nor the consequence of anything specific which may or may not have happened; it is purely a request for a private opinion. Which strikes you as more—shall we say euphonious— J. & D. Walsh & Son, or J., D. & R. Walsh?"

Roan felt one of his fingernails bite through his glove as he clasped his hands behind him. He hoped his voice would not shake when he answered. "I could not presume to express an opinion on such a matter to one as familiar with . . ." and, beyond that, his voice would not go.

He flashed a glance at his father, and almost extraneously it occurred to him that if the old man ever smiled, he might not be able to see it at all through the beard. Chalk yet one more advantage up to the enviable state of being head of a family.

He thought for a moment that his father was about to

say something pleasant, but the impossibility remained impossible, and the old man merely nodded at the door. "You're expected at my Mam's this evening," he said curtly. "Be prompt there, at least."

It stung, and the old man followed it up. "Lying abed immersed in company problems, even if they are of doubtful value, speaks well of an employee's devotion to his work. Unpunctuality speaks badly of it. A Private—" he squared his shoulders—"can be on time *and* be inspired."

Roan lowered his chin another notch and shuffled backward to the panel. It opened. He went through. When the panel clicked home, Roan leaped straight up in the air, his whole being filled with a silent shout. *The partnership! He's going to shake loose that gorgeous, beautiful, blossomy old partnership!* His gloved hands pounded silently and gleefully together. *Oh, Roan, you dog you, how do you do it? What makes that fuzzy head of yours tick when you get in a jam? Oh, you're a—*

He stopped, his mouth slack and his eyes abulge. There on his desk, in precisely the same pose, sat the golden-haired vision he had seen during the night and whose number he had dialed by error in the morning.

She was dressed—if one could call it dressed—in a long garment which fell from her throat and cascaded softly around her, rolling and folding and completely unlike the wrinkle-free, metrical cone-thrust-in-a-cone of conventional garb. Her arms were entirely bare and so, incredibly, were the feet which peeped out from under the flowing hem. She sat with both hands crossed on one knee and regarded him gravely. She smiled and was for a second transparent— and then she vanished.

Roan saw people and huge cargoes vanish every day— but not sixty meters from the nearest transplat! And not people indecently clad in outlandish fabrics which fell close to the body instead of standing properly away from it!

There was a heat in his face, and he became aware that he had not breathed in—how long? There was a straining ache about him and he realized that, at some point in this extraordinary experience, he had slumped to his knees on the carpet.

He got shakily to his feet and let himself be preoccupied with the reflex of adjusting his pantalets. They were neat and glossy and perfectly cylindrical, and not at all like the delicate pink taper of her—her limb. She'd had toes, too. Had it ever occurred to him before to wonder if women had toes? Surely not! Yet they had. *She had.*

Then reaction struck him and he staggered to his desk.

His first lucid thought was to wonder what this vision would look like properly clad and he found that he could not possibly imagine it. He found, further, that he did not want to imagine it, and he descended into a scalding shame at the discovery. Oh, cried every ounce of upbringing within him, the Private was right in withholding the partnership for so long; he'd be so wrong in trusting me with it! What am I, he sobbed silently, what horrible thing am I?

II

Private Whelan Quinn
Quinn and Glass,
Level 4,
Matrix 124-10-9783.

Honored Private:

In reference to yours of the seventeenth instant, we regret to inform you that the supply of chromium-plated ventilator girls is, at the moment, insufficient to complete the minimum mass for transplat shipment to you, which must total two toes. However, knowing that you use prefab paneling in considerable amounts, we are prepared to make up the weight in standard sheets if this is marriageable to you. We have the material in white, gold, dream and ivory. Please inform the undersigned as soon as possible if a doctor would be any help.

Yours in Privacy,

Roan stared dully at the words which glowed on the voicewriter screen, his hand hovering over the SEND button of his telefax. He was wondering mistily whether that line about radiator grilles was quite right when the annunciator hummed.

"Yes?"

Corsonmay's giggly voice then emerged. "Greenbaum

Grofast just called, Roan Walsh. Query on a 'fax transmitted at 1013 from your matrix. They want to know what is meant by item eleven on it."

"What's item eleven?"

"It says here, 'smiling toenails.' "

"Whatever it means, it's wrong. Is there a price on the item?"

"Just a blank."

"Then it doesn't matter. Tell them to cancel the line and up-number the other items. You could have thought of that."

"I'm sawrrree," she said in such a disgustingly ingratiating tone that, had she been in the room with him, he would certainly have bashed her head clear down to her bedroom —no, *backbone.*

"Listen," he snapped, "lift the copy of every 'fax I've sent out since I got here this morning and bring them in."

Roan growled. The shot of adrenalin his irritation yielded up cleared his mind and his vision, and he stared appalled at the letter on his screen. Shuddering, he cleared it. He could just see old Quinn puzzling out *"if this is marriageable to you."* Further, he could see the deep, secret ripplings at the base of his father's beard if by any chance Quinn happened to check through to him.

Corsonmay minced in with a sheaf of copies. "This one says—"

"Give me those. Byemay," he rapped.

"Well, bye." At the panel, she stopped and said solicitously, "Roan Walsh, you look—I mean is there anything . . ."

"Byemay!" he roared.

She gulped. "You could tell *me.*" Then her eyes widened as she watched his face. That odd, detached part of himself which irrepressibly wondered about such things wondered now just what expression he was wearing. Whatever it was, it blew her out of the office as if the room were a cannon and she the shell.

He looked at the top sheet *". . . your question as to how many support poles in a lading ton. The clerk in charge will supply the information. What is her number anyway?"* Then there was another reference to gold, this time *with the light behind it,* and a fantastic paragraph about shipping a generator *complete with ankling bolts.*

Going through the sheets, the most recent first, he was relieved to see that his preoccupation had noticeably affected only the last four messages. He settled himself down to a grim and careful enunciation of the corrections, worded with apologies but without explanations, checked them carefully and sent them. Then he destroyed the copies he had corrected.

When he straightened up, his face was flushed and his head spun. Noon already. Thank the powers for that.

Then he saw the note on his desk, at the corner on which the vision had appeared. In beautifully firm calligraphy was a transplat number—nothing more.

Hussy!

But he put it in his pocket.

On the way out, he said to Corsonmay, without looking at her, "Won't be back today. Field work."

"Oh, but you're not scheduled for—"

Before she could finish, he whirled and glared at her. She gulped so hard, he had the mad conviction that she was about to swallow her own lips. He strode to the dial-post, spun a number and got out of there.

He stood for a moment under the sky—well, under the metal-glas canopy—drinking in the sights of Grosvenor Center. There were shops and a restaurant and a library, and a theater as well, an immense structure honeycombed from top to bottom with its one-seat cells and one-man screens. Something called *The Glory of Stasis* was playing. He remembered the reviews—a two-hour prose poem dedicated to the fantasy of eternal afternoons, permanent roses and everlasting youthfulness. He should see it, he thought. After all, wasn't that what he needed—a reaffirmation in the permanence of things and his place in this eternal society?

How comforting the Center was! People moved from one shop to another, not hurrying, not idling, each as sure of where he was going as where he had come from. Each dressed alike, walked alike, the rectangular feet unhesitating, the tubular limbs alternating, the cone-in-cone clothing never rippling, never draping, never clinging close to bodies . . .

He shook himself.

. . . And concealed under the decent capes, stockinged hands were folded, unused until needed—just as Godmade as a bird's wing—and hidden when they worked, as all working mechanisms were housed. And as far as the eye could see them, these sane folk were identifiable, correct. One was never in doubt, for that smooth-faced one was a Bachelor like himself, and the long hair yonder was a May, and the bound hair a Mam, and the bearded ones were Privates.

Noble title, Private—constant reminder of the great principle of Privacy, which was the very essence of all order. It was born, he had been taught, of the people themselves when, in the days of the barbarities, they had formed great armies—millions upon millions of just people in a single organization—and their majority were called Private. Magnificent then and magnificent today.

He saw the bank of transplats and felt a surge of pride. Someone had used the term "keystone." A good one. For the transplat covered the Earth like a great clean cape, standardizing language, dress, customs and ambitions. Every spot on Earth was but a step and a split-second away from every other, and all resources lay ready for the seeking glove. He had been curious enough, at one time, to attempt an orientation in geographic distances. He soon gave it up as profitless. What did it matter that the company offices were in Old New Mexico and his home near what had once been called Philadelphia? Could it be important that Corsonmay arrived each morning from Deutsch Polska and Hallmay, the Private's secretary, slept each night in Karachi?

The population was stabilized below its resources. Why, there was enough copper to supply power fuel for seven centuries—copper which, so they said, was once used to carry feeble little pulses of electricity. And when the copper was gone, it would be simple enough to synthesize more. Food—filthy, necessary, secret stuff—was no longer a problem. And for delicacies of mind and heart, there were the spaceships, roaring away to the stars and returning years later, carrying strange fossils and odd stones, after having traveled every laborious inch out and every inch back again, aging their crews and enriching the world.

Once, he knew, there had been talk of an interplanetary transplat, but it was now unshakably established that the effect was possible only in a gravitic field of planetary "viscosity." Once the immense task of establishing the dial central was finished, the system could be extended anywhere on a planet, but never between them. And a good thing, too, as his father had explained to him. What would happen to the beautifully balanced cultural structure if humanity were suddenly free to scatter through the Universe as it is now scattered over the Earth? And why leave? What could there possibly be for anyone—except a crazy spaceman—off Earth?

He had read this, too: *A species which can build perfection as fast as we have done is a species capable of maintaining perfection forever.* It took fifteen thousand years to populate the Earth and then explode it in a mighty war. It took half a thousand years to concentrate the few hundred thousand survivors in Africa, the only continent left in which men could live. It took the African Colony six hundred years to reach the transplat stage in its technology. But *that* was only a hundred and fifty years back. The transplat built cities in days, floated them on impervious bedplates and shielded them with radiation-proof domes when necessary. People could settle anywhere—and they did. People could work the Earth for its resources almost anywhere—and they did.

Roan sighed, feeling much better. He looked away from the calm but busy Center and idly took in what could be seen of the horizon. There a snowcapped mountain hung like a cloud, and yonder was blue water as far as the eye could see. He wondered what mountain it might be, what sea; and then he laughed. It was all the same to a man, all the same to humanity.

He paced out the Center, from one end to the other, delighted, proud. He was young and vital and marriageable—perhaps all such as he suffered from the equivalent of his blonde apparition when that time of life came upon them. Marriage, after all, held certain animal mysteries, and like those of his flower-shop, where he cleaned his body and teeth and stoked himself with food concentrates, they just could not be discussed. He would wait and see; when the time came, the mysteries would be explained, even as had all the others.

He came out into the walkway loving everybody, even, for a moment, Granny.

Granny! He stopped and closed his eyes, his face twisted. He'd very nearly forgotten about her. Well, she could blossom well wait. He'd had a bad time this morning and the very thought of Granny then had been unbearable. Who, in the throes of self-abasement, wanted contact with a veritable monolith of respectability? And who, having regained his respectability, needed the monolith? Either way, the visit was insupportable. He'd make his sister Valerie go. Someone from the family had to make the visit once a week. Why, he didn't know and had never asked. Let Valerie do it. What was the use of having a sister if you couldn't get her to do the dirty work once in a while?

He crossed the walkway, went to the phone banks and dialed Valerie's number after a glance at his watch. She should be back at work from noonrest by now.

She was. As soon as she saw his face, she said, "Roan Walsh, if you're calling up to palm that visit to Granny off on *me*, you have another think coming. I do my duty by the family and I'm blessed if I can see why I should do any more than my duty or why you should do any less so don't even say a word about it." He opened his mouth, but before anything came out of it, she said, "And don't be late either. And especially, don't be early."

Roan opened his mouth again, but the screen went black.

Out in the filtered sunlight again, he let the chagrin fade and the amusement grow. It grew into something rare in Roan—an increasing glow of heady resentment and conscious command. How did these magnificent human beings get so magnificent in the first place? Why, by asking if everything was all right or if it weren't—and, if it weren't, then they changed things until it was. Now everything was all right with him, except this Granny business. They ask the question—why should he go see Granny? Because someone always had to. That was no answer. Put it another way, then—what would happen if he just didn't go?

He strode buoyantly down the walkway, beaming fiercely at the passersby, and the wonderful thought defeated him in exactly seven minutes, twenty seconds. Because the answer to "What if he just didn't go?" was:

From Mam, that hurt look and then an avalanche of "understanding."

From Val, a silent, holier-than-thou waspishness, day after day.

And from the Private, thunder and lightning. And no partnership. Well, buds with the partnership!

At this point, he stopped walking. What did you do when you walked out on your family's business?

He'd never known anyone who had. Where did you go? What did you do?

His other, inner self said, banteringly, *Aw, come off it. Are you going to kick over the Cosmos to save yourself sixty minutes with the old woman?*

Roan said nothing to that. So the voice added, *What have you got against Granny, anyway?*

"She bothers me," Roan said aloud. He turned and went into a decorator.

What for? demanded the inner Roan.

"To buy something for Granny," he replied. And the inner voice, damn its stinking stamens, chuckled and said, *Know what, Roan? You're a crawling coward.*

"Why can't you be on my side for once?" he demanded. but its only answer was a snigger so smug that even his sister Valerie might have envied it.

The decorator was an old bachelor with a fierce countenance. Roan bought roses and hybrid jonquils, paid for them and started out. Suddenly he went back, prodded by his weird questioning mood, and said, "What did they call a place where you buy roses before they called it a decorator?"

The man uttered a soprano nickering which, Roan deduced, was laughter. He leaned across the counter and, looking over each of his shoulders in turn, said in a shrill whisper, "Flower shop." He clung to the counter and twisted up his face until the tears spurted.

Roan waited patiently until the man calmed down and then asked, "Well, then, why do they call the you-know-what a flowershop?"

This seemed to sober the man. He scratched his pale, cropped head. "I don't know. I guess because, whatever they called it before, people used to make jokes and cusswords about it. Like now with—Flower Shops."

Roan shuddered. Its motivation was beyond definition for him, but with it came a feeling of having taken a ludicrous path to a great truth, and somehow he knew he would never joke or swear about flower shops again. Or, for that matter, about whatever new name they gave the plumbing after they got through with muddying up this one. For this much he could say aloud, "There ought to be something else to curse and make jokes about."

The man's fierce face yielded for a moment to puzzlement, and then he shrugged. To Roan, it was a disgusting gesture and an alarming one, the one his father had made years ago, when Roan's tongue was a little more firmly attached to his curiosity than it had been of late. It was transplat this and transplat that, until he had suddenly asked his father how the thing worked. The Private had stopped dead, hesitated, then shrugged just that way. It was a gesture which said, "That's how things are, that's all."

On the way to the transplats, Roan stopped where people clustered. There was a shop there dealing in, according to its sign, FAD AND FASHION. Having passed through a number of engrossing fads in his life—Whirlstick and Chase and Warp and, once, a little hand loom on which he had woven a completely useless strip of material twice his length and two fingers wide—he stopped to see what people were buying.

It was a motion-picture of white-gloved hands manipulating two thick needles and a sort of soft heavy thread. No one would have dared to do such a thing in the open, but the picture was acceptable, though giggle-making.

On a shelf at waist height were many samples of the fabric which seemed to be the product of this exercise. He stepped forward until his cape covered enough of the shelf for him to pick up a piece of the material.

It was loosely woven, with a paradoxical texture, very rough, yet very soft.

It fell on and around his hand and draped away like— like . . .

"What is it? What's this called?" he blurted.

A woman next to him said, "They call it knitting."

III

He skipped to the laFarge yards and Kimberley, Danbury Marble and Krasniak, checking inventories and consulting accountants. He did it all without notes, which he had left in his office when he charged out at noon. He did it efficiently and he did it, without at first knowing why or even how, in the most superb cross-spoor fashion, so that, by quitting time, it would take far more trouble than it was worth for the office to discover he had used the first two hours of the afternoon for his own purposes.

This small dishonesty troubled him more than a little. Honor was part of the decency-privacy-perfection complex, and yet, to a degree, it seemed to be on the side of good business and high efficiency to operate without it. Did this mean that he was not and could not be what his father called a gentleman? If not, how much did it matter?

He decided it didn't matter, cursed silently and jovially at the inner voice which sneered at him, and went to see his grandmother.

There was very little difference between one transplat court and another. A business might have a receptionist and homes might have a larger or smaller facility, but with the notable exception of the blonde's apartment in his dream— surely it *was* a dream—when he first found walls covered with drapes, he had never noticed much difference between courts.

Granny's, however, always gave him a special feeling of awe. If it could be found anywhere on Earth, here, right here in this court, was the sum and symbol of their entire culture—neat, decent, *correct*.

He stepped off the transplat and went to the dialpost to check the time, and was pleased. He could hardly have been any more punctual.

There was a soft sound and a panel stood open. It was the same one as always and he wondered, as he had many times before, about the other rooms in Granny's house. He would not have been surprised if they all proved to be empty. What could she need but her rectitude, her solitude and a single room?

He entered and stood reverently. Granny, all ivory and white wax, made a slight motion with her hooded eyes and he sat opposite her. Between them was a low, bare table.

"Great Mam," he said formally, "good Stasis to you."

"Hi," she said quaintly. "How you doing, boy?" For all his patient irritation with Granny, as always he felt the charm of her precise, archaic speech. Her voice was loud enough, clear enough, but always had the quality of a distant wind. "You look like you hoed a hard row."

Roan understood, but only because of many years of experience to her odd phrasing. "It's not too bad. Business."

"Tell me about it." The old woman lived in some hazy, silent world of her own, separated incalculably in time and space from the here and now, and yet she never failed to ask this question.

He said, "Just the usual . . . I've brought you something." From the pocket under his cape, he took the decorations he had bought, twisted the tube which confined them and handed the explosion of roses and daffodils to her. The other package clattered to the table.

There was the demure flash of a snowy glove and she had the stems. She put her face down into the fragrant mass and he heard her breath whisper. "That was very kind," she said. "And what's this?" She popped the wrapping and peeped down between the edge of the table and the hem of her cape to see. *"Knitting!* I didn't know anyone remembered knitting. Used to be just the thing for the old folk, when I was a sprout like you. Sit in the Sun and rock and knit, waiting for the end."

"I thought you'd like it." He caught the slight movement of her shoulders and heard the snap of the wrappings as she closed the package again and slid it to the undershelf.

They beamed at each other and she asked him, "Aren't you working too hard? You look—well, you were going to tell me about the business."

He said. "It's about the same. Oh, I had an idea this morning and told the Private about it. I think he's going to use it. He was pleased. He talked about the partnership."

"That's fine, boy. What was the idea?"

She wouldn't understand. But he told her anyway, choosing his words carefully, about his plan to eliminate the transplat operators. She nodded gravely as he spoke, and at one point he had a mad impulse to start making up nonsense technological terms out of his head, just to see if she'd keep nodding. She would; it was all the same to her. She was just being polite.

He restrained himself and concluded, "So, if it works out, it will be a real economy. There just wouldn't be any way for a shipment to go astray the way—" he almost blurted out the story of the arrival of the passenger van at the monastery, and caught himself just in time; the old lady would have been shocked to death—"the way some have in the past."

"I reckon they couldn't," she agreed, nodding as if she understood.

He ought to return her courtesy, he thought, and said, "And what has occupied you, Great Mam?"

"I do wish you'd keep calling me Granny," she said, a shade of petulance creeping into the weary whisper. "What have I been doing? What might I be doing at my age? Know how old I am, Roan?"

He nodded.

"A hundred and eighty-three come spring," she said, ignoring him. "I've seen a lot in my time. The stories I could tell you . . . Did you know I was born in the Africa Colony?"

He nodded again, and again she ignored him. "Yes indeedy, I was about your age when all this started, when the transplat broke the bubble we lived in and scattered us all over the world."

Yes, you saw it happen! he thought, for the first time fully realizing something he had merely knew statistically before. *You saw folk dancing chest to chest and having food together and no one thinking a thing about it. You knew the culture before there was any real privacy or decency—you, who are the most private and decent of people today. The stories you could tell? Oh, yes—couldn't you, though! What did they call them before they called them 'flower shops'?*

Certainly she couldn't conceivably divine his motivations, he asked, "What did people *do* then, Granny? I mean— today, if you could name one single job all of us had to do, it would be keeping the perfection we have. Could you say that you folks had any one thing like that?"

Her eyes lighted. Granny had the brightest eyes and the whitest, soundest teeth of anyone he knew. "Sure we had." She closed her eyes. "Can't say we thought much about perfection—not in the early days. I think the main job was the next step up. The next step up," she repeated, savoring the phrase. "You know, Roan, what we have today—well, we're the first people in human history that wasn't working on that, one way or another. They'd ought to teach human history nowadays. Yes, they should. But I guess most folks wouldn't like it. Anyway, folks always wanted to be a bit better in those days.

"Sometimes they stopped dead a couple hundred years and tried to make their souls better, and sometimes they forgot all about their souls and went ahead gettin' bigger and faster and tougher and noisier. Sometimes they were real wrong and sometimes they did right just by accident; but all the time they worked and worked on that next step up. Not now," she finished abruptly.

"Of course not. What would we do with a step up? What would we step up to?"

She said, "Used to be when nobody believed you could stop progress. A grass seed can bust a piece of granite half in two you know. So can a cup o' water if you freeze it in the right place."

"We're different," he said smugly. "Maybe that's the real difference between us and other kinds of life. We can stop."

"You can say that again." He did not understand her inflection. Before he could wonder about it, she said, "What do you know about psi, Roan?"

"Psi?" He had to search his mind. "Oh—I remember it. Fad and Fashion was selling it a couple of years ago. I thought it was pretty silly."

"That!" she said, with as much scorn as her fragile, distant-wind voice could carry. "That was a weejee-board. That thing's older'n anyone knows about. It didn't deserve the name of psi. Well, look here—for ten thousand years, there've been folks who believed that there was a whole world of powers of the mind—telepathy, telekinesis, teleportation, clairvoyance, clairaudience . . . lots more. Never mind, I'm not going to give you a lecture," she said, her eyes suddenly sparkling.

He realized that he had essayed a yawn—just a small one—with his mouth closed, and that she had caught him at it. He flushed hotly. But she went right on.

"All I'm saying is this—there's plenty of proof of this power if you know where to look. One mind talks to another, a person moves in a blink from place to place without a transplat, a mind moves material things, someone knows in advance what's going to happen—all this by mind power. Been going on for thousands of years. All that time, nobody understood it—and now nobody needs to. But it's still around."

He wondered what all his had to do with the subject at hand. As if she had heard him wonder, she said, "Now you wanted to know what the next step up might be, in case anybody was interested. Well, that's it."

"I can't see that as a step upward," he said, respectfully but positively. "We already do move things—speak over distances—all those things you mentioned. We even know what's going to happen next. Everything is arranged that way. What good would it be?"

"What good would it be to move the operators off the transplats?"

"Oh, that's an economy."

"What would you call it if telekinesis and teleportation moved goods and people without the transplat?"

"*Without the transplat?*" he almost shouted. "But you— but we—"

"We'd all be in the same boat with those operators you're replacing."

"The op—I never thought about them!"

She nodded.

Shaken, he mused, "I wonder why the Private never thought of that when I told him about it this morning."

There was a dry, delighted sound from deep in the old chest. "He wouldn't. He never did understand how anything works. He just rides it."

Roan controlled himself. One did not listen to criticism of one's parents. But this was Great Mam herself. The effort for control helped bring the whole strange conversation into perspective and he laughed weakly. "Well, I hardly think we're going to have any such—economy—as that."

She raised her eyebrows. "This progress we were talking about. You know, even in my time most folks had the idea that humans planned human progress. But when you come to think of it, the first human who walked upright didn't do it because he wanted to. He did it because he already could." When she saw no response on his face, she added, "What I mean is that *if* the oldtimers were right and progress *can't* be corked up, then it's just going to bust loose. And if it busts loose, it's going to do it whether you're the head of J. & D. Walsh or a slag-mucker, whether you're happy about it or not."

"Well, I don't think it will happen."

"Haven't you been listening to me? It's *always* been with us."

"Then why didn't they—why should it show up now and not a thousand years from now?"

"We never stopped progressing before—not like this," she said, with a sweeping glance at the walls and ceiling which clearly indicated the entire planet.

"Granny, do you *want* this to happen? *You?*"

"What I want doesn't matter. There've always been people who had—powers. All I'm suggesting is that now, of all times, is the moment for them to develop—now that we don't develop in any other way."

He was persistent. "You think it's a good thing, then?"

She hesitated. "Look at me, how old I am. Is that a good thing? It doesn't matter—it happened—it had to happen."

"Why have you told me this?" he whispered.

"Because you asked me what was occupying me," she said, "and I figured to tell you, for a change. Frighten you?"

Sheepishly, he nodded.

She did, too, and laughed. "Do you good. In my day, we were frightened a whole lot. It took us a long way."

He shook his head. *Do you good?* He failed to see what good could come of any so-called "progress" that threatened the transplat. Why, what would happen to things? What would happen to their very way of life—to privacy itself, if anyone could—what was it, teleport?—teleport into a man's office or cubicle . . .

"Look, boy, you don't have to wait until it's your turn to come chat with your old Granny, you know. Come over anytime you have something to talk about. Just let me know first, that's all."

There was nothing in life he wanted less than another session like this one, but he remembered to thank her. "Byemam."

"Byeboy."

He rushed out to the dialpost and feverishly got the number of his home. He stepped up on the platform and the last he saw of Granny's face through the open panel was her expression of—was it pity?

Or perhaps compassion was a better name for it.

IV

He went straight to his cubicle, brushing past his sister as she stood at the edge of the court. He thought she was going to speak, but deliberately showed his back and quickened his stride. Her kind of smugness, her endless, placid recitations of her day's occupations, were the prime thing he could do without at the moment. He needed privacy, lots of it, and right now.

He leaned back against the panel when it closed. His head spun. It was a head which had the ability to thrust indigestible ideas into compartments, there to seal them off from one another until he had time to ruminate. This was how he was able to handle so many concurrent business affairs. It was also how he had been able to get through this extraordinary day—till then. But the compartments were full; nothing else must happen.

He had awakened before daylight to see, in the soft glow of the walls, a girl in a flowing garment who regarded him gravely. Her hair had been golden and her hands were clasped over one knee. He had not been able to see her feet—not then.

He had stepped on the 'plat to get to the office and had arrived, instead, in an unmentionable place containing drapes and this same girl. She had spoken to him.

He had seen her again, perched on his desk.

He had lost two hours in an unwonted self-examination, which had left him bewildered and unsure of himself, and had gone most respectably to see his most respectable grandmother, who had filled him full of the most frightening conjectures he had ever experienced—including the one which brought this mad business full circle. For she had suggested to him that, by a force called tele-something-or-other, certain people might appear just anywhere, transplat or no transplat.

He snorted. You didn't need a transplat to have a dream! He had dreamed the girl here and in the draped court. He had dreamed her in the office. "There!" he said to himself. "Feel better?"

No.

Anyone who had dreams like that had to be off his 'plat.

All right: they *weren't* dreams.

In which case, Granny was right; someone had something so much better than a transplat that the world—his world—would come to an end. If only this were a technological development, it could be stopped, banned, to maintain the Stasis. But it wasn't—it was some weird, illogical uncontrollable mystery known to only certain people *and he, Roan, wasn't one of them.*

It was unthinkable, insupportable. Indecent!

Going into his flower shop, he reached for his dinner ration. He grunted in surprise, for instead of the usual four tablets and tumbler of vitabroth, his hand fell on something hot, slightly greasy and fibrous. He lifted it, turned it over. It was like nothing edible he had ever seen before. On the other hand, there had been innovations from time to time, as the Nutrient Service saw fit to allow for this or that change in the environment, the isolation of mutated bacteria and their antibiotics, the results of their perpetual inventory of sample basals.

But this thing was far too big to be swallowed. Maybe, he thought suddenly, it was a combination of nutrients and roughage.

His teeth sank readily into it. Hot, reddish juice dribbled down his chin and a flavor excruciatingly delectable filled his mouth and throat, his nostrils and, it seemed, his very eyes. It was so good, it made his jaw-hinges ache.

He demolished the entire portion before it had a chance to get cold, then heaved a marveling sigh. He fumbled about the food-shelf in the vain hope of finding more—but that was all, except for the usual broth. He lifted the cup, then turned and carefully poured it down the sink. Nothing was going to wash that incredible flavor out of his mouth as long as he could help it.

He slipped into his dressing shield and changed rapidly. As he transferred his wallet, he paused to glance into it to see if it needed replenishing.

He grunted with the impact of memory. As he had left the Private's office, he had come face to face with his—with that—well, dream or no, there she had been. And had disappeared. And on the corner of his desk, just where she had sat, had been the 'plat number—*this* number, here in his hand.

Like the dream she was—wasn't she?—the girl had not

spoken to him here in his cubicle or in the office. But in the
draped court she had. That episode, improbable as it
seemed, could hardly have been a dream. He had dialed
that transplat to get there. He might have misdialed, but
he had been wide awake when he did it.

She must be one of those—those next-step-upward monsters Granny was talking about, he decided. He had to
know, had to speak to her again. Not because of her hair,
of course, or the brazen garment. It was because of the
transplat, because of the hard-won Stasis that held society
together. It was a citizen's simple duty to his higher pink
toes. No, his higher self.

He adjusted a fresh pair of gloves and strode out to the
court. Valerie was still there, looking wistful.

"Roan!"

"Later," he barked, already spinning the dial.

"*Please!* Only a minute!"

"I haven't got a minute," he snapped and stepped up on
the platform. The flicker of blackness cut off her pleading.

He stepped down from his arrival platform and stopped
dead.

No drapes! No perfume! No—oh, holy Private in
Heaven!

"Roan *Walsh!*" squeaked Corsonmay. The secretary's
eyeballs all but stood out on her dry cheekbones. Under
them, her hands—decently gloved, thank the powers—were
pressed, and in her hair obscenely hung a comb which, he
deduced, he had interrupted in midstroke. He saw instantly what had happened, and a coruscation of fury and
embarrassment spun dazzlingly inside him.

She must have seen him throw away the number she had
written down for him and supplied him with another. And
he had had to go and assume that it was . . . oh, to expect
the drapes, the arms, the—and all that—and to come face
to face with *this!*

"Private!" she shrilled. "*Mam! Mam!*" Calling her parents. Well, of course. Any decent girl would.

He dived for the dialpost. So did she, but he got there
first.

"Don't go, Roan Walsh," she panted. "Corsonmay and
my father, they're not here, they would have been if only
I'd known, they'll be back soon, so *please* don't go."

"Look," he said, "I found the number on my desk and

I thought Grig Labine had left it there. I was supposed to
see him and I'm late now. I'm sorry I invaded your privacy,
but it was a mistake, see? Just a mistake."

The eagerness faded from her almost-wrinkled face and
homely hot eyes. She seemed to shrink two inches in a
tenth of a second. Her mouth pouted, wet and pathetic,
and quivering puckers appeared at its sides. *Oh, you
stinker, what did she ever do to you?* he said to himself.

"Be serene," he blurted. He dialed his home.

"Oh-h-h-h . . ." Her wail was cut off by the transplat.

He stood where he was, his eyes squeezed closed on his
embarrassment, and breathed hard.

And then he became aware of a whimpering "Please . . ."
and, for one awful moment, thought Corsonmay's transplat had not operated. He opened his eyes cautiously and
then sighed and stepped down. He was home. It was Valerie who was whimpering.

"Well, what's the matter with you?" he asked.

"Roan," she wept, *"please* don't be angry with me. I
know I was a beast. It was just—oh, I meant it, but I didn't
have to be so . . ."

"What are you talking about?"

"When you called about wanting me to go to Granny's."

That seemed so long ago and so completely trivial. "Forget it, Val. You were absolutely right. I went, so forget it."

"You're not mad?"

"Of course I'm not."

"Well, I'm glad, because I want to talk to you. Can I?"
she begged.

This was unusual. "What about?"

"Can we go out, Roan?"

"Where are the parents?"

"In the Family Room. We can be right back. Please,
Roan," she pleaded.

He yielded. In his cosmos, Val was merely a perennial
and harmless irritation; this was probably the first time he
had consciously realized that she might be a person, too,
with personal problems.

"Grosvenor Center?" he asked.

She nodded. He dialed it and stepped up on the platform
and down again at Grosvenor. It was still daylight there and
he wondered vaguely where on Earth it might be. The sea
on one side was an evening blue, the mountaintop a glory.

Val appeared on the transplat and stepped down. They walked silently past the decorator and the Fad and Fashion and the restaurant until they reached the park. They sat down side by side on a bench, with its shoulder-high partitions between each seat, and looked at the fountain.

She was very pale and her shoulders were moving under the cape, a complex motion that was partly stifled sobs and partly the kneading of hands.

He said, as gently as he could, "What's up?"

"You don't like me."

"Aw, sure I do. You're all right."

"No, please don't like me. I don't *want* you to. I came to you because you don't like me."

This was completely incomprehensible to Roan. He decided that listening might extract more data than talking.

Valerie said in a low voice, "I've got to tell you something that would make you hate me if you didn't already, so that's why. Oh, Roan, I'm no *good*!"

He opened his mouth to deny this, but closed it silently. He had the wit not to agree with her, either.

"There's somebody I—saw. I have to see him again, talk with him. He's—I want—*Oh!*" she cried, and burst into tears.

Roan fumbled for a clean handkerchief and passed it deftly around the front of the partition, down low. He felt it taken from his fingers.

"A May's supposed to wait," she said brokenly, "and one day her Private will come looking for her, and he will be her Private, and she will be his help and service until the end. But I don't want to be help and service to the Private who comes. Who knows, one might come any minute. I want *this* one to come!"

'Maybe he will," soothed Roan. "Who is he?"

"I don't *know!*" she said in agony. "I only saw him. Roan, you have to find him for me."

"Well, where—"

"He's tall, as tall as you," she said hurredly. "His eyes are green. He has—" she gulped and her voice sank—"long hair, only not like a May. And right on the bottom of his chin there's a little cleft and on one side—yes, on the left side—there's a little curl of a scar."

"Hair? Men don't have long hair!"

"This one has."

"Now look," he said, suppressing his laughter at the outlandish concept. "If there were such a man, long hair and all, *everybody'd* know where he is."

"Yes," she said miserably.

"So there you are. There's no such man."

"But there *is*! I saw him!"

"Where?" She was silent. He said impatiently, "If you don't tell me where, how can I find him?"

"I can't tell you," she said at last, painfully. "It doesn't matter—you'd never find him—there?" She colored. "He must be somewhere else, too. Please find him, Roan. His name. Where he is. Even if he never—I'd like to know what his name is," she finished wistfully. She stood up. "The Private will miss us."

On the way back to the transplat, she said to the air straight in front of her, "You think I'm just awful, don't you?"

"No!" he said warmly. "Sometimes I think everyone's just a little different from what the Stasis expects. It isn't 'awful' to be a little different." And his subconscious, instead of objecting, dropped its prim jaw in astonishment.

V

The Family Room was the heart of their house, as such rooms were to every house on Earth. A chair—virtually a throne—dominated one wall. It held the video controls and the audio beams which came to audible focus in their proper places in the room—the miniature of the throne at the right wall, which was the place of the son of the house; the wooden bench at the left, which was the daughter's; and the small stool at the throne's foot, where the mother sat.

The room, because of its beams and its padded floor and acoustically dead walls and ceiling, was a silent one and it was the custom for each family to convene there for two hours at the end of the day. There were stylized prayers, such reading as the Private chose, whatever conversation he dictated and, when he was so moved, transmitted entertainment of his choice for the clan.

When Roan and Valerie entered, the original silence was compounded by towering disapproval. The Private's hand lay on the video control, which he had just switched off. The Mam's head had bobbed once, sidewise, so engrossed had she been in the program; it was if a prop had been snatched away.

Son and daughter separated and went to their places. Roan felt the old hovering terror as the Private's gaze flicked across his withers like a rowel. He sat down and glanced quickly at his sister. She huddled on her bench so oppressed, so indrawn, that even her wrinkle-free, fold-less garments could not conceal her crushed look. Roan, with hands properly folded, swallowed apprehensively.

"Late," said the Private. "*Both* of you. This sort of thing can hardly help in my recommendations, Valerie, you unwanted creature." This was an idiom used in chastising all Mays and passed Valerie by. Then, to Roan, "One would assume that my generosity and forgiveness"—that would be the hint about the partnership—"would result in at least a minimal effort not to repeat the offense. You are thirty years of age—old enough to know the difference between Stasis and chaos. You will be confined, by my personal lock, to your cubicle for forty-eight hours, where you may reflect on the consequences of disorganization. *Valerie!*"

She twitched and gave the proper response, which was to meet his eyes. Roan said nothing. In such occasions, there was no appeal.

"Valerie, were you and your brother together in whatever escapade it was that led you to flout the organization of this house?"

"Yes, Private, but it was really my—"

"Then you must bear the same punishment—not primarily for being tardy, which is not one of your habitual defects, but for your failure to use your influence on your irresponsible sibling. I assume you failed to try, since it would be too painful for me to conclude that both my offspring lacked the basic elements of decency."

Another massive silence followed. The mother, sitting at his feet, rolled her eyes upward to the cushions, where his gloved hand lay. With a slight, unconscious movement, her ear sought the focal point of the currently non-existent audio beam. The Private's beard bulged as he dropped his glare upon her.

"And since I must cling to a single shred of satisfaction," he said, "let it be my faith in *your* knowledge of correct behavior, Mam. Assuming that this knowledge exists, the circumstance clearly indicates that you too have not properly applied it. There will therefore be no video for you tonight." He unleashed a semi-circular glare in which his beard smote across their presences like the back of a hand. "Leave me."

They rose and shuffled out. The panel slid shut behind them. "I'm sorry." Val barely breathed the apology.

"*Silence!*" roared the grille over the door.

They hung their heads and waited. Walshmam tiptoed away and returned in a moment with two small cubes. She led Valerie to her cubicle and stood aside. Valerie glanced once at Roan, who twitched a dismal smile at her. Then the panel slid shut on her and Walshmam pressed one of the cubes into its socket, effectively sealing the door until removed again from this side. True to custom, Roan waited until she passed him and then shuffled along behind her to his own cubicle.

"And furthermore," enounced the grille over the door, "I herewith refuse to consider the merits of the suggestion you made this morning. For, if good, it issues from an unworthy source and is tainted—if bad, it deserves no consideration."

Walshmam seemed very sad, but then few Mams were anything else. Their lives alternated between silent patience and silent regret, with only an occasional flicker of preventive action. He grimaced in an effort to convey a certain camaraderie, but she misunderstood and looked away, and he knew she had taken it as a rebellious or unrepentant expression.

He wondered, as he dropped the dressing shield over his head, what would happen if he got up and hauled on the Private's beard.

Reaching for his brief nightshirt and sleeping shorts and bedshoes, he told himself, "I bet he hasn't even got anything in his rulebook to cover that. And he never was so good with a new idea."

That reminded him of what Granny had said—the Private "never did understand how anything works. He just rides it." He sure rides his family, Roan thought.

So he himself would be a Private some day, have a family and get it all back again, he thought sleepily, and

let himself sink down and down into a place where he
sat on a monstrous throne with a beard to his knees, and
watched his father, who sat on the boy's chair, weeping.
At his feet was—well, for heaven's sake, *it was Granny!*

At some point, it must have turned into a nightmare—
a dreadful fragment involving being lost in the flicker of
final black that one experienced on the transplat. Here,
however, he was immersed in it, with dimensionless space
at his freezing back and the unyielding "inner" surface of
reality pressing into his face. He cried out and struggled—
and thumped his cheekbone on solid rock. He yelped and
pressed away from the rock and sat up.

Not an inch from his head was the lintel of a shimmer-
ing, rectangular rock. Beyond it, a pale, green, alien sky
which brightened by the moment.

He glanced behind him and saw nothing but purple
plain, cracked and crevassed, from which cactuslike spears
sprouted grotesquely.

He stepped through the doorway and, a few yards beyond, the desolation abruptly ended. Before him stretched
rolling parkland, then a curving line of trees following a
brook. Across the brook were fields—one brown, one tan,
one a tender green—and they seemed, at this distance, as
smooth as the surface of a cup of milk. To the right were
mountains, one with a flaming cap so brilliant, his eyes
stung. He recognized it as dawnlight on snow. To the left
was a broad rolling valley. The air was warm but spar-
kling-fresh.

He paused and inhaled deeply, seeking comprehension,
then saw, to his right, a boulder as big as a Private chair.
On the boulder sat a girl with golden hair and strange
eyes. She wore a belted singlet that revealed far more girl
than Roan had ever seen before. She held one delicately
bronzed, bare knee in both hands. Her bare feet acknowl-
edged the snowfire pinkly, and they were wet with dew.

She laughed a greeting and rose and flowed over to him.
"Come along," she said.

He clutched himself and hid his naked hands. With a
swift, strong movement, she had his hands in hers.

"Up we go," she sang and, before he could think, she
was leading him.

His cheek touched her bare shoulder. He smelled her
perfume and her sweet breath, and his eyes rolled up and

his knees sagged. Her arm went briefly round his shoulders and she laughed again.

"It's all right, it's only a dream," she told him.

"A dre—" he coughed—"eam?"

"Thirsty?" She held out her hand, and he started violently when a cup appeared in it. "Here you are."

He took it, hesitated, then raised it. She still stood, smiling at him. Modestly he turned his back and drank. It was bright orange, cold, sweet-acid and delicious. He patted his lips carefully and turned back, waving the cup helplessly.

"Throw it," she said.

"Th—what?"

She gestured. Obediently, he tossed the cup straight up. It vanished.

"Feel better? Come on, they're all waiting for you."

Gaping up at the spot into which the cup had vanished, Roan said. "I want to go home."

"You can't. Not until the dream's finished."

He put his arms straight down and fluttered his hands until the cuffs concealed them. "I want to go home," he said forlornly.

"Why?"

"I just . . ." He looked longingly over his shoulder at the doorway. When he looked back, she was gone. And suddenly, urgently, he wanted her back. He took a step forward.

"*Boo!*" she said, her lips just touching the nape of his neck.

He whirled, and there she stood. "Where were you?"

"Here—anywhere." She vanished and reappeared instantly at his right.

"Please," he said, "don't do that any more. And just let me stand here quietly for a minute."

"All right." She wandered away, picked a snowdrop and a strange green-and-purple flower, added a fern-frond and came back toward him, her fingers deft and a-dance. She held out the flowers, woven into a tiny circular wreath, and spun them on her finger. Then she set them into her golden hair.

"Pretty?"

"Yes." His eyes fell away from her and were dragged

back again. "Why don't you cover your arms?" he blurted.

"We wear what we please here."

"Where is *here?*"

"Sort of another world." He glanced back at the gateway. "It wouldn't do any good," she explained. "There isn't anything in there now but blackness. The way out is a time, not a place. Don't be afraid. You'll go back when it's time."

"When?"

"How long did you have to sleep?"

"Forty-eight hours, though I'd never—"

"Maybe you can stay that long. Who's to know?"

"You're—sure I'll get back in time?"

"Sure as sure. Is it all right now?"

Shyly, he smiled. "Fine. Everything's fine."

She took his hand, and skipped two paces, so he had to follow. He tried politely to tug his hand free, but she held fast and seemed not to notice. A giggle, a blush, the slightest sign of self-consciousness in her, and he would have found the contact unbearable.

But she was so completely at ease that the revulsion would not come, and she chattered so gaily, making him answer, keeping him busy, that, even had he felt like asking her to let go, he had no space for the words, nor the words with which to do it.

"You were in my cubicle," he said breathlessly, as she hurried him down the slope.

"Oh, yes—more than you know. I watch you sleep. You sleep nicely. There's a tanager." She stopped, balancing, something flowing out of her shining face to the blazing bird and back again. "I came to see you at your office, too. Everything's straight and hard there, and sort of lonely. But all you people are lonely."

"We're not!"

"You wait until the dream's finished and you won't say that. Want to see a magic?" She stooped, still walking, and brushed her long fingers across a thick growth of tiny spiked leaves. They all closed up like little green fists.

"Why'd you come?" he asked.

"Because you were ready to wonder."

"Wonder what?"

She appeared not to consider this worth answering, but

released his hand and bounded like a deer once, twice, then high over a brook. He floundered through it, soaking his bedshoes.

When he caught up with her, she touched his chest. "Shh!"

On the wind floated a note, then another note and, high and sweet, another, so that they became a chord. Then a note changed, and another, and another, and the chorus of voices modulated softly, like the aurora, which is the same as long as one looks, but changes if one looks away and back.

"What's your name?" he asked abruptly.

"What would you like it to be?"

"Flower!" he cried, the strange pressures of a dream asserting themselves; and with it he felt a liberation from the filth with which custom had clothed the word.

"And you're Roan, and a roan is a horse with wind in his mane and thunder in his feet, sweet-nostriled, wild-eyed, all courage and speed."

He thought it was a phrase from a song, yet it could have been speech—her speech. He squished the water in his muddy shoes and almost whinnied with delight at the thought of the thunder in his feet. She took his hand again and they leaped together to the brow of a foothill. Ahead, the song finished in a roar of good laughter.

"Who is it?" he wanted to know.

"You'll see. There—*there!*"

Where the hill shouldered into the forest was a clear, deep pool. In the forest and on the hillside, buildings nestled. Their walls were logs and their roofs were thatch. They were low and wide, and very much part of the hill and the woods. In the clearing between woods and slope, by the pool, was a great trestle table and, around the table, were the people who had been singing—you could tell by the sound of their laughter.

"I can't—I *can't!*" Roan croaked miserably.

"Why, what's the matter?" asked Flower.

"They have no decency!"

"There are only two things which are indecent—fear and excess—and you'll see neither here. Look again."

"So many limbs," he breathed. "And the colors—a green-and-red man, a blue woman . . ."

"A blue dress and a harlequin suit. It's grand to wear colors."

"There are some things one shouldn't even dream."

"Oh, no! There's nothing you can't dream. Come and see."

They went to see. They were made very welcome.

VI

At dusk, on the second day, Flower and Roan walked a shadowed aisle in the forest. Roan's sleeping garments were tattered and seam-gutted, for he would not give them up, though they had not been designed for the brutality they had suffered. Yet he did not mind the rips and gapes, for no one else did. His bedshoes were long gone and he felt that if he were told he would never again feel the coolth of moss under his bare feet, or the tumble of brook-sand, he would die. He knew the Earth as something more than a place on which to float sealed cities. He had worked till he hurt, laughed till he cried, slept till he was healed. He had helped with a saw, with a stone, with a song. Wonder on wonder, and greatest wonder of all—the children.

He had never seen any before. He did not know where children came from except that, when they were twelve, they went to their families from the crèches. He did not know how they were born. He did know that each child was educated specifically for a place in his Family and in the Stasis, and that the largest part of this education was a scrubbing and soaking and rubbing in of the presence of the father—his voice, features, manners of living and speaking and working. When the child emerged, there was a place for him in the home, by then very little different from his last place in the crèche, and he was fitted to it, not by the accidental authority of parentage, but through the full-time labors of a bank of specialists.

Each family had one boy, one girl—one trade, one aim. This was how an economy could be balanced and kept balanced. This was how the community could raise its young and still maintain the family.

But here, in this dream . . .

Children babbled and sang and burned their fingers. They ran howling underfoot and swam like seals in the pool. They fought and, later, loved. They grieved, sweated, made their music and their mistakes. It was all very chaotic and perplexing and made for a strong, sane settlement which knew how to laugh and how to profit from an argument. It was barbarous and very beautiful.

And it had a power—for these people quite casually did what Roan had seen Flower do. They seemed to have a built-in transplat and could send and receive from anywhere to anywhere. They could reach up into nothingness and take down bread or a hatchet or a book. They could stand silently for a time and then know what a wife would serve for nutrient—which they brazenly sat together to eat, though they went privately for other functions no more disgusting—or the tune of a new song or news of a find of berries.

They seemed willing enough to tell him how all this was done, yet his questions got him nowhere. It was as if he needed a new language or perhaps a new way of thinking before he could absorb the simple essence. But for all their power, they had callouses on their hands. They burned wood as fuel and ate the yield of the land around them. To put it most simply, they made their bodies function at optimum because it made them joyful. They never let the *psi* factor turn, cancerlike, from a convenience to a luxury.

So Roan walked quietly in the dusk, Flower at his side, thinking about these things and trying to shake them down into a shape he could contain. "But, of course, this isn't real," he said suddenly.

"Just a dream," nodded Flower.

"I'll wake."

"Very soon." She laughed then and took his hands. "Don't look so mournful. We're never very far away!"

He couldn't laugh with her. "I know, but I feel that this is—I can't say it, Flower. I don't know how!"

"Then don't try for now."

Before he knew it, his arms were around her. "Flower—please let me stay."

She stirred in his arms. "Don't make me sad," she whispered.

"Why can't I? Why?"

"Because it's your dream, not mine."

"I won't let you go! I'll hold onto you and I won't wake up!" He staggered then and fell heavily. Flower stood calmly ten feet away.

"Don't make me sad," she said again. "It hurts me to push you away like this."

He climbed slowly to his feet and held out his hand. "I won't spoil any more of it," he said huskily.

They walked silently in the dimness, toward the shaft of light which the Sun laid up the valley to the settlement each evening at this season.

"How soon?" he asked, because he could not help himself.

"When it's time," she said. She released his hand, put her arm through his and took his hand again. They came to the light.

Roan looked slowly from one end of the clearing to the other, trying to see it as it had been to him at first, then as it was with the familiarity of two days. There was the kettle they used, they said, to make sugar from the maples, and he pretended he had seen it boil, seen the frantic dogs snapping the caramelized sweetmeat up from the snow and running in circles frantically until it melted and they could get their silly mouths open again. There was the buckwheat field which would carpet the spring snow with quick emerald on a warm day. There was the pond, there the ducks with old-ivory webs and mother-of-pearl lost in their necks. He saw—

"There!" he yelled and twisted away from Flower, to go racing across the clearing. "You!" he shouted. "You! *Stop!* You by the pool!"

But the man did not turn. He was tall, as tall as Roan; his hair was very long, his eyes were green and at the side of his cleft chin, was a curl of a scar. In the water, there was a chuckle of laughter, a flash of white.

"You with the scar," Roan gasped. "Your name—I've got to know your—"

As the man turned, Roan looked past his shoulder, down at the water, straight into the startled eyes of his sister Valerie.

And that was the end of the dream.

Only one good thing had happened since his mother

had removed the block from his cubicle door. The cubicle itself had been the most depressing conceivable place to wake up in; its walls crushed him, its filtered air made him cough. It had no space, no windows, The dressing shield brought out a thudding in his temple and he hurled it to the floor, turning violently away from it, physically and mentally. He felt that if he itemized the symbolism of that tubular horror, he would go berserk and tear this coffin-culture apart corpse by corpse. Breakfast was an abhorrence. The clothes—well, he put them on, not daring to be angry about them, or he never would have gotten to the office.

Corsonmay looked his way only long enough to identify, then stuck her silly flaccid face in a file-drawer until he was safely in his office. He looked at the desk, its efficient equipment, at the vise-jaws called walls and the descending heel called a ceiling, and he shook with anger. But he was weak with it when the heavy voice issued from the grille: "Step in here, Roan Walsh."

Trouble again. Out of the prison into the courtroom.

He took four great breaths, three for composure, one a sigh. He went to the panel and it admitted him. His father sat back, his head and beard vying texture against texture. Before him was a scattering of field reports, and he looked as if he had nibbled the corner off one of them and found it unexpectedly good.

"Good Stasis, Private."

The old man nodded curtly. "Your absence made it necessary for me to take up the threads of your work as well as my own. You will find what I have done on reports subsequent to yours." He stacked the cards neatly and scattered them. "On reviewing these, I found to my surprise—my pleasant surprise, I may add in all fairness—that you have done a phenomenal amount of work. Kimberley, Krasniak, that warehouse tangle in Polska. And in spite of its speed, the work is good. I investigated it in detail."

This, thought Roan, sounded *really* bad. He put his hands behind him, lowered his chin in The Stance, and set his teeth.

"The investigation brings out," lumbered the vocal juggernaut, "that the work was done in roughly speaking four hours, three and one-half minutes. Very good. It seems, further, that the elapsed time involved was five hours, forty-eight minutes and some odd seconds. Approximately, that is." He tapped the edges of the cards on the desk, flickered the lightning at Roan, then snapped forward and roared, "One hour and forty-five minutes seem to have disappeared here!"

Roan wet his lips and croaked, "There was noonrest, Private."

The Private leaned back and stretched jovially. "Splendid, my efficient young scoundrel. Superb! And what is the noonrest permitted us at our present altitude in the organization?"

"Forty minutes, Private."

"Good. Now all we have to account for is one hour and five minutes. Sixty-five precious, irredeemable minutes, which the resources of Stasis itself could not buy back. Over an hour unreported, yet somehow a double-time dock from your wages is not entered here. Or perhaps it is entered and, in my haste, I overlooked it."

"No, Private."

"Then either one or more transactions of company affairs were handled on that afternoon and not reported—which is gross inefficiency—or the time was spent on idling and personal indulgence, with every intention of accepting payment from the firm for this time—which is stealing."

Roan said nothing except to himself, and that was, almost detachedly, "I think I can stand about four minutes, thirty-two and three-tenths seconds—approximate—more of this."

"The picture is hardly a pleasant one," said the Private conversationally, and smiled. "The records give me the choice of three courses of action. First, the time owed may be made up. Second, the value of these hours may be paid back. Third, I can turn you over to Central Court with a full indictment, and thereby wash my hands of you. You might be given a bow and arrow and left to make your way in the wilderness between segments of Stasis. You could survive a long time with your training. Days. Weeks even."

"Eighteen, seventeen, sixteen . . ." Roan counted silently.

"However, I am going to give you every opportunity to ameliorate this—this frightful crime. Take these cards into your office. You have between now and 1600—a punctual 1600, that is—in or out of the office, to revise any slight miscalculations you may have made and to refresh your memory in the event that you did useful work for the firm in any of these lost minutes. Every alteration you make, of course, will be checked to the tenth of a second. Until 1600—be serene."

Roan, quite numb, tottered forward, took the cards, muttered, "Byepry," and awkwardly backed out.

Why, he wondered, did he stand for it?

Because there was no place to go, of course.

There was . . .

No, there wasn't. That had been a dream.

He sank into a black paralysis of rage.

VII

The phone roused him. He received, ready to tear the head off the caller, any caller. But it was Valerie.

She said, "It's nearly noonrest." She would not meet his eyes. "Could you—would you mind . . . ?"

"Same place, right away?"

"Oh, *thank* you, Roan!"

He growled affectionately and broke off.

She was not at the Grosvenor transplat when he got there, so he stalked straight to the park. She was waiting for him. He dropped down next to her and put his head in his hands—and damn the passers-by. Never seen a man's hands before?

He sat up after a while, however; Valerie's silence positively radiated. He wondered if he should tell her about the man in the dream, and almost laughed. But he could not laugh at Valerie. Not now. In the dream, there had been love. Valerie, in her crushed, priggish way, had fallen in love. All right, tell her you still haven't found the guy and then sympathize with her and get it over with. You have some real worrying to do.

He turned to her. "I haven't been able to—"

"His name's Prester." She leaned close to the partition and whispered, "Oh, Roan, you saw me like that, in the pool. They hadn't meant for you to see me at all. Oh, what you must *think!*"

He said, just as softly, "I hadn't let myself believe it."

"I know," she said desperately. "I'm surprised you even came here."

"What do you mean—Oh, the pool! Do you know, it never occurred to me until this minute that you were— that you'd be—oh, forget it, Val. I'm just glad you found him. Prester, hm? Nice-looking fellow."

Her face lit up like a second sun. "Roan—*really?* I'm not a—hussy?"

"You're grand and the only person I know in this whole sterile, starched world who's managed to live a little! I'm *glad*, Val! You don't know—you can't—what I've been through. Enough to make a dozen dreams. And it came like a dream—I mean parts and chunks of real-life things —things Granny was maundering about, things I'd seen, a girl I met once wrong-dialing—an accident, you little prude! I believed it was just a dream—I had to, I guess. I had to believe Flower and she *told* me it was." Lord, he'd said the word right out loud in front of his sister!

But she was quite composed, cheeks excitement-red, not disgusted-red, eyes bright and distant. "She's lovely, Roan, just *beautiful*. She loves you. I *know*."

"Think she does?" He grinned till it hurt. "Oh, Val, Val —the maplesugar kettle."

"Mmm—the oat-field!"

"The big table and the singing!"

"Yes, and the children—all those children!"

"What happened?" he cried. "How could such a thing happen?"

She whispered fervently, "We could both be crazy. Or the whole world could be coming apart and we slipped in and out through a crack into—or maybe it really was a dream, but we had it together. But I don't care, it was beautiful and—and if you'd said I was a—because of— you'd have *spoiled* it and killed me, too. Is it all right then, Roan, is it really all right? Really?"

"You're sort of beautiful yourself. For a sister, that is."

"*Oooh!*" she squeaked, blushing and enormously pleased. Then, happily, "I'm glad I'm not you."

"Uh—why?"

"How does it work, what makes it go, is it a dream, and, if not, what could it be? Be like me, Roan. It happened—for the rest of my life it has *happened!* But—I hope there'll be more."

"If I find out how it works, what makes it go and so on, there *will* be more. So you just be glad *I'm* like me in that respect."

"If you found it, you—wouldn't keep me out?"

"If I couldn't take you," he said warmly, "I wouldn't go. Now do you feel better?"

"I'm going to kiss you!"

He roared with laughter at the very idea in a place like this and, under the stares this attracted, she cried, "Be quiet —thunderfeet!" At the phrase from Flower's little song, his heart twisted.

She peeped at his face and said, "I'm sorry, Roan."

"Don't be," he said hoarsely. "For that second, she was right here." He put out his hands, made fists, stared at them, then got them out of sight again. Flower—well, he'd have plenty of time to find her after 1600. "Val . . ."

"I didn't know anyone could be so happy!" she said. "What, Roan?"

"Nothing. Just that I really am late," he said, abruptly changing his mind. No need to air his troubles to her now —the news services would take care of that about 1612. Meanwhile, let her stay happy.

They walked back to the transplat.

"Roan, let's come here every day and talk about it. I don't know a thing you did and you don't know what I did. Like the time—"

"Sure I will, sure," he said. "Take something pretty big to stop me."

She stopped dead. "There's something the matter."

"Get on your 'plat. Everything's fine. Hurry now."

She dialed and stepped up and was gone. He stood looking at the empty air, where her anxious face had been, until another passenger filled it. He hoped he hadn't worried her.

He walked slowly back to the bench and sat down, and that was where he had his big idea.

"Whoever *is* that?" The thin old voice was edgy.

"Me. Roan," he said from the court.

The top panel of a door slid back and the voice floated to him, gentle now, and firm. "You know you're welcome here, son, but you also know you're to call first. Just spin that dial and clear out of here for an hour. Then you can come and stay as long as you like."

"Petals to that. I haven't *got* an hour. Come on out here or I'm coming in."

"Don't you use that language on me, you leak-brained snipe, or I'll lift your hair with a blunt nailfile!"

The instant she began to shout, he began to roar, "Decent or not, just get on out here. *If you'd shut off your low-fidelity mouth for twelve lousy seconds, you'd stop wasting your own time!*"

They stopped yelling together and the silence was deafening. Suddenly, Granny laughed, "Boy, where'd you learn that type language?"

"For years, I've been hearing you talk, Great Mam," he said diffidently. "It only just now occurred to me that I never really listened. And about being decent—if you're comfortable, come as you are."

"Damfidon't!" She came out of the room and kicked the door closed with a flip of her heel. She wore an immense wrapper of an agonizing blue and seemed to be barefooted. Her hair, instead of lying sleekly away from the center part in two controlled wings, flew free like a May's. Roan had one frozen moment, and then she tossed the hair back on one side with an angry twitch of her head. "Well?" she blazed. There seemed to be nothing left of the gentle talc-on-ivory quality in her voice.

Slowly, he smiled. "Damfidon't like you better the way you are."

She sniffed, but she was pleased. "All you can do to keep your eyes from rolling out onto the carpet. Ah, well, you've found my secret. Reckon I'm old enough to have just one eccentricity?" she demanded challengingly.

"You've lived long enough to earn your privileges."

"Come on in here," she said, starting down the court. "Most folks don't or can't realize I've spent the least part of my life in that cone-in-cone getup. Everybody else around's practically born in it. I just don't *like* it. Chest-padding the men so they won't look different from women!" she snorted. "I wasn't brought up that way." She opened the manual door in the corner. "Here we are."

It was an odd-shaped room, an isoscles triangle. He had

never seen it before. "What happened to your voice, Granny? You feeling all right?"

In the familiar wind-in-the-distance tones, she said, "You mean you miss this little gasp?" Then, stridently, "Something I picked up for company. Had to. Nobody'd take me seriously when I talked natural. They cast me as a frail little pillar of respectability and, by the Lord, I was stuck with it. It's hot in here."

He missed the hint, waited for her to sit down, and then joined her. "Know why I'm here?"

She regarded him closely. "Sleeping well?"

"That wasn't a dream."

"No? What then?"

"I came to find out what it was. Where it is."

She fluttered the lapel of the wrapper. "You got this part of my secret life out of me, but that don't guarantee you all of it. What makes you so sure it wasn't a dream?"

"You just don't go to bed healthy and sleep for two days! Besides, there's Valerie. I saw her there, right at the very last second."

She grunted. " 'Fraid of that. No one was sure." She laughed. "Must've been a picnic when you two got your heads together. You come here to kill me?"

"What?"

"Outraged brother and all that?"

"Valerie's happier than she's ever been in her life and so much in love, she can't see straight. I'm just as happy for her as she is for herself."

"Well!" she smiled. "This changes things. So you want to take your sister and go live out your lives in a dreamland."

"It's more than that," he said. "I need one of your telekinesis operators. I mean *now.*"

"The best I can do for you is a little girl who can knock down a balancing straight-edge at any distance under fifteen feet."

He made no attempt to conceal his scorn.

She pursed her lips thoughtfully. "How'd you mix me up in this, anyway?"

"We're wasting time," he said. "But if you must know, it was your hints to me last time I was here—the transplat obsolete, people appearing in any room anywhere, communication without phones. I'd already seen telekinesis twice, when you told me that. And since then . . ." he shrugged. "You *had* to be in it. Maybe you'd like to tell me why *I'm* mixed up in it."

"Hadn't planned to for a while. Maybe we'll step up the schedule. Now what's the all-fired rush?"

"I have an appointment in—" he checked—"less than two hours that is going to put me under the ground unless I can get help."

He told her, rapidly, about the lost time and his father's threat.

"You're dead right," she said after a moment. "He's afraid of you. I don't know why he should be *that* afraid. He's just like his father, the potbellied old—" She stopped, shocked, as a large hand closed over her wrist.

"I can't listen to that."

"All right," she said with surprising swiftness. "I'm sorry. Given one of my TKs, what would you do?"

He leaned forward, put his elbows on his knees, bringing his gloved hands into plain sight.

"Do? I'm going to take this wrinkle-free civilization and turn it out into the woods. I'm going to clutter up the Family Rooms with the family's own children. I'm going to turn Stasis itself upside down and shake it till the blood runs into its head and it finds out how to sweat again."

Granny's eyes brightened. "Why?"

"I could tell you it was for the good of all the people— because you're Great Mam and lived through it all and had a chance to think about things like that. But I'm not going to say anything like that to you. No—I'll do it because I want to live that way myself, head of a family of hard-handed, barefoot, axe-swinging people who are glad to get up in the morning.

"I thought of finding the dream-people again. I even thought of going out into the wilderness between cities and living that way myself. But if I did, I'd always be afraid that some day a resources survey crew might find me, scoop me up and bring me back. Stasis wouldn't let people live like that, so let's make Stasis live our way."

He took a deep breath. "Now Stasis is built around the transplat. There can't ever be a better machine. But if I go in there today and claim I've spent years secretly developing one—if I get one of your people to start transmitting things all over his office and claim I have a new machine to do it with—why, the Private's got to listen. I'll save my job and spot your people through and through the whole culture till it falls apart. And one day maybe I'll be the Private at Walsh & Co.—and, Stasis, look out!"

"You know," she said. "I *like* you."

"Help me," he said bluntly. "I'll like you, too."

She rose and punched his arm with sharp knuckles. "I'll have to think. You know, if you can fast-talk your way out of this you'll only stall things a little. The old—your father—wouldn't buy any parlor tricks. He'd want to see that machine."

"Then let's stall. Can you fix me up with a telekin—telekineticist? That what you call them?"

"TK," she said absently. "I've got something a heap better than any TK. How'd you like a stationless transplat —a matter transmitter that will lift anything from any-where to anywhere without centrals or depots?"

"There's no such thing, Granny."

"Why do you say that?"

"All my life I've been a transplat man, that's why. There's a limiting factor on matter transmission. It must have a planetary field; it must have a directing central; it must have platforms built of untransmissible material and—"

"Don't tell *me* how transplat works," she snapped. "Sup-pose a machine was designed on totally different principles. A force-pump instead of a suction pump. Or an Archi-medes screw."

"There isn't any other principle! Don't you think I *know?*"

"I'll show you the damn machine!" She marched to the angled wall of the little room and bumped a scuff-plate near the floor. The entire wall slid upward into the ceiling, swift and silent. Lights blazed.

It was quite a laboratory. Much of its equipment he had thought existed only in factories. Most was incompre-hensible to him.

Granny walked briskly down an aisle and stopped at the far wall. Ranged against it was a glittering cluster of equipment beneath a desk-sized control panel. The desk surface seemed to be a vision screen, though it was hinged at the top. At the side, he saw what looked like manipulator controls of the kind used in radiation laboratories.

"There's a servo-robot this size on a hill about forty miles from here," said Granny.

She turned a switch, sat down over the screen and began to spin two control wheels.

"Tell you what it does," she said abstractedly as she worked, "though this ain't really the way it does it. Plot a straight line out from this machine and a line from the other. Where they intersect, that's your transmission point. Now draw two more lines from the equipment and where *they* cross, that's the arrival point. When they're set up, you haul on this snivvy and what was *here* is now *there*. The stuff doesn't travel any more than it does with a transplat. It ceases to exist at one point and conservation of matter makes it appear at another.

"But you've created just the strain in space which makes it show up where you want it to."

"Show me."

"All right. Call it."

"My old wallet. Top drawer, left side in the office. Drawer's locked by the way," he said.

"What's the matrix?"

He reeled off the address coordinates. She tapped them on a keyboard and bent over the screen. It showed a Stasis unit. She spun a wheel and the buildings rushed closer. Her hand dropped back to a vernier and the view slowed, seemed to press through the roof and hover over a desk.

"Right?"

"Go on," he said. "Pretty fair spy-ray you have there."

"You don't know!" She reached and from a speaker came the quiet bustle of the office. She went back to the controls and the view sank into the desktop. Suddenly, the contents of the drawer were there. With the manipulators, she deftly hooked the wallet, raised it a fraction. Then the scene disappeared as she shifted to another set of controls.

"Receiver location," she murmured. The garbled picture cleared, became a mass of girders and then a bird's-eye view of the room they stood in, so clear that Roan looked up with a start. He could see nothing. "Stick out your stupid hand," said Granny.

He obeyed and she brought the scene down to it until its image hung in the center of the picture. Roan wiggled his fingers. Granny cut back to the other view, checked

it, then threw over the "snivvy" she had shown him earlier.
The wallet dropped into his hand.

She switched off, turned and looked up at him. "Well?"

He said, "Why play around like this?"

"What do you mean?"

"This thing doesn't do what you say it does. I got the
wallet, sure, but not with that thing."

"Do tell. All right, how *did* you get the wallet?"

He considered the instrument carefully. "It's a sort of
amplifier—yes, and range-finder, too. It just gets a fix for
your TK man. Right?"

"You really think I've got a high-powered psychic hiding
around here who does the work after I get to it with the
finder?"

"*You're* the TK!"

She slumped resignedly at the controls. "If you can't lick
'em, join 'em. Old Roman saying. If that's what you say it
is, then that's what it is."

"Why didn't you say so in the first place?" he grumbled,
looking at his watch. "So now what do we do?"

"Wait a minute—I've got to get used to something." She
hung over the console and then glanced up brightly. "I'll
break out the pilot model. You can't tote this thing under
your arm."

She went to a storage wall and dragged out a bin. In it
was a long box. Roan helped her open it and lift out the
spindly collection of coils and bars, setting it on a bench.

"I'll check you through this." She flung off her wrapper
and advanced on the machine. "Just turn it on its side for
me," she said. "What are you gawping at? Oh!" She looked
down at her shorts and halter, and laughed. "I *told* you it
was too hot in here."

It was not that age had left no marks on her compact
body, but certainly not two centuries' worth. Holding a
light-duty soldering iron near her cheek, she slapped herself on the bare midriff.

"One thing you might keep in mind about women as you
get to know 'em, Roany—the parts that the decent people
expose are exactly the ones that get old first. This face of
mine was gone at 75, but the tummy's good for another
hundred yet." She bent over the device. "Maybe it's better
that way, maybe not—who's to say? Hand me the millivolt-
meter there."

After a time, her work with the machine took precedence over everything else in Roan's cosmos. "You sure can get around in there," he said, awed, as he held the light for her. "Think so?' she grunted, and went on working steadily.

VIII

At 1451, Roan Walsh arrived at the Walsh Building. His head spun with its lopsided weight of advice, technical data and strategy. His arrival was in the warehouse, not in the office, for he brought a long wooden box on casters. He pushed the box himself up the long corridor to the office wing.

"Oh, Roan Walsh, can I help?"

"No, Corsonmay. Wait—yes, come in." He put his hands on the end of the box and nodded at the dithering secretary. "Grab hold here."

She came close, tittered and let the tips of her gloves show for an instant before she slipped them clumsily under the end of the box.

Not that end up, you addlehead.

Roan yelped and let go. Corsonmay, now bearing most of the not inconsiderable weight, began to mew rapidly. Roan, sitting flat on the floor, gasped, "Who said that?"

"*Ewp!*" squeaked Corsonmay. "It's heavy!"

"Let it down. My God, Corsonmay, you're as strong as a horse!"

"That's the nicest thing you ever said to me," she beamed without sarcasm.

He turned to her, found himself face to face with her withered ardency. "What did you say about lifting up the wrong end, Corsonmay?"

"I didn't say anything."

I did.

"Byemay," he said, and forestalling her, added, "Really —nothing more. Byemay."

She left and he whirled, hunting futilely in midair. "Granny! Where are you?"

Briefly, just at eye-level, the business end of a needle-focus audio beam projector appeared. Roan patted it happily and it disappeared. Bless her, she'd be watching everything through her big machine, her audio aimed for his inner ear every second.

At 1559.5, the ceiling said, "Roan Walsh, you may step in now."

"Coming, Private." He all but started at the sound of his own voice. How was it that, though he seemed increasingly able to cope with anyone or anything, his father's voice still turned him to mush?

But that could wait. He stepped just inside the room.

"Come, come—stand close. I intend to do one of several things, but biting is not one of them."

Roan stayed where he was. "May I have the Private's permission to bring a piece of equipment in?"

"You have my permission to bring those cards in, revised or not. Nothing more."

"The Private deprives me of the use of evidence he himself assigned me to bring," Roan said stiffly.

"Do I now?" The beard, its lower end invisible under the privacy hood, was pulled thoughtfully. "Very well. But I should warn you—you have no leeway, young man. None!"

Roan wheeled the box through the doorway. He was shaking with apprehension, but Granny's voice pleaded inaudibly. *Trust me.*

Even in front of his father, he nearly smiled. He locked the casters and, with a tremendous effort, heaved the box up on end. The right end, this time.

"What the devil's *that?*" demanded the beard.

"My evidence, Private." Outwardly calm, inwardly aquiver, he drew out the top section of the box with its two knobs and their two sets of horns. Each horn was hollow and had a light inside. Roan turned them on.

"I asked you a question," rumbled the Private.

"Your patience," Roan responded.

What patience? Granny's chuckle did more good for Roan than a week's delay.

"Ready now, Private. May I have the use of some small object—your stylus, perhaps, or a small book?"

"You have taken my money and you are taking my time. Is it now your intention to take my property?"

Whyncha spit in his eye?

Roan threw up a glance of such extreme annoyance that the inaudible voice apologized.

Sorry. It's just that I'm on your side, honey.

Honey! He had tasted his very first honey in his "dream." That was a nice thing to call someone. He wondered if anyone had ever thought of it before. To the Private, he said, "If I use my own property, there could be some suspicion of previous preparation."

"I suspect the previous preparation with which you are cluttering up my office already," growled the old man. "Here's the old paperweight. It dates from the time when buildings had sliding panels opening to the outside air. If anything happens to it—"

"It will do," said Roan levelly, taking it without thanks. The Private's eyebrow ridges moved briefly. "Would you kindly point out a spot on the floor?"

With an expression of saintly patience, the Private drew out his stylus and threw it. It fell near the far wall. Roan placed the paperweight near the point of the stylus, on the carpet.

"And one more indulgence. A point on your desk—somewhere with enough area to support that paperweight."

"Damn it, no! Go get those cards and we'll settle the matter in hand. I fail to see—"

Don't let him rant. Find your own spot and ask him if it suits him.

Like a man in a hailstorm, Roan advanced through the booming and shrieking syllables and pointed.

"Will this do?" he shouted, just loud enough to be heard over the storm.

The Private stopped just then and Roan's voice was like an airfoil crashing the sound barrier. Both men recoiled violently; to his own astonishment, Roan found that he recovered first. The old man was still sunk deep in his chair, the base of the beard quivering. In Roan's ear, Granny cackled.

Roan grasped the two horns protruding from one of the two spheres on his machine and turned them so that the beam from each rested on the center of the paperweight.

"The production model would have other means of aiming," he explained as he worked. "This is for demonstration only." The other two beams were aimed at the indicated spot on the desk. "Ready now, Private."

"For what?" snarled the Private, then choked as if he had swallowed a triple ration of roughage, for when Roan touched the control, there was a soft click and the paperweight appeared on the desk, exactly in the small pool of light from the beams. He put out a hand, hesitated, dropped back in his chair. "Again."

Roan threw the lever the other way. The paperweight lay quietly on the carpet. "For years, I have used every available minute on the research needed for this device and in building it. If the Private feels that the machine is of no use to this firm and the industry, that the time spent on it was wasted or stolen, then I shall be satisfied with his previously suggested—"

"Now come off it, son," said the beard. He rose and approached Roan, but kept his eyes glued on the machine in fascination. "You know the old man was just trying to throw a scare into you."

Got 'im!

"Could a large model be built?"

"Larger than a transplat," Roan said.

"Have you built any larger than this?"

Tell him yes!

"Yes, Private."

Slowly the Private's eyes left the machine and traveled to Roan's face. Roan would have liked to retreat, but his back was against the wooden case.

Watch out!

"You feel this could be better than the transplat?"

Yes. Tell 'im yes—even if it hurts, tell 'im!

Roan found he could not speak. He tremblingly nodded his head.

"Hmm." The Private walked around the machine and back, though there was nothing to be seen. "Tell me," he said gently, "is this machine built on the same principle as the transplat?"

Sweat broke out on Roan's brow. He wished he could wipe it off, but to raise his glove would have been a rudeness. He let it trickle.

"No," he whispered.

"You are telling me that this is a new kind of machine, better than the transplat!" When Roan neither moved nor spoke, the Private suddenly shouted, "Liar!"

Roan, white, dry-mouthed, with a great effort brought his eyes up to meet those of the livid Private. "A transplat can't do that," he said, nodding to the paperweight.

"You've got to be lying! If there was such a machine as

this, you couldn't build it. You couldn't even conceive it! Where did you get it?"

Say you built it—quick!

"I built it," Roan breathed.

"I can't understand it," mumbled the Private.

Roan had never seen him so distressed and his curiosity got the better of his own tension. "What is it that you want me to say, Private?"

The Private swung around, face to face with his son. "You're holding something back. What is it?"

This is it! Now hold tight, honey. Tell him it works by PK.

Roan shook his head and set his lips, and the Private roared at him. "Are you refusing to answer me?"

Tell him, tell him about the PK. Tell him!

Roan had never felt so torn apart. There had to be more to this than he knew about. What was pushing him? What tied his tongue, knotted his stomach, swelled his throat?

Trust me, Roan. Trust me, no matter what.

It broke him. He choked out, "This is only a direction-finder. It works by psychokinetic energy."

"By what? What?" The Private fairly bounced with eagerness.

"It's called PK. Mental power."

"Then it really isn't a machine at all!"

"Well—yes, you might say so. That's my theory, anyway." And where were the tied tongue, the aching throat? Gone!

"And you believe in that psycho-stuff?"

Roan found himself smiling. "It works."

"Why were you hiding it?"

"Would you have believed in such a thing, Private?"

"I confess I wouldn't."

"Well, then—I wanted to get it finished and tested, that's all."

"Then what?"

Give it to him. I mean it—give it to him!

"Why, it's yours. Ours. The company's. What else?"

The dry sound was the slow rubbing of gloved hands together. The other, which only Roan heard, was Granny's acid chuckle. *And he didn't even ask where the psychic operator was—notice? And he never will.*

The Private said, "Would you like to work with the Development Department on the thing?"

Sure, honey. I'll never let you down.

"Fine," Roan said.

"You'll never know—you can't know what this really means," said the Private. For a moment, Roan was sure he was going to clap him on the shoulder or some such unthinkable thing. "I can own up to a mistake. You should've been on the nuts-and-bolts end right from the start. Instead I had you chasing inventories and consignments. Well, you've shown up the old man. From now on, your time's your own. You just work on anything around here that amuses you."

"I couldn't do that!"

Yes, by God, you could! snapped the voice in his ear. *And while he's down, hit him again. Get your own home.*

His own home! With one of those PK machines, he could go anywhere, anytime. He could take Val—and find Flower again!

IX

It was warm and windy and very dark. The village was asleep and only a handful of people sat around the great trestle table in the clearing. The stars watched them and the night-birds called.

"To get grim about it," said the old lady in a voice a good deal less than grim, "breaking up a culture isn't something you can do on an afternoon off. You've got to know where it's been and where it is, before you know where it's going. That takes a good deal of time. Then you have to decide how much it needs changing and, after that, whether or not you were right when you decided. Then it's a good idea to know for sure—but for *sure*—that you don't push it so far, it flops over some other gruesome way."

"But I was right all the same, wasn't I?" Roan insisted.

"Bless you, yes. You don't know how right."

"Then tell me."

"Some of it'll hurt."

"Don't hurt him," said Flower, half-seriously. Roan took her hand in the dark, feeling, as always, the indescribable flood within him brought by the simple touch of living flesh.

"Have to, honey," said Granny. "Blisters'll hurt him too, and his joints will ache at plowin' time, but in the long run he'll be all the better for it. Who's there?" she called.

A voice from the darkness answered, deep and happy, "Me, Granny. Prester."

"Hi, Granny," said Val. They came into the dim, warm glow of the hurricane lamp guttering on the table. Val was wearing a very short sleeveless tunic, which looked as if a spider had spun it. She and Prester moved arm in arm like a single being. Looking at her face, Roan felt dazzled. He squeezed Flower's hand and found her smiling. ....

"Sit down, kids. I want you to hear this, too. Roan, would you do something for me—something hard?"

"What is it?"

"Promise to shut up until I've finished, no matter what?"

"That's not hard."

"No, huh? All right, Flower, tell us just exactly what psi powers you have."

Roan closed his eyes in delight, picturing again Flower's appearance in his cubicle, her birdlike flitting about the gateway during his dream, the cup she had drawn out of thin air for him. She said, "None that I know of, Granny."

"What!" he exploded.

Granny snapped, "You have promised to shut up!" To Flower, she went on, "And who's got the most psi potential in the place, far as we know?"

"Annie," said Flower.

"The fifteen-year-old I told you about," Granny explained to Roan. "The one who can knock over a straightedge. Shut up! Let me finish!"

With a great effort, he subsided.

"In a way, we've lied to you," said Granny, "and, in a way, we haven't. I once told you some of what I've been thinking of—the new race of people that has to be along some day, if we let it—the next step up. I believe in them, Roan; call that a dream if you like. And when you had your dream those two days, we made the dream come true for a little while. We worked that thing out like a play—I had you in the frame of that new machine of mine all the time.

"It *is* a new machine, Roan, built on a new principle

that the transplat boys never thought of. It's just what I told you it was—a stationless matter transmitter—no central, no depots, no platforms. I used it on every psi incident you witnessed in those two days. Believe me?"

"No!"

"Val?"

"I'd like to," she said diffidently. "But I've always thought—"

"There's no use being tactful about this," said Granny. "For the rest of your life, this is going to bother you, Roan, Val—and, later, a lot of other people we'll bring in. You'll rationalize it or you won't, but you'll never believe I have a new kind of machine. Shut *up*, Roan!

"You two and the rest of your generation are the first group to get really efficient crèche conditioning. You don't remember it, but ever since you were suckling babes, you've been forced into one or two basic convictions. Maybe we'll find a way to pry 'em loose from you. One of these convictions is that the transplat is the absolute peak of human technology—that there's only one way to make 'em and that there are only certain things they can do.

"You got it more than Val did, Roan, because you males in the transplat families were the ones who might be expected to develop such a machine. That's why, when this new one was built, *women* built it. Don't fight so, son! We have it, whether you believe it or not. We always will have it from now on. I'm sorry—it hurts you even to hear about it and I know what you went through when you had to sell it to your father. You damn near choked to death!"

Roan breathed heavily, but did not speak. Flower put her arm across his shoulders.

"We had to do it to you, boy we *had* to—you'll see why," said Granny, her old face pinched with worry and tenderness. "I'm coming to that part of it. Like I said, you don't break up a culture just all at once, boom. I wanted to change it, not wreck it. Stasis is the end product of a lot of history. Human beings had clobbered themselves up so much for so long, they developed what you might call a racial phobia against insecurity. When they finally got the chance—the transplat—they locked themselves up tight with it. That isn't what the transplat was for, originally. It was supposed to disperse humanity over the globe again, after centuries of huddling. *Hah!*

"About the time they started deep conditioning in the crèches, walling each defenseless new generation off from new thoughts, new places, new ways of life, a few of us started to fear for humanity. Stasis was the first human culture to try to make new ideas impossible. I think it might have been humanity's first eternal culture. I really do. But I think it would also have been humanity's worst one.

"So along came Roan—the first of the deep-conditioned transplat executives, incapable of believing the service could be improved. There were—are—plenty more in other industries and we're going after 'em now, but transplat is the keystone. Roan, believe it or not, you were a menace. You had to be stopped. We couldn't have you heading the firm without introducing the new machine, yet if it weren't introduced in your generation, it never would be.

"Your father is the last weak link, the last with the kind of imperfect conditioning that would let him even consider an innovation—remember your suggestion for eliminating freight operators? Only he would be unconditioned, just enough to put our new machine into Development before realizing that, once in use, every cubicle in the whole human structure will suddenly be open to the sky. And it's all right—he can be trusted with it, because his 'decency' won't let him abuse privacy. *We'll* take care of that side of it!"

"I wish you wouldn't talk like that about him," said Roan miserably.

"I'm sorry, boy. Does it do any good to tell you that subservience and blind respect for your father are conditioned, too? I wish I could help you—you'll have that particular sore toe tramped on all your life. Anyway, enter Roan, just when we've perfected the new machine. There would have been no problem if we could have broken your conditioning against it, but the only alternatives seemed to be—either you'd see the machine operate and think you had lost your sanity, or you'd use your position in the firm to eliminate all trace of it."

He objected, "But you were wrong both ways."

"That's because we discovered that the conditioning against any new transplat was against any new *machine*— any new *device*," Granny replied. "They'd never thought of matter transmission by a method *which was in no way a device!*

"Can you see now why your father was so upset when he was faced with you and your pilot model? One of the props of his decent little universe was that the conditioning would stick—that of all people on Earth, you'd be the last to even think of a new machine, let alone build one. And when at last you came out with that gobbledegook about psychic power, he recognized the rationalization for what it was and felt safe again. Stasis was secure.

"I don't mind telling you that you made us jump the gun a bit. Our initial plan was to recruit carefully, just the way we did you. Dreams—unexpected and high-powered appeals to everything humanity has that Stasis is crushing. Then when there were enough of us wilderness people, maybe the gates would open. But ultimately we'd win—we have all nature and God Himself on our side.

"But you came along—what a candidate! You responded right down the line—so much so that, if we'd given you your head, you'd have dynamited Stasis and probably yourself and us along with it! And you took to that psi idea the way you took to the steak we planted in your nutrient that day, testing for food preference before the dream sequence. All of a sudden, you wanted to plant our machine spang in the middle of Stasis! It was chancy, but—well, you've seen what happened."

"Can I talk now?" Rowan asked uncomfortably.

"Sure, boy."

"I'm not going to argue with you about the new machine—how it works, I mean. All you've done is give Stasis a more efficient machine. You can interfere with the new network, but you could do that anyway with the one you already had. So what's the big advantage?"

Granny chuckled. From a side pocket, she dug a white object and tossed it across the table. It left a powdery spoor as it rolled. "Know what that is?"

"Chalk?" asked Val.

"No, it isn't," Roan said. "It's Lunar pumice. I've seen a lot of that stuff."

"Well, you'll have to take my word for it," said Granny, "though I'll demonstrate any time you say—but I got that at 1430 this very afternoon—off the Moon, using only the machine you saw in the lab."

"Off the *Moon!*"

"Yup. That's the advantage of the new machine. The

transplat operates inside a spherical gravitic field, canceling matter at certain points and recreating it at others—a closed system. But the new machine operates on paragravitic lines—straight lines of sub-spatial force which stretch from every mass in the Universe to every other. Mass canceled at one point on the line recurs at another point. Like the transplat, the new machine takes no time to cross any distance, because it doesn't actually cover distance.

"The range seems to be infinite—there's a limitation on range-finding, but it's a matter only of the distance between the two parts of the machine. I got the Moon easily with a forty-mile baseline. Put me a robot on the Moon and I can reach Mars. Set up a baseline between here and Mars and I can spit on Alpha Centauri. In other words, an open system."

They were silent as Roan raised his eyes and, for a dazzling moment, visualized the stars supporting a blazing network of lines stretching from each planet, each star, to all the others—a net that pulsed with the presence of a humanity unthinkably vast.

Prester murmured, "Anybody want to buy a good spaceship?"

"Why did you do it?" whispered Val, ever so softly, as if she were in a cathedral.

"You mean why couldn't I mind my own business and let the world happily dry up and blow away?" Granny chuckled. "I guess because I've always been too busy to sit still. No, I take that back. Say I did it because of my conscience."

"Conscience?"

"It was Granny who built the first transplat," Flower explained.

"And *you* were telling her what could and couldn't be be done, Roan!" gasped Val.

"I still say—" he objected in irritation, and then he began to laugh. "I once took a politeness present to Granny. Knitting. Something for the old folk to do while they watch the Sun sink."

They all laughed and Flower said, "Granny won't knit."

"Not for a while yet," Granny said, and grinned up at the sky.

WHEN
YOU'RE
SMILING

It must be apparent by this time that I tend to write about nice guys. But I also believe (as you will discover later on) that I believe in the yin and the yang, and that from time to time one must turn the coin over and investigate what lives under the sun-warmed rock.

I also believe that although ultimate justice will be done (even if only statistically, even if later than sooner) it is, as often as not, done for selfish reasons and benefits the universe by accident.

Never tell the truth to humans.

I can't recall having formulated that precept; I do know I've lived under it all my life.

But *Henry*?

It couldn't matter with Henry.

You might say Henry didn't count.

And who would blame me? Being me, I'd found, was a lonely job. Doing better things than other people—and doing them better to boot—is its own reward, up to a point. But to find out about those murders, those dozens and dozens of beautiful scot-free murders, and then not to be able to tell anyone . . . well, I act like a human being in so many other ways—

And besides, it's only Henry.

When I was a kid in school, I had three miles to go and used roller skates except when it was snowing. Sometimes it got pretty cold, occasionally too hot, and often wet; but rain or shine, Henry was there when I got to the building. That was twenty years ago, but all I have to do is close my eyes to bring it all back, him and his homely, doggy face, his odd flexible mouth atwist with laughter and welcome. He'd take my books and set them by the wall and rub one of my hands between his two if it was cold, or toss me a locker-room towel if it was wet or very hot.

I never could figure out why he did it. It was more than just plain hero-worship, yet Lord knows he got little enough from me.

That went on for years, until he graduated. I didn't do so well and it took me longer to get out. I don't think I really tried to graduate until after Henry did; the school suddenly seemed pretty bleak, so I did some work and got clear of it.

After that, I kicked around a whole lot looking for a

regular income without specializing in anything, and found it writing features for the Sunday supplement of one of those newspapers whose editorial policies are abhorrent to decent people, but it's all right; no decent person reads them.

I write about floods, convincingly describing America's certain watery grave, and I write about drought and the vanishing water table, visualizing our grandchildren expiring on barren plains that are as dry as a potato-chip. Then there's the perennial collision with a wandering planet, and features about nuts who predict the end of the world, and biographies of great patriots cut to size so they won't conflict with the editorial page. It's a living, and when you can compartment it away from what you think, none of it bothers you.

So a lot of things happened and twenty years went by, and all of a sudden I ran into Henry.

The first funny thing about him was that he hadn't changed. I don't think he had even grown much. He still had the coarse hair and the ugly wide mouth and the hot happy eyes. The second funny thing was the way he was dressed, like always, in hand-me-downs: a collar four sizes too large, a baggy suit, a raveled sweater that would have fought bitterly with his old herringbone if both weren't so faded.

He came wagging and panting up to me this early fall day when everyone in sight but Henry was already wearing a topcoat. I knew him right away and I couldn't help myself; I just stood there and laughed at him. He laughed, too, glad to the groveling point, not caring why I was laughing, but simply welcoming laughter for its own sake. He said my name indistinctly, again and again; Henry almost always spoke indistinctly because of that grin he wore half around his head.

"Well, come on!" I bellowed at him, and then cussed at him. It always made him wince, and it did now. "I'll buy you a drink. I'll buy you nine drinks!"

"No," he said, smiling, backing away a little, bobbing his head in that funny way, as if he was about to duck. "I can't right now."

It seemed to me he was looking at my sharp-creased dacron suit, or maybe the pearl homburg. Or maybe he just caught my eye on his old set of threads. He waggled his hands aimlessly in front of him, like an old woman caught naked and not knowing what to cover up. "I don't drink."

"You'll drink," I said.

I took him by the wrist and marched him down to the corner and into Molson's, while he tugged ineffectually at me and mumbled things from between his solid, crooked teeth. I wanted a drink and I needed a laugh, right *now,* and I wasn't going to drag all the way down to Skid Row just to keep him from feeling conspicuous.

Somebody was sitting in a back booth—someone I especially didn't want to see. Be seen by. I don't think I broke stride when I saw her, though. Hell, the day won't come when I can't handle the likes of her . . .

"Siddown," I said, and Henry had to; I pushed him and the edge of the seat hit the backs of his knees. I sat down, too, giving him the hip hard enough to slide those worn old tweeds of his back into the corner where he wouldn't be able to get out unless I moved first. "Steve!" I roared, just as though I didn't care if anyone in the place knew I was there. Steve was on his way, but I always yelled like that; it bothered him. Steve's also sort of a funny guy.

"Awright, awright," he complained. "What'll you have?"

"What are you drinking, Henry?"

"Oh, nothing—nothing for me."

I snorted at him and said to Steve, "Two sour-mash an' soda on the side."

Steve grunted and went away.

"Really," Henry said, with his maybe-I-better-duck wobble, "I don't want any. I don't drink."

"Yes, you do," I told him. "Now what's with you? Come on, right from the beginning. From school. I want the story of your life—trials and triumphs, toil 'n' tragedies."

"*My* life?" he asked, and I think he was genuinely puzzled. "Oh, I haven't done anything. I work in a store," he added. When I just sat there shaking my head at him, he looked down at his hands and pulled them abruptly down into his lap as if he was ashamed of the nails. "I know, I know, it's nothing much." He looked at me with that peculiar hot gaze. "Not like you, with a piece in the paper every week and all."

Steve came with the bourbon. I shut up until he'd gone. With Steve, I like to pretend I have big business and don't trust him to listen in. I swear sometimes you can hear him grinding his teeth. He never says anything though. A good customer's got just a little more rights than just anybody else, so there's nothing he can do about it. He just works there.

When he'd gone, I said, "Here's to the twist that don't exist, and her claim there's a game that can't be played. Here's to the wise old lies we use—"

"Honest, I don't want any," said Henry.

"If I'm going to be hospitable, you're going to be house-broke," I told him, and picked up his glass and shoved it at his face.

He got his lips on it just in time to keep it from falling into that oversize collar. He didn't take but a sip, and that great big mouth snapped down to button-size as if it had a drawstring on it. His eyes got round and filled wtih tears; he tried to hold the liquor on his tongue, but he sneezed through his nostrils and swallowed and started to cough.

Laugh? I got my breath back just this side of hernia. Some day I'll plant a sound camera and do that again and make an immortal out of old Henry.

"Gosh!" he gasped when he could.

He wiped his eyes with his frayed sleeves. I guess he didn't have a handkerchief. "That *hurt*." But he was grinning the old grin all the same. "You drink that all the time?" he half whimpered.

"All the time, like so," I said, and drank the rest of his, "and like so," and drank mine down. "Steve!" Steve already had the refills on a tray and I knew it, which is why I yelled at him. "Now about what you started to say—" and I broke off while Steve got to the table and put down the drinks and picked up the empties and went away again— "the story of your life. You sit there and tell me 'Oh, nothing,' and you say you work in a store, period. Now *I* am going to tell *you* the story of your life. First of all, I'm going to tell you who you are. You're Henry. Nobody else in God's great gray-green Universe was ever this particular Henry. We start with that. No—"

Henry said, "But I—"

"No mountain," I went on, "no supernova, no collapsing, alpha-splitting nucleus was ever more remarkable than the simple fact of you, Henry, just being Henry. Name me an earthquake, an oak tree, a racehorse or a Ph.D. thesis and I will, by God, name you one just like it that happened before. You," I said, leaning forward and jamming my forefinger into his collarbone, "you, Henry, are unique and unprecedented on this planet in this galaxy."

"No. I'm not," he laughed, backing off from the finger, which did him no good once I had him pinned to the wall behind him.

"No supernova," I said again, having just discovered that the phrase is a delightful way of sending the flavor of good bourbon through the nostrils. "That's what we only begin with," I went on. "Just by being, you're a miracle, aside from everything you've ever said or done or dreamed about." I took away the finger and sat back to beam at him.

"Ah," he said; I swear he blushed. "Ah, there's plenty more like me."

"Not a single one." I tipped up my glass, found it was empty already, so drank his because I had my mouth all set for it. "Steve!" I sat silently watching Henry aimlessly rubbing his collarbone while the drinks arrived and the empties left. "So we start with a miracle. Where do we go from there? How do you cap that?"

He made a sort of giggle. It meant, "I don't know."

"You never heard anybody talk like this about you before, did you?"

"No."

"All right." I put out the forefinger again, but did not touch him with it because he expected I would.

Over his shoulder, in the wall mirror, I could see that woman sitting alone in the back booth, crying. Always a great one for crying, she was.

"I'll tell you why I talk like this, Henry," I said. "It's for your own good, because you don't know what you are. Here you walk around the place telling people 'Oh, nothing' when they ask for the story of your life, and you're a walking miracle just to start with. Now what do we go on with?"

He shrugged.

"You feel better, now you know what you are?"

"I don't . . . I never thought about it." He looked up at me swiftly, as if to find out what I wanted him to say. "I guess I do."

"All right then. That makes it better. That makes it easier on you, because I am now going to tell you what you are, Henry. Henry, what are you?"

"Well, you said—" he swallowed— "a miracle."

I brought down my fist with a bang that made everybody jump, even her in the mirror, but especially Henry. "*No!* I'll tell you what you are. You are a nowhere type, a *nudnick* type *nothing!*" I quickly bent forward. He shrank from the finger like a snail from salt. "And now you're going to tell me that's a paradox. You're going to say I contradicted myself."

"I'm not." His mouth trembled and then he was smiling again.

"Well, all right, but it's what you're thinking. Drink up." I raised my glass. "Here's to the eyes, blue brown and brindle, and here's to the fires that those eyes kindle; I don't mean the fires that burn down shanties, I mean the fires that pull down—"

"Gee, no, thanks," he said.

I drank my drink. "But I mean," I said aloud to myself, "really a nothing." I took his drink and held it and glared at him. "You will, by God, stop stepping on my punchlines."

"I'm sorry. I didn't even notice." He pointed vaguely. "I didn't know that anyone could handle so much of that— that whiskey."

"I got news for you, boy," I said, and winked at him. "Here it is past quitting time and this whiskey is all I had for lunch, and it's what I had for a snack—high tea, wot? —and it's what I'm having for dinner, and well should you envy this mighty capacity. Among other things. Now I will show you why I have uttered no paradox in describing you as a miracle and as a simultaneous, coexistent, concurrent nothing."

I smelled his drink and lowered it. "You started out being everything I described—unique, unprecedented. If you thought about it at all, which I doubt, you thought of yourself as having been born naked and defenseless, and having gained constantly since—the power of speech, the ability to read, an education of sorts (you can see by my calling it that that I'm in a generous mood) and, lately some sort of a job in some sort of a store, the right to vote, and that . . . well, unusual suit you're wearing. No matter how modest you are about these achievements—and you are, you really are—they seem to add up to more than you started with.

"Well, they don't. Since the day you were born, you've lost. What the hell is it that you keep looking at?"

"That girl. She's crying. But I'm listening to what you're saying."

"You better listen. I'm doing this for you, for your own good. Just let her cry. If she cries long enough, she'll find out crying doesn't help. Then she'll quit."

"You know why she's crying?"

Did I! "Yes, and it's a pretty useless procedure. Where was I?"

"I've been losing since I was born," Henry obediently reminded me.

"Yeah, yeah. What you've lost is potential, Henry. You started out with the capability of doing almost anything and you've come to a point where you can do almost nothing. On the other hand, I started out being able to do practically nothing and now I can do almost anything."

"That's wonderful!" he said warmly.

"You just don't know," I told him. "Now, mind you, we're still talking about you. You'll see the connection. I just want to illustrate a point . . . These days, everybody specializes or doesn't make it, one or the other. If you're lucky enough to have a talent and find work where you use it, you go far. If your work is outside your talent, you can still make out. If you have no talent, hard work in one single line makes for a pretty fair substitute. But in each case, how good you are depends on how closely you specialize and how hard you work inside a specialty. Me, now, I'm different. *Steve!*"

"None for me," Henry insisted plaintively.

"Do it again, Steve. Henry, stop interrupting when I'm doing you a favor. What *I* am, I'm what you might call a specializing nonspecialist. We're few and far between. Henry—guys like me, I mean. Far as work's concerned, I got a big bright red light in here—" I tapped my forehead —"that lights up if I accidentally stay in one line too long. Any time that happens, I quick wind up what I'm doing and go do something else instead. And far as talents are concerned, talents I got, I guess. Only I don't use 'em. I avoid 'em. They're the only thing that could ever trap me into specializing and I just won't be trapped, not by anybody or anything. Not me!"

"You have a real talent for writing," Henry said diffidently.

"Well, thanks, Henry, but you're wrong. Writing isn't a talent. It's a skill. Certain kinds of thinking, ways of thinking—you might call them based on talent; but writing's just a verbalization, a knack of putting into an accepted code what's already there in your head. Learning to write is like learning to type, a transformation of a sort of energy into a symbol. It's what you write that counts, not how you do it. What's the matter, did I lose you?"

He was looking out into the room over my shoulder and smiling. "She's still crying."

"Forget it. Every day, women lose their husbands. They get over it."

"Lose—her husband's dead?"

"Altogether."

He looked again and I watched his wide mouth, the show of strong, uneven teeth. I couldn't blame him. She's a very unusual-looking girl and here the coast was clear. I wondered next what you'd ever say to Henry so he wouldn't smile.

Then he was looking at me again. "You were talking about your writing," he said.

"Oh. Now suppose, Henry, you had the assignment to write a piece every week and you wrote every single one so the man who reads it believes it. And suppose one piece says: 'The world will end.' And another one says: 'The world will not end.' One says: 'No man is good. He can only struggle against his natural evil.' And another says: 'No amount of evil can alter the basic goodness of human beings.' See what I mean? Yet every single word of every piece comes out like a revelation. The whole series just stinks of truth. Would you say that you, the writer of all this crud, believes or does not believe in what he writes?"

"Well, I guess . . . I don't know. I mean I—" He looked into my eyes swiftly, trying again to discover what I wanted him to say. "Well," he said clumsily, when I just sat and wouldn't help, "if you, I mean, I, writing that way, if I said white was white and then it was blue . . . well, I guess I couldn't believe 'em both?" His voice put the question mark shyly at the end and he pretended to duck.

"You mean to say that kind of writer doesn't believe anything he writes. Well, I knew you were going to say

that, and you're one hundred and three per cent *wrong*."
And I leaned forward and glared at him.

He looked into his lap. "I'm sorry." Then, "He believes
some of it?"

"No!"

"Oh," Henry said. Miserably, he moved his glass an inch
to the left. I took it away from him.

I said, "A writer like that learns to believe *everything* he
writes about. Sure, white is white. But look: go down as far
as you can into the microscopic, and still down, and what
do you find? Measurements that can only be approximated;
particles that aren't particles at all, but only places where
there is the greatest probability of an electric charge . . . in
other words, an area where nothing is fact, where nothing
behaves according to the rules we set up for the proper
behavior of facts.

"Now go up in the other direction, out into space,
farther than our biggest telescopes can reach, and what do
you find? Same thing! The incommensurable, the area of
possibility and probability, where the theoretical computa-
tion (that's scientese for 'wild guess') is acceptable mathe-
matics. So okay: all these years, we've been living as if
white was white and a neat *a* plus *b* equals a respectable *c.*

"There might be an excuse for that before we knew that
in the microcosm and in the macrocosm all the micro-
meters are made of rubber and the tapemeasures are
printed on wet macaroni. But we do know that now; so
by what right do we assume that everything's vague up
there and muzzy down yonder, but everything *here* is all
neat as a pin and dusted every day? I maintain that nothing is altogether anything; that nothing proves anything,
nothing follows from anything; nothing is really real, and
that the idea we live in a tidy filling of a mixed-up sand-
wich is a delusion.

"But you can't go around not believing in reality and at
the same time do your work and get your pay. So the only
alternative is to believe *everything* you run into, everything
you hear, and especially everything you think."

Henry said, "But I—"

"Shut up. Now, belief—faith, if you like—is a peculiar
thing. Knowledge helps it along, but at the same time it can
only exist in the presence of ignorance. I hold as an axiom
that complete—*really* complete—information on any given

subject would destroy belief in it. It's only the gaps between the steppingstones of logic that leave room for the kind of ignorance called intuition, without which the mind can't move. So back we come to where we started: by not specializing in anything, I am guarding my ignorance, and as long as I keep that ignorance at a certain critical level, I can say anything or hear anything and believe it. So living is a lot of fun and I have more fun than anybody."

Henry smiled broadly and shook his head in deep admiration. "I'm glad if it's so, I mean, you're happy."

"What do you mean, *if*? I get what I want, Henry; I always get what I want. If that isn't being happy, what is?"

"I wouldn't know." Henry closed his eyes a moment and then said again, "I wouldn't know . . . Let me out, would you?"

"You going some place? I'm not through with you, Henry, me boy. I don't *begin* to be through with you."

He looked wistfully at the door and, without moving, seemed to sigh. Then he smiled again. "I just want to, uh, you know."

"Oh, that. The used beer department is down those steps over there." I got up and let him by. There was no way out of Molson's except past me; he wouldn't get away.

Why shouldn't he get away?

Because he made me feel good, that's why. There was something about Henry, a sort of hair-trigger dazzle effect, that was pretty engaging. Recite the alphabet to him and I swear he'd look dazzled. Not that the line I'd been slinging wouldn't dazzle anyone.

It was just then I decided to tell him about the murderer.

The room tilted suddenly and I hung to the edges of the table and stopped it. I recognized the symptom. Better get something to eat before soaking up any more of that sourmash. I didn't want to get offensive.

Just then I felt, rather than heard, a sort of commotion. I looked up. Henry, that damn fool, was leaning with his palms on the table where what's-her-name sat, the one who cried all the time. I saw her glance up and then her face went all twisted. She sprang up and fetched him one across the chops that half spun him around. Next thing you know, she was through the door, with Henry staring after her and grinning and slowly rubbing his face.

"Henry!"

Turning my way, Henry looked again at the door, then came shambling over.

"Henry, you ol' wolf; you've been holding out on me," I said. "Since when have you been chasing tomatoes?"

He just sat down heavily and fondled his cheek. "Gosh!"

"Whyn't you tell me you wanted to make a pass? I'd have saved you the trouble. She won't be good for anything for weeks yet. She can't think of anything but—"

"It wasn't anything like that. I just asked her if there was anything I could do. She didn't seem to hear me, so I asked her again. Then she got mad and hit me. That's all."

I laughed at him. "Well, you probably did her a favor. She's better off mad at something than sitting there tearing herself apart. What made you think you could get to first base with her, anyway?"

He grinned and shook his head. "I told you, honest I didn't want anything, only to see if I could help." He shrugged. "She was crying," he said, as if that explained something.

"So what's in it for you?"

He shook his head.

"I thought so!" I banged him on the shoulder. "That's where we'll start, Henry. We're going to make you over, that's what we're going to do. We're going to get you out of oversize second-hand shirts and undersize Boy Scouts ideas. We're going to find out what you really want and then we're going to see that you learn how to get it."

"But I'm all—I mean I don't really—"

"Shut up! And the first and rock-bottom basic and important thing you'll learn till you're blue in the face is, never do nothing for nothing. In other words, always ask 'What's in it for me?' and do nothing about anything until the answer comes up 'Plenty!' *Steve! The check!* That way you'll always have a new wallet to put in your new suit and nobody, especially girls, is going to clobber you in a filthy joint like this."

Actually it wasn't a filthy joint, but Steve came up just then and I wanted him to hear me say it. I gave him what the check said, to the penny, and told him to keep the change. Once in a while, I'd tip Steve—not often—and then I'd make it a twenty or better. What he didn't know was, if you total all the bills and all the tips, the tips came out to exactly nine per cent. Either he'd find that out for himself some day or I'd tell him; one way or the other, it would be fun. The secret of having fun is to pay attention to the details.

Out on the street, Henry stopped and shuffled his feet. "Well, good-by."

"Good-by nothing. You're coming home with me."

"Oh," he said, "I can't. I got to——"

"You got to what? Come on now, Henry—whether you know it or not, you need help; whether you like it or not, you're going to get it. Didn't I say I was going to tear you down and make you over?"

He stepped to the right and he stepped to the left. "I can't be taking up your time. I'll just go on home."

I suddenly saw that if I couldn't change his mind, the only way I'd get him to come along would be to carry him. I could do it, but I didn't feel like it. There's always a better way than hard work.

"Henry," I said, and paused.

He waited, not quite jittering, not exactly standing still. Guys like Henry, they can't fight and they can't run; you can do whatever you want with them. So—think. Think of the right thing to say. I did, and I said it.

"Henry," I said, real sudden, real soft, sincere, and the change must have hit him harder than a yell, "I'm in terrible trouble and you're about the only man in the world I can trust."

"Gosh." He came a little closer and peered up at me in the thickening twilight. "Why didn't you say so?"

Sticking out the marrow of his soul, every man has an eyebolt. All you have to do is find it and drop your hook in. This was Henry's. I almost laughed, but I didn't. I turned away and sighed. "It's a long story . . . but I shouldn't bother you with it. Maybe you'd better——"

"No. Oh, no. I'll come."

"You're a pal, Henry," I whispered, and swallowed as noisily as I could.

We walked down to the park and started across it. I walked slowly and kept my eyes on the middle distance, like a hired mourner, while Henry trotted alongside, looking anxiously up into my face every once in a while.

"Is it about that girl?" he asked after a while.

"No," I said. "She's no trouble."

"Her husband. What happened to him?"

"Same thing that happened to the ram who didn't see the ewe turn." I hit him with my elbow. "U-turn, get it? Anyway, he drove over a cliff." We were passing under a street light at the time and I saw Henry's face. "Some day you're going to split your head plumb in two just by grinning. What do you go around showing your teeth for all the time, anyway?"

He said, "I'm sorry." And when we were almost through the park, "Why?"

"Why what?" I asked vacantly.

"The husband . . . over the cliff."

"Oh. Well, she had a sort of a roll in the hay with somebody, and when she told him, he up and knocked himself off. Some people take themselves pretty seriously. Here we are." I led him up the walk and through the herculite doors. In the elevator, he gulped around at the satinwood paneling. "This is nice."

"Keeps the rain off," I said modestly. The doors slid open and I led the way down the hall and kicked open my door. "Come on in."

In we went and there, of course, stood Loretta with The Look on her face, the damned anger always expressed as hurt. So I pushed Henry ahead of me and watched The Look be replaced by tight Company Manners.

"My wife," I told Henry.

He stepped back and I pushed him forward again. He grinned and bobbed his head and wagged his figurative tail. "Huh-huh-huh—" he said, swallowed, and tried again. "Huh-how do?"

"It's Henry, my old school pal Henry that I never told you about, Loretta." I'd never told her a thing. "He's hungry. I'm hungry. How's for some food?" Before she could answer, I asked, "A couple paper plates in the den would be less trouble than setting the table, hm?" and at this she must nod, so I shoved Henry toward the den and said, "Fine, and thanks, o best of good women," which made her nod a promise. We went in and I closed the double doors and leaned against them, laughing.

"Gosh," said Henry, his eyes heating up. "You never told me you had a—uh—were married." The smile flickered, then blazed.

"Guess I didn't. One of those things, Henry. The air you

breathe, a post-nasal drip, the way you walk from here to the office—same thing. Part of the picture. Why talk about it?"

"Yes, but maybe she . . . maybe it's trouble for her. Why are you laughing?"

I was laughing because of the change in Loretta's face as we had come in. I was late and dinner was ruined, and I'd been drinking to boot; and primed as she was to parade hurt feelings all over the apartment, she hadn't expected me to bring anyone home. Ah, Loretta; so mannered, so polite! She'd have died rather than show her feelings before a stranger, and to see her change from hostility to hospitality in three point five seconds was, to me, very funny. There's always a way of getting out from under. All you have to do is think of it. In time.

"I'm laughing," I told Henry, "at the idea of Loretta's having trouble."

"You mean I'm no bother?"

"I mean you make everything all right. Sit down."

He did. "She's pretty."

"Wh—oh. Loretta. Yep, nothing but the best. Henry, I am a man different from all other men."

He fumbled with some facial expressions and came up with a slow grinning puzzlement. "Isn't everybody?" he asked timidly.

"Yes, you idiot. But by different, I mean *really* different. Not necessarily better," I added modestly. "Just different."

"How do you mean, different?" Good old Henry. What a straight man!

By way of answering him, I took out my key-case, zipped it open, thumbed out the flat brass key of my filing drawer and dangled it. "I'll show you, soon as we have something in our stomachs and no interrruptions."

"Is this the . . . the trouble you said you were in, you wanted my help?"

"It is, but it's so strictly private and confidential that I don't want you even thinking about it until I can lock that door and go into detail."

"Oh," he said. "All right." Visibly, he cast about for something else to talk about. "Can I ask you something about that girl who was . . . whose husband . . ."

"Fire away," I said. "Not that it matters. You have the

damnedest knack, Henry, of combining the gruesome with the trivial."

"I'm sorry. She seemed so, well, sad. What was it you said, I don't think I understood it?" His voice supplied the question mark to his odd phrasing. "She and somebody . . ." His words trailed off and he went pink. "And her husband found out—"

"She sure did. And he didn't exactly find out; she *told* him. She was mixed up in some research, see. Field-test of a new drug, a so-called hypnotic. So there she was, awake and aware and absolutely subject to any and all suggestions. And as you saw for yourself, she's not a bad-looking chick, not bad at all. So nature just took its course. *Carpe diem*, as the Romans used to say, which means drill not and ye strike no oil."

He looked at me foggily, but smiling broadly, too. "The researcher, the one who gave her the drug. But that wasn't exactly her fault. I mean her husband didn't have to—"

"Her husband did have to," I mimicked, "being what he was. One of those idealistic, love-is-sacred characters, who, besides all this, was sensitive about the side of his face he left in Korea. Love," I said, harpooning Henry's collarbone with my finger again, "is cornflakes."

I leaned back. "Besides, he had no way of knowing how it happened. This drug, it's something like sodium amytal, though chemically unrelated. You know, 'truth serum!' Only it doesn't leave the subject groggy or doped. She went straight home, walking and talking just like always, and incapable of concealing what had happened. She didn't even know she'd been—ah—medicated. It was in her coffee. All she could say was that such-and-such had happened to her and it was all so easy that, from now on, she could never know when it might happen again. He chewed on it for most of the night and then got up and got in his car and drove over the cliff."

Henry smiled twice, one smile right on top of the other. "Now all she does is drink in bars?"

"She doesn't drink. Ever read that William Irish book, *Phantom Lady*, Henry? There's a girl in there who cracks a character just by haunting him—by being there, wherever he is, day and night, for weeks. This chick in the bar, in her goofed-off ineffectual way, is trying to do the same thing to me. She sits where I can see her and hates me. And cries."

"*You?*"

I winked at him and made a *giddap* sort of cluck-cluck with my back teeth. "Research, Henry. A scientific project. It covers a multitude. And covering multitudes is a happy hobby, especially if you do it one by one. Sure, I know chemistry—told you I was a specializing non-specialist. Now wipe that grin off your face or you won't be able to chew: here comes the food."

Loretta carried in a tray. Butter-fried shrimp with piquant orange sauce, a mixed-greens salad with shallots and grated nuts, and an Arabian honey-cake.

"Oh!" gulped Henry, and bounced to his feet. "Oh, that's just beautiful, Mrs.—"

"You didn't bring a drink first, but I guess we can have it along with the food," I said.

"I don't want any, really," Henry said.

"He's being polite. We don't let our guests be polite, do we, Lorrie?"

For a moment, she had only one lip because she had sucked in the lower one to bite on. Then she said, "I'm sorry. I'll mix—"

"Don't mix," I told her. "Bring the bottle. We wouldn't think of troubling you any more, would we, Henry?"

"I really don't want—"

"Right away, *dar*ling." Two out of five times when I say *dar*ling, I roar at her. She set the tray down on the coffee table and fairly scurried out. I laughed. "Wonderful, wonderful. She doesn't exactly hide the liquor, but she sure tidies it away. Now, by God, she'll bring it to me."

I could actually hear the soft sound at the corners of Henry's mouth as his smile stretched it.

Loretta came back and I took the bottle. "No chaser; we're *men* in here. Okay, *dar*ling, you can leave the dishes here for the night."

She wouldn't back to the door and she wouldn't—maybe she was frightened just then—she wouldn't take her eyes off me, so she got out sidewise, not forgetting to flip the crumpled fragment of a hostess's smile to Henry.

Henry was saying, "Well, thank you very much, Mrs.—" but by the time he got it all stammered out, I had the door closed.

I went to the settee, rubbing my hands. "Bring the bottle, Henry."

He brought it, and sat down by me, and we ate. It was very good, which is the least a man can expect. I toyed with the idea of yelling for some tabasco, but I'd had enough fun with Loretta for the time being. Enveloping that food, my stomach felt well pleased with itself. Silent, unsmiling and intent, Henry absorbed what was on his plate.

I poured a slug for Henry, knowing I could afford to be generous, and one for myself. I leaned back and enjoyed a belch, which made Henry jump, threw down the bourbon, poured another and went to the desk.

On my desk is a typewriter, and under the typewriter is a sound-absorbing mat, and in the mat I keep a sewing-machine needle, the best toothpick Man ever made. It's strong and it's sharp and it has a base you can get a grip on without snapping it. I sat in the swivel chair and leaned my elbows on the typewriter and picked my teeth and watched Henry mopping the honey off his dessert plate with a piece of bread.

"That was—your wife certainly can—"

"Like I said, Henry, nothing but the best. Sit down over here. Bring your drink."

He hesitated, then brought it over and put it on the desk where I could reach it. He sat down on the edge of the easy chair. He looked like a worrisome kitten making its first try at sitting on a fence. I laughed in his face and he smiled right back at me.

"What I'm going to do, Henry," I told him, I told average, stupid, fearful, dogface Henry, "I'm going to let you in on some things that no human being on Earth knows. I'm going to tell you at the same time that these things are known to a number of people. Not a large number, but—a number. Could both those statements be true?"

"Well, I—" he said. Then he blushed.

"You're sort of slow, so I'll keep it simple and easy for you. I just got off a paradox. But it isn't a paradox. Don't sit there and smile and shake your head at me. Just listen. You'll catch on. Now you and I—are we different from each other?"

"Oh, yes," he breathed.

"Right. At the same time, all human beings are alike. And you know what? No paradox there, either."

"No?"

"No. And here's why. You're like my wife and the bartender and my city editor and all the billions of creepers and crawlers on Earth who call themselves human beings. And as you just so perceptively pointed out, I'm not like you. And for your information, I'm not like Loretta or Steve or the city editor. Now do you see why there's no paradox?"

Henry shifted unhappily. He absolutely astonished me. How could a guy like that, without bluff, without deftness, without, as far as I could see, even the ability to lie a little—how could he live three consecutive days in a world like this? Look at him, worrying away at my question, wanting *so* much to get the right answer.

It came like an abject apology: "No, I don't see. No, I don't." His eyes flickered, the embarrassed heat stirring and waning. "Unless what you mean is you're not a human being." He snickered weakly and again made that odd warding-off, half-ducking motion.

Leaning back, I beamed at him. "Now isn't it a relief to know you're not so dumb, after all?"

"Is that really what you mean? You're not . . . but I thought *everybody* was a human being!" he cried pathetically.

"Don't get all churned up," I told him gently.

I leaned forward very suddenly to startle him, and I did, too. I stuck my finger in my whiskey, lifted the glass with the other hand, and drew a wet circle on the desk-top, about eight inches in diameter.

"Let's say that anywhere in this circle—" I moved the glass around inside the mark—"this glass is what you call human. When it's here or *here* or a little bit forward, it's still human; it's just not the same human—the same *kind* of human. You're different from Steve the bartender because everything he is is here, and everything you are is over on the other side, *here*. You're different because you're placed differently in the circle, but you're the same because you're both inside it. Presto—no paradox." I moved the glass far enough to empty it and set it aside and put my hand in the circle. The wet wood was bleaching slowly, which was okay; Loretta would polish it up in the morning.

"Inside this circle," I said, "a man can be smart or stupid, musical, aggressive, tall, effeminate, mechanically apt, Yugoslavian, a mathematical genius or a strudel baker —but he's still human. Now by what Earthly conceit do we conclude that a man just *has* to live within that circle? What about a guy who's born here, on the outside edge? Why can't he be here, right on the line? Who's to say he can't live way out here?" And I banged my hand down a foot away from the circle.

Henry said, "I—"

"Shut up. Answer: there *are* people outside this border. Not many, but some. And if you're going to call the ones inside 'human,' the ones outside have to be—something else."

"Is that what you are?" Henry whispered.

"That's me."

"Is that what they call a moot . . . mute . . ."

"Mutation? No! Well, damn it, yes; that's as good a name as any. But not in any way you ever thought of. No atom-dust, no cosmic rays, nothing like that. Just normal everyday variation. Look, you have to go farther from one side of this circle to the other than from just inside to just outside—right? Yet the distance across is within the permissible variation; the difference between human beings which leaves them still human beings together. But one small variation this way—" I slid my finger outside the circle— "and you have something quite new."

"How—new?"

I shrugged. "Any one of a zillion ways. Take any species. Take kittens from the same litter. You'll find one has sharper claws, another has sharper eyes. Which is the best kitten?"

"Well, I guess the one with the—"

"No, you mumbling Neanderthal." That made him smile. "Neither one is best. They're just different, each in a way that makes him hunt a bit better. Now say another of the litter has functional gills and another has mat-scales like an armadillo, there's your . . ."

"Supercat?" he beamed.

"Just call it 'uncat.' "

"You—you're, uh, un—"

"Unhuman." I nodded.

"But you look—"

"Yeah, a cat with sweat-glands in its skin would look like a cat, too—most of the time. I'm different, Henry. I've always known I was different." I poked my finger toward him and he curled from its imaginary touch. "You, for example—you have, like nobody else I ever met, that stuff called 'empathy.' "

"I have?"

"You're always feeling with other people's fingertips, seeing through other people's eyes. Laugh with 'em, cry with 'em. Empathy."

"Oh. Yes, I guess—"

"Now me, I have as much of that as my armadillo-cat has fur. It's just not in me. I have other things instead. Do you know I was never angry in my life? That's why I have so much fun. That's why I can push people around. I can make anybody do anything, just because I always have myself under control. I can roar like a lion and beat my fists on the wall and put up a hell of a show, yet always know exactly what I'm doing. You knew me when, Henry. You've read my stuff. You've seen me operate. You going to call a man like me human?"

He wet his lips, clasped his hands together, blankly made the knuckles crack. Poor Henry! A brand-new idea and it was splitting his skull-seams.

"Couldn't you be," he ventured at last, "just sort of—talented, not really different at all?"

"Ah! Now we come to the point. Now we get the big proof. Speaking of proof, where's the bottle? Oh, here." I poured. "See I'm a real modest boy, Henry. When I figured this all out, I didn't do the human thing—conclude that I was the only super—uh, unhuman in captivity. There's just too many people being born, too much variation this way and that. Law of averages. There just *has* to be more like me."

"You mean just like—"

"No! I mean more unhumans—all kinds, any kind. So, because I can think like an unhuman, I thought my way after others of my kind."

Trying to heave up out of my chair, I quit and slumped back. "Damn it. You know, I'm hungry as a . . . imagine, a dinner like that. Why can't she cook up something that sticks to a man's ribs? I swear I'm as empty as a paper sack. Henry, check that door for me, see that it's locked."

He went to the door and tried it. It was locked. As he came back, I picked up the brass key. "This will open your eyes, Henry, old boy, old boy," I said.

I unlocked the file drawer. It got heavier all the time, I thought. Well, if you're going to have fun, you've got to take care of the details.

I lifted out the "Justice" file and banged it down beside the typewriter. "So I found me another unhuman. Takes one to catch one, Just you listen now and tell me what human being would even start this line of thinking, let alone carry it through." I opened the file.

"This all started," I said, "when I did a piece on unsolved murders. You know that no city releases figures on unsolved murders; well, not easily, anyway. You should see 'em—69 per cent in one city, 73 in another. Some bring it down to 40—our town got it to 38 per cent one year. But that's a whole lot of scot-free murderers, hm? All over the country. Imagine!

"So what I did—for the feature story, you know—I dug up everything I could find on a whole drawerful of these cases. What I wanted was an angle. What's the most obvious? Whodunit, that's what. So threw that out. What next? Who could have done it, but didn't. Throw that out, too.

"So then it occurred to me to see if there wasn't some sort of lowest common denominator to them—here a second-string advertising man with no enemies, there a teen-age hood with a knife in him, yonder a rich boy found floating next to his yacht—all kinds of people get murdered, you know.

"Mind you, I'm still just looking for an angle.

"Next, I threw out all the cases where people had a lot of enemies, and all the cases where a lot of people had an opportunity as well as a motive. This left a pretty strange stack. All of them were, apparently, reasonless, purposeless murders, all done differently at different places.

"Well, I phoned and I legged and I sat and thought, and I interviewed God knows how many people. Couple of times, I came pretty close to finding new stuff, too, but who cares whodunit? Not me. I wasn't looking for crimes with a reason behind them. I was looking for killings with no motive. Any time the scent got hot, I threw that case out. By this time, I had a feature shaping up—I'd call it 'Murder for What?' Good for a couple spreads—maybe even a series."

I thumped the file. "I guess I had the answer for weeks before I even knew it. Then, one night, I sat here and read everything through. And what do you know: in each and every one of these cases, someone was happy because of the murder! Or, anyway, happier. And I'm *not* talking about people who inherited the victims' loot, or poor persecuted wives and children who would no longer have to put up with the old man's payday drunks. Reach me the bottle, Henry.

"Now not a single one of this final stack showed motive or opportunity for the—let's say 'beneficiary' of these murders. Like this one, where the old woman, her with a constitution like a buffalo, she'd been lying in bed for eight months pretending to be sick so her daughter wouldn't marry. The girl was nine miles away when someone cut the old biddy's throat.

"And this one here, an engineering student and a good one, working his own way through school and then had to quit and come home because his old man had doubled the size of the ancestral hardware store for no reason but that it had been small enough to handle by himself. So one warm Sunday, the kid is, no fooling, in church in front of eighty witnesses while, down the road, somebody parts the old man's head with a tire iron. They never did find out who.

"And this one, this is practically the best of all: a little old guy for years ran a flea circus, gluing costumes on 'em and making 'em turn little merry-go-rounds and all that kind of thing. Used to feed 'em off his arm. One fine day, someone swipes one of his pets and replaces it with *pulex cheopis*—a rat flea, to you—loaded to the eyeballs, or cephalothorax, as the case may be, with bubonic plague. First and only case of black plague in these parts in a hundred and eighty years." I laughed.

"Someone was happier?" Henry asked wonderingly.

"Well, the other fleas were. And besides, the old guy used to get a large charge out of cracking fleas in his tweezers right under the noses of the most squeamish women in the audience. You know how they go—*blip!*"

Henry grinned. "Blip," he half-whispered.

"It's hot in here," I said uncomfortably. "Well, this is

the part I was getting to, I mean about thinking unhumanly. I said to myself, now suppose, just for the sake of argument, that there's this guy, see, a sort of mutant, a slight variation to just outside the circle, and he has this special way of thinking; he goes around killing people who stand in other people's way. He never kills the same way or the same kind of person or in the same place. So how could anyone ever catch up with him?

"Right away, I began looking into other deaths—the 'natural causes' ones. Why? Well, here, whoever he is, he might do some murders that look like murders, but he'd also do some that looked like natural causes; he'd have to; there's only just so many ways you can kill people and this busy, busy boy would have to try all of 'em. So I smelled around looking not for a killer, but for happy people, innocent people, who had benefited from these deaths.

"Whenever I found a situation like that, I checked back on the death. Sometimes it was a perfectly genuine croak, but time and again I found what you might find if you knew what you were looking for . . . scarlet fever, for instance. People shouldn't die of scarlet fever, but you know what? Feed somebody just enough belladonna and a doctor will write a scarlet fever certificate for the late lamented, nice as you please, if he has no reason to be suspicious. And in these deaths—my busy boy's work, I mean—there's never any reason to be suspicious. Where's the—you pour it for once, Henry.

"Hey, Henry! I'm getting tighter'n a ticklish tick with an alum stick, haha . . .

" 'Course, by this time, the feature story was up the spout: I had better use for the situation than a lousy feature or even a series. Yep. For weeks now. I've been following the meat-wagons and morguing around. All I do, I write 'em up when they look funny to me. I keep it to myself; it's all in the files here, every one of 'em. Oh, man, if the papers or the coroner or somebody got hold of those files, what a *hassle!* They'd dig up the marble orchards around here like potato patches! They'd find more little old embolisms and post-syncopes!

"Say, did you know that *Acontium Napellus,* which is wolfsbane, which is aconite, has a root that grates up into a specially nippy kind of horseradish for them as likes it strong for a few brief seconds? There's a woman just down the street who curled up and died last Tuesday and they called it heart failure; her daughter's already headed for Hollywood where she won't make anything but carhop, second class, but anyway it's what she wanted.

"Sooner or later, taking the notes I do the way I do at the deaths I investigate, this boy, this busy, busy fellow who is bringing so much sunshine into so many brutalized innocent lives, this boy will come over to me and say, 'Hi, chum, you looking for somebody?' "

"What will you do," gasped Henry without the question mark.

"What do you think?" I prodded.

"A reward, maybe? Or a big scoop—is that what they call it in newspapers?"

"Yes, in the movies. *Catch it, Hen*—hey, thanks. First time I knocked over a bottle in nine years, so help me. Mop up the ol' 'Justice' file—I call it the 'Justice' file; you like that, boy? Ooo . . . ooh. I'm adrift, kid, and you know what? I love it. Pour me another. Do it m'self only I'm not myself if you see what I—mmm. Good.

"So where was I? Oh, yes, you say I'd nab this busy boy and get a reward. Well, there you go thinking like a human being. I, sir Henry, will do no such a thing. Now I don't know exactly why this boy does this bit and I don't much care, long's I can get him to do it for me. He wants to knock off obstacles from the path of poor imprisoned souls. I got just the chore for him. Just some justice is all.

"You see that scared rabbit came in here a while back with the tray, that Loretta? Now that thing with Loretta, it was great while it lasted, and it lasted too long about four months back. All the time around, oh, please don't drink so much, where have you been, but I was worried . . . you know the routine, Henry. Now I could handle this myself, but even I can't think of a way which wouldn't be either expensive or messy.

"When you come right down to it, I'd just as soon keep her around.

"Loretta's not much trouble. She leaves me alone pretty much and comes in here about the time I'm bottle dippy every night and gets me into bed, talking on bright and cheery as anything, just as if I wasn't hooked over the desk here, green as a gherkin and just as pickled . . .

"The reason, the *real* reason I'd like to introduce this other unhuman type to my lovely wife is that I'd get more of a kick than you'd understand, just making him do it. Humans I can handle; this boy would be a real challenge. You can talk anybody into anything, and yourself out of anything, if you can just think of the right thing to say—and I'm the boy who can do it. Was your mother frightened by a keyboard?"

"What?" he asked, startled.

"That grin. What I'd like to know, I'd like to know how that busy boy covers so much territory. First he has to find 'em, then he has to plan how to knock 'em off, then he has to wait his chance . . . so *many*, Henny! Five already this week and here it's only Thursday!"

"Maybe there's more than one," Henry suggested tentatively.

"Say, I never thought of that!" I exclaimed. "I guess it's because there's only one of me. Gosh, what a lovely idea—squads of unhumans thinking unhumanly, doing whatever they unhumanly want all over the lot. But why should the likes of them take chances just to make some humans happy?"

"They don't care if anyone gets happy," said Henry. "Why are you whispering?"

"Must be getting pretty tight, I guess; can't seem to do much better. Whee-ooo! Such a gorgeous load! *What?* What's that you said about the unhumans, that they don't care about making people happy? Listen, son, don't go telling me about unhumans. Who's the expert around here? I tell you, every time they knock somebody off, someone around stops getting mistreated. Those files there—"

"Right files, wrong conclusion. You keep worrying about what you are; we don't. We just *are*."

"*We?* Are you classifying yourself with *me?*"

"I wasn't," said Henry, not smiling. "Just what you are, human or not, I don't know and I don't care. You're a blowhard, though."

I snarled and heaved myself upward. But a whispered snarl doesn't amount to much and you can heave all you like and get nowhere when your arms are deadwood and your legs are about as responsive as those old inner tubes in your neighbor's back yard.

"What's the matter with me?" I rasped.

"You're about nine-tenths dead, that's all."

"Nine—what do you mean, Henry? What are you talking about? I'm just drunk, not—"

"Dicoumarin," he said. "You know what that is?"

"Sure I know what it is. Capillary poison. All the smallest blood vessels rupture and you bleed to death internally before you even know you're sick. Henry, you've poisoned *me!*"

"Well, yes."

I tried to struggle up, but I couldn't. "You weren't supposed to kill *me,* Henry! It was Loretta! That's why I brought you home—I guessed that the killer would be the opposite of the likes of me and you're about as opposite as anybody could be. And you know I can't stand her and killing her would make me happier. It's *her* you're supposed to kill, Henry!"

"No," he answered stubbornly. "It couldn't be her. I told you we don't care if somebody's made happier. It had to be you."

"Why? *Why?*"

"To stop the noise."

I looked at him, frowned foggily, shook my head.

"Self-defense," he explained patiently. "I'm a—I suppose you'd call it a telepath, though it isn't telepathy like you read about. No words, no pictures. Just a *noise,* I guess is the best word. There's a certain kind of mind—human or not, who cares?—it can't get angry, and it enjoys degrading other people and humiliating them, and when it's enjoying these things, it sets up . . . that noise. We can't stand the noise. You—you're special. Hear you for miles. When we get rid of one of you, of course it makes a human happy—whoever it was you were humiliating." Then he said again. "We can't stand the noise."

I whispered, "Help me, Henry. Whatever it is, I'll stop. I promise I'll stop."

"You can't stop," he said. "Not while you're alive . . . Oh, damn you, damn you, you're even enjoying dying!" He put forearms over his head—not over his ears—and rocked back and forth, and smiled and smiled.

"You smile all the time," I hissed. "Even now. *You* enjoy *killing.*"

"It isn't a smile and I kill only to stop the noise." He was breathing hard. "How can I explain to anything like you? The noise—it's—some people can't stand the screek of a fingernail on a blackboard, some hate the scrape of a shovel on a cement sidewalk, most can't take the rasp of a file on metal."

"They don't bother me a bit," I said.

"Here, damn you, look here!" He snatched my sewing-machine needle and plunged it under his thumbnail. His lips spread wider. "It's *pain . . . pain!* Only, with you, it's agony! I can't stand your noise! It puts all my teeth on edge, it hurts my head, it deafens me!"

I remembered all the times he had smiled since I brought him home. And each time like the nail on the blackboard, like the shovel, like the rasp of the file, like the needle under the nail . . .

I made a sort of laugh. "You'll come with me. They'll find the poison in me."

"Dicoumarin? You know better than that. And there won't be any in the whiskey glass, if that's what you're thinking. I gave it to you three hours ago, in Molson's, in the drink I didn't want and you took."

"I'll hang on and tell Lorrie."

"Tell me," he jeered, leaning toward me, his smile that wasn't a smile as huge as a boa's about to bite.

My tongue was thick, numb and wobbly. "Don't!" I gasped. "Don't . . . jump me . . . now, Henry."

Again he clutched his head. "Get mad! If you could get mad, it would go away, that noise! Argh, you snakes, you freaks . . . all of you who enjoy hating! The girl, remember her, in the bar? She was making that noise until I got her angry . . . she's going to get better now that you're dead."

I was going to say I wasn't dead, I wasn't yet, but my mouth wouldn't work.

"I'll take these," Henry said. I watched him stack the files right under my nose. "Everything's nice and tidy," he told me. "You were due to drink yourself to death, anyway, and here you are just like always. Only you won't sleep this one off . . . I wish I could have got you sore."

I watched him unlock the door, saw him go, heard him talking to Lorrie briefly. Then the outer door banged.

Loretta came into the room and stopped. She sighed. "Oh, dear, we're in a *special* mess tonight, aren't we?" she said brightly.

I tried, how I tried to yell, to scream at her, but I couldn't, and it was growing dark.

Loretta bent and pulled my arm around her neck. "You'll have to help just a little now. *Up*sy-daisy!" Strong shoulders and a practiced hip hauled me upright, lolling. "You know, I do like your friend Henry. The way he smiled when he left—why, it made me feel that everything's going to be all right."

THE
CLAUSTROPHILE

We are a hero-hungry culture, and it has been a convention to visualize our heroes—especially in the early days of science fiction—to give our heroes bulging deltoids, perfect teeth, and a short temper. The transference of this hero to the controls of spacecraft is understandable but hardly rational. Why a man who is best qualified for bare-handed conflict with a Siberian tiger is the ideal spaceman defies logic.

"Show me a man who cannot be by himself," said my dear old mother, "and I'll show you a man who is not good company." It was this cogitation that led me to wonder why, in so much science fiction, the spaceman had to be the intellectual heir of Conan the Conqueror.

Or, for that matter, why had he to be a man at all? Despite the proven preferences of NASA, women really are as smart as human beings, and by and large, are smaller and lighter.

This is the line of thought that produced The Claustrophile.

"Pass Mr. Magruder the *hominy*, Chris!" His mother's mild, tired voice at last penetrated. "For pity's sakes, son, how many times—"

But Tess Milburn came to his rescue, reaching a thin arm, a sallow hand, to the dish of grits and passing it down to the boarder. Mr. Magruder didn't say anything. He never said anything. He never ate hominy grits, either, but that wasn't the point. When Miz Binns set out the dinner, everything had to be passed to everybody, no matter what.

Chris sighed and mumbled he was sorry. He let his mind drift back to the three-body problem. He knew he couldn't solve the three-body problem, but he couldn't be satisfied that it was impossible. Chris Binns was a computer mechanic, a good one, and what he was really pursuing was (a) the right question to ask the (b) right kind of machine.

He frowned at the problem as if he could squeeze an answer out of his brow, and almost had what he wanted when he became aware that he had impaled Tess Milburn with his unseeing gaze and was scowling fiercely at her. She smiled, that brief, weak showing of teeth that she did instead of blushing. It was Chris who blushed, a very little, but already he was sliding back into his thoughts, away from embarrassment, apology, even from the dinner table.

The solution, he thought, lies here: that it's fair to consider all three orbits as ellipses and the final solution as a predictable relationship between the lengths of one focal axis of each. He saw, clearly, a circular cam riding a parabolic track, and the linkage between three such tracks and their cams trembled in the wings of his intellect, ready for the spotlight, the entrance—

Wham!

The screen door slammed back against the verandah wall and a heavy suitcase simultaneously struck the floor by the table.

"Hit the blockhouse!" roared a heavy baritone. " 'Ware my tailjets! I'm a-comin' *in*!"

"Billy! Oh, Billy!" cried Miz Binns.

She was on her feet with her arms out, but couldn't use them before she was caught up and swung around by the laughing giant who had hit the floor right by the suitcase.

Tess Milburn sat astonished, stopped, like some many-functioned machine when its master switch is thrown; chewing, breathing, blinking, probably heartbeat, certainly cerebration, all ceasing at once in the face of something she had no reflexes for.

Mr. Magruder made a sound that would have been a grunt if it had been vocalized, and bent to pick up the fork he had dropped. With no change of expression, he scrubbed it with his napkin and then went on eating.

Chris Binns sat with his eyes closed, to all appearances as frozen as the girl, but inwardly in an agony of activity as he pursued his vanished thought, humbly asking only for their shape and texture, not their whole substance, something he could find again and rebuild on. But it was not possible; the lights were out inside, the doors closed. He blew gently through his nostrils, making up his mind to try again some time, and opened his eyes. "Hi, Bill."

The cadet put his mother down. "Contact, shipmate!" he said thunderously. His hair was crisp, sun-colored; his shoulders bulged under the short, full cape of the space-blue topcoat. Its four buttons, gold, white, green, red for the inner planets, glittered in their midnight background as he flung himself on his brother. Chris, flailing away the accurate and painful pounding of the cadet's greeting, suddenly giggled foolishly, slid his chair back, bent sideways.

"Hi. Hi."

"And if it isn't little old Tessie Heartburn," Billy roared, bestowing an explosive kiss on Tess Milburn's cheek. "And Old Faithful himself, star boarder extraordinary, conversationalist par ex—" His heavy hand was stopped abruptly in its descent to the old man's shoulder apparently by nothing more than Mr. Magruder's quick glance upward.

The hand raised again, to be a facetious, almost insulting salute. "Mr. Magruder."

Mr. Magruder nodded once, curtly, and went about the business of eating.

Miz Binns fluttered and clucked and cried. "Billyboy, oh, it's so *good* to, why didn't you *tell* us you were, have you had your, now, Tess, if you'll just move a little this way and, Chris, just, and I'll set you another—"

"You wired you'd be here in the morning," said Chris.

"Sun always comes up when little Billee walks in," grinned the cadet. "But ack-shull, shipmate, I got a ride in a supply truck, begged off final inspection, and jatoed out." He looked swiftly around the table. "Where's Horrible Horrocks?"

"Billy!" squeaked his mother.

"Miss Horrocks got transferred to another school," said Chris. "Thought we wrote you about it."

"Oh, yes. Forgot. Read through the home gossip real fast," said Billy carelessly.

Miz Binns said, "Mr. Magruder found us a new boarder for her room. A Miss Gerda Stein. We thought she'd be settled in by the time you arrived. But you didn't arrive tomorrow, did you?"

Billy laughed and kissed her. "I sure didn't arrive tomorrow. I'm going to arrive ten minutes ago."

"Oh-h, you know what I . . . silly-Billy. Chris, come help me."

Chris looked at her numbly for a moment, then got to his feet, jostling the table. Billy laughed and said, "I know you, Mom. You don't need help. You've got secrets." He turned grinning to Tess Milburn. "They're prolly going to talk about you."

"Oh, Billy, you're awful, just awful," his mother said pinkly. Mr. Magruder only steadied his water glass as Chris bumped the table, and then began to butter a roll. Tess Milburn gave her embarrassed lip-flicker, and Miz Binns said, "Don't you listen to that wicked boy, Tess," and shook a fond finger at Billy. She made an abrupt beckoning motion and disappeared into the kitchen.

Chris followed her out. She stood by the door, and when he was in the room, she reached out a practiced hand and stopped the door from swinging. With the ignorance of acoustics apparently possible only to mothers, she began speaking intensely in a whisper which was totally inaudible to him, pointing and flapping toward the dining room, moving her lips too much and her jaw not at all.

"What?" he asked, not too softly. He was mildly irritated.

She cast her eyes up to heaven and shushed him violently. She took his arm and backed across the kitchen, looking past his shoulder all the while as if she expected everyone in the dining room to be pressing ears to the door. "I *said* what did you have to go and have *her* for dinner tonight of all nights, Billy home and all?"

"We had a date. Besides, I didn't know Billy was—"

"It's very inconsiderate," she complained.

"Well, what do you want me to do?"

"It ought to be sort of a family thing, your brother home from school."

The irritation rose to as high as it ever got with Chris—not very high. "Then let's get rid of Mr. Magruder, too."

"That's different and you know it."

He did know it. Mr. Magruder had his own bubble of life within the lives they all led and he stayed unbreakably within it. He communed with himself, his newspaper and his habits, which were so regular that, once established, they required no imagination or conjecture from anyone else in the place. He could talk: but he needn't. They hardly saw him, which led them all to believe that he didn't see them much either.

"Well, all right," said Chris. "I'll just explain it to her and take her home and come right back."

"You can't, you can't," she fretted. It was what she wanted him to do, but that disqualified it; she wouldn't have that on her conscience.

He shrugged and said, "Then what did you call me out here for?" The question was not rude, but a genuine request for information.

"It's a shame, that's all," she answered. She squeezed her hands together and looked at them unhappily. There seemed to be nothing else for him to say and certainly nothing he could do. He turned to go back to the dining room, but she said, "Why is she here so much, Chris?"

"I don't know, Mom. She—" He made a vague gesture. He really didn't know. Tess dropped around occasionally—

hadn't it been to visit Miz Binns, anyway at first? And since she was around so much, he talked to her.

Talked about what? Again, he couldn't recall clearly. Anything. Whatever was on his mind that could be talked about. His work—some of it; most of it couldn't be expressed in words; it was conceptual, or technical, or mathematical, or all three. His feelings—some of them; most of them couldn't be expressed in words, either; they were too conceptual, or unidentified, or occluded, or all three.

"We go to the movies sometimes," he said at length. And, "It's nice sometimes to have somebody to talk to." He said that, not "talk with." He would have wondered why, but his mother interrupted his thinking the way people always did.

"I know this is no time to discuss it," she said in that urgent whisper, "but what's she want? I mean are you, do you, are you planning to, you know." She finished it like a statement, not a question.

"I—never thought about it."

"You better. The way she acts."

"All right. But like you say, Mom, it's not the time to think about it now." The limited irritation was back again. He turned to the door which exploded inward and struck him a stinging blow on the right pelvis.

"Now what's going on in th' black hole?" Billy roared. "You engineers precessin' my gyros again?"

"Tell Mom what you want to eat," said Chris painfully. He walked stiffly back to the table and sat down. He rubbed his hip covertly. He didn't look at Tess Milburn. He couldn't.

He picked at his food. She picked at her food. Mr. Magruder, who drank tea with his meals, drank his tea. And all the while, voices came from the kitchen. Chris was acutely embarrassed, but at the same time he was wondering about the filtering effect of the swinging door, because it passed Miz Binns' high frequencies—the sibilants and the hiss of her stage whisper—and Billy's lows, the woofs, the chest tones—all without transmitting a single intelligible syllable. But when Billy laughed, he understood it. He had heard that laugh before.

Billy bumped the door and surged through without touching it again as it swung open and back. His mother caught it and held it open on her side and bleated, "No, Billy, no!" and Billy laughed again and said, "Don't you worry your pretty little head about it, Mom. Billy fix." Miz Binns stood in the doorway wringing her hands, then sighed and went back in to get Billy's dinner.

Billy plumped down at the table and passed Chris a wide wink. "Well, Tess," he said expansively. "So long since I've seen you. Grown a bit, filled out a bit. Hell around a bit too, I bet." He ignored the silent drop of her jaw and the quick frightened smile that followed it. "You've been walled up in this haymow too long, girl. A little hurry an' noise will do you a world of good. How about you and me, we couple up right after chow and buzz this burg?"

Stricken, she looked at Chris.

Chris said, "Look, Billy, we—"

Just then, Miz Binns came in with a plate heaped and steaming. Serving dishes on the table not good enough for little Billee, Chris thought bitterly. Cold by now.

"Mom, what do you know! Tess and I got a date for right away!" Billy announced.

"Oh, now, *Billy!*" said Miz Binns in that he's-naughty-but-he's-so-sweet tone. "Your very first night and we haven't had a chance to chat even, and you have so little time, and—"

"Mom," said the cadet cheerfully, "you and I, we have two solid weeks in the daytime to blow tubes and scavenge tanks to our hearts' delight, in the daytime when all good slaves are out digging gold. I hate to deprive you tonight, but gosh, Mom, don't be stingy. Spread it around. It's okay, isn't it Chris?"

It's okay, isn't it, Chris? All his life, that special laugh and then this question. For a while, when he was nine and Billy was seven, he used to burst into tears when he heard that question. For a while before that and afterward, he had responded with a resounding "No!" And a little later on, he had reasoned, argued, or silently shaken his head. Nothing ever made any difference. Billy would watch .him and smile happily through his countermeasure, no matter what, and when he was finished would go right ahead and take, or do, or not do whatever the thing was that he wanted and Chris didn't. He had outweighed Chris since he was four years old, outtalked him always.

But this one time, this one lousy time, he wasn't going to get away with it.

Chris looked at his mother's anxious face, at Tess with a spot of pink on each of her sallow cheeks, a shine in her eyes that he had never been able to put there. *No, by God, no.*

He filled his lungs to say it out loud when the impossible happened. A hard hand closed on his left wrist, under the table. A voice spoke in his left ear: "Let him!"—soft but commanding. He looked down at the hand, but it had already gone. He looked at the face to his left, and Mr. Magruder impassively poured more tea. No one else seemed to have seen or heard.

It was Mr. Magruder, all right, with some knack of directional, perfectly controlled speech, two syllables formed and aimed from the side of the thin dry lips for Chris and Chris alone. It was unusual for the old man to say anything at all beyond "Pass the salt." It was unprecedented for him to enter a conversation, advise.

Chris looked at Tess's troubled, almost beseeching face, the pink, the shine. "You want to go?"

She looked at Billy and back to him, and then dropped her eyes. Chris felt rather than saw the slight movement of Mr. Magruder's foot against the floor. He did not touch Chris, but the movement was another syllable of command; there was no question in Chris's mind about that. "Go ahead if you want to."

Mr. Magruder nodded, or simply dropped his chin to watch his hands fold a napkin. Miz Binns said, "I still think you're *awful*, Billy," and did not quite add, "dear boy." Tess Milburn giggled.

Billy began to eat heartily, and what might have been a very strained silence indeed was canceled before it could become a problem.

The doorbell rang.

"I'll get it," Chris said relievedly. He got up and turned to the open, screened doorway.

It must be a trick of the light was the thought that flashed through his mind, but there wasn't time to pursue it. "Yes?"

"I'm Gerda Stein. Mr. Magruder—"

"Oh, it's Miss Stein," his mother called. "Come in, do come in."

It had been no trick of the light. Chris opened the screen door and stood back, speechless. He had known there were human beings like this. TV and the movies were full of them. They smiled from magazines and book-jackets, crooned and called and sold coffee, crockery and cosmetics on the car radio. All these are the proper and established places for such creatures; they don't, they just *don't* stand breathtakingly under the porch light on warm summer evenings and then walk straight into your own familiar house.

Someone nudged him out of his daze—Miz Binns. "Dinner's on, I can warm up something, and your room's all, my son from the Space Academy just, no, this is Chris. Billy's the—"

"How do you do, Chris," said Gerda Stein.

"Uh," said Chris. He followed the girl and his mother through the foyer into the dining room.

"You already know Mr. Magruder and *this*, this is Billy."

Billy shot up out of his chair like one of the Base rockets, and again Mr. Magruder steadied his water glass.

"Well-l-l," Billy breathed, a sound like the last descending tones of a mighty alert siren.

Gerda Stein smiled at him and Chris could see him blink. "No," she said in answer to something Miz Binns was saying, "I've had dinner."

Chris came around the table and found his eyes on Tess Milburn's face. It was wistful. "And this is Tess Milburn," he blurted. In that instant of empathy for the ignored girl, so shadowed by the great light cast by the newcomer, he fairly shouted. He looked like a fool and knew it.

Gerda Stein smiled warmly and took Tess's hand. Surprisingly, Tess smiled, too, and went on smiling after she had been released—a real smile, for once, substitute for nothing.

Chris felt embarrassed to see it—a strange embarrassment, starting with the consciousness of how hot his ears were, then going through a lightning intuitive chain to the insight that he was embarrassed when he made someone happy, and that it had been worth the effort of thought because it was so rare, and then the conclusion that anyone who made people happy so rarely couldn't be worth much. Which led him, of course, to look at his younger brother.

Billy had stopped chewing when Gerda Stein came in and he had not swallowed. He seemed for these long seconds as preoccupied as Chris was most of the time, and the slight flick of his blue eyes from Tess's face to Gerda Stein's indicated the source of his deep perplexity. And suddenly Chris saw it, as if it had been imprinted across the golden tan of the cadet's bland forehead in moving lights.

If Billy now went on with his idea of a date with Tess, this vision would be left here with Chris and Mom and Mr. Magruder and—very soon now, Mr. Magruder and Mom would retire, and . . .

On the other hand, Billy shared with his mother a deep reluctance to face anyone with "Beat it, I don't need you around," or any variation thereof.

Chris sat down slowly before his cold dinner and waited. He felt some things which taught him a great deal. One of them was that it was good to be involved with Billy in a situation where Billy couldn't win. If Billy backed out of the date, Chris would go; if not, not; and by this Chris learned that the date didn't really matter to him. This was a great relief to him. His mother's questions had disturbed him more than he had known until he felt the relief.

Billy sighed through his nostrils and finally swallowed his mouthful. "I'm backin' off my gantry, girl," he said to Tess, "so start the count-down."

Chris caught a quick puzzled flicker of expression on Gerda Stein's face. Miz Binns said, "He always talks like that. He means he and Tess are going out. Space talk." Chris thought she was going to run and hug him, but with obvious effort she controlled her feelings and said to Miss Stein, "Well, come settle in the parlor until I can take you up to your room."

"Have fun, kids," said Chris, and got up and followed into the parlor.

In the foyer, he turned and glanced back. He met Mr. Magruder's penetrating gaze, a startling experience for one used to seeing only the man's cheek or lowered eyelid. He wished he could get some message, some communication from it, but this time he couldn't. He felt very strange, as if he had been given absolute alternatives: chaos, or obedience to an orderly unknown. He knew he had chosen obedience and he was inexpressibly excited.

"Always wanted a spaceman in the family," Miz Binns was saying proudly to Gerda Stein, "and Billy's always wanted to be one, and now look."

From the couch, Gerda Stein said politely, "He seems to be doing very well."

"Well? Why, he's in the top twentieth of his class, nobody ever did that before except one fellow that was an air marshal's son, Billy's born for it, that's what he is, born for it."

Chris said, "He was running around in a space helmet when he was two years old."

At his voice, Gerda Stein turned and smiled at him. "Oh, hello."

"I declare I don't know how I could've had two boys so different," said Miz Binns. "Years, I just couldn't guess what Chris here would wind up doing, he's nicely settled down though, fixing adding machines."

"Computers," Chris said mildly.

"Really! That must be very interesting. I use a computer."

"What kind?"

"KCI. It's only a very simple little one."

"I know it. Mechanical binary. Clever little machine," said Chris and, to his intense annoyance, found himself blushing again.

"Oh, well, you have something in common," said Miz Binns. "I'll just scoot along upstairs and see that your room's just right. You keep Miss Stein happy till I call, Chris."

"Don't go to any—" the girl began, but Miz Binns had fluttered out.

Chris thought, *we have something in common, have we?* He was absolutely tongue-tied. Keep Miss Stein happy, hah! He flicked a glance at her and found with something like horror that she was watching him. He dropped his eyes, wet his lips, and sat tensely wishing somebody would say something.

Billy said something. Leaving Tess standing in the foyer, he stepped into the parlor, winked at Gerda Stein and said to Chris, "I heard that last test-firing of yours, shipmate— 'Have fun!' Well, *you* have fun." He looked at Gerda Stein with open admiration. "Just remember, brer pawn—first move don't win the game; it's only an advantage. You told me that yourself."

"Shucks," Chris said inanely.

"I'll see *you* soon," said Billy, stabbing a forefinger toward her.

"Good night," Gerda Stein said courteously.

Billy left the room, bellowing, "C'mon, Venus-bird, let's go git depraved." Tess Milburn squeaked, then tittered, and they went out. Miz Binns came downstairs just then and stopped at the front door.

"You Tess Milburn," she called in what she apparently hoped was mock severity, "you don't go keepin' that boy up until all hours!" From the warm dark came Billy's rich laughter.

"That boy," breathed Miz Binns, coming into the parlor, "I do declare, he's a caution, come on upstairs now if you want to and see your room, Miss Stein. That your bags out there on the stoop? Chris, just nip out and get Miss Stein's bags in like a good boy."

"All right, Mom." He was glad to have something to do. He went out and found the bags, two of them, a large suitcase and what looked like an overnight case. The suitcase was no trouble, but the little one weighed perhaps fifty pounds and he grunted noisily when he lifted it.

"Here," called Miz Binns, "I'll—"

"No!" he barked. "I can handle it." Mom wouldn't learn, couldn't learn that a man might be humiliated in front of strangers.

He lifted the bags abruptly, knowing just how Bill—how a fellow could walk, sing, surge them up to the landing, lift and surge again to the top, breathing easily. He took a step and swung, and got all tangled with the screen door, and banged the overnight case noisily against the jamb; his arms and back wouldn't do the easy graceful thing his mind knew how to do with them. So he didn't lift and swing, or breathe easily, but plodded and hauled, and came into the north bedroom blowing like a grampus. All in the world he hoped for was that he wouldn't catch Gerda Stein smiling.

He caught Gerda Stein smiling.

He put the bags down by the bed and went blindly back down the stairs. Mr. Magruder was just then pacing his leisurely way into the parlor, his newspaper under his arm, and Chris became painfully aware of how hard he was still breathing and how it must look. He controlled it and fled to the dining room.

He stood against the table for a long moment, pulling himself together, and then, with his glazed eyes fixed on the dish of cold hominy grits, slid gratefully into the familiar aloneness of his conjectures.

Hominy is corn, is dry before cooking, absorbs moisture softens swells steams gets cold loses moisture gets gummy if left long enough would set like concrete anyway until more moisture came along. Deeper he went into a lower level, seeing the hydroscopes, the thirsty molecular matrices, yearning and getting, satiated, yielding, turning again to thirsty horn. Down again to a lower level and the awareness all about him of the silent forces of the capillary, the unreasonable logic of osmosis, the delicate compromise called meniscus.

Water, water, everywhere . . . in the table-legs and the cloth, water fleeing from the edges of a pool of gravy, flying to the pores of a soda-cracker, all the world sere and soggy, set, slushy, slippery and solid because of water.

Down in this level there were no pipestem arms nor unready tongues nor fumblings for complex behavior codes known reflexively to all the world but Christopher Binns, and he was comforted.

"What you *dreaming* about, boy, I do declare!"

He came up out of it and faced her. He felt much better. "I'll give you a hand washing up, Mom."

"Now you don't have to do any such of a thing, Chris. Go on into the parlor and chat with Mr. Magruder."

He chuckled at the thought and began to stack the dirty plates. His mother went into the kitchen to clear the sink, shaking her head. Her woeful expression, he divined, was only superficial, a habit, an attitude; he could sense the core excitement and delight with which Billy always filled her.

Billy can do no wrong; he syllogized—
Billy does everything well; THEREFORE:
Billy does no wrong well.

He carried the plates into the kitchen.

"I'm going to bed, dear."

"Good night, Mom."

"Thanks for helping. Chris—"

"?"

"You're not angry at Billy, are you, about Tess, I mean?"

"Why should I be angry?" he asked.

"Well, I'm glad, then." She thought he had answered her. "He doesn't mean it, you know that."

"Sure, Mom." He wondered dispassionately how her remark could possibly be applied to the situation, and gave up. He wondered also, with considerably more interest, how and why he had been aware that while he was in the kitchen, Gerda Stein had come down and re-entered the parlor and that Mr. Magruder had gone up to bed. He wondered also what use the information would be to him, he who had the Sadim touch. The Sadim touch was a recurrent whimsy with him; it was Midas spelled backward and signified that everything he touched, especially gold, turned to—"Shucks."

"What, dear?"

"Nothing. Good night, Mom."

Palely she kissed him and tiredly toiled up the stairs. He stood by the dining room table, looking at the cut glass sugar-bowl, now turned out to pasture in its old age and holding two dozen teaspoons, handles down, looking like something a robot bride in a cartoon might carry for a bouquet. He scanned the orderly place-setting around the table, the clean inverted cups mouthing their saucers, each handle a precise sixty degrees off the line of the near table edge; the bread plates with the guaranteed 14K 100% solid gold edging absent from every convexity, wanly present in the concave.

And he couldn't lose himself in these things. Below the level of the things themselves, there was nowhere he could go. Something had closed his usual ready road to elsewhere and he felt a strange panic. He was unused to being restrained in the here and now, except on company time.

All right, then, he admitted.

He walked slowly through the foyer and into the parlor. Gerda Stein sat on the couch. She wasn't knitting, or reading, or doing anything. Just sitting quietly, as if she were waiting. What on Earth could she be waiting for?

He looked for the right place to sit, a chair not too close (not because he was afraid of being "forward" but because he would have absolutely no resources if she thought he was) and not too far away (because it was late and everyone was in bed and they would have to keep their voices low. In case they talked).

"Here," she said, and put her hand on the cushion beside her.

In his own house, he said, "Thank you, thank you very much," and sat down. When the silence got to be too much for him, he faced her. She looked back gravely and he turned again and stared at the print of the sentinel at Pompeii which had hung there since before he was born.

"What are you thinking?"

You're the most beautiful thing I've ever seen. But he said, "You comfortable?" He considered his statement, hanging there untouched in the room, and added with something like hysteria, "In your room, I mean."

She shrugged. It conveyed a great deal. It was, "Quite what I expected," and "There's certainly nothing to complain about," and "What can it possibly matter?" and, more than anything else, "I won't be here long enough to have any feelings about it one way or the other."

Any of these things, spoken aloud by anyone else, would have made him wildly defensive, for all he may not have been able to express it. Spoken by her, perhaps it would be different. He couldn't know. But transmitted thus mutely—he had nothing to say. He put his hands together between his knees and squeezed, miserable and excited.

"Why did your brother go to the Space Academy?" she asked.

"Congressman Shellfield got him the appointment."

"I didn't mean that."

"Oh," he said, "you mean *why*." He looked at her and again had to look away. "He wanted to, I guess. He always wanted to."

"You can't always want to do anything," she said gently. "When did it start?"

"Gosh . . . I dunno. Years back. When we were kids."

"What about you?"

"Me?" He gave a short, uncertain laugh. "I can't remember wanting anything specially. Mom says—"

"I wonder where he ever got the idea," she mused.

He guessed she had been thinking about Billy up in her room and had come down to find out more about him, had sat here waiting until he could come and tell her more. He made a sad, unconscious little gesture with his hands. Then he remembered that she had asked a question. When he didn't answer questions, why did she just wait like that?

"We used to play spaceman before Billy could talk," he recalled. He glanced her way and laughed surprisedly. "I'd forgotten all about that. I really had."

"What kind of games?"

"Games, you know. Rocket to the Moon and all. I was the captain and he was the crew. Well, at first I was the . . . I forget. Or I was the extraterrestrial and he was the explorer. Games." He shrugged. "I remember the takeoffs. We'd spread out on the couch and scream when the acceleration pressed the air out of our lungs. Mom didn't much like that screaming."

She laughed. "I can imagine. Tell me, do all spacemen talk the way he does?"

"You mean that 'shipmate' and 'gantry' and 'hit the blockhouse'?"

He paused for such a long time that she asked quietly, "Don't you want to tell me?"

He started. "Oh, sure, sure. I had to think. Last year, Easter vacation, he brought another cadet with him, name of Davies. Nice fellow, quiet, real black hair, sort of stoop-shouldered. I'd heard Billy talking that way before, thought it was the way to talk. But when I used it on Davies, he'd just look at me—" unconsciously, Chris was mimicking the wonderstruck Davies—"as if I was crazy. Harmless, but crazy." He gave his soft, embarrassed chuckle. "I guess I didn't do it right. I guess there's just exactly a right way of saying those things. You have to be a cadet to do it."

"Oh? Do all the cadets talk that way?"

"Davies didn't. Not to us, anyway. I never met any others."

"Maybe Billy's the only one who talks that way."

Chris had never considered the possibility. "That would sure sound funny at the Academy."

"Not if he never did it there."

Chris made a sudden awkward movement of the head, trying to brush away the idea. Stubbornly, it wouldn't brush. It was, after all, the first hypothesis his kind of logic had been able to accept for Cadet Davies' odd reactions. In itself, this was welcome, but it opened up an area of thinking about his brother he disliked to indulge in.

He said as much: "I wouldn't like to think of Billy that way, talking like—like when we were seven, eight years old."

"Why not? How do you like to think of Billy?"

"He's—getting what he wants. Going where he wants to go. He always has."

"Instead of you?"

"I don't know what you mean." *Or,* he added silently, *why you ask or why you want to know any of this.* He shifted his feet and turned to meet that disconcerting, warm, open, unjeering smile. "What do you want me to say?" he demanded, with a trace of irritation.

She settled back slightly. He knew why; she was going to wait again. He wouldn't be able to cope with that, he knew, so he said quickly, "It's all right for Billy to be that way. He can do things I—other people can't do. I'm not mad about that, not mad at him. There's nothing to be mad at. It would be like—being mad at a bird because it had wings. He's just different."

He realized that he had wandered from the area of her question, so he stopped, thought back, located it. Billy gets what he wants—*instead of you.*

He began again: "It's all right for Billy to get what he wants, even if it's something I happen to want, too, and don't get . . . How can I explain it?"

Rising suddenly, he began pacing, always turning away from her, passing her with his eyes downcast. It was as if the sight of her chained him, and with his eyes averted, he could run with his own thoughts again.

"It's as if Billy wasn't something separate at all, but just another side of me. Part of me wants to go to the Academy —Billy goes. Part of me wants to go out with Tess, not just to the movies, but *out* with her, make her feel—you know. Well, Billy does it. Or talk like Billy, look like him, all that racket and fast gab." He laughed, almost fondly. He sounded, then, just like his mother. "Sometimes he's a nuisance, but mostly I don't care. There's other things, lots of them, that I do that Billy couldn't. There's another part of me that does those things."

He allowed himself another quick look at Gerda Stein. She had turned to follow his pacings. He was in the far corner of the room and she sat with her cheek on her bare forearm, her head inclined as on a pillow and her hair hung down over the arm of the couch, heavy and bright.

"What things?" she asked.

He came back then and sat down beside her. "It's hard to say. It's very hard to say."

He sat for a long time performing the totally unprecedented task of verbalizing what he had never given words to before, the thoughts and feelings, ideas and intuitions so intimately, so mutely his own; all the things he set aside when he talked to Tess, all the things which occupied and preoccupied him during that ninety per cent of his life when he must commune and could not communicate. He sat there striving with it while she waited. Her waiting was no longer a trial to him. He realized that, but would not think about it. Yet.

"The nearest I can get to it," he said when he was ready, "is this: I've found out something that's at the root of everything anyone can think about, something that all thinking gets to sooner or later, and starts from, too. One simple sentence . . . Now wait." He put his simple sentence in front of his mind and looked at it for a long studious time. Then he spoke it. "Nothing is always absolutely so."

He turned to her. She nodded encouragingly but did not speak.

"It's a—help. A big help," he said. "I don't know when I first found it out. A long time back, I suppose. It helps with people. I mean the whole world is built on ideas that people say are so, and about all the troubles people have are caused by finding out that one thing or another around them just *isn't* so. Or it isn't so any longer. Or it's almost so, but not absolutely."

On receipt of another encouraging nod from Gerda Stein, "Nothing is always absolutely so," he said again. "Once you know that, know it for sure, you can do things, go places you never thought about before. Everything there is gives you some place to go, something to think about. Everything. Take a—a brass rivet, say. It's brass; you start with that. And what's brass? An alloy. How much change of what metal would make it not be brass? Given enough time, would radioactive decay in one of the metals transmute it enough so it wouldn't be brass any more?

"Or take the size. How big is it? Well, doesn't that depend? It's smaller after it's been used than when it was new. What color is it? That depends, too. In other words, if you're going to describe to me exactly what that rivet is, you're going to have to qualify and modify and get up a list of specs half as long as a tide chart and half as wide as Bowditch. And then all I have to do is sweat one drop of sweat on that rivet and wait twenty-four hours and you'll have to revise your specs.

"Or drop down a level. Pass a current through my rivet. The copper has this resistance and the zinc has another and a trace of iron has still more. What's the velocity of electromagnetic force through all this mess, and what kind of arguments do the atoms have about it? Or use a strong magnetic field. Why—really why, aside from 'It just happens'—is the copper so shy magnetically in brass and so out-and-out ferrous in alnico?"

He stopped to breathe. He breathed hard. It recalled to him how she had smiled when he had puffed into her room with the bags.

He realized suddenly that he had been altogether wrong in his estimate of that smile. He had feared it because he was ready to fear any smile. Now he knew that it was not just any smile, but the one he saw now—warm, encouraging, much like the smile which Tess Milburn had found and kept.

"What I'm driving at is, with this idea, that nothing is always absolutely so. You don't really need people or anything about them—movies, TV, talk; anyway, not for hours at a time, days. You don't have to hate people; I don't mean that at all. It's just that people's worries don't matter so much. People's troubles you can answer every time by saying 'Nothing is always absolutely so,' and go on to something else.

"But when you see that the wet half of a towel is darker than the dry half, or hear the sound of a falling bomb descending when all reason says it ought to rise in pitch, and you know where you're going to start: *Why?* and where you'll wind up: *Nothing is always absolutely so,* and challenge yourself to find the logic betwen start and finish— why, then you have your hands full; then you have a place to go."

"Isn't that a sort of escape?" the girl asked quietly.

"Depends on where you're standing at the time. Mixing

yourself up with human problems is maybe escaping from these other things. Anyway, these other things *are* human problems.'

"Are they?"

"$E=MC^2$ turned out to be. First it had to be thought out, with the thinking all the reward in sight, and after that it had to be applied, but don't tell me it isn't a human problem! Someone, for instance, had to put pineapple rings on a ham before baking, for the very first time! Or eat a raw oyster. That seems to me to be the kind of thinking I'm talking about." He brought his hand down for emphasis on the arm of the couch; it fell right on hers. "That's why Billy's at the Academy, because someone, and then some people, and then mankind began to want space."

She curled her fingers around his hand, not quite clasping it, and looked down contemplatively. "A good hand," she said in an impersonal voice, and gave it back to him.

"Huh? It's crummy—solder burns, ground-in bench dirt . . ." He held it as if it no longer completely belonged to him. *And it doesn't*, he thought with a start.

"Tell me," she asked lazily, "is the Academy's way the right way to get to space?"

"The only way," he said positively, and then, because his reason caught up with his honesty, he amended, "that's being tried."

Suddenly she sat up straight, leaned forward. She tossed her hair back as she turned toward him, with a gesture he knew he'd never forget.

She said, "I wonder about that. I wonder about fine-tuning men physically until they're all muscle and bounce, just to coop them up in a cabin for months on end. I wonder about all the training in astrogation when even primitive computers can do better, and no training at all in conversation, which we don't have a machine for yet. I wonder at the thinking behind hundred per cent male complements on those ships. I wonder about 10G stress tests on man who will have to develop an inertialess drive before they can think about *real* space travel. But most of all, I wonder—I worry—about putting extraverts on spacecraft."

She settled back again, looking at him quizzically.

"All right," he said, "I can play that game. Suppose I took every one of those wonderments of yours and turned them over to look at the other side. What would you do instead—man your ships with soft-bellied bookworms with no reflexes? Train them in philosophy and repartee in an eighteenth-century salon? Teach them to rely on their computers and never know what the machines are doing? Put women on the ships for them to get jealous about and fight over? Lay in a pack of brooding introverts, neuroses and all?"

"Neuroses," she repeated. "I'm glad you mentioned them. I imagine you're pretty sure that humanity is by and large a pretty neurotic species."

"Well, if your definition—"

"Never mind the specs," she said, interrupting him.

There was a new, concise ring to her voice that affected him much as had the first sight of her, standing out there under the porch light. Breathless, he fell silent.

"Yes, humans are neurotic," she answered her own question. "Insecure, disoriented, dissatisfied, fearful, full of aggressions against their own kind, always expecting attack, always afraid of being misunderstood, always in conflict between the urge to fly like a bird and the urge to burrow like a mole. Now why should all this be?"

He simply shook his head, bewildered.

"You have a very special mind, Chris, with your hypotheses and your lower levels and your quarreling atoms. Can you take a really *big* hypothesis?"

"I can try."

"Hypothesis," she said, making it sound like a story title. "There is a space-traveling species that achieved space flight in the first place because, of all species, it was the most fit. It established a commerce throughout a system, systems of systems, a galaxy, another. It had an inertialess faster-than-light drive, a suspended animation technique, sub-etheric communications—why go on listing all its achievements? Just say it was technologically gifted and its gift was only one facet of the whole huge fact that it was born and bred for space travel.

"Now, expanding as it must, it spread itself thin. It compensated as well as it could by learning to breed fast, by reducing to the minimum the size of its crews and increasing the efficiency of its ships. But each of these expedients only increased the spread; there's an awful lot of business in this universe for the sole qualified species.

"The only way out was to locate planets similar to their

own home world and seed them with people. That way, crews could be formed from one end of the explored universe to the other. The best way to do this would be to put down large colonial ships on suitable planets, complete with everything they might need to raise six or seven generations while acclimating to the planet. Thereafter, the colonies could be self-sustaining. That's the overall pic—uh—hypothesis. Are you still with me?"

"N-no," said Chris dazedly, "but go on."

She laughed. "Now suppose one of these big colonial vessels had some trouble—an impossible series of unlikely happenings that threw it out of control, while in faster-than-light flight with the personnel in suspended animation and all automatic orientation gear washed out. Centuries go by. If it encounters a galaxy, it will search out the right kind of planet, but it doesn't encounter anything until—"

Her voice died down. Chris looked at her, bent closer. Her eyes were closed and she was breathing very slowly, very deeply. As if she sensed him near her, she opened her eyes suddenly and gave a queer twisted smile.

"Sorry," she murmured, and took his hand so he would not move away. "This is the part I—don't like to think about, even—hypothetically."

For a moment, all the senses in Chris's body seemed to concentrate and flow together, to lie ecstatic in the hollow of her hand. Then she began to speak again.

"The ship was old, old by then, and the machinery badly butchered. It found a galaxy all right, and, in time, a planet. It snapped into normal space; it started the gestators . . ."

"Gestators?" he echoed blankly.

"Artificial placentae. Easier to carry fertilized ova and nutrients than children or even parents. But the revitalizers, for the suspendees—they failed, about ninety-eight per cent of them."

She sighed. It was a mourning sound. "No one knows what happened, not all of it. No one . . . should. The ship wasn't designed to make planetfall; it was an orbital, true-space vessel. They landed it, somehow, the few that were left. The crash took more lives—most, perhaps. The scout ships, the ferries, neatly stacked in the gimbal locks—all wrecked. Stores, *books*—call them books, it's simpler—everything lost. And all that was left, all that lived . . . a couple of hundred babies, helpless, hungry, many hurt, and a handful of maimed adolescents to care for them.

"The ship didn't last long; it wasn't built to take what a corrosive oxygen atmosphere could do to it. The boats hadn't been coated and they went, too, in weeks.

"But this is a hardy breed. Most died, but not all. Perhaps, to some, this would be a fascinating study in the old heredity-environment haggle; personally, I wouldn't have the stomach for it. They lost their language, their culture, their traditions and age-old skills. But they kept their genes. And in time, two prime characteristics showed through their savagery, come straight from their heritage: They bred fantastically and they reached for the stars.

"Unlike any other civilized species, they would breed beyond the ability of the land to support them, breed until they had to kill one another to survive at all—a faculty developed through eons of limitless *lebensraum,* but a deadly quality for a planet-bound race. It decimated them and they outbred even their own deadliness, so that in a brief time—twenty, twenty-two thousand years—they went from the dozens to the billions, threatening to carpet the planet with their bodies. Meanwhile the suicidal otherworldly urge to breed colored their mores and their literature until it stood unique among the galactic cultures.

"But they reached for the stars. They excused their hunger for the stars in a thousand ways, and when they grew too rational for excuses, they made no more and still went starward.

"And now, today, they are on the verge of it, by themselves, struggling along in their own terrified, terrifying way, ignorant of their origins, mystified by the drive in their blood . . . yes, Chris, a neurotic people."

After a time, Chris said, "How did you—uh—where did you hear—uh—read this . . ."

She laughed and looked down again at his hand. She patted it with her free one and then held it for a moment in both. "Hypothesis, remember?"

He shuddered, the late, large impact of her vivid voice and the pictures it evoked. It was somehow a delightful sensation.

"Will . . . did they ever find their own people?"

"They were found. Contact was made—oh, four hundred years ago."

Chris exhaled explosively. "Then it isn't—" He looked closely at her face. Even now, he was afraid of what her laughter might be like. ". . . Earth?" he finished in a small voice.

"Isn't it?"

"Four hundred years . . . everybody would know."

She shook her head soberly. "Consider: twenty thousand years of genetic drift, mutation, conditioning. The old drives may be there—statistically, and in the majority. But figure it out for yourself—what are the chances of a proto-typical spaceman after all that time? You'd find most of the desirable characteristics in some, some in most. You'd find all of them as a statistic, in a numerical sample. But if you were a captain looking for a crew, how would you find the man you wanted?"

"You already described the spacebound neurotic."

"It can't be just any neurotic, only because he's neurotic! He has to be a very special—very *specialized* neurotic indeed. They're rare."

"Then you'd have to announce yourself, advertise for what you wanted, have screenings, a training program—"

"Don't you know what would happen if all the world found out about the spaceman?"

"There'd be a riot, I guess—everyone wanting to go."

"There'd be a riot, all right," she said sadly, "but not that kind. There's one thing mankind is afraid of, sight unseen. It's a fear born of his slow growth on a strange and hostile planet, with only his brains as weapons and shelter."

"One fear—"

"The alien. Xenophobia—virtually a racial disease. All through your history, you have it, and it's always there under the surface, waiting to break out again like an ugly fire. There would be an attack on the spacemen themselves, and then a witch-hunt the like of which even this planet has never seen before. First the ones who fully qualify as spacemen, though they were born here; next anyone who has some of spaceman's characteristics—and everyone has!"

"I don't believe it!" Chris protested hotly. "I don't think human beings would go that far, be that stupid!"

"Humanity lets itself live on bare sufferance as it is," Gerda Stein said sorrowfully. "No, publicity isn't the answer."

"Then what's been going on these four hundred years?"

She said, "Surveys. Spaceman still desperately needs recruits, especially in this galaxy, which is new, unexplored, practically. So spacemen come here, live among you, and every once in a while a candidate is spotted. He's observed for—well, long enough to determine if he's the right kind."

"What's the right kind?" he asked.

"You gave a pretty good description yourself a while ago."

"The introspective neurotic?"

"With special mechanical and computing skills, and an inner resource that needs no books or teleplays or joy-riding or depravitiy to keep from being bored."

"And what happens when someone like that turns up?"

"The—agent reports, and after a while the space captain shows up. If the candidate is willing, he goes. He disappears from Earth and just goes."

"He has to be willing."

"Of course! What good would he be if he was shang-haied?"

"Well," said Chris primly, "that's something, anyway."

She did laugh at him, after all. It didn't hurt. While she was laughing, he was so disarmed that he asked her a question. He hadn't meant to; it just slipped out.

"Why did you want to know all those things about Billy?"

"Don't you have any idea?"

He looked at his hands. He said, a little sullenly, "You seem to think Billy never started anything by himself. You don't seem to think he can. You—well, I got the idea you think he gets pushed into things." He turned to her briefly. "By *me*, for Pete's sake!"

"And you don't think so?"

He gave a snort, embarrassed and negative. "If I could believe that, I—I could believe everything else you've been saying."

She smiled a very special smile. "Why don't you try it, then, and find out who's right?"

Quietly, for a long time, he thought.

"I will," he whispered at last. "I will." He straightened and looked at her. "Gerda, where do you come from?"

She rose and, spectacularly, stretched. "A little place

called Port Elizabeth," she said. "Not very far from here.
Port Elizabeth, New Jersey."

"Oh."

She laughed at him again and took his hand. "Good
night, Chris. Can we talk some more about this?"

He shook his head. "Not until I really—*really* think
about it."

"You will."

He watched her cross the foyer to the stairs. She put one
hand on the newel post and waved to him, crinkling her
eyelids in a way he would find as unforgettable as that turn
and sweep and uncovering when she threw back her hair
to face him. He found himself quite incapable of a wave
or anything else.

For a long time after he heard her door close, he stood
in the parlor looking at the stairs. At last he shook himself, turned out the lights in the parlor and all but the night
lamp in the foyer. He turned on the porch light for Billy
and went upstairs to the room they shared.

He undressed slowly and absent-mindedly, looking
around his room as if he had never seen it.

The orrery which he had started to build when he was
ten, and which Billy had taken away from him and finished,
all except the painting, which he did after all because Billy
grew tired of it.

The charts of the Solar System from the celestial north
(over Billy's bed) and from the south (over his). The
Smithsonian photo-map of the Moon, carefully pasted to
the ceiling, which Billy had moved to another spot, apparently because he hadn't been consulted, so Chris had had to
plaster up the first spot. The spaceships and Billy's toy
space helmet. (Hadn't it been Chris's for his twelfth birthday? But somehow "your" helmet had become "our" helmet and then "mine.") Anyway, it was all space stuff,
everything in sight, and space meant Billy, so somehow it
was all Billy. And Billy not back long enough even to
open his bag.

Chris got the pattern suddenly, but very late. Years late.
He lay back on his bed and grinned, then got up and
switched on the light over the desk. He went into the lava-
tory and got a big cake of white soap and spread newspaper on the desk and went to work on the soap with a
pocketknife, carving a cat's head.

Billy came in about two, clumping heavily, yawning noisily on the stairs. He banged into the room and kicked the door closed.

"Now you didn't have to wait up, shipmate," he said facetiously.

"I wasn't." Chris got up from the desk, put the knife down, and crossed to his bed.

Billy flung off his cape and tossed it on the easy-chair. "Well, I tilted that chick clean off the orbit, shipmate. You can take your meteor screens. She won't be dustin' around you *no* more."

"Why do me a favor like that?" Chris asked tiredly.

"You and Mom, you mean," said Billy, shucking out of his space boots. "You hadn't oughta worry Mom like that."

"Like what?"

"She computed you an' li'l Heartburn on a collision orbit. Well, Billy fix. She'll have nothin' in her viewplates from now on but Space Academy blue." He went to his cape and arranged it carefully on the chair-back. "It's not me, y'unnerstan', shipmate, not me pers'nal. It's just no one man can compete against the Space Corps. Not on a Venus sighting anyway," he said with labored modesty. Chris could see his mind wandering away from the subject before he had gotten the whole sentence out. "How'd you make out?"

"Make out? Oh—Miss Stein."

"Oh—Miss Stein. Fair warning, shipmate—that there's Target the Next."

Chris lay back and closed his eyes.

"You ever satisfied?"

"Look, shipmate," Billy said over his shoulder, " 'satisfied' didn't come inboard yet. These things I play straight and square, gyros on the ship's long axis and a-pointin' down the main tube. So get the brief, mudbound: tonight's mission was for you and for Mom. Tomorrow's for me. Over." He banged open his kit and pulled out a pajama zip-on. It was then that the carved bar of soap caught his eye. "What you riggin', shipmate?"

"Nothing," said Chris, as tiredly before, but watching like a lynx.

"Sculptin' soap. I heard of it. Often wondered." He bent over the work and, suddenly, laughed. That laugh. "Hey, high time we got a new hobby. This ain't bad for a beginner." He rocked the desk lamp back and forth to get shadows. "Think I'll square it away a bit for you. It's okay, isn't it, Chris?"

"I was going to fin—"

"That's all right, don't let it worry you. You won't know I touched it." He had stopped listening to Chris while Chris spoke, stopped listening to himself before he himself finished. He leaned over and flicked the carving with the point of the knife, then again. He bent closer, considering. Abruptly he sat down, got his elbows solidly planted on the desk, pulled the light closer and went to work.

Behind him, Chris nodded once, then smiled himself into his thoughts, level on lower level—the very first being the knowledge of who did start (and usually complete) things —until he slept.

It was Mr. Magruder's habit to take no breakfast at home, but to mount his stately and ludicrous old three-tone Buick and drive into town, where he would have tea sent up to the office. He did these things at such an unbearably early hour that his tacit offer of transportation to any who wanted it was almost always refused.

But this was an exception. Miz Binns greeted the change with polite protests but inner satisfaction; Billy was sleeping late, having been doing something up in the room until all hours, and now she would be able to take her time and compose a really fabulous tray for him. And Chris, looking uncharacteristically bright and cheerful for that hour, held Gerda Stein's elbow for her as she negotiated the front steps, and opened the ancient Buick's chrome-slashed door for her.

As soon as they were away from the curb, Chris took a deep breath and said, "I'm sure you won't be needing Miss Stein today at all, Mr. Magruder."

The old man said nothing and did nothing but continue to drive at his less-than-lawful and undeviating rate.

Gerda Stein turned expressionless and watchful eyes to Chris's face. Nobody said anything for a two-block interval.

"Also," said Chris firmly, "I'd appreciate it if you'd have someone in your office call my plant around 9:15 and tell them I won't be in today. I could do it myself, but I want it off my mind right now."

Mr. Magruder took his foot off the accelerator and let the car glide to a stop at the curb before applying the brakes. It took a long silent time. Chris opened the door and handed Gerda Stein out. He shut the door. "Thank you, Mr. Magruder."

As soon as the car was out of sight, Chris Binns began to laugh like a fool. Gerda Stein held on to him, or sturdily held him up, and after a time laughed, too.

"What was that for?" she asked when she could.

Chris wiped his eyes. "Damn if I know. Too much of ... too much all at once, I guess." Impulsively he reached out and ran his hand gently from her temple to the hinge of her jaw, not quite cupping her chin.

She held quite still while he did this, and when he dropped his hand, she said, "Well, hello."

He wished he had something like it to say, but after two trials all he could utter was, "B-breakfast," so they laughed together again and strode off, Chris holding her hand tight to the inside of his elbow. She walked well with him, long steady paces. "Can you dance in a spaceship?" he asked.

"With slow rolls," she twinkled.

They had waffles with cherry syrup and the best coffee in the world. He watched his thoughts and smiled, and she watched his face. When they had finished and fresh coffee arrived, he said, "Now, questions."

"Go ahead."

"You say the colony ship was wrecked here about twenty-five thousand years ago. How do you account for Swanscombe and Pekin and Australopithecus and all?"

"They're indigenous."

She touched his hand for emphasis. "Chris, if you'll think on galactic terms, or larger, you'll be quite satisfied. When one of those seeking mechanisms is set for a planet of this type, it isn't satisfied with an *almost*. And in multi-galactic terms, there's plenty of choice. Homo sap, or something very like him, grows on many of those planets, if not most. In Earth's case, they have even have interbred. We're not sure, but there have been cases. Whether or not, though, Spaceman's presence here was no boon to the other races. He's a pretty nice fellow in his own element, but he makes for a fairly critical mass when you let him pile up."

"All right. Now a little more about this neurosis business. Why should Spaceman be so out of kilter on a planet? I'd think of him as pretty adaptable."

"He certainly is! He survived for twenty-five thousand

years here, didn't he? But about these neuroses—they're easy enough to account for, once you understand the basic drives. Look:

"One characteristic that has been the subject of more worry, more sneers, more bad jokes than anything else here—except sex itself—is the back-to-the-womb movement. Introspection and introversion and agoraphobia and heaven knows what else, from the ridiculous—like the man who can't work in an office where he can't have his back to the wall—to the sublime—like the Nirvana concept—is traced to a desire for the womb—*the enclosed, sustaining, virtually gravityless womb.* As soon as you discover that the womb itself is only a symbol for this other heritage, what explanation do you need instead?"

"Bedamned," whispered Chris.

"Another almost universal inner tension has to do with people, though some of us compensate admirably. What's the most ideal state for most people? The family—the enclosed, familiar, mutually responsive family unit. Only strangers cause communication to break down; only outsiders are unpredictable. Hence our cultural insanities—as I told you before, xenophobia, the fear of the foreigner. Spaceman travels in sexually balanced small-family units, the young getting their own ships and their own mates as the ships meet and cross the Universe over."

"Bedamned again," said Chris.

"Now your ideal spaceman: He'd have to be a neurotic on Earth, just as—if you can imagine it—a person brought up from birth to walk nothing but tight wires would be neurotic on solid ground. He'd wear himself out with unnecessary compensatory reflexes. Your true spaceman wants knowledge, not pastimes. His reaction to outside pressures is to retreat into his own resources—first, his ship (like you in your job); next, his own thoughts and where they might lead him (like you on your own time). And he wants a—"

Chris looked up into her eyes.

He said gently, "Go on."

"He wants, not women, but a mate," she said.

"Yes."

It took a while, but she then could smile and say, "Any more questions?"

"Yes . . . What's going to become of Billy?"

"Oh, he'll be all right," she said confidently. "He and all his kind. He'll graduate, and train some more, and graduate again. He'll stay where he is, perhaps, and train others. Or he'll get a big job—skipper of a Moon ferry, maybe, or second officer on the first Mars ship. Space will make him sick—tense, always apprehensive, never comfortable—but he'll be strong and stick it out. And after a while, he'll retire with honors and a pension."

"And he'll never know?"

"That would be too cruel . . . Any more?"

"Only one big one and I haven't been able to think around it. One of the most permeating fears of human-kind—some say the only one we're actually born with and don't have to learn—is the fear of falling. How do you equate that with Spaceman?"

She laughed. "You can't see that?"

He shook his head.

She leaned forward, capturing him with her eyes and her urgency. "You are home, where you belong, in space, with all of safe immensity around you, and it's the way you live, and work, and sleep . . . and suddenly, *right there*, there's a *planet* under you!"

It hit him so suddenly, he gasped and actually strained upward to get away from the floor, the great pressing obtrusive bulk of Earth. "You're not falling," she whispered into the heart of his terror. "*It's trying to fall on you!*"

He closed his eyes and clutched at the table and forced himself to reorient. Slowly, then, he looked at her and managed to grin. "You've got yourself a boy," he said. "Let's get *out* of here, Captain."

My dear Chris and Gerda: I do declare I have never had my life turned so upsy turvy all at once in my life. What with you getting married so quick like that and then Mr. Magruder finding you that wonderful job but I still dont know what's so wonderful about New Zealand of all places. Still if your happy.

Then on top of that Billy running out to marry Tess Milburn like that just because you two did it I don't understand, I always thought Billy had his own ideas and couldn't be led, its as if somebody just pushed a button and bang he did it, come to think of it thats the way he decided to go after the Academy thing and he says it was you started him on this soap carving even. What with keeping the marriage secret until he graduates and trying to find a new bar of soap in the house I do declare I don't know where I am.

Speaking of Mr. Magruder which I was, he's no longer with me, just paid up his month and left without a howdy do. I hear he's with Mrs. Burnett over to Cecil Street, all she has is that little house and that hopeless son who designs cameras and whatnot and hides in his room all the time, which is pretty insulting after all I did for him for eight solid years.

Well my dears take care of yourselves and send pictures of you and your pet sheep or goats or whatever it is you crazy kids are into.

Much love,
Mom.

Subscript by Etheric Radio
Operator Grout X 3115
CAPTAIN GERDA STEIN
2ND CHRISTOPHER STEIN
YOUR THIRD PREPARED LETTER DESPATCHED TO MIZ BINNS AS PER INSTRUCTIONS ALSO SHEEP FARM PHOTOS SUPPLIED. MAGRUDER SENDS REGARDS AND SAYS HE HAS A LIVE ONE IN THE BURNETT KID. PASS THE WORD. SEE YOU IN TEN YEARS OR SO.
    GROUT
    AUCKLAND NEW ZEALAND
    TERRA (SOL 3)
    TERC 348
    QUAD 196887
    OCT 384
(Untranslatable)
13996462597

THE
OTHER
MAN

A great many scientists and technologists are involved in science fiction. During the Big War, the largest block of subscriptions to Astounding Science Fiction *was in Oak Ridge, Tennessee, and the next largest in Hanford, Washington—facts, John Campbell told me, that the German military intelligence never discovered or noticed. Whenever I appear on radio or television, the interviewer may or may not know anything about the field, but you can bet the guys behind the glass wall do. Many famous scientists, like astronomer Fred Hoyle, anthropologist Chad Oliver, rocket designer G. Harry Stine, and the late Willy Ley, have written it, and some, like Carl Sagan and M.I.T.'s brilliant Marvin Minsky, have come to science through an early love for it. And I had the heady experience of being told by a Nobel caliber scientist that he became a microbiologist because of a single story I wrote.*

Such being the case, why doesn't some psychiatrist or psychotherapist pick up on the technique suggested by this story? Intuitively I know that it, or something like it, just has to work. Intuition, of course, is no substitute for expertise. In other words, if I knew enough I'd be doing it instead of writing about it. But it's a valid notion just the same.

When he saw her again, he all but yelled—a wordless, painful bleat, one concentrated syllable to contain five years of loneliness, fury, self-revilement and that agony peculiar to the victim of "the other man." Yet he controlled it, throwing it with a practiced reflex to a tensing of his abdomen and the transient knotting of thigh muscles behind the desk, letting the impact strike as it should, unseen.

Outwardly, he was controlled. It was his job to know the language of eyelids, jaw muscles, lips, and it was his special skill to make them mute. He rose slowly as his nurse ushered her in and while she took the three short paces to meet him. He studied her with an impassive ferocity.

He might have imagined her in old clothes, or in cheap clothes. Here she was in clothes which were both. He had allowed, in his thoughts of her, for change, but he had not thought her nose might have been broken, nor that she might be so frighteningly thin. He had thought she would always walk like something wild . . . free, rather . . . but with stateliness, too, balanced and fine. And indeed she still did so; somehow that hurt him more than anything else could.

She stopped before the desk. He moved his hands behind him; her gaze was on them and he wanted her to look up. He waited until Miss Jarrell discreetly clicked the door shut.

"Osa," he said at last.

"Well, Fred."

The silence became painful. How long did that take—two seconds, three? He made a meaningless sound, part of a laugh, and came around the desk to shift the chair beside it. "Sit down, for heaven's sake."

She sat down and abruptly, for the first time since she

had entered the office, she looked directly at him. "You look—you look well, Fred."

"Thanks." He sat down. He wanted to say something, but the only thing that would come readily to his lips was, "You're looking well, too"—such a patent lie that he couldn't tell it. And at last he found something else to say: "A lot has happened."

She nodded and her gaze found a corner of the tooled leather blotter frame on the desk. She studied it quietly.

"Five years," she said.

Five years in which she must have known everything about him, at first because such a separation is never sharp, but ragged, raveled, a-crackle with the different snaps of different threads at different times; and later, because all the world knew what he was, what he had done. What he stood for.

For him, five years at first filled with a not-Osa, like a sheet of paper from which one has cut a silhouette; and after that, the diminishing presence of Osa as gossip (so little of that, because anyone directly involved in gossip walks usually in a bubble of silence); Osa as rumor, Osa as conjecture. He had heard that Richard Newell had lost —left—his job about the time he had won Osa, and he had never heard of his working again.

Glancing at Osa's cheap clothes now, and the new small lines in her face, he concluded that whatever Newell had found to do, it could not have been much. Newell, he thought bitterly, is a man God made with only one victory in him and he's used it up.

"Will you help me?" Osa asked stridently.

He thought: Was I waiting for this? Is this some sort of reward, her coming to me for help? Once he might have thought so. At the moment, he did not feel rewarded.

He sat looking at her question as if it were a tangible object, a box of a certain size, a certain shape, made of some special material, which was not to be opened until he had guessed its contents.

Will you help me? Money? Hardly—Osa may have lost a great deal, but her towering pride was still with her. Besides, money settles nothing. A little is never enough and helps only until it is gone. A little more puts real solutions a bit further into the future. A whole lot buries the real problem, where it lives like a cancer or a carcinogen.

Not money, then. Perhaps a job? For her? No, he knew her well. She could get her own jobs. She had not, therefore she didn't want one. This could only mean she lived as she did for Newell's sake. Oh, yes, he would be the provider, even if the illusion starved her.

Then a job for Newell? Didn't she know he couldn't be trusted with any responsible job and was not constituted to accept anything less? Of course she knew it.

All of which left only one thing. She must be sure, too, that Newell would accept the idea or she would not be here asking.

He said, "How soon can he start therapy?"

She *flickered*, all over and all at once, as if he had touched her with a high voltage electrode—the first and only indication she had evinced of the terrible tensions she carried. Then she raised her head, her face lit with something beyond words, something big enough, bright enough, to light and warm the world. His world. She tried to speak.

"Don't," he whispered. He put out his hand and then withdrew it. "You've already said it."

She turned her head away and tried to say something else, but he overrode that, too.

"I'll get paid," he said bluntly. "After his therapy, he'll earn more than enough—" (For both of us? For my bill? To pay you back for all he's done to you?) "—for everything."

"I should have known," she breathed. He understood. She had been afraid he wouldn't take Newell as a patient. She had been afraid, if he did take him, that he might insist on doing it free, the name of which was charity. She need not have worried. *I should have known.* Any response to that, from a shrug to a disclaimer, would destroy a delicacy, so he said nothing.

"He can come any time you say," she told him. This meant, *He isn't doing anything these days.*

He opened a desk book and riffled through it. He did not see it. He said, "I'd like to do some pretty intensive work with him. Six, eight weeks."

"You mean he'd stay here?"

He nodded. "And I'm afraid—I'd prefer that you didn't visit him. Do you mind very much?"

She hesitated. "Are you sure that . . ." Her voice trailed off.

"I'm sure I want to do it," he said, suddenly rough. "I'm sure I'll do everything I can to straighten him out, bar nothing. You wouldn't want me to say I was sure of anything else."

She got to her feet. "I'll call you, Fred." She watched his face for a moment. He did not know if she would want to shake his hand or—or not. She took one deep breath, then turned away and went to the door and opened it.

"Thank you . . ."

He sat down and looked at the closed door. She had worn no scent, but he was aware of her aura in the room, anyway. Abruptly he realized that she had not said "Thank you."

He had.

Osa didn't call. Three days, four, the phone ringing and ringing, and never her voice. Then it didn't matter—rather, she had no immediate reason to call, because the intercom whispered, and when he keyed it, it said in Miss Jarrel's clear tones, "A Mr. Newell to see you, doctor."

Stupidly he said, "Richard A. Newell?"

Bzz, Psss, Bzz. "That's right, doctor."

"Send him in."

"I beg your pardon?"

"Send him in," said the doctor. *I thought that's what I said. What did it sound like?* He couldn't remember. He cleared his throat painfully. Newell came in.

"We-ell, Freddy boy." (Two easy paces; cocked head, half smile.) "A small world." Without waiting to be asked, he sat down in the big chair at the end of the desk.

At first glance, he had not changed; and then the doctor realized that it was the—what word would do?—the symphonic quality of the man, the air of perfect blending—it was that which had not changed.

Newell's diction had always suited the clothes he chose and his movements were as controlled as his speech. He still wore expensive clothes, but they were years old—yet so good they hardly showed it. The doctor was immediately aware that under the indestructible creases and folds was a lining almost certainly frayed through; that the elegant face was like a cheap edition printed from worn plates and the mind behind it an interdependence of flimsy parts so exactly matched that in the weak complex there was no weakest component. A machine in that condition might run indefinitely—idling.

The doctor closed his eyes with a brief impatience and consigned the concepts to the limbo of oversimplified analogies. "What do you want?"

Newell raised his eyebrows a fraction. "I thought you knew. Oh, *I* see," he supplemented, narrowing his eyes shrewdly. "One of those flash questions that are supposed to jolt the truth out of a man. Now let's see, just what did pop into my head when you asked me that?" He looked at the top of the window studiously, then leaned forward and shot out a finger. "More."

"More?"

"More—that's the answer to that question. I want more money. More time to myself. More fun." He widened his eyes and looked disconcertingly into the doctor's. "More women," he said, "and better. Just—more. You know. Can do?"

"I can handle only so much," said the doctor levelly. His thighs ached. "What you do with what I give you will be up to you . . . What do you know about my methods?"

"Everything," said Newell off-handedly.

Without a trace of sarcasm, the doctor said, "That's fine. Tell me everything about my methods."

"Well, skipping details," said Newell, "you hypnotize a patient, poke around until you find the parts you like. These you bring up by suggestion until they dominate. Likewise, you minimize other parts that don't suit you and drive them underground. You push and you pull and blow up and squeeze down until you're satisfied, and then you bake him in your oven—I'm using a figure of speech, of course—until he comes out just the proper-sized loaf. Right?"

"You—" The doctor hesitated. "You skipped some details."

"I said I would."

"I heard you." He held Newell's gaze soberly for a moment. "It isn't an oven or a baking."

"I said that, too."

"I was wondering why."

Newell snorted—amusement, patronization, something like that. Not irritation or impatience. Newell had made a virtual career out of never appearing annoyed. He said, "I watch you work. Every minute, I watch you work; I know what you're doing."

"Why not?"

Newell laughed. "I'd be much more impressed in an atmosphere of mystery. You ought to get some incense, tapestries in here. Wear a turban. But back to you and your bake-oven, what-do-you-call-it—"

"Psychostat."

"Yes, psychostat. Once you've taken a man apart and put him together again, your psychostat fixes him in the new pattern the way boiling water fixes an egg. Otherwise he'd gradually slip back into his old, wicked ways."

He winked amiably.

Not smiling, the doctor nodded. "It is something like that. You haven't mentioned the most important part, though."

"Why bother? Everybody knows about *that*." His eyes flicked to the walls and he half-turned to look behind him. "Either you have no vanity or you have more than anyone, Fred. What did you do with all the letters and citations that any human being would frame and hang? Where's all the plaques that got so monotonous on the newscasts?" He shook his head. "It can't be no vanity, so it must be more than anyone. You must feel that this whole plant—you yourself—are your citation." He laughed, the professional friendly laugh of a used-car salesman. "Pretty stuffy, Freddy."

The doctor shrugged.

"I know what the publicity was for," said Newell. "A fiendish plot to turn you into a personality kid for the first time in your life." Again the engaging smile. "It isn't hard to get you off the subject, Freddy boy."

"Yes, it is," said the doctor without heat. "I was just making the point that what I do here is in accordance with an ethical principle which states that any technique resulting in the destruction of individual personality, surgical or otherwise, is murder. Your remarks on its being publicly and legally accepted now are quite appropriate. If you must use that analogy about taking a patient all apart and putting him together again in a different and better way, you should add that none of the parts are replaced with new ones and none are left out. Everything you have now, you'll have after your therapy."

"All of which," said Newell, his eyes twinkling, "is backed up by the loftiest set of ethics since Mohandas K. Gandhi."

The twinkle disappeared behind a vitreous screen. The voice was still soft. "Do you suppose I'd be fool enough to put myself in your hands—*your* hands—if I hadn't swallowed you and your legendary ethics down to here?" He jabbed himself on the chest. "You're so rammed full of ethical conduct, you don't have room for an honest insult. You have ethics where most people carry their guts."

"Why did you come here," asked the doctor calmly, "if you feel that much animosity?"

"I'll tell you why," smiled Newell. "First, I'm enjoying myself. I have a sense of values that tells me I'm a better man than you are, law, fame and all, and I have seventy-odd ways—one of which you were once married to—to prove it. Why wouldn't anyone enjoy that?"

"That was 'first.' You've got a 'secondly'?"

"A beaut," said Newell. "This one's for kicks too: I think I'm the toughest nut you've ever had to crack. I'm real happy about the way I am—all I want is *more,* not anything *different.* If you don't eliminate my lovable character or any part of it—and you won't; you've stacked the deck against yourself—you'll wind up with just what you see before you, hi-fi amplified. And just for a little salt in the stew, I might as well tell you that I know you can't operate well without hypnosis, and I can't be hypnotized."

"You can't?"

"That's right. Look it up in a book. Some people can't be hypnotized because they won't, and I won't."

"Why not?"

Newell shrugged and smiled.

"I see," said the doctor. He rose and went to the wall, where a panel slid aside for him. He took up a shining hypodermic, snicked off the sterile sheath and plunged the needle into an ampoule. He returned to the desk, holding the hypodermic point upward. "Roll up your sleeve, please."

"I also happen to know," Newell said, complying readily, "that you're going to have one hell of a time sorting out drug-reaction effects from true responses, even with neo-scopolamine."

"I don't expect my work to be easy. Clench your fist, please."

Newell did, laughing as the needle bit. The laugh lasted four syllables and then he slumped silently in his chair.

The doctor took out a blank case book and carefully entered Newell's name and the date and a few preliminary notes. In the "Medication" column, he wrote, *10 cc neutral saline solution.*

He paused then and looked at the "better" man and murmured, "So you can run a mile faster than Einstein."

"All ready, doctor."

"Right away."

He went to the rack in the corner and took down a white coat. Badge of office, he thought, cloak of Hippocrates, evolved through an extra outdoor duster we used to wear to keep the bodily humours off our street clothes . . . and worn today because, for patients, the generalization "doctor" is an easier departure point for therapeutics than the bewildering specific "man." Next step, the juju mask, and full circle.

He turned into the west corridor and collided with Miss Thomas, who was standing across from Newell's closed door.

"Sorry!" they said in unison.

"Really my fault," said Miss Thomas. "I thought I ought to speak to you first, doctor. He—he's not completely dismantled."

"They very frequently aren't."

"I know. Yes, I know that." Miss Thomas made a totally uncharacteristic, meaningless flutter of the hands and then welded them angrily to her starched flanks.

The doctor felt amusement and permitted it to show. Miss Thomas, his head technician, was neither human nor female during working hours, and the touch of color, of brightness in her lack of ease pleased him somehow.

She said, "I'm familiar with the—uh—unexpected, doctor. Naturally. But after eighty hours of machine catalysis, I don't expect a patient to resemble anything but a row of parts laid out on a laboratory bench."

"And what does this patient resemble?"

There was a sudden, soft pedal of delighted feminine laughter from the closed door. Together they looked at its bland surface and then their eyes met.

"Two hundred cycles," said Miss Thomas. "Listen to her."

They listened: Miss Jarrell's voice, a cooing, inarticulate Miss Jarrell, was saying, "Oh . . . you . . . you!" And more laughter.

Miss Thomas said severely, "I know what you're thinking about Hildy Jarrell, but don't. That's exactly what I did myself." Again she made the uncharacteristic fluttery gesture. "Oh-h!" She breathed impatiently.

Because his impulses were kind, the doctor ignored most of this and picked up only, "Two hundred cycles. What do you get at the other frequencies?"

"Oh, that's all right, all of it. Average response. Pre-therapeutic personality responds best at eighty cycles. Everywhere else, he's nice and accessible. Anyway," she said a little louder, obviously to drown out another soft sudden chuckle from behind the door, "I just wanted you to know that I've done what I can. I didn't want you to think I'd skipped anything in the spectrum. I haven't. It's just that there's a personality in the 200-cycle area that won't dismantle."

"Yet," he corrected mildly.

"Oh, *you* can do it," she said in rapid embarrassment. "I didn't mean . . . I only meant . . ."

She drew a deep breath and started over. "I just wanted you to be sure *my* job's done. As to what you can do, you'll handle it, all right. Only—"

"Only what, Miss Thomas?"

"It's a pity, that's all," she blurted, and pushed past him to disappear around the corner.

He shook his head, puzzlement and laughter wrestling gently deep inside him. Only then did something she had said fully register with him: ". . . *there's a personality in the 200-cycle area that won't dismantle*."

That woman, he thought, has the kind of precision which might be clouded by emotion, but nothing would eliminate it. If she said there's a personality in the 200-cycle area, she meant just that. A personality, not a component or a matrix or a complex.

As she herself had put it, after catalysis a patient should resemble nothing more than a row of parts on a lab bench. Down through the levels of hypnosis, audible frequencies would arbitrarily be assigned to various parts of the personality, and by suggestion each part would respond to its frequency throughout the therapy. Any part could be summoned, analyzed, then minimized, magnified, stressed or quelled in the final modulation and made permanent in the psychostat. But at the stage Newell was in—should be in—these were *parts*, sub-assemblies at most. What did she mean "a personality" in the 200-cycle area?

She was wrong, of course. *Oh, God,* he thought, *she's wrong, isn't she?*

He opened the door.

Miss Jarrell did not see him. He watched for a long moment, then said, just loud enough to be heard over the soft thrumming of the 200-cycle note from the speakers, "Don't stop, Miss Jarrell. I'd like to see a little more of this."

Miss Jarrell flung up a scarlet face.

The doctor said again, quietly but with great force, "Go on, please."

She turned away to the bed, her back held with a painful rigidity and her ears, showing through her hair, looking like the tips of bright little tongues.

"It's all *right,*" soothed the doctor. "It's all right, Miss Jarrell. You'll see him again."

She made a soft sound with her nostrils, grinned ruefully and went to the controls. She set one of them for the patient's allotted sleep-command frequency and hit the master switch. There was a gentle explosion of sound—"white" noise, a combination of all audio frequencies, which served to disorient the dismantled patient, his reflexive obedience attempting to respond to all commands at once—for ten seconds, and then it automatically faded, leaving the 550-cycle "sleep" note. The patient's face went blank and he lay back slowly, his eyes closing. He was asleep before his head reached the pillow.

The doctor stood suspended in thought for some time. Miss Jarrell gently arranged the patient's blanket. It was not done dutifully nor as part of the busyness of waiting for his next move. For some reason, it touched the doctor deeply and pulled him out of his reverie. "Let's have the P.T., Miss Jarrell."

"Yes, doctor." She consulted the index and carefully set the controls. At his nod, she touched the master switch. Again the white noise, and then deep moo of the 80-cycle tone.

The P.T.—pretherapeutic—personality would be retained untouched throughout the treatment, right up until the final setting process in the psychostat, except, of course, for the basic posthypnotic command which kept all segments under control of the audio spectrum. The doctor watched the sleeping face and was aware of a most unprofessional desire to have something other than that untouched P.T. appear.

He glanced at Miss Jarrell without turning his head. She should leave now, and ordinarily she would. But she was not behaving ordinarily just now.

The patient's eyes half-opened and stayed that way for a time. It was like the soft startlement of a feline which is aware of something, undecided whether the something deserves more attention than sleep, and therefore simply waits, armed and therefore relaxed.

Then he saw the eyes move, though the lids did not. This was the feline taking stock, but deluding its enemies into thinking it still drowsy. The man changed like an aurora, which is ever the same while you watch, but something quite different if you look away and look back again. *I think in analogies,* the doctor childed himself, *when I don't like the facts.*

"Well, Freddy boy," drawled Richard A. Newell.

Behind him, he heard Miss Jarrell's almost inaudible sigh and her brisk quiet footsteps as she turned on the speech recorder, crossed the room and closed the door behind her.

Newell said, "Nurse is an odd term for a woman built like that. How you doing, Freddy?"

"Depends," said the doctor.

Newell sat up and stretched. He waved at the red eye of the recorder. "Everything I say is taken down and may be used against me, hm?"

"Everything is used, yes. Not—"

"Oh, spare me the homilies, Fred. Transcribe them yourself, do you?"

"I—no." As he caught Newell's thought, and knew exactly the kind of thing the man was going to do next, he felt himself filling up with impotent rage. It did not show.

"Fine, fine." Projecting his voice a bit, Newell said over an elaborate yawn, "Haven't waked up like this since I was a kid. You know, disoriented, wondering for a moment where I was. Last bed I was in wasn't so lonesome. Missed thirty of those last forty winks, the way she was all over me. 'Dick, oh, Dick, please . . .' " he mimicked cruelly. "Told her to shut up and get breakfast."

He laughed outright, obviously not at anything he had said, but at the writhing silent thing within the doctor, which he could not see but knew must be there.

He glanced again at the pilot light on the recorder and said, "Mentioning no names, of course," and the doctor understood immediately that names would be mentioned, places, dates and interrelationships, whenever Newell chose . . . which would be when the suspense ceased to entertain him. Meanwhile, the doctor could prepare himself for the behind-the-back gossip, the raised eyebrows of the transcribing typist, the afterhours debates as to the ethical position of a doctor's practicing on the man who had . . . who was . . .

The sequence spiraled down to a low level of his personal inferno and flickered there, hot and smokeless.

"You didn't tell me," said Newell. "How you doing? Find the secret of my success yet?"

The doctor shrugged easily, which was not easy to do. "We haven't begun."

"Thought not." Newell snorted. "By the time you're finished, you won't have begun, either."

"Why do you say that?"

"I extrapolate it. I come here, you give me a shot of knockout drops, I get a sound sleep and wake up rested and cheerful. Otherwise, nothing. Yet I know that you've taken my slumbering corpus, poked it, prodded it, checked in it and wrung it out, tooted on your tooters, punched cards and clicked out four miles of computer tapes—for what? I'm still me, only rested up a little."

"How do you know we did all that?"

"I read the papers." When the doctor made no reply, Newell laughed again. "You and your push-button therapy." He looked up in recall, as if reading words off the ceiling. "What's the claim—82% of your patients cured?"

"Modulated."

"Pretty word, modulated. Pretty percentage, too. What kind of a sieve do you use?"

"Sieve?"

"Don't tell me you don't select your patients!"

"No, we take them as they come."

"Ha. You talk like the Lysenkoists. Remember them? Russian genetics experts fifty years back. They claimed results like that. They claimed nonselective methodology, too, even when some of the people supposed to be breeding split-kernel corn were seen splitting the kernels with a knife. Even the Communists rejected them after a while." He flicked a wolfish glance at the recorder and grinned. "But then," he said clearly, "no Communist would reject *you*, Freddy."

Of the four possible responses which came to him, the doctor could find none that would sound unlike a guilty protest, so he said nothing. Newell's widening grin informed him that his silence was just as bad.

"Ah, Fred, m'boy, I know you. I know you well. I knew a lot about you five years ago and I've learned a lot more since." He touched the dark wiry tuft between his collarbones. "Like, for example, you haven't a single hair on your chest. Or so I've been told."

Again the doctor used silence as a rejoinder. He could examine his feelings later—he knew he would; he inescapably must. For now, he knew that any answer would fall into Newell's quiver as new arrows. Silence was a condition Newell could not maintain nor tolerate; silence made Newell do the talking, take the offensive . . . inform on and expose his own forces. Silence Newell could use only sometimes; words, always.

Newell studied him for a moment and then, apparently deciding that in order to return to a target, it was necessary to leave it temporarily, looked at the compact control panel. "I've read a lot about that. Push one button, I'm a fighting engine. Push another, I lie down with the lamb. Who was it once said humanity will evolve into a finger and a button, and every time the finger wants anything, it will push the button—and that will be the end of humanity, because the finger will get too damn lazy to push the button?" He wagged his head. "You're going to gadget yourself clear out of a living, Fred."

"Did you read what was written over the entrance when you came here?" the doctor asked.

"I noticed there was something there," said Newell amiably, "and no, I didn't read it. I assumed it was some saw about the sanctity of the personality, and I knew I'd get all I could stand of that from you and your acolytes."

"Then I think you ought to know a little more about what you call 'push-button therapy,' Newell. Hypnosis isn't therapy and neither is the assigned audio-response technique we use. Hypnosis gives us access to the segments of personality and creates a climate for therapy, and that's all. The therapy itself stands or falls on the ability of the therapist, which is true of my school as it is of all others short of the lobotomists."

"Well, well, well. I goaded a real brag out of you at last. I didn't know you had it in you." Newell chuckled. "82% effective and you do it all your little self. Now ain't you something? Tell me, able therapist, how do you account for the 18% who get by you?"

"Why do you want to know?"

"I might alter the figures for you. Who are these sturdy souls?"

"Organic defectives," said the doctor. *And certain others* . . . but he kept that to himself.

Newell shouted, "Touché!" and fell back with a roar of appreciative laughter. But the doctor saw his eyes before he closed them, little windows with all the faces of hate looking out.

The doctor was delighted. He braced himself for the reaction against his own pleasure which he could always expect from his austere professionalism, but it did not come. He put this fact away with the others he knew he must examine later.

Newell was saying, "You can't have it both ways, Fred. About hypnosis not being therapy, I mean. What's this I heard somewhere about certain frequencies having certain effects, no matter who you are?"

"Oh, that. Yes, some parts of the audio spectrum do affect most people. The subsonics—fourteen to around twenty cycles, for example, if you use enough amplitude—

they scare people. And beat frequencies between two tones, where the beat approaches the human pulse, sometimes have peculiar psychological effects. But these are byways, side phenomena. We use the ones we can rely on and ignore or avoid the others. Audio frequencies happen to be convenient, accurate and easy for patients and therapists to identify.

"But they're not essential. We could probably do the same thing with spoken commands or a spectrum of odors. Audio is best, though; the pure electronic tone is unfamiliar to most people and so has no associations except the ones we give it. That's why we don't use 60 cycles—the hum you're surrounded by all your life from AC devices."

"And what about if you're tone-deaf?" asked Newell, with an underlay of gloating which could only mean that he was talking about himself.

"Nobody's *that* tone-deaf, except the organic defectives."

"Oh," said Newell disappointedly, then returned to the half-sneering search for information. "And so the patient walks out of here prepared for the rest of his life to go into a state of estrus every time an English horn sounds A-440?"

"You know better than that," retorted the doctor for once not concealing his impatience. "That's what the psychostat is for. Every frequency the patient responds to is recorded there—" he waved at the controls—"along with its intensity. These are analyzed by a computer and compared by another one with a pattern which shows which segments are out of line—like too much anger or unwarranted fear, in terms of patient's optimum. The psychostat applies dampers on the big ones and amplifies the atrophied ones until the response matches the master pattern. When every segment is at optimum—the patient's, mind you; no one else's—the new pattern is fixed by an overall posthypnotic which removes every other suggestion that has been applied."

"So the patient *does* go out of here hypnotized!"

"He walks in here hypnotized," said the doctor. "I'm surprised at you, Newell. For a man who knows so much about my specialty, you shouldn't need to be lectured on the elementals."

"I just like the sound of your voice," Newell said acidly, but the acid was dilute. "What do you mean, the patient walks in here hypnotized?"

"Most people are, most of the time. In the basic sense, a man is under hypnosis whenever any one of his senses does not respond to a present stimulus, or when his attention is diverted even slightly from his physical surroundings. You're under hypnosis when you read a book, or when you sit and think and don't see what you're staring at, or when you bark your shin on a coffee table you didn't see under bright lights."

"That's so much hairsplitting." Newell didn't even pause before his next sentence, which came from quite a different area than his scoffing incredulity. "Why didn't you tell me all this when I said I couldn't be hypnotized?"

"I preferred to believe you when you said you knew it all."

Every pretense of joviality disappeared. "Listen, you," Newell grated, in the ugliest tone of voice the doctor had ever heard, "you better watch what you are doing."

It was time again for silence and the doctor used it. He gave Newell no choice but to lie there and stare at his own words. He watched the man regaining his poise, laboriously, hand over hand, then resting, testing, waiting to be sure he could speak again.

"Well," Newell said at length, and the doctor almost admired him for the smoothness of his tone, "it's been fun so far and it'll wind up more so. If you really can do what you say, I'll make it right with you, Freddy boy. I'll really pay off."

"That's nice," said the doctor guardedly.

"Nice? Just nice? Man, I'll give you a treasure you couldn't get any other way. *You* could never get," he amended. He looked up into the doctor's face brightly. "Nearly five solid years a-building and it's all yours. Me, I'll start a new one."

"What are you talking about?"

"My little black book. Got everything in it from pig to princess. Whoever you are, however you feel from time to time, there's a playmate in there for you. You could really use it, Freddy. You must have stored up quite a charge since you-know-what," he said, grinning at the recording machine. "Fix me up, I fix you up. Fair enough?"

The silence this time was unplanned. The doctor walked to the controls, dialed 550 and hit the master. The 80-cycle note died, the white noise took over, and then the 550-cycle sleep command. The doctor felt that gleaming grin leave the room like a pressure off his back.

He is a patient, the doctor thought at last, out of his hard-held numbness. He is a patient in a therapeutic environment as detached from the world as a non-Euclidean theorem. There is no Newell; there is only a patient. There is no Fred, only a doctor. There is no Osa, only episodes. Newell will be returned to the world because he has a personality and it has an optimum, because that is what I do here and that is what I am for.

He touched the annunciator control and said, "Miss Jarrell, I want you."

She opened the door almost immediately; she must have been waiting in the corridor. "Oh, doctor, I *am* sorry! I know I shouldn't do anything like that. It's just—well, before I knew it . . ."

"Don't apologize, Miss Jarrell. I mean it—don't. You may even have done some good. But I have to know exactly what influences were . . . no, don't explain," he said when she tried to speak. "Show me."

"Oh, I couldn't! It's so—*silly!*"

"Go on, Miss Jarrell. It isn't silly at all."

Flushing, she passed him with her eyes averted and went to the controls. She dialed a frequency and activated the master, and as the white noise roared out, she went to the foot of the bed, waiting. The audio faded, all but a low, steady thrum—200 cycles.

The patient opened his eyes. He *smiled*. It was a smile the like of which the doctor had never seen before, though he might have imagined one. Not, however, on the face of Richard A. Newell. There was nothing conceivable in Richard A. Newell to coexist with such an expression.

The patient glanced down and saw Miss Jarrell. Ecstatic recognition crossed his face. He grasped the covers and whipped them over his head, and lay stiff and still as a pencil.

"You . . .!" crooned Miss Jarrell, and the blanket was flung down away from the patient's head, and he gurgled with laughter. She snatched at his toes, and he bucked and chortled, and covered up again. "The bumble bee—"

she murmured, and he quivered, a paroxysm of delighted anticipation—"goes round the tree . . . and goes bzz . . . *bzzz* . . . BZZ!" and she snatched at his toes again.

He whipped the blanket away from his face and gave himself up to an explosion of merriment which was past vocalization—in fact, but for that soft and intense chuckle, he had made hardly a sound.

"You . . ."

The doctor watched and slowly felt a vacuum in the scene somehow, and a great tugging to fill it with understanding, and the understanding would not come until the word "ridiculous" slipped through his mind . . . and that was it: This should be ridiculous, a grown man reacting like a seven-month infant. What was extraordinary was that it was *not* ridiculous and that it was indeed a grown man, not a mere infantile segment.

It was a thing to be felt. There was a—a radiance in these bursts of candid merriment which, though certainly childlike, were not childish. It was a quality to be laughed with, not laughed at.

He glanced at the audio selector. Yes, this was the 200-cycle response that Miss Thomas had mentioned. "A personality—" He began to see what she had meant. He began, too, to be afraid.

He went to the wall rack where the technician's response-breakdown was clipped. It was a standard form, one column showing the frequencies arbitrarily assigned to age levels (700 cycles and the command suggestion: "You are eleven years old") and another column with the frequencies assigned to emotional states (800 cycles and "You are very angry;" 14 cycles, "You are afraid").

Once the patient was completely catalyzed, response states could readily be induced and their episodic material extracted—fear at age three, sexuality at fourteen, fear plus anger plus gratification at age six, or any other combination.

The 200-cycle area was blotchy with Miss Thomas's erasures, but otherwise blank.

The doctor inwardly shook himself and got a firm grip. He went to the bed and stood looking down at that sensitive, responsive face.

"Who are you?" he asked.

The patient looked at him, eyes bright, a glad, antici-

patory smile on his lips. The doctor sensed that the man
did not understand him, but that he was eager to; further,
that from the bottom of his heart the man was prepared
to be delighted when he did understand. It filled the doctor
with an almost tender anxiety, a protectiveness. This creature could not be disappointed—that would be inartistic
to the point of gross injustice.

"What's your name?" the doctor pursued.

The patient smiled at him and sat up. He looked into
the doctor's eyes with an almost unbearable attention and
a great waiting, ready to treasure whatever might come
next if only—if only he could identify it.

One thing's certain, mused the doctor: this was no infantile segment. Child, yes, but not quite child.

"Miss Jarrell."

"Yes, doctor."

"The initial, the middle initial on the chart. It's 'A'.
What does that stand for?"

After a moment, "Anson," she said.

To the patient, he said, "I'm going to call you Anson.
That will be your name." He put his hand on the patient's
chest. "Anson."

The man looked down at the hand and up, expectantly,
at the doctor.

The doctor said, touching his white coat, "Doctor.
Doctor." He pointed at Miss Jarrell. "Miss—"

"Hildy," said Miss Jarrell quickly.

The doctor could not help it; he grinned briefly. This
elicited a silent burst of glee from the patient, which was
shut off instantly, to be replaced by the anticipation, the
watchful and ready attentiveness. He burdened the doctor
with his waiting and the necessity to appreciate. Yet what
burden was it, really? This creature would appreciate the
back of a hand across the face or two choruses of the
Londonderry Air.

The doctor poised over the bed, waiting for an answer,
and it came:

The burden lay in the necessity not to please this entity,
but to do this thing properly, in ways which would never
have to be withdrawn later. *He trusts me*—there, in three
words, was the burden.

The doctor took the patient's hand and put the fingertips

close to his lips. "An-son," he said. Then he put the hand to the patient's own mouth, nodding encouragingly.

The patient obviously wanted to do it right, too—more, even, than the doctor. His lips trembled. Then, "An-son," he said.

Across the room, Miss Jarrell clapped her hands and laughed happily.

"That's right," smiled the doctor, pointing. "Anson. You're Anson." He touched his own chest. "Doc-tor." He pointed again. "Miss Hildy."

The man in the bed sat up slowly, his eyes on the doctor's face. "An-son. Anson." And then a light seemed to flood him. He hit his chest with his knuckles. "Anson!" he cried. He felt his own biceps, his face, and laughed.

"That's right," said the doctor.

"Doc . . . tor," said Anson, with difficulty. He looked wistful, almost distraught.

"That's okay. That's good. Doctor."

"Doc-tor." Anson turned brightly to Miss Jarrell and pointed. "Miss Hildy!" he sang triumphantly.

"Bless you," she said, saying it like a blessing.

While Anson grinned, the doctor stood for a moment grinning back like a fool and feeling frightened and scratching his head.

Then he went to work.

"Richard," he said sharply, and watched for a reaction. There was none, just the happy eagerness.

"Dick."

Nothing.

"Newell."

Nothing.

"Hold up your right hand. Close your eyes. Look out of the window. Touch your hair. Let me see your tongue."

Anson did none of these things.

The doctor wet his lips. "Osa."

Nothing.

He glanced at Miss Jarrell. "Anson," he said, and Anson increased his attention. It was startling; the doctor hadn't known he could. "Anson, listen." He pulled back his sleeve and showed his watch. "Watch. Watch." He held it close, then put it to Anson's ear.

Anson gurgled delightedly. "Tk tk," he mimicked. He cocked his head and listened carefully to the doctor repeating the word. Then, "Wats. Watts. *Watch,*" he said, and clapped his hands exactly as Miss Jarrell had done before.

"All right, Miss Jarrell. That's enough for now. Turn him off."

He heard her intake of breath and thought she was going to speak. When she did not, he faced her and smiled. "It's all right, Miss Jarrell. We'll take good care of him."

She looked for the sarcasm in his face, between his words, back in recall, anywhere, and did not find it. She laughed suddenly and heartily; he knew she was laughing at herself, spellbound as she had been, anxious for the shining something which hid in the 200-cycle area.

"I could use a little therapy myself, I guess," she said wonderingly.

"I would recommend it to you if you had reacted any other way."

She went to the door and opened it. "I like working here," she said, blushed, and went out.

The doctor's smile disappeared with the click of the latch. He glanced once at the patient, then moved blindly to the controls. He locked them and went back to his office.

Miss Thomas knocked. Getting no answer, she entered the doctor's office. "Oh, I beg your pardon, I thought you were still——"

The expression on his face halted her. She took the reports she carried and put them down on the desk. He did not move. She went to the cabinet, which slid open for her, and shook two white pills from a vial. She broke a beam with a practiced flick of the wrist. A paper cup dropped and filled with ice water. She took it to the doctor. "Here."

He said rapidly, "What? What? What?" and, seeking, looked the wrong way to find her voice. He turned again, saw her. "What?" and put his hand for a moment over his eyes, "Oh, Miss Thomas."

"Here," said the technician again.

"What is it?" He seemed to be trying to identify the cup, as if he had never seen one before.

Because she was kind, Miss Thomas took it another way. "Dexamyl."

"Thank you." He took them, swallowed water, and looked up at her. "Thank you," he said again. "I seem to be . . ."

"It's all right," said Miss Thomas firmly. "Everything's all right."

Some of his control returned and he chuckled a little. "Using my own therapy on me?"

"Everything *is* all right, far as I know," she said, in the grumpy tone under which she so often concealed herself. She folded her arms with an all but audible snap and glared out of the window.

The doctor glanced up at her rigid back and, in spite of himself, was amused. She was daring him to order her out, challenging him not to tell her what the trouble was. He recalled, then, that she was doubtlessly gnawed like the Spartan boy by the fox of curiosity she was hiding under her starch. *There's a personality in the 200-cycles area that won't dismantle . . . oh, you can do it, but . . . it's a pity, that's all,* he recalled.

He said, "It's one of those things of Prince's."

She was quiet for so long that she might not have heard him, and I'm damned, he thought, if I'm going to spell it out for her.

But she said, "I don't believe it," and, into his continued silence, "Morton Prince's alternate personality idea might be the only explanation for some cases, but it doesn't explain this one."

"It doesn't?"

"Two personalities in one mind—three or more sometimes. One of his case histories was of a woman who had five distinct egos. I'm not quarreling with the possibility, doctor."

Every time Miss Thomas surprised him, it was in a way that pleased him. He would, he thought, think that through some day.

"Then why quarrel with this one?" he asked.

Unmasked and unabashed, she sat down in the big chair. They sat for a time in a companionable, cerebral quiet.

Then she said, "Prince's case histories show a lot of variation. I mean one ego will be refined, educated, another rough and stupid. Sometimes the prime was aware of the others, sometimes not; sometimes they hated each other. But there was this denominator: If the condition existed at all, it existed because the alternate ego *could* communicate and did. Had to."

THE STARS ARE THE STYX

"Morton Prince wasn't equipped for segmentation under tertiary hypnosis."

"I think that's beside the point," Miss Thomas said flatly. "I'll say it again: Prince's alternate egos *had* to emerge. I think that's the key. If an ego can't communicate and won't emerge unless you drag it out by the scruff of the neck, I don't think it deserves to be called an ego."

"You can say that and yet you've seen Ans—the alternate?"

"Anson. Hildy Jarrell told me about the christening. Yes, I can say that."

He looked at her levelly and she dropped her eyes. He remembered again their encounter in the corridor in front of Newell's door. *Don't blame Hildy Jarrell—that's exactly what I did myself.*

"Miss Thomas, why are you trying to herd me away from this case?"

"Doctor!"

He closed his eyes and said, "You find a segment that you can't break. It's a particularly—well, let's say that whatever it is, you like it." He paused and, exactly in time, said, "Don't interrupt me. You know very well that the rock bottom of my practice is that personality is inviolate. You know that if this is a genuine case of alternate ego, I wouldn't touch it—I couldn't, because the man has only one body, and to normalize him, I'd have to destroy one ego or the other.

"Now you knew perfectly well that I'd discover the alternate. So the first thing you do is call my attention to it, and the next thing you do is give me an argument about it, knowing I'd disagree with you, knowing that if there was any doubt in my mind, it would disappear in the argument."

"Why on earth would I do a thing like that?" she challenged.

"I told you—so I'd get off the case—reset the P.T. and discharge him."

"Damn it," said Miss Thomas bitterly.

"That's the trouble with knowing too much about a colleague's thought processes," he said into midair. "You can't manipulate somebody who understands you."

"Which one of us do you mean?" she demanded.

"I really don't know. Now are you going to tell me why you tried this, or shall I tell you?"

"I'll tell you," said Miss Thomas. "You're tired. I don't want anything to happen to that Anson. As soon as I found him, I knew exactly what would happen if you went ahead with Newell's therapy. Anson would be the intruder. I don't care how—how beautiful an intruder he might be, he could only show up as an aberration, something extraneous. You'd pack him down to pill size, and bury him so deep in a new-model Newell that he'd never see daylight again. I don't know how much consciousness he has, but I do know I couldn't bear to have him buried alive.

"And supposing you committed therapy on Anson alone, brought him up like a shiny young Billy Budd and buried that heel Newell—if you'll pardon the unprofessional term, doctor—down inside him somewhere? You think Anson would be able to defend himself? You think he could take a lane in the big rat race? This world is no place for cherubim.

"So there isn't a choice. I don't know what Anson shares with Newell and I never will. I do know that however Anson has existed so far, it hasn't spoiled him, and the only chance he has to go on being what he is is to be left alone."

"Quod erat demonstrandum," said the doctor, spreading his hands. "Very good. Now you know why I've never treated alternate ego cases. And perhaps you also know how useless your little machination was."

"I had to be sure, that's all. Well, I'm glad. I'm sorry."

He smiled briefly. "I follow that." He watched her get up, her face softened by content and her admiration of him unconcealed.

She bent an uncharacteristically warm gaze on him and moved toward the door. She looked back once on the way, and once there, she stopped and turned to face him. "Something's the matter."

There were, he knew, other ways to handle this, but at the moment he had to hurt something. There were several ways to do the hurt, too, and he chose the worst one, saying nothing.

Miss Thomas became Miss Thomas again, her eyes like one-way mirrors and her stance like a soldier. She looked out of herself at him and said, "You're going on with the therapy."

He did not deny it.

"Are you going to tell me which one gets it?"

"Depends on what you mean by 'gets it,' " he said with grim jocularity.

She treated the bad joke as it deserved to be treated and simply waited for it to go away.

He said, "Both."

She repeated the word in exactly his inflection, as though she could understand it better if it were as near as her own lips. Then she shook her head impatiently. "You can apply just so much therapy and then there's a choice to make."

"There's this choice to make," he said, in a constricted tone that hurt his throat. "Newell lives in a society he isn't fit for. He's married to a woman he doesn't deserve. If it is in my power to make him more fit and more deserving, what is the ethical choice?"

Miss Thomas moved close to the desk. "You implied that you'd turned down cases like this before. You sent them back into society, untreated."

"Once they sent lepers back untreated," he snapped. "Therapy has to start somewhere, with someone."

"Start it on rats first."

I am, he said, fortunately to himself. He considered her remark further and decided not to answer it, knowing how deeply she must regret saying it.

She said, "Hildy Jarrell will quit when she finds this out."

"She will not quit," said the doctor immediately and positively.

"And as for me—"

"Yes?"

Their gazes locked like two steel rods placed tip to tip, pressing, pressing, knowing that some slight wavering, some side drift, must come and must make a break and a collision.

But instead, she broke. She closed her eyes against tears and clasped her hands. "Please," she whispered, "do you have to go through with this? Why? Why?"

Oh, God, he thought, I hate this. "I can't discuss it." That, he thought painfully, is altogether the truth.

She said heavily, "I don't think you should." He knew it was her last word.

"It is a psychological decision, Miss Thomas, and not a technological one." He knew it was unfair to fall back on rank and specialty when he no longer had an argument he could use. But this had to stop.

She nodded. "Yes, doctor." She went out, closing the door too quietly. He thought, What do you have to be to a person so you can run after someone crying, Come back! Come back! Don't hate me! I'm in trouble and I hurt!

It took Miss Jarrell about forty minutes to get to the office. The doctor had figured it at about thirty-five. He was quite ready for her.

She knocked with one hand and turned the knob with the other and flew in like an angry bee. Her face was flushed and there was a little pale tension line parenthesizing each nostril. "Doctor—"

"Ah, Miss Jarrell," he said with a huge jovlality. "I was just about to call you. I need your help for a special project."

"Well, I'm sorry about *that*," she began. Her eyes were wide and aflame, and the rims were slightly pink. He wished he could magic a few minims of azacyclonol into her bloodstream; she could use it. "I've come to—"

"The Newell case—"

"Yes, the Newell case. I don't think—"

He had almost to shout this time. "And *I* think you're just the one for the job. I want that 200-cycle entity—you know, Anson—I want him educated."

"Well, I think it's just—*what?*" And as the angry syllable ricocheted around the office, she stared at him and asked timidly, "I beg your pardon?"

"I'd like to relieve you of your other duties and put you with Anson full time. Would you like that?"

"Would I like . . . what will I do?"

"I want to communicate with him. He needs a vocabulary and he needs elementary instruction. He probably doesn't know how to hold a fork or blow his nose. I think you can do a good job of teaching him."

"Well, I—why I'd love to!"

"Good. Good," he said like a department store Santa Claus. "Just a few details. I'll want every minute on sound film, from white noise to white noise, and I'll want to review the film every day. And, of course, I'd have to ask you not to discuss this with anyone, on or off the staff. It's a unique case and a new therapy, and a lot depends on it. On you."

"Oh, you can depend on me, doctor!"

He nodded agreement. "We'll start tomorrow morning. I'll have the first word lists and other instructions ready for you by then. Meanwhile, I've got some research to do. Contact the Medical Information Service in Washington and have them key in Prince, Morton, and Personality, Multiple, on their Big Brain. I want abstracts of everything that has been published in the last fifty years on the subject. No duplicates. An index. Better order microfilm and send it by telefax, AA priority."

"Yes, doctor," said Miss Jarrell eagerly. "Foreign publications too?"

"Everything any researcher has done. And put a Confidential on the order as well as the delivery."

"*Really* secret."

"Really." He concealed the smile which struggled to show itself; in his mind, he had seen the brief image of a little girl hiding jelly beans. "And get me the nurses' duty list. I have some juggling to do."

"Very well, doctor. Is that all?"

"All for now."

She nearly skipped to the door. He saw a flash of white as she opened it; Miss Thomas was standing in the outer office. He could not have been more pleased if she had been there by his explicit orders, for Miss Jarrell said, as she went out, "And thank you, doctor—thank you *very* much."

Chew on that, Thomas, he thought, feeling his own small vindictiveness and permitting himself to enjoy it for once.

And: Why am I jumping on Thomas?

Well, because I have to jump on somebody once in a while and she can take it.

Why don't I tell her everything? She has a good head. Might have some really good ideas. Why not?

Why not? he asked again into a joyless voice. Because I could be wrong. I could be so wrong. That's why not.

The research began, and the long night work. In addition to the vast amount of collateral reading—there was much more material published on the subject of multiple personality than he had realized—he had each day's film to analyze, notes to make, abstracts to prepare for computer coding, and then, after prolonged thought, the next day's lessons to outline.

The rest of the clinic refused to stop and wait for this

job to be done, and he had an additional weight of consciousness as he concealed his impatience with everything else but the Newell case. He was so constituted that such a weight made him over-meticulous in the very things he wished to avoid, so that his ordinary work took more time rather than less.

As for the research, much of it was theory and argumentation; the subject, like reincarnation, seemed to attract zealots of the most positive and verbose varieties, both pro and con. Winnowing through the material, he isolated two papers of extreme interest to him. One was a theory, one an interim report on a series of experiments which had never been completed due to the death of the researcher.

The theory, advanced by one Weisbaden, was based on a search through just such material as this. Indeed, Weisbaden seemed to have been the only man besides himself who had never asked the Medical Information Service for this complete package.

From it, he had abstracted statistics, weighted then to suit his theory, and come up with the surprising opinion that multiple personality was a twinning phenomenon, and that if a method were found for diagnosing all such cases, a correspondence would be found between the incidence of multiple births and the incidence of multiple personalities. So many births per thousand are twins, so many per hundred thousand are triplets, and the odds with quads and quints are in the millions.

So, too, said Weisbaden, would be the statistical expectation for the multiple personality phenomenon, once such cases stopped being diagnosed as schizoids and other aberrants.

Weisbaden had not been a medical man—he was some sort of actuary—but his inference was fascinating. How many twins and triplets walked the Earth in single bodies, without any organic indication that they were not single entities? How many were getting treatment for conditions they did not have; how many Siamese twins were being penalized because they would not walk like other quadrupeds; how many separate entities were being forced to spend their lives in lockstep?

Some day, thought the doctor—as so many doctors have thought before—some day, when we can get closer to the genetic biologists, when psychology becomes a true science, when someone devises a cross-reference system between the disciplines which really works . . . and some day, when I have the time—well, maybe I could test this ingenious guess. But it's only a guess, based on neither observation nor experiment. Intriguing though—if only it could be tested.

The other paper was of practical value. A certain Julius Marx—again not a medical man, but a design engineer with, apparently, hobbies—had built an electro-encephalograph for two (would anyone ever write a popular song about *that?*) which graphed each of the patients through a series of stimuli, and at the same time drew a third graph, a resultant.

Marx was after a means of determining brain wave types, rather than individual specimens, and had done circuitry on machines which would handle up to eight people at once. In a footnote, with dry humor, he had qualified his paper for this particular category: "Perhaps one day the improbable theories of Dr. Prince might approach impossibility through the use of such a device upon a case of multiple personality."

Immediately on reading this, the doctor ordered EEGs on both Anson and Newell, and when he had both before him, he wished fervently that Julius Marx had been there with him; he suspected that the man enjoyed a good laugh, even on himself.

The graphs were as different as such graphs can possibly be.

The confirmation of his diagnosis was spectacular, and he left a note for Miss Jarrell to track down every multiple personality case he had rejected for the past eight years and see what could be done about some further tests. What would come after the tests, he did not know—yet.

The other valuable nudge he got from the Marx paper was the idea of a resultant between two dissimilar electro-encephalograms. He made one from the Newell-Anson EEGs—without the use of anything as Goldbergian as Marx's complicated device, but with a simple computer coupling. He kept it in his top desk drawer, and every few days he would draw it out and he would wonder . . .

Therapy for Anson wasn't therapy. Back at the very beginning, Miss Thomas had said that his was a personality that wouldn't dismantle; she had been quite right. You can't

get episodic material from an entity which has had no sub-
jective awareness, no experience, which has no name, no
sense of identity, no motility, no recall.

There were many parts to that strange radiance of Anson's and they were all in the eye of the beholder, who
protected Anson because he was defenseless, who was con-
tinually amazed at his unself-consciousness as if it were an
attribute rather than a lack. His discovery of the details
of self and surroundings was a never-ending delight to
watch, because he himself was delighted and had never
known the cruel penalties we impose on expressed delight,
nor the masking idioms we use instead: *Not a bad sunset
there. Yeah. Real nice.*

"He's good," Miss Jarrell said to the doctor once. "He's
only good—nothing else."

Therapy for Newell was, however, therapy, and not re-
warding. The properly dismantled and segmented patient
is relatiively simple to handle.

Key in anger (1200 cycles) and demand "How old are
you?" Since anger does not exist unsupported, an episode
must emerge; the anger has an object, which existed at a
time and place; and there's your episode. "I'm six," says
your patient. Key in the "You are six years old" note for
reinforcement and you're all ready for significant recall. Or
start with the age index: "You are twelve years old." When
that is established, demand, "How do you feel?" and if
there is significant material in the twelfth year, it will
emerge. If it is fear, add the "fear" note and ask "Where
are you?" and you'll have the whole story.

But not in Newell's case. There was, of course, plenty of
conflict material, but somehow the conflicts seemed secondary; they were effects rather than causes. By far the largest
category of traumas is the unjustified attack—a severe beating, a disease, a rejection. It is traumatic because, from the
patient's point of view, it is unjustified. In Newell's case,
there was plenty of suffering, plenty of defeat; yet in every
single episode, he had earned it. So he was without guilt.
His inner conviction was that his every cruelty was justified.

The doctor had an increasing sense that Newell had lived
all his life in a books-balanced, debts-paid condition. His
episodes had no continuity, one to the other. It was as if
each episode occurred at right angles to the line of his existence; once encountered, it was past, like a mathematical

point. The episodes were easy to locate, impossible to relate to one another and to the final product.

The doctor tried hard to treat Anson and Newell in his mind as discreet, totally unconnected individuals, but Miss Jarrell's sentimental remark kept echoing in his mind: "He's good; he's only good—nothing else," and generating an obverse to apply to Newell: *He's evil, he's only evil—nothing else.*

This infuriated him. How nice, how very nice, he told himself sarcastically, the spirits of good and evil to be jonied together to make a whole man, and how tidily everything fits; black is totally black and white is white, and together the twain shall make gray. He found himself telling himself that it wasn't as simple as that, and things did not work out according to moral evaluations which were more arbitrary even than his assigned audio.

It was about this time that he began to doubt the rightness of his decision, the worth of his therapy, the possibility of the results he wanted, and himself. And he had no one to advise him. He told that to Miss Thomas.

It was easy to do and it surprised both of them. He had called her in to arrange a daily EEG on both facets of the Newell case and explain about the resultant, which he also wanted daily. She said yes, doctor, and very well, doctor, and right away, doctor, and a number of other absolutely correct things. But she didn't say why, doctor? or that's good, doctor, and suddenly he couldn't stand it.

He said, "Miss Thomas, we've got to bury the hatchet right now. I could be wrong about this case, and if I am, it's going to be bad. Worse than bad. That's not what bothers me," he added quickly, afraid she might interrupt, knowing that this must spill over or never emerge again. "I've been through bad things before and I can handle that part of it."

Then it came out, simple and astonishing to them both: "But I'm all alone with it, Tommie."

He had never called her that before, not even to himself, and he was overwhelmed with wonderment at where it might have come from.

Miss Thomas said, "No, you're not," gruffly.

"Well, hell," said the doctor, and then got all his control back. He dropped a film cartridge into the viewer and brought out his notes. Using them as index, he sat with his hand on the control, spinning past the more pedestrian material and showing her the highlights. He presented no interpretations while she watched and listened.

She heard Newell snarling, "You better watch what you're doing," and Anson pointing about the room, singing, "Floor, flower, book, bed, bubble. Window, wheel, wiggle, wonderful." (He had not known at that stage what a wonderful was, but Miss Jarrell said it almost every hour on the hour.) She saw Newell in recall, aged eleven, face contorted, raging at his fifth-grade teacher, "I'll bomb ya, y'ole bitch!" and at thirteen, coolly pleased at something best unmentioned concerning a kitten and a centrifuge.

She saw Anson standing in the middle of the room, left elbow in right hand, left thumb pressed to the point of his chin, a stance affected by the doctor when in perplexity: "When I know everything there is to know," Anson had said soberly, "there'll be two Doctor Freds."

At this, Miss Thomas grunted and said, "You wouldn't want a higher compliment than that from anybody, anytime." The doctor shushed her, but kindly. The first time he had seen that sequence, it made his eyes sting. It still did. He said nothing.

She saw it all, right up to yesterday's viewing, with Newell in a thousand pieces from what appeared to be a separate jigsaw puzzle for each piece, and Anson a bright wonder, learning to read now, marveling at everything because everything was new—teaspoons and music and mountains, the Solar System and sandwiches and the smell of vanilla.

And as he watched, doors opened in the doctor's mind. They did not open wide, but enough for him to know that they were there and in which walls. How to describe the indescribable *feeling* of expertness?

It is said that a good truck driver has nerve endings which extend to the bumper and tail light, tire tread to overhead. The virtuoso pianist does not will each separate spread and crook of each finger; he wills the notes and they appear.

The doctor had steered this course of impossible choices by such willing and such orientation; and again he felt it, the urge that this way is right now, and there is the thing to do next. The miracle to him was not the feeling, but that it had come back to him while he watched the films

and heard the tapes with Miss Thomas, who had said nothing, given no evaluation or advice. They were the same
films he had studied, run in the same sequence. The difference was only in not being alone any more.

"Where are you going?" Miss Thomas asked him.

From the coat closet, he said, "File that material and
lock it up, will you, Miss Thomas? I'll call you as soon as
I return." He went to the door and smiled back at her. It
hurt his face. "Thanks."

Miss Thomas opened her mouth to speak, but did not.
She raised her right hand in a sort of salute and turned
around to put the files away.

The doctor called from a booth near the Newell apartment. "Did I wake you, Osa? I'm sorry. Sometimes I don't
know how late it gets."

"Who . . . Fred? Is that you, Fred?"

"Are you up to some painful conversation?"

Alarmed, she cried, "Is something the matter? Is Dick—"

He mentally kicked himself for his clumsiness. What
other interpretation could she have put on such a remark?
"He's okay. I'm sorry. I guess I'm not good at the light
banter . . . Can I see you?"

She paused for a long moment. He could hear her breathing. "I'll come out. Where are you?"

He told her.

She said, "There's a café just around the corner, to your
left. Give me ten minutes."

He put up the phone and went to the corner. It was on a
dingy street which seemed to be in hiding. On the street,
the café hid. Inside the café, booths hid. In one of the
booths, the doctor sat and was hidden. It was all he could
do to keep himself from assuming a fetal posture.

A waiter came. He ordered collinses, made with light
rum. He slumped then, with his forearms on the table and
his chin on them, and watched bubbles rise in the drinks
and collect on the underside of the shaved ice, until the
glasses frosted too much for him to see. Then he closed his
eyes and attempted to suspend thought, but he heard her
footsteps and sprang up.

"Here I am," he said in a seal-like bark far louder than
he had intended.

She sat opposite him. "Rum collins," she said, and only
then did he remember that it had always been the drink

they shared, when they had shared things. He demanded of himself, Now why did I have to do that? and answered, You know perfectly well why.

"Is he really all right?" she asked him.

"Yes, Osa. So far."

"I'm sorry." She turned her glass around, but did not lift it. "I mean maybe you don't want to talk about Dick."

"You're very thoughtful," he said, and wondered why it had never occurred to him to see her just for himself. "But you're wrong. I did want to talk about him."

"Well . . . if you like, Fred. What, especially?"

He laughed. "I don't know. Isn't that silly?"

He sipped his drink. He was aware that she did the same. They never used to say "cheers" or "skoal" or anything else, but they always took that first sip together.

He said, "I need something that segmentation or hypnosis or narcosynthesis just won't give me. I need to flesh out a skeleton. No, it's more refined than that. I need tints for a charcoal portrait." He lifted his hands and put them down again. "I don't know what I need. I'll tell you when I get it."

"Well, of course I'll help if I can," she said uncertainly.

"All right. Just talk, then. Try to forget who I am."

He met her eyes and the question there, and elaborated, "Forget I'm his therapist, Osa. I'm an interested stranger who has never seen him, and you're telling me 'bout him."

"Engineering degree, and where he comes from, and how many sisters?"

"No," he said, "but keep that up. You're bound to stumble across what I want that way."

"Well, he's . . . he's been sick. I think I'd tell a stranger that."

"Good! What do you mean, sick?"

She glanced quickly at him and he could follow the thought behind it: *Why don't you tell* ME *how sick he is?* And then, *But you really want to play this game of the interested stranger. All right.*

She stopped looking at him and said, "Sick. He can't be steered by anything but his own—pressures and they—they aren't the pressures he should have. Not for this world."

"Why do you suppose that is?"

"He just doesn't seem to care. No," she denied forcefully, "I don't mean that, not at all. It's more like—I think he would care if he—if he was allowed to, and he isn't allowed to." She got his eyes again. "This is very hard to do, Fred."

"I know and I'm sorry. But do go on; you're doing fine. What do you mean, he isn't allowed to care about the world and the way it wags? Who won't allow him?"

"It isn't a who; it's a—I don't know. You'd have a term for it. I'd call it a monster on his back, something that drives him to do things, be something he really isn't."

"We strangers don't have any terms for anything," he reminded her gently.

"That's a little refreshing," she said with a wan half-smile. "I live . . . mystified . . . people. They make me feel like one of the crowd. You know who's lucky?" she asked, her voice suddenly wild and strained and, by its tone, changing the subject. "Psychotics are lucky. The nuts, the real buggy ones. (I talk like this to layman strangers.) The ones who see butterflies all the time, the ones who think the president is after them."

"Lucky!" he exploded.

"Yes, lucky. They have a name for the beast that's chewing on them. Sometimes they can see it themselves."

"I don't quite—"

"I mean this," she said excitedly. "If I see grizzly bears under every lamp post, I'm *seeing* something. It has a name, a shape; I could draw a picture of it. If I do something irrational, the way some psychos do—run a nonexistent railroad or shoot invisible pheasant with an invisible gun, I'm *doing* something. I can describe it and say how it feels and write letters about it. See, these are all *things* plaguing the insane. Labels, handles. Things that *you* can hold up to reality to demonstrate that they don't coincide with it."

"And that's lucky?"

She nodded miserably. "A mere neurotic—Dick, for example—hasn't a *thing* he can name. He acts in ways we call irrational, and has a sense of values nobody can understand, and does things in a way that seems consistent to him but not to anyone else. It's as if there were a grizzly bear, after all, but we'd never heard of grizzly bears—what they are, what they want, how they act. He's driven by some monster without a name, something that no one can see and that even he is not aware of. That's what I mean."

"Ah."

They sat for minutes, silent and careful.

Then, "Osa—"

"Yes, Fred."

"Why do you love him?"

She looked at him. "You really meant it when you said this would be a painful conversation."

"Never mind that. Just tell me."

"I don't think it's a thing you can tell."

"Then try this: What is it you love in him?"

She made a helpless gesture. "Him."

He sat without responding until he knew she felt his dissatisfaction with the answer.

She frowned and then closed her eyes. "I couldn't make you understand, Fred. To understand you'd have to be two things: a woman, and—Osa." Still he sat silent. Twice she looked up to his face and away, and at last yielded.

She said in a low voice, "It's a . . . tenderness you wouldn't believe, no matter how well you know him. It's a gentle, loving something that no one ever born ever had before and never will again. It's . . . I hate this, Fred!"

"Go on, for heaven's sake! This is exactly what I'm looking for."

"It is? Well, then . . . But I hate talking like this to you. It doesn't seem right."

"Go on!"

She said, almost in a whisper, "Life is plain hell sometimes. He's gone and I don't know where, and he comes back and it's just awful. Sometimes he acts as if he were alone in the place—he doesn't see me, doesn't answer. Or maybe he'll be the other way, after me every second, teasing and prodding and twisting every word until I don't know what I said or what I should say next, or who I am, or . . . anything, and he won't leave me alone, not to eat or to sleep or to go out. And then he—"

She stopped and the doctor waited, and this time realized that waiting would not be enough. "Don't stop," he said.

She shook her head.

"Please. It's impor—"

"I would, Fred," she burst out frantically. "I'm not refusing to. I *can't,* that's all. The words won't—"

"Don't try to tell me what it is, then," he suggested. "Just say what happens and how it makes you feel. You can do that."

"I suppose so," she said, after considering it.

Osa took a deep breath, almost a sigh, and closed her eyes again.

"It will be hell," she said, "and then I'll look at him and he . . . and he . . . well, it's *there*, that's all. Not a word, not a sign sometimes, but the room is full of it. It's . . . it's something to love, yes, it's that, but nobody can just love something, one-way, forever. So it's a loving thing, too, from him to me. It suddenly arrives and everything else he is doing, the cruelty, the ignoring, whatever might be happening just then, it all stops and there's nothing else but the—whatever it is."

She wet her lips. "It can happen any time; there's never a sign or a warning. It can happen now, and again a minute from now, or not for months. It can last most a day or flash by like a bird. Sometimes he goes on talking to me while it happens; sometimes what he actually says is just nothing, small-talk. Sometimes he just stands looking at me, without saying anything. Sometimes he—I'm sorry, Fred— he makes love to me then and that's . . . Oh, dear God, that's . . ."

"Here's my handkerchief."

"Thank you. He—does that other times, too, when there's nothing loving about it. This—this thing-to-love, it—it seems to have nothing to do with anything else, no pattern. It happens and it's what I wait for and what I look back on; it's all I have and all I want."

When he was quite sure she had no more to say, he hazarded, "It's as if some other—some other personality suddenly took over."

He was quite unprepared for her reaction. She literally shouted, *"No!"* and was startled herself.

She recoiled and glanced guiltily around the café. "I don't know why," she said, sounding frightened, "but that was just—just *awful*, what you said. Fred, if you can give any slightest credence to the idea of feminine intuition, you'll get that idea right out of your head. I couldn't begin to tell you why, but it just isn't so. What loves me that way may be part of Dick; but it's Dick, not anybody or anything else. I *know* that's so, that's all. I know it."

Her gaze was so intense that it all but made him wince. He could see her trying and trying to find words, rejecting and trying again.

At last, "The only way I can say it that makes any sense to me is that Dick could be such a—a louse so much of the time and still walk a straight line without something just as extreme in the other direction. It's—it's a great pity for the rest of the world that he only shows that side to me, but there it is."

"Does he show it only to you?" He touched her hand and released it. "I'm sorry, but I must ask that."

She smiled and a kind of pride shone from her face. "Only to me. I suppose that's intuition again, but it's as certain as Sunday." The pride disappeared and was replaced by a patient agony. "I don't delude myself, Fred— he has other women; plenty of them. But that particular something is for me. It isn't something I wonder about. I just—know."

He sat back wearily.

She asked, "Is all this what you wanted?"

He gave her a quick, hurt glance and saw, to his horror, her eyes filling with tears.

"It's what I asked for," he said in a flat voice.

"I see the difference." She used his handkerchief. "May I have this?"

"You can have—" But he stopped himself. "Sure." He got up. "No," he said, and took the damp handkerchief out of her hand. "I'll have something better for you."

"Fred," she said, distressed, "I—"

"I'm going, forgive me and all that," he said, far more angrily than he had thought he would. But polite talk and farewells were much more than he could stand. "The layman stranger has to have a long interview with a professional acquaintance. I don't think I'd better see you again, Osa."

"All right, Fred," she said to his back.

He had hurt her, he knew, but he knew also that his stature in her cosmos could overshadow the hurt and a hundred more like it. He luxuriated in the privilege and stamped out, throwing a bill to the waiter on the way.

He drove back and plodded up the ramp to the clinic. For some obscure reason, the inscription over the door caught his attention. He had passed it hundreds of times without a glance; he had ordered it put there and he was satisfied with it, and why should it matter now? But it did. What was it that Newell had said about it? *Some saw about the sanctity of personality.* A very perceptive remark, thought the doctor, considering that Newell hadn't read it:

ONLY MAN CAN FATHOM MAN

It was from Robert Lindner and was the doctor's answer to the inevitable charges of "push-button therapy." But he wondered now if the word "Man" was really inclusive enough.

He shook off the conjecture and let himself into the building.

Light gleamed from the translucent door of his office at the far end of the corridor. He walked down the slick flooring toward it, listening to his heels and not thinking otherwise, his mind as purposively relaxed as a fighter's body between rounds. He opened the door.

"What are you doing?"

"Waiting," said Miss Thomas.

"Why?"

"Just in case."

Without answering, he went to the closet and hung up his coat. Back at his desk, he sat down and straightened his tired spine until it crackled. Then he looked at Miss Thomas in the big chair. She put her feet under her and he understood that she was ready to leave if he wished her to.

He said, "Hypothesis: Newell and Anson are discreet personalities."

While he spoke, he noticed Miss Thomas's feet move outward a little and then cross at the ankles. His inner thought was, Of all the things I like about this woman, the best is the amount of conversation I have with her without talking.

"And we have plenty of data to back that up," he continued. "The EEGs alone prove it. Anson is Anson and Newell is Newell, and to prove it, we've crystallized them for anyone to see. We've done such a job on them that we know exactly what Anson is like without Newell. We've built him up that way, with that in mind. We haven't done quite the same with Newell, but we might as well have. I mean we've investigated Newell as if Anson did not exist within him. What it amounts to is this: In order to demonstrate a specimen of multiple personality, we've separated and isolated the components.

"Then we go into a flat spin because neither segment looks like a real human being . . . Miss Thomas?"

"Yes?"

"Do you mind the way I keep on saying 'we'?"

She smiled and shook her head. "Not at the moment."

"Further," he said, answering her smile but relentlessly pursuing his summation, "we've taken our two personalities and treated each like a potentially salvable patient—one neurotic, one retarded. We've operated under the assumption that each contained his own disorder and could be treated by separate therapies."

"We've been wrong?"

"*I* certainly have," said the doctor. He slapped the file cabinet at his left. "In here, there's a very interesting paper by one Weisbaden, who theorizes that multiple personalities are actually twins, identical twins born of the same egg-cell and developing within one body. One step, as it were, into the microcosm from *foetus in foetu.*"

"I've read about that," said Miss Thomas. "One twin born enclosed in the body of another."

"But not just partly—altogether enclosed. Whether or not Weisbaden's right, it's worth using as a test hypothesis. That's what I've been doing, among other things, and I've had my nose stuck so far into it that I wasn't able to see a very important corresponding part of the analogy: namely, that twinning itself is an anomaly, and any deviation in a sibling of multiple origin is teratological."

"My," said Miss Thomas in mock admiration.

The doctor smiled. "I should have said 'monstrous,' *but* why drag in superstitions? This thing is bad enough already. Anyway, if we're to carry our twinning idea as an analogy, we have got to include the very likely possibility that our multiple personalities are as abnormal as Siamese twins or any other monstrosity—I *hate* to use that word!"

"I'm not horrified," said Miss Thomas. "Abnormal in what way?"

"Well, in the crudest possible terms, what would you say was the abnormality suffered by one Siamese twin?"

"The other Siamese twin."

"Mmm. And by the same analogy, what's the name of Newell's disorder?"

"My goodness!" gasped Miss Thomas. "We better not tell Hildy Jarrell."

"That isn't the only thing we'll have to keep from her—for a while, at least," said the doctor. "Listen: did you run my notes on Newell?"

"All of them."

"You remember the remark she made that bothered me, about Anson's being only and altogether good, and the trouble I had with the implication that Newell was only and altogether bad?"

"I remember it."

"It's a piece of childishness that annoys me whenever I find it and I was damned annoyed to be thinking at all along those lines. The one reason for its being in the notes at all is that I had to decant it somewhere. Well, I've been euchred, Miss Thomas. Because Anson appeared in our midst shining and unsullied, I've leaned over backward trying to keep away from him the corruptions of anger, fear, greed, concupiscence and all the other hobbies of real mankind. By the same token, it never occurred to me to analyze what kindness, generosity, sympathy or empathy might be lurking in Newell. Why bother in such a—what was the term you used?"

"Heel," said Miss Thomas without hesitation.

"Heel. So what we have to do first is to give each of these—uh—people the privilege of entirety. If they are monsters, then let us at least permit them to be whole monsters."

"You don't mean you'll—"

"We," he corrected, smiling.

She said, through her answering smile, "You don't mean we'll take poor Anson and—"

He nodded.

"Offhand, I don't see how you're going to do it, Doctor. Anson has no fear. He'd laugh as he walked into a lion's cage or a high-tension line. And I can't imagine how you'd make him angry. You of all people. He—he loves you. As for . . . oh, dear. This is awful."

"Extremes are awful," he agreed. "We'll have to get pretty basic, but we can do it. Hence, I suggeste Miss Jarrell be sent to Kalamazoo for a new stove or some such."

"And then what?"

"It is standard practice to acquaint a patient with the name and nature of his disorder. In our field, we don't tell him, we show him, and when he absorbs the information, we call it insight. Anson, meet Newell. Newell, meet Anson."

"I do hope they'll be friends," said Miss Thomas unhappily.

In a darkness within a darkness in the dark, Anson slept his new kind of sleep, wherein he now had dreams. And then there was his own music, the deep sound which lit the darkness and pierced the dark envelopes, one within the other; and now he could emerge to the light and laughter and the heady mysteries of life and communication with Miss Hildy and Doctor Fred, and the wonder on wonder of perception. Gladly he flung himself back to life to—

But this wasn't the same. He was here, in the bed, but it wasn't the same at all. There was no rim of light around the ceiling, no bars of gold pouring in a sunlit window; this was the same, but not the same—it was dark. He blinked his eyes so hard, he made little colored lights, but they were inside his eyes and did not count.

There was noise, unheard-of, unbearable noise in the form of a cymbal-crash right by his head in the dark. He recoiled from it and tried to bounce up and run, and found he could not move. His arms were bound to his sides, his legs to the bed, by some wide formless something which held him trapped. He fought against it, crying, and then the bed dropped away underneath him and stopped with a crash, and rose and dropped again. There was another noise—not a noise, though it struck at him like one: this was a photo-flash, though he could not know it.

Blinded and sick, he lay in terror, waiting for terror again.

He heard a voice say softly, "Turn down the gain," and his music, his note, the pervasive background to all his consciousness, began to weaken. He strained toward it and it receded from him. Thumpings and shufflings from somewhere in the dark threatened to hide it away from him altogether. He felt, without words, that the note was his life and that he was losing it. For the first time in his conscious life, he became consciously afraid of dying.

He screamed, and screamed again, and then there was a blackness blacker than the dark and it all ceased.

"He's fainted. Lights, please. Turn off that note. Give him 550 and we'll see if he can sleep normally. God, I hope we didn't go too far."

They stood watching the patient. They were panting with tension.

"Help me with this," said the doctor. Together, he and Miss Thomas unbuckled the restraining sheet. They cleared away the flash-gun, the cymbals, and readjusted the bed-raising control to its normal slow operation.

"He's all right, physically anyway," said the doctor after a swift examination. "I told you it would work if we got basic enough. He wouldn't fear a lion because he doesn't know what a lion is. But restraint and sudden noise and falling—he doesn't have to know what they are. Okay, button him up again."

"What? You're not going to—"

"Come on, button him up," he said brusquely.

She frowned, but she helped him replace the restraining sheet. "I still think—" she began, and earned a "Sh!"

He set up the 200-cycle note again at its usual amplitude and they waited. There was a lag in apparent consciousness this time. The doctor realized that the patient was awake, but apparently afraid to open his eyes.

"Anson . . ."

Anson began to cry weakly.

"What's the matter, Anson?"

"D-doctor Fred, Doctor Fred . . . the big noise, and then I couldn't move and all the black and white smash lights." He wept again.

The doctor said nothing. He simply waited. Anson's sobs stopped abruptly and he tried to move. He gasped loudly and tried again.

"Doctor Fred!" he cried in panic.

Still the doctor said nothing.

Anson rolled his head wildly, fell back, tried again. "Make it so I can get up," Anson called piteously.

"No," said the doctor flatly.

"Make so I—"

"No."

Piercingly, Anson shrieked. He surged upward so powerfully that for a second the doctor was afraid for the fastenings on the restraining sheet. But they held.

For nearly ten minutes, Anson fought the sheet, screaming and drooling. Fright turned to fury, and fury to an intense, witless battle. It was a childish tantrum magnified by the strength and staying power of an adult.

At about the second minute, the doctor keyed in a supplementary frequency, a shrill 10,500 cycles which had been blank on the index. Whenever Anson paused for breath, the doctor intoned, "You are angry. You are angry." Grimly he watched until, a matter of seconds before the patient had to break, he released him to sleep.

"I couldn't stand another minute of that," said Miss Thomas. Her lips were almost gray. She moistened a towel and gently bathed the sleeping face. "I didn't like that at all."

"You'll like the rest of it," promised the doctor. "Let's get rid of this sheet."

They took it off and stored it.

"How'd you like me to hit the ten-five cycles with that sheet off?" he asked.

"Build him a cage first," she breathed in an awed tone.

He grinned suddenly. "Hit eighty cycles for me, will you?"

She did and they watched Richard Newell wakening. He groaned and moved his head gingerly. He sat up suddenly and yelped, and covered his face for a moment with both hands.

"Hello, Newell. How do you feel?"

"Like the output of a garbage disposal unit. I haven't felt like this since the day I rowed a boat for fourteen hours."

"It's all right, Newell. All in a day's work."

"Work is right. I know—you've had me out pulling a plow while I was hypnotized. Slave labor. Lowers the overhead. Damn it, Fred, I'm not going to take much more of this."

"You'll take as much as I choose to give you," snapped the doctor. "This is my party now, Dicky boy."

Miss Thomas gasped. Newell slowly swung his legs out and sat looking at the doctor, an ominous and ugly half-smile on his face.

"Miss Thomas," said the doctor, "ten-five, please."

With his amusement deeply concealed, he watched Miss Thomas sidle to the controls and dial for the 10,500 supplementary note. He knew exactly what was going on in her mind. Ten-five was a fury motif, the command to Anson to relive the state of unbearable anger he had been in just moments ago.

"Miss Thomas," said Newell silkily, "did I ever tell you the story of my life? Or, for that matter, the story of the doctor's life?"

"Why—no, Mr. Newell."

"Once upon a time," said Newell, "there was a doctor who . . . who . . ." As the shrill note added itself to the bumble of the 80-cycle tone, Newell's voice faltered. Behind him, the doctor heard the rustle of Miss Thomas's starch as she braced herself.

Newell looked at the doctor with astonishment. "What the hell am I up to?" he murmured. "That isn't a funny story. 'Scuse me, Miss Thomas." He visibly relaxed, swung his feet back up on the bed and rested on one elbow. "I haven't felt like this since . . . Where's Osa?" he asked.

"Home. Waiting for you."

"God. Hope she doesn't have to wait much longer. Is she all right?"

"She's fine. So are you, pretty near. I think we have the thing whipped. Like to hear about it?"

" 'Talk about me,' " Newell quoted. " 'Talk nice if you can, but talk about me.' "

The doctor saw Miss Thomas staring incredulously at the controls, checking to be sure she had keyed the right note. He laughed. Newell laughed with him; it was one of the most pleasant of imaginable sounds. And it wasn't Anson's laugh, either—not even remotely. This was Richard Newell to the life, but warm, responsive, considerate.

The doctor said, "Did Osa ever tell you she thought you had a nameless monster pushing you around?"

"Only a couple hundred times."

"Well, you have. I'm not joking, Dick—you really have. Only you've never suspected it and you don't have a name to call it by."

"I don't get you." He was curious, anxious to learn, to like and be liked. It was in the way he spoke, moved, listened. Miss Thomas stood with her hand frozen near the controls, ready to shut him off at the first sign of expected violence.

"You will. Now here's the picture." And in simple terms, the doctor told him the story of Anson, the theory of multiple personality as a phenomenon of twinning, and at last his theory of the acrobatic stabilization the two entities had achieved on their own.

"Why acrobatic?" asked Newell.

"You know you act like a heel most of the time, Dick."

"You might say so." It was said quite without resentment.

"Here's why. (Just listen, now; you can test it any way you like after you've heard it all.) Your alter ego (to coin a phrase) had been walled in, excluded from consciousness and expression and even self-awareness, ever since you were born. I won't attempt to explain that; I don't know. Anyway, there it lay, isolated but alive, Dick, alive—*and just as strong as you!*"

"I . . . can't picture such a thing."

"It isn't easy. I can't either, completely. It's like trying to get into the mind of another species, or a plant, if you can imagine such a thing. I do know, though, that the thing is alive, and up until recently had nothing—no knowledge, no retained experience, no mode of expression at all."

"How do you know it's there, then?"

"It's there all right," said the doctor. "And right this very minute, it's blowing its top. You see, all your life it's lived with you. It has had a blind, constant urge to break through, and it never could make it until it popped up here and we drew it out. It's a fascinating entity, Dick. I won't go into that now; you'll know it—him—thoroughly before you leave. But believe it or not, it's pretty nice. More than nice: it's positively angelic. It's lain there in the dark all these years like a germinated seed, pushing up toward the light. And every time it came near—you battled it down again."

"I did?"

"For good sound survival reasons, you did. But like a lot of survival impulses yours were pretty irrational. A lion roars, a deer runs. Good survival. But if he runs over a cliff? What I'm getting at is that there's room for both of you in Richard Anson Newell. You've coexisted fairly well, considerng, as strangers and sometimes enemies. You're going to do a lot better as friends and partners. Brothers, if you want the true term, because that's just what the two of you are."

"How does this—if true—explain the way I've been mucking around with my life?"

Looking for an image, the doctor paused. "You might say you've been *cantilevered* out from a common center. Way out. Now your alter—we call him Anson—is, as I've said, a very nice fellow. His blind strugglings have been almost all toward something—call it an aura, if you like—in people around you. The pressures are everything that's warm and lovable and good to be with.

"But you—man, you felt invaded! You could never reach out toward anything; Anson was there ahead of you, pressing and groping. You had to react, immediately and with all your might, *in the opposite direction*. Isn't it true that all your life you've rejected and tramped on anything that attracted you—and at the same time you've taken only things you couldn't really care about?"

"Well, I . . ."

"Just hold onto the idea. This speech I'm making is for your intellectual understanding; I don't expect you to buy it first crack out of the barrel."

"But I haven't always . . . I mean what about Osa? Are you telling me I didn't really want Osa?"

"That's the cantilever effect, Dick. Anson never felt about Osa the way you did. I think she must have some confining effect on him; he doesn't like to be confined, does he, Miss Thomas?" He chuckled. "She either leaves him cold or makes him angry. So angry that it's beyond belief. But it's an infant's anger, Dick—blind and furious and extreme. And what happens *then*, when you react in the *opposite* direction?"

"Oh, my God," breathed Newell. "Osa . . ." He turned his suddenly illuminated gaze up. "You know, sometimes I—we—it's like a big light that . . ."

"I know, I know," said the doctor testily. "Matter of fact, that's happening right now. Turn off the ten-five, please, Miss Thomas."

"Yes, doctor."

"That high note," the doctor explained. "It's for Anson—induced anger. You're being pretty decent at the moment, Newell. You realize that?"

"Well, why wouldn't I? You've done a lot for me."

The note faded. Newell closed his eyes and opened them again. There was a long, tense silence.

Finally Newell said in his most softly insulting tone, "You spin a pretty tale, Freddy boy. But I'm tired of listening. Shall I blackmail you the hell out of here?"

"Five-fifty, Miss Thomas."

"Yes, doctor." She turned Newell off.

Back in the office again, Miss Thomas jittered in indecision. She tried to speak and then looked at the doctor with mute pleading.

"Go ahead," he encouraged.

She shook her head. "I don't know what comes next. Morton Prince was wrong; there are no multiple egos, just multiple siblings sharing the same body, the same brain." She halted, waiting for him to take it from there.

"Well?" he said.

"I know you're not going to sacrifice one for the other; that's why you never handled these cases before. But—" she flapped her hands helplessly—"even if Newell could carry the equipment around, I'd never sleep nights thinking that Anson had to go through the agony of that ten-five note just so Newell would be a decent human being. Or even, for that matter, vice versa."

"It wouldn't be either humane or practical," he said. "Well?"

"Do they take turns being dominant, one day on, one day off?"

"That still would be sacrificing each half the time."

"Then what? You said it would be 'Newell, meet Anson. Anson meet Newell.' But you don't have the same problem you'd have with Siamese twins or the same solution."

"Which is?"

"Separating them without killing either one. All these two have is a single brain to share and a single body. If you could cut them free—"

"I can't," he said bluntly. "I don't intend to."

"All right," she conceded in defeat. "You're the doctor. You tell me."

"Just what you said—the Morton Prince cases were in communication."

"And Newell and Anson are, just because we gave Anson

a vocabulary? What about that cantilever effect you explained to Newell? You can't let them go through life counterbalancing each other—Newell pulling violently to the other side of Anson's reactions, Anson doing the same with Newell's. Then *what?*" she repeated almost angrily. "If you know, why put me through this guessing game?"

"To see if you'd come up with the same answer," he said candidly. "A check on my judgment. Do you mind?"

She shook her head again, but this time with a little complimentary smile. "It's a painful way to get cooperation, only it works, damn you." She frowned then, considering. "The two of them are compartmented. Are they different in that way from the other multiples?"

"Some, yes—the ones that are detected because there is communication. But not the others. And those cases rate treatment (because all people in difficulty do) and Newell-Anson, if we work it out properly, will show us how to help them. There's an obvious answer, Miss Thomas. I'm hoping—almost desperately—that you come up with the one I thought of."

She made a self-impatient gesture. "*Not* the psychostat. *Definitely* not eliminating one or the other. *Not* making them take turns." She looked up with a questioning awe on her face. "The *opposite* of treating Siamese twins?"

"Like what?" he asked urgently, leaning forward.

"Like what?' he asked urgently, leaning forward.

"Don't separate them. *Join* them. Make a juncture."

"Keep going," he pressed. "Don't stop now."

"Surgical?"

"Can't be done. It isn't one lobe for Newell, the other for Anson, or anything that simple. What else?"

She thought deeply, began several times to say something, dismissed each intended suggestion with a curt headshake. He waited with equally deep intensity.

She nodded at last. "Modulate them separately." She was no longer asking. "Then modulate them in relation to each other so they won't be in that awful cantilever balancing act."

"Say it!" he nearly yelled.

"But that isn't enough."

"No!"

"Audio response."

"Why?" he rapped out. "And which?"

"Sixty cycles—the AC tone they'll be hearing almost all the time. Assign it to communication between them."

The doctor slumped into a chair, drained of tension. He nodded at her, with the tiredest grin she had ever seen.

"All of it," he whispered. "You got everything I thought of . . . including the 60 cycles. I knew I was right. Now I *know* it. Or doesn't that make sense?"

"Of course it does."

"Then let's get started."

"Now?" she asked, astonished. "You're too tired—"

"Am I?" He jacked himself out of the chair. "Try stopping me and see."

They used the EEG resultants, made two analogs and another, and used all three as the optimum standard for the final fixing process in the psychostat. It was a longer, more meticulous process than it had ever been and it worked; and what shook the doctor's hand that last day was an unbelievable blend—all of Newell's smoothness and a new strength, the sum of powers he had previously exhausted in the dual struggle that neither had known of; and, with it, Anson's bright fascination with the very act of drawing breath, seeing colors, finding wonderment in everything.

"We're nice guys," said Richard Anson Newell, still shaking the doctor's hand. "We'll get along great."

"I don't doubt it a bit," the doctor said. "Give my best to Osa. Tell her . . . here's something a little better than a wet handkerchief."

"Whatever you say," said Richard Anson Newell.

He waved to Miss Thomas, who watched from the corridor, and behind her, Hildy Jarrell, who wept, and he went down the steps to the street.

"We're making a mistake, doctor," said Miss Thomas, "letting him—them—go."

"Why?" he asked, curious.

"All that brain power packed in one skull . . ."

The doctor wanted to laugh. He didn't. "You'd think so, wouldn't you?" he agreed.

"Meaning it's not so at all," she said suspiciously. "Why not?"

"Because it isn't *twice* the amount of brains any individual has. It's only as much as any *two* distinct individuals have. Like you and me, for instance. Mostly we supplement each other—but just here and there, not everywhere, adding up to a giant double brain. Same with Newell and Anson. And any two people can be counted on to jam one another occasionally. So will they—but not like before treatment."

They watched until Richard Anson Newell was out of sight, then went back to check the multiple personality cases that Miss Jarrell had dug out of the files.

Four months later, the doctor got a letter:

> Dear Fred,
> I'll write this because it will do me good to get it off my chest. If it doesn't do enough good, I'll send it. If that doesn't help, I don't know what I'll do. Yes, I do. Nothing.
> Dick is . . . incredible. He takes care of me, Fred, in ways I'd never dreamed of or hoped for. He cares. That's it, he cares—about me, about his work. He learns new things all the time and loves old things over again. It's . . . could I say miracle?
> But, Fred—this is hateful of me, I know—the thing I told you about, the thing I used to wish for and live to remember, no matter what . . . it's gone. That's probably good, because of what happened between times.
> But sometimes I'd trade my perfect husband for that louse and a wet handkerchief, if I could have the other thing along with it somehow.
> There, I've said it.
>
> > Osa

The doctor galloped through the clinic until he found his head technician in the electrical lab.

"Tommie," he said jovially, "did you ever go out and get drunk with a doctor?"

The tears were streaming down his face. Miss Thomas went out and got drunk with the doctor.

THE STARS
ARE
THE STYX

I've written elsewhere about the strange way things that I write about seem to happen about fifteen years later. It's a small thing, but writing this in 1950 I had no idea in the world that in fifteen years couples would be dancing separately, each more or less doing their own thing. In '65 they began doing just that. Nor did I dream that this, of all the stories I was writing at the time, would one day be the title story of a collection like this.

I'd like to restate my gratitude to Rowena Morrell for the beautiful painting she has done for this first edition. Not only have I not met the lady at this writing—she has not met me; yet she has produced an astonishing likeness of me from photographs. This is especially gratifying since some demon has decreed, ever since Emsh's portrait in 1962, that someone else's face must always appear on my books. I could not be more pleased.

Every few years someone thinks to call me Charon. It never lasts. I guess I don't look the part. Charon, you'll remember, was the somber ferryman who steered the boat across the River Styx, taking the departed souls over to the Other Side. He's usually pictured as a grim, taciturn character, tall and gaunt.

I get called Charon, but that's not what I look like. I'm not exactly taciturn, and I don't go around in a flapping black cloak, I'm too fat. Maybe too old, too.

It's a shrewd, gag, though, calling me Charon. I do pass human souls Out, and for nearly half of them, the stars are indeed the Styx—they will never return.

I have two things I know Charon had. One is that bitter difference from the souls I deal with. They have lost only one world; the other is before them. But I'm rejected by both.

The other thing has to do with a little-known fragment of the Charon legend. And that, I think, is worth a yarn.

It's Judson's yarn, and I wish he was here to tell it himself—which is foolish; the yarn's about why he isn't here. "Here" is Curbstone, by the way—the stepping-off place to the Other Side. It's Earth's other slow satellite, bumbling along out past the Moon. It was built 7800 years ago for heavy interplanetary transfer, though of course there's not much of that left any more. It's so easy to synthesize anything nowadays that there's just no call for imports. We make what we need from energy, and there's plenty of that around. There's plenty of everything. Even insecurity, though you have to come to Curbstone for that, and be someone like Judson to boot.

It's no secret—now—that insecurity is vital to the Curbstone project. In a cushioned existence on a stable Earth, volunteers for Curbstone are rare. But they come in—the adventurous, the dissatisfied, the yearning ones, to man the tiny ships that will, in due time, give mankind a segment of space so huge that even mankind's voracious appetite for expansion will be glutted for millennia. There is a vision that haunts all humans today—that of a network of force-beams in the form of a tremendous sphere, encompassing much of the known universe and a great deal of the unknown—through which, like thought impulses through the synaptic paths of a giant brain, matter will be transmitted instantly, and a man may step from here to the depths of space while his heart beats once. The vision frightens most and lures a few, and of those few, some are chosen to go out. Judson was chosen.

I knew he'd come to Curbstone. I'd known it for years, ever since I was on Earth and met him. He was just a youngster then, thirty or so, and boiling around under that soft-spoken, shockproof surface of his was something that had to drive him to Curbstone. It showed when he raised his eyes. They got hungry. Any kind of hunger is rare on Earth. That's what Curbstone's for. The ultimate social balance—an escape for the unbalanced.

Don't wince like that when I say 'unbalanced.' Plain talk is plain talk. You can afford to be mighty plain about social imbalance these days. It's rare and it's slight. Thing is, when a man goes through fifteen years of primary social —childhood, I'm talking about—with all the subtle tinkering that involves, and still has an imbalance, it's a thing that sticks with him no matter how slight it is. Even then, the very existence of Curbstone is enough to make most of 'em quite happy to stay where they are. The handful who do head for Curbstone do it because they have to. Once here, only about half make the final plunge. The rest go back—or live here permanently. Whatever they do, Curbstone takes care of the imbalance.

When you come right down to it, misfits are that way either because they lack something or because they have something *extra*. On Earth there's a place for everything and everything's in its place. On Curbstone you find someone who has what you lack, or who has the same extra something you have—or you leave. You go back feeling that Earth's a pretty nice safe place after all, or you go

Out, and it doesn't matter to anyone else, ever, whether you're happy or not.

I was waiting in the entry bell when Judson arrived on Curbstone. Judson had nothing to do with that. I didn't even know he was on that particular shuttle. It's just that, aside from the fact that I happen to be Senior Release Officer on Curbstone, I like to meet the shuttles. All sorts of people come here, for all sorts of reasons. They stay here or they don't for all sorts of other reasons. I like to look at the faces that come down that ramp and guess which ones will go which way. I'm pretty good at it. As soon as I saw Judson's face I knew that this boy was bound Out. I recognized that about him even before I realized who it was.

There was a knot of us there to watch the newcomers come in. Most were there just because it's worth watching them all, the hesitant ones, the damn-it-alls, the grim ones. But two Curbstones I noticed particularly. Hunters both. One was a lean, slick-haired boy named Wold. It was pretty obvious what he was hunting. The other was Flower. It was just as obvious what she had her long, wide-spaced eyes out for, but it was hard to tell why. Last I had heard, she had been solidly wrapped up in an Outbounder called Clinton.

I forgot about the wolf and the vixen when I recognized Judson and bellowed at him. He dropped his kit where he stood and came bounding over to me. He grabbed both my biceps and squeezed while I thumped his ribs. "I was waiting up for you, Judson," I grinned at him.

"Man, I'm glad you're still here," he said. He was a sandy-haired fellow, all Adam's apple and guarded eyes.

"I'm here for the duration," I told him. "Didn't you know?"

"No, I—I mean. . . ."

"Don't be tactful, Jud," I said. "I belong here by virtue of the fact that there's nowhere else for me to go. Earth isn't happy about men as fat and funny-looking as I am in the era of beautiful people. And I can't go Out. I have a left axis deviation. I know that sounds political; actually it's cardiac."

"I'm sorry." He looked at my brassard. "Well, you're Mr. Big around here, anyway."

"I'm just big around *here*," I said, swatting my belt-line.

"There's Coördination Office and a half-squad of Guardians who ice this particular cake. I'm just the final check on Outbounders."

"Yeah," he said. "You don't rate. Much. The whole function of this space-station waits on whether you say yes to a departure."

"Shecks now," I said, exaggerating my embarrassment to cover up my exaggerated embarrassment. "Whatever, I wouldn't worry too much if I were you. I could be wrong—we'll have to run some more tests on you—but if ever I saw an Outbounder, it's you."

"Hi," said a silken voice. "You already know each other. How nice."

Flower.

There was something vaguely reptilian about Flower, which didn't take a thing from her brand of magnetism. Bit by bit, piece by piece, she was a so-so looking girl. Her eyes were too long, and so dark they seemed to be all pupil and the whites too white. Her nose was a bit too large and her chin a bit too small, but so help me, there never was a more perfect mouth. Her voice was like a 'cello bowed up near the bridge. She was tall, with a fragile-in-the-middle slenderness and spring-steel flanks. The overall effect was breathtaking. I didn't like her. She didn't like me either. She never spoke to me except on business, and I had practically no business with her. She'd been here a long time. I hadn't figured out why, then. But she wouldn't go Out and she wouldn't go back to Earth—which in itself was all right; we had lots of room.

Let me tell you something about modern women and therefore something about Flower—something you might not reason out unless you get as old and objective as I've somehow lived to become.

Used to be, according to what I've read, that clothes ran a lot to what I might call indicative concealment. As long as clothes had the slightest excuse of functionalism, people in general and women in particular made a large fuss over something called innate modesty—which never did exist; it had to be learned. But as long as there was weather around to blame clothes on, the myth was accepted. People exposed what the world was indifferent to in order to whip up interest in the rest. "Modesty is not so simple a virtue as honesty," one of the old books says.

Clothes as weatherproofing got themselves all mixed up with clothes as ornament; fashions came and went and people followed them.

But for the past three hundred years or so there hasn't been any "weather" as such, for anyone, here or on Earth. Clothes for only aesthetic purposes became more and more the rule, until today it's up to the individual to choose what he's going to wear, if anything. An earring and a tattoo are quite as acceptable in public as forty meters of iridescent plastiweb and a two-meter coiffure.

Now, most people today are healthy, well-selected, and good to look at. Women are still as vain as ever. A woman with a bodily defect, real or imagined, has one of two choices: She can cover the defect with something artfully placed to look as if that was just the best place for it, or she can leave the defect in the open, knowing that no one today is going to judge her completely in terms of the defect. Folks nowadays generally wait until they can find out what kind of a human being you are.

But a woman who has no particular defect generally changes her clothes with her mood. It might be a sash only this morning, but a trailing drape this afternoon. Tomorrow it might be a one-sided blouse and clinging trousers. You can take it as a very significant thing when such a woman *always* covers up. She's keeping her natural warmth, as it were, under forced draft.

I didn't go into all this ancient history to impress you with my scholastics. I'm using it to illustrate a very important facet of Flower's complex character. Because Flower was one of those forced-draft jobs. Except on the sun-field and in the swimming pools, where no one ever wears clothes. Flower always affected a tunic of some kind.

The day Judson arrived, she wore a definitive example of what I mean. It was a single loose black garment with straight shoulders and no sleeves. On both sides, from a point a hand's-breath below the armpit, down to the hip-bone, it was slit open. It fastened snugly under her throat with one magne-clasp, but was also slit from there to the navel. It did not quite reach to mid-thigh, and the soft material carried a light biostatic electrical charge, so that it clung to and fell away from her body as she moved. So help me, she was a walking demand for the revival of the extinct profession of peeping Tom.

This, then, was what horned in on my first few words with Judson. I should have known from the way she looked that she was planning something—something definitely for herself. I should have been doubly warned by the fact that she took the trouble to speak up just when she did—just when I told Jud he was a certifiable Outbounder if I ever saw one.

So then and there I made my big mistake. "Flower," I said, "this is Judson."

She used the second it took me to speak to suck in her lower lip, so that when she smiled slowly at Jud, the lip swelled visibly as if by blood pressure. "I *am* glad," she all but whispered.

And then she had the craft to turn the smile on me and walk away without another word.

". . . Gah!" said Judson through a tight glottis.

"That," I told him, "was beautifully phrased. Gah, indeed. Reel your eyeballs back in, Jud. We'll drop your duffel off at the Outbound quarters and—*Judson!*"

Flower had disappeared down the inner ramp. I was aware that Judson had just started to breathe again.

"What?" he asked me.

I waddled over and picked up his gear. "Come on," I said, and steered him by the arm.

Judson had nothing to say until after we found him a room and started for my sector. "Who is she?"

"A hardy perennial," I said. "Came up to Curbstone two years ago. She's never been certified. She'll get around to it soon—or never. Are you going right ahead?"

"Just how do you handle the certification?"

"Give you some stuff to read. Pound some more knowledge into you for six, seven nights while you sleep. Look over your reflexes, physical and mental. An examination. If everything's all right, you're certified."

"Then—Out?"

I shrugged. "If you like. You come to Curbstone strictly on your own. You take your course if and when you like. And after you've been certified, you leave when you want to, with someone or not, and without telling anyone unless you care to."

"Man, when you people say 'voluntary' you're not just talking!"

"There's no other way to handle a thing like this. And

you can bet that we get more people Out this way than we ever would on a compulsory basis. In the long run, I mean, and this is a long-term project . . . six thousand years long."

He walked silently for a time, and I was pretty sure I knew his thoughts. For Outbounders there is no return, and the best possible chance they have of survival is something like fifty-four per cent, a figure which was arrived at after calculations so complex that it might as well be called a guess. You don't force people Out against those odds. They go by themselves, driven by their own reasoning, or they don't go at all.

After a time Judson said, "I always thought Outbounders were assigned a ship and a departure time. With certified people leaving whenever they feel like it, what's to prevent uncertified ones from doing it?"

"That I'm about to show you."

We passed the Coördination offices and headed out to the launching racks. They were shut off from Top Central Corridor by a massive gate. Over the gate floated three words in glowing letters:

SPECIES
GROUP
SELF

Seeing Jud's eyes on it, I explained, "The three levels of survival. They're in all of us. You can judge a man by the way he lines them up. The ones who have them in that order are the best. It's a good thought for Outbounders to take away with them." I watched his face. "Particularly since it's always the third item that brings 'em this far."

Jud smiled slowly. "Along with all that bumbling you carry a sting, don't you?"

"Mine is a peculiar job," I grinned back. "Come on in."

I put my palm on the key-plate. It tingled for a brief moment and then the shining doors slid back. I rolled through, stopping just inside the launching court at Judson's startled yelp.

"Well, come on," I said.

He stood just inside the doors, straining mightily against nothing at all. "Wh—wh—?" His arms were spread and his feet slipped as if he were trying to force his way through a steel wall.

Actually he was working on something a good deal stronger than that. "That's the answer to why uncertified people don't go Out," I told him. "The plate outside scanned the whorls and lines of my hand. The door opened and that Gillis-Menton field you're muscling passed me through. It'll pass anyone who's certified, too, but no one else. Now stop pushing or you'll suddenly fall on your face."

I stepped to the left bulkhead and palmed the plate there, then beckoned to Judson. He approached the invisible barrier timidly. It wasn't there. He came all the way through, and I took my hand off the scanner.

"That second plate," I explained, "works for me and certified people only. There's no way for an uncertified person to get into the launching court unless I bring him in personally. It's as simple as that. When the certified are good and ready, they go. If they want to go Out with a banquet and a parade beforehand, can. If they want to roll out of bed some night and slip Out quietly, they can. Most of 'em do it quietly. Come on and have a look at the ships."

We crossed the court to the row of low doorways along the far wall. I opened one at random and we stepped into the ship.

"It's just a room!"

"They all say that," I chuckled. "I suppose you expected a planet-type space job, only more elaborate."

"I thought they'd at least *look* like ships. This is a double room out of some luxury hotel."

"It's that, and then some." I showed him around—the capacious food lockers, the automatic air recirculators, and, most comforting of all, the synthesizer, which meant food, fuel, tools and materials converted directly from energy to matter.

"Curbstone's more than a space station, Jud. It's a factory, for one thing. When you decide to go on your way, you'll flip that lever by the door. (You'll be catapulted out—you won't feel it, because of the stasis generator and artificial gravity.) As soon as you're gone, another ship will come up from below into this slot. By the time you're clear of Curbstone's gravitic field and slip into hyper-drive, the new ship'll be waiting for passengers."

"And that will be going on for six thousand years?"

"More or less."

"That's a powerful lot of ships."

"As long as Outbounders keep the quota, it is indeed. Nine hundred thousand—including forty-six per cent failure."

"Failure," said Jud. He looked at me and I held his gaze.

"Yes," I said. "The forty-six per cent who are not expected to get where they are going. The ones who materialize inside solid matter. The ones who go into the space-time nexus and never come out. The ones who reach their assigned synaptic junction and wait, and wait, and wait until they die of old age because no one gets to them soon enough. The ones who go mad and kill themselves or their shipmates." I spread my hands. "The forty-six per cent."

"You can convince a man of danger," said Judson evenly, "but nobody ever believed he was really and truly going to die. Death is something that happens to other people. I won't be one of the forty-six per cent."

That was Judson. I wish he was still here.

I let the remark lie there on the thick carpet and went on with my guided tour. I showed him the casing of the intricate beam-power apparatus that contained the whole reason for the project, and gave him a preliminary look at the astrogational and manual maneuvering equipment and controls. "But don't bother your pretty little head about it just now," I added. "It'll all be crammed into you before you get certified."

We went back to the court, closing the door of the ship behind us.

"There's a lot of stuff piled into those ships," I observed, "but the one thing that can't be packed in sardine-size is the hyper-drive. I suppose you know that."

"I've heard something about it. The initial kick into second-order space comes from the station here, doesn't it? But how is the ship returned to normal space on arrival?"

"That's technology so refined it sounds like mysticism," I answered. "I don't begin to understand it. I can give you an analogy, though. It takes a power source, a compression device, and valving to fill a pneumatic tire. It takes a plain nail to let the air out again. See what I mean?"

"Vaguely. Anyway, the important thing is that Outbound is strictly one way. Those ships never come back. Right?"

"So right."

One of the doors behind us opened, and a girl stepped out of a ship. "Oh . . . I didn't know there was anyone here!" she said, and came toward us with a long, easy stride. "Am I in the way?"

"You—in the way, Tween?" I answered. "Not a chance."

I was very fond of Tween. To these jaded old eyes she was one of the loveliest things that ever happened. Two centuries ago, before variation limits were as rigidly set as they are now, Eugenics dreamed up her kind—olive-skinned true-breeds with the silver hair and deep ruby eyes of an albino. It was an experiment they should never have stopped. Albinoism wasn't dominant, but in Tween it had come out strongly. She wore her hair long—really long; she could tuck the ends of it under her toes and stand up straight when it was loose. Now it was braided in two ingenious halves of a coronet that looked like real silver. Around her throat and streaming behind her as she walked was a single length of flame-colored material.

"This is Judson, Tween," I said. "We were friends back on Earth. What are you up to?"

She laughed, a captivating, self-conscious laugh. "I was sitting in a ship pretending that it was Outside. We'd looked at each other one day and suddenly said, 'Let's!' and off we'd gone." Her face was luminous. "It was lovely. And that's just what we're going to do one of these days. You'll see."

" 'We'? Oh—you mean Wold."

"Wold," she breathed, and I wished, briefly and sharply, that someone, somewhere, someday would speak my name like that. And on the heels of that reaction came the mental picture of Wold as I had seen him an hour before, slick and smooth, watching the shuttle passengers with his dark hunting eyes. There was nothing I could say though. My duties have their limits. If Wold didn't know a good thing when he saw it, that was his hard luck.

But looking at that shining face, I knew it would be her hard luck.

"You're certified?" Judson asked, awed.

"Oh, yes," she smiled, and I said, "Sure is, Jud. But she had her troubles, didn't you, Tween?"

We started for the gate. "I did indeed," said Tween. (I loved hearing her talk. There was a comfortable, restful quality to her speech like silence when an unnoticed, irritating noise disappears.) "I just didn't have the logical aptitudes when I first came. Some things just wouldn't stick in my head, even in hypnopedia. All the facts in the universe won't help if you don't know how to put them together." She grinned. "I used to hate you."

"Don't blame you a bit." I nudged Judson. "I turned down her certification eight times. She used to come to my office to get the bad news, and she'd stand there after I'd told her and shuffle her feet and gulp a little bit. And the first thing she said then was always, 'Well, when can I start retraining?' "

She flushed, laughing. "You're telling secrets!"

Judson touched her. "It's all right. I don't think less of you for any of his maunderings. . . . You must have wanted that certificate very much."

"Yes," she said. "Very much."

"Could—could I ask why?"

She looked at him, in him, through him, past him. "All our lives," she said quietly, "are safe and sure and small. This—" she waved back towards the ships—"is the only thing in our experience that's none of those things. I could give you fifty reasons for going Out. But I think they all come down to that one."

We were silent for a moment, and then I said, "I'll put that in my notebook, Tween. You couldn't be more right. Modern life gives us infinite variety in everything except the magnitude of the things we do. And that stays pretty tiny." And, I thought, big, fat, superannuated station officials, rejected by one world and unqualified for the next. A small chore for a small mind.

"The only reason most of us do puny things and think puny thoughts," Judson was saying, "is that Earth has too few jobs like his in these efficient times."

"Too few men like him for jobs like his," Tween corrected.

I blinked at them both. It was me they were talking

about. I don't think I changed expression much, but I felt as warm as the color of Tween's eyes.

We passed through the gates, Tween first with never a thought for the barrier which did not exist for her, then Judson, waiting cautiously for my go-ahead after the inside scanning plate had examined the whorls and lines of my hand. I followed, and the great gates closed behind us.

"Want to come up to the office?" I asked Tween when we reached Central Corridor.

"Thanks, no," she said. "I'm going to find Wold." She turned to Judson. "You'll be certified quickly," she told him. "I just know. But, Judson—"

"Say it, whatever it is," said Jud, sensing her hesitation.

"I was going to say get certified first. Don't try to decide anything else before that. You'll have to take my word for it, but nothing that ever happened to you is quite like the knowledge that you're free to go through those gates any time you feel like it."

Judson's face assumed a slightly puzzled, slightly stubborn expression. It disappeared, and I knew it was a conscious effort for him to do it. Then he put out his hand and touched her heavy silver hair. "Thanks," he said.

She strode off, the carriage of her head telling us that her face was eager as she went to Wold. At the turn of the corridor she waved and was gone.

"I'm going to miss that girl," I said, and turned back to Judson. The puzzled, stubborn look was back, full force. "What's the matter?"

"What did she mean by that sisterly advice about getting certified first? What else would I have to decide about right now?"

I swatted his shoulder. "Don't let it bother you, Jud. She sees something in you that you can't see yourself, yet."

That didn't satisfy him at all. "Like what?" When I didn't answer, he asked, "You see it, too, don't you?"

We started up the ramp to my office. "I like you," I said. "I liked you the minute I laid eyes on you, years ago, when you were just a sprout."

"You've changed the subject."

"Hell, I have. Now let me save my wind for the ramp." This was only slightly a stall. As the years went by, that ramp seemed to get steeper and steeper. Twice Coördination had offered to power it for me and I'd refused haughtily. I could see the time coming when I was going to be too heavy for my high-horse. All the same, I was glad for the chance to stall my answer to Judson's question. The answer lay in my liking him; I knew that instinctively. But it needed thinking through. We've conditioned ourselves too much to analyze our dislikes and to take our likes for granted.

The outer door opened as we approached. There was a man waiting in the appointment foyer, a big fellow with a gray cape and a golden circlet around his blue-black hair. "Clinton!" I said. "How are you, son? Waiting for me?"

The inner door opened for me and I went into my office, Clinton behind me. I fell down in my specially molded chair and waved him to a relaxer. At the door Judson cleared his throat. "Shall I—uh. . . ."

Clinton looked up swiftly, an annoyed, tense motion. He raked a blazing blue gaze across Jud, and his expression changed. "Come in, for God's sake. Newcomer, hm? Sit down. Listen. You can't learn enough about this project. Or these people. Or the kind of flat spin an Outbounder can get himself into."

"Clint, this's Judson," I said. "Jud, Clint's about the itchy-footedest Outbounder of them all. What is on your mind, son?"

Clinton wet his lips. "How's about me heading Out—*alone?*"

I said, "Your privilege, if you think you'll enjoy it."

He smacked a heavy fist into his palm. "Good, then."

"Of course," I said, looking at the overhead, "the ships are built for two. I'd personally be a bit troubled about the prospect of spending—uh—however long it might be, staring at that empty bunk across the way. Specially," I added loudly, to interrupt what he was going to say, "if I had to spend some hours or weeks or maybe a decade with the knowledge that I was alone because I took off with a mad on."

"This isn't what you might call a fit of pique," snapped Clinton. "It's been years building—first because I had a need and recognized it; second because the need got greater when I started to work toward filling it; third because I found who and what would satisfy it; fourth because I was so wrong on point three."

"You *are* wrong? Or you're *afraid* you're wrong?"

He looked at me blankly. "I don't know," he said, all the snap gone out of his voice. "Not for sure."

"Well, then you've no real problem. All you do is ask yourself whether it's worthwhile to take off alone because of a problem you haven't solved. If it is, go ahead."

He rose and went to the door. "Clinton!" My voice must have crackled; he stopped without turning, and from the corner of my eye I saw Judson sit up abruptly. I said, more quietly, "When Judson here suggested that he go away and leave us alone, why did you tell him to come in? What did you see in him that made you do it?"

Clinton's thoughtfully slitted eyes hardly masked their blazing blue as he turned them on Judson, who squirmed like a schoolboy. Clinton said, "I think it's because he looks as if he can be reached. And trusted. That answer you?"

"It does." I waved him out cheerfully. Judson said, "You have an awesome way of operating."

"On him?"

"On both of us. How do you know what you did by turning his problem back on himself? He's likely to go straight to the launching-court."

"He won't."

"You're sure?"

"Of course I'm sure," I said flatly. "If Clinton hadn't already decided *not* to take off alone—not today, anyhow —he wouldn't have come to see me and get argued out of it."

"What's really bothering him?"

"I can't say." I wouldn't say. Not to Judson. Not now, at least. Clinton was ripe to leave, and he was the kind to act when ready. He had found what he thought was the perfect human being for him to go with. She wasn't ready to go. She never in all time and eternity would be ready to go.

"All right," said Jud. "What about me? That was very embarrassing."

I laughed at him. "Sometimes when you don't know exactly how to phrase something for yourself, you can shock a stranger into doing it for you. Why did I like you on sight, years ago, and now, too? Why did Clinton feel you were trustworthy? Why did Tween feel free to pass you some advice—and what prompted the advice? Why did—" No. Don't mention the most significant one of all. Leave her out of it. "—Well, there's no point in itemizing all afternoon. Clinton said it. *You can be reached.* Practically anyone meeting you knows—feels, anyhow—that you can be reached . . . touched . . . affected. We like feeling that we have an effect on someone."

Judson closed his eyes, screwed up his brow. I knew he was digging around in his memory, thinking of close and casual acquaintances . . . how many of them . . . how much they had meant to him and he to them. He looked at me. "Should I change?"

"God, no! Only—don't let it be *too* true. I think that's what Tween was driving at when she said not to jump at any decisions until you've reached the comparative serenity of certification."

"Serenity . . . I could use some of that," he murmured. "Jud."

"Mm?"

"Did you ever try to put into one simple statement just why you came to Curbstone?"

He looked startled. Like most people, he had been living, and living ardently, without ever wondering particularly what for. And like most people, he had sooner or later had to answer the jackpot question: "What am I doing here?"

"I came because—because . . . no, that wouldn't be a simple statement."

"All right. Run it off, anyway. A simple statement will come out of it if there's anything really important there. Any basic is simple, Jud. Every basic is important. Complicated matters may be fascinating, frightening, funny, intriguing, worrisome, educational, or what have you; but if they're complicated, they are, by definition, not important."

He leaned forward and put his elbows on his knees. His hands wound tightly around one another, and his head went down.

"I came here . . . looking for something. Not because I thought it was here. There was just nowhere else left to look. Earth is under such strict discipline . . . discipline by comfort; discipline by constructive luxury. Every need is taken care of that you can name, and no one seems to understand that the needs you *can't* name are the important ones. And all Earth is in a state of arrested development because of Curbstone. Everything is held in check. The *status quo* rules because for six thousand years it must and will. Six thousand years of physical and social evolution will be sacrificed for the single tremendous step that Curbstone makes possible. And I couldn't find a place for myself in the static part of the plan, so the only place for me to go was to the active part."

He was quiet so long after that, I felt I had to nudge him along. "Could it be that there *is* a way to make you happy on Earth, and you just haven't been able to find it?"

"Oh, no," he said positively. Then he raised his head and stared at me. "Wait a minute. You're very close to the mark there. That—that simple statement is trying to crawl out." He frowned. This time I kept my mouth shut and watched him.

"The something I'm looking for," he said finally, in the surest tones he'd used yet, "is something I lack, or something I have that I haven't been able to name yet. If there's anything on Earth or here that can fill that hollow place, and if I find it, I won't want to go Out. I won't need to go—I *shouldn't* go. But if it doesn't exist for me here, then Out I go, as part of a big something, rather than as a something missing a part. Wait!" He chewed his lower lip. His knuckle-joints crackled as he twisted his hands together. "I'll rephrase that and you'll have your simple statement."

He took a deep breath and said, "I came to Curbstone to find out. . . whether there's something I haven't had yet that belongs to me, or whether I . . . belong to something that hasn't had me yet."

"Fine," I said. "Very damned fine. You keep looking, Jud. The answer's here, somewhere, in some form. I've never heard it put better: Do you owe, or are you owed? There are three possible courses open to you no matter which way you decide."

"There are? Three?"

I put up fingers one at a time. "Earth. Here. Out."

"I—see."

"And you can take the course of any one of the words you saw floating over the gate to the launching court."

He stood up. "I've got a lot to think about."

"You have."

"But I've got me one hell of a blueprint."

I just grinned at him.

"You through with me?" he asked.

"For now."

"When do I start work for my certificate?"

"At the moment, you're just about four-ninths through."

"You dog! All this has been—"

"I'm a working man, Jud. I work all the time. Now beat it. You'll hear from me."

"You dog," he said again. "You old *hound*-dog!" But he left.

I sat back to think. I thought about Judson, of course. And Clinton and his worrisome solo ideas. The trip can be done solo, but it isn't a good idea. The human mind's communications equipment isn't a convenience—it's a vital necessity. Tween. How beautiful can a girl get? And the way she lights up when she thinks about going Out. She's certified now. Guess she and Wold will be taking off any time now.

Then my mind spun back to Flower. Put those pieces together . . . something should fit. Turn it this way, back— Ah! Clinton wants Out. He's been waiting and waiting for his girl to get certified. She hasn't even tried. He's not going to wait much longer. Who's his girl now . . . ?

Flower.

Flower, who turned all that heat on Judson.

Why Judson? There were bigger men, smarter, better-looking ones. What was special about Judson?

I filed the whole item away in my mind—with a red priority tab on it.

The days went by. A gong chimed and the number-board over my desk glowed. I didn't have to look up the numbers to know who it was. Fort and Mariellen. Nice kids. Slipped Out during a sleep period. I thought about them, watched the chain of checking lights flicker on, one after another. Palm-patterns removed from the Gate scanner; they'd never be used there again. Ship replaced. Quarters cleared and readied. Launching time reported to Coördination. Marriage recorded. Automatic machinery calculated, filed, punched cards, activated more automatic machinery until Fort and Mariellen were only axial alignments on the molecules of a magnetic tape . . . names . . .

memories . . . dead, perhaps; gone, certainly, for the next six thousand years.

Hold tight, Earth! Wait for them, the fifty-four per cent (I hope, I ardently hope) who will come back. Their relatives, their Earthbound friends will be long dead, and all their children and theirs; so let the Outbounders come home at least to the same Earth, the same language, the same traditions. They will be the millennial traditions of a more-than-Earth, the source of the unthinkable spatial sphere made fingertip-available to humankind through the efforts of the Outbounders. Earth is prepaying six thousand years of progress in exchange for the ability to use stars for stepping-stones, to be able to make Mars in a minute, Antares and Betelgeuse afternoon stops in a delivery run. Six thousand years of sacred stasis buys all but a universe, conquers Time, eliminates the fractionation of humanity into ship-riding, minute-shackled fragments of diverging evolution among the stars. All the stars will be in the next room when the Outbounders return.

Six thousand times around Sol, with Sol moving in a moving galaxy, and the galaxy in flight through a fluxing universe. That all amounts to a resultant movement of Earth through nine Möllner degrees around the Universal Curve. For six thousand years Curbstone flings off its tiny ships, its monstrous powerplant kicking them into space-time and the automatics holding them there until all—or until enough—are positioned. Some will materialize in the known universe and some in faintly suspected nebulae; some will appear in the empty nothingnesses beyond the galactic clusters, and some will burst into normal space inside molten suns.

But when the time comes, and the little ships are positioned in a great spherical pattern out around space, and together they become real again, they will send to each other a blaze of tight-beam energy. Like the wiring of a great switchboard, like the synapses of a brain, each beam will find its neighbors, and through them Earth.

And then, within and all through that sphere, humanity will spread, stepping from rim to rim of the universe in seconds, instantaneously transmitting men and materials from and to the stars. Here a ship can be sent piecemeal and assembled, there a space-station. Yonder, on some unheard-of planet of an unknown star, men light years away from Earth can assemble matter transceivers and hook them up to the great sphere, and add yet another world to those already visited.

And what of the Outbounders?

Real time, six thousand years.

Ship's time, from second-order spatial entry to materialization—*zero*.

Fort and Mariellen. Nice kids. Memories now; lights on a board, one after another, until they're all accounted for. At Curbstone, the quiet machinery says, "Next!"

Fort and Mariellen. Clinging together, they press down the launching lever. Effortlessly in their launching, they whirl away from Curbstone. In minutes there is a flicker of gray, or perhaps not even that. Strange stars surround them. They stare at one another. They are elsewhere . . . else*when*. Lights glow. This one says the tight-beam has gone on, pouring out toward the neighbors and, through them, to all the others. That one cries *"emergency"* and Fort whips to the manual controls and does what he can to avoid a dust-cloud, a planet . . . perhaps an alien ship.

Fort and Mariellen (or George and Viki, or Bruce, who went Out by himself, or Eleanor and Grace, or Sam and Rod—they were brothers) may materialize and die in an intolerable matter-displacement explosion so quickly that there is no time for pain. They may be holed by a meteor and watch, with glazing freezing eyes, the froth bubbling up from each other's bursting lungs. They may survive for minutes or weeks, and then fall captive to some giant planet or unsuspected sun. They may be hunted down and killed or captured by beings undreamed of.

And some of them will survive all this and wait for the blessed contact; the strident heralding of the matter transceiver with which each ship is equipped—and the abrupt appearance of a man, sixty centuries unborn when they left Curbstone, instantly transmitted from Earth to their vessel. Back with him they'll go, to an unchanged and ecstatic Earth, teeming with billions of trained, mature humans ready to fill the universe with human ways—the new humans who have left war and greed behind them, who have acquired a universe so huge that they need exploit no creature's properties, so rich and available is everything they require.

And some will survive, and wait, and die waiting because

of some remotely extrapolated miscalculation. The beams never reach them; their beams contact nothing. And perhaps a few of these will not die, but will find refuge on some planet to leave a marker that will shock whatever is alive and intelligent a million years hence. Perhaps they will leave more than that. Perhaps there will be a slower, more hazardous planting of humanity in the gulfs.

But fifty-four per cent, the calculations insist, will establish the star-conquering sphere and return.

The weeks went by. A chime: Bark and Barbara. Damn it all, no more of Barbara's banana cream pie. The filing, the sweeping, the recording, the lights. Marriage recorded.

When a man and a woman go Out together, that is marriage. There is another way to be married on Curbstone. There is a touch less speed involved in it than in joined hands pressing down a launching lever. There is not one whit less solemnity. It means what it means because it is not stamped with necessity. Children derive their names from their mothers, wed or not, and there is no distinction. Men and women, as responsible adults, do as they please within limits which are extremely wide. *Except. . . .*

By arduous trial and tragic error, humanity has evolved modern marriage. With social pressure removed from the pursuit of a mate, with the end of the ribald persecution of spinsterhood, a marriage ceases to be a rubber stamp upon what people are sure to do, with or without ceremonies. Where men and women are free to seek their own company, as and when they choose, without social penalties, they will not be trapped into hypocrisies with marriage vows. Under such conditions a marriage is entered gravely and with sincerity, and it constitutes a public statement of choice and—with the full implementation of a mature society—of inviolability. The lovely, ancient words "forsaking all others" spell out the nature of modern marriage, with the universally respected adjunct that fidelity is not a command or a restriction, but a chosen path. Divorce is swift and simple, and—almost unheard of. Married people live this way, single people live that way; the lines are drawn and deeply respected. People marry because they intend to live within the limits of marriage. The fact that a marriage exists is complete proof that it is working.

I had a word about marriage with Tween. Ran into her in the Gate corridor. I think she'd been in one of the ships again. If she was pale, her olive skin hid it. If her eyes were bloodshot, the lustrous ruby of her eyes covered it up. Maybe I saw her dragging her feet as she walked, or some such. I took her chin in my hand and tilted her head back. "Any dragons I can kill?"

She gave me a brilliant smile, which lived only on her lips. "I'm wonderful," she said bravely.

"You are," I agreed. "Which doesn't necessarily have anything to do with the way you feel. I won't pry, child; but tell me—if you ever ate too many green apples, or stubbed your toe on a cactus, do you know a nice safe something you could hang on to while you cried it out?"

"I do," she said breathlessly, making the smile just as hard as she could. "Oh, I do." She patted my cheek. "You're . . . listen. Would you tell me something if I asked you?"

"About certificates? No, Tween. Not about anyone else's certificate. But—all he has to do is complete his final hypnopediae, and he just hasn't showed up."

She hated to hear it, but I'd made her laugh, too, a little. "Do you read minds, the way they all say?"

"I do not. And if I could, I wouldn't. And if I couldn't help reading 'em, I'd sure never act as if I could. In other words, no. It's just that I've been alive long enough to know what pushes people around. So's I don't care much about a person, I can judge pretty well what's bothering him.

" 'Course," I added, "if I do give a damn, I can tell even better. Tween, you'll be getting married pretty soon, right?"

Perhaps I shouldn't have said that. She gasped, and for a moment she just stopped making that smile. Then, "Oh, yes," she said brightly. "Well, not exactly. What I mean is, when we go Out, you see, so we might as well not, and I imagine as soon as Wold gets his certificate, we'll . . . we kind of feel going Out is the best . . . I seem to have gotten something in my eye. I'm s-sor. . . ."

I let her go. But when I saw Wold next—it was down in the Euphoria Sector—I went up to him very cheerfully. There are ways I feel sometimes that make me real jovial.

I laid my hand on his shoulder. His back bowed a bit and it seemed to me I felt vertebrae grinding together. "Wold, old boy," I said heartily. "Good to see you. You haven't been around much recently. Mad?"

He pulled away from me. "A little," he said sullenly. His hair was too shiny and he had perfect teeth that always reminded me of a keyboard instrument.

"Well, drop around," I said. "I like to see young folks get ahead. You," I added with a certain amount of emphasis, "have gone pretty damn far."

"So have you," he said with even more emphasis.

"Well, then." I slapped him on the back. His eyeballs stayed in, which surprised me. "You can top me. You can go farther than I ever can. See you soon, old fellow."

I walked off, feeling the cold brown points of his gaze.

And as it happened, not ten minutes later I saw that *kakumba* dance. I don't see much dancing usually, but there was an animal roar from the dance-chamber that stopped me, and I ducked in to see what had the public so charmed.

The dance had gone through most of its figures, with the caller already worked up into a froth and only three couples left. As I shouldered my way to a vantage point, one of the three couples was bounced, leaving the two best. One was a tall blonde with periwigged hair and subvoltaic bracelets that passed and repassed a clatter of pastel arcs; she was dancing with one of the armor-monkeys from the Curbstone Hull Division, and they were good.

The other couple featured a slender, fluid dark girl in an open tunic of deep brown. She moved so beautifully that I caught my breath, and watched so avidly that it was seconds before I realized that it was Flower. The reaction to that made me lose more seconds in realizing that her partner was Judson. Good as the other couple were, they were better. I'd tested Jud's reflexes, and they were phenomenal, but I'd had no idea he could respond like this to anything.

The caller threw the solo light to the first couple. There was a wild burst of music and the arc-wielding blonde and her arc-wielding boy friend cut loose in an intricate frenzy of disjointed limbs and half-beat stamping. So much happened between those two people so fast that I thought they'd never get separated when the music stopped. But they untangled right with the closing bars, and a roar went up from the people watching them. And then the same blare of music was thrown at Jud and Flower.

Judson simply stood back and folded his arms, walking out a simple figure to indicate that, honest, he was dancing, too. But he gave it all to Flower.

Now I'll tell you what she did in a single sentence: she knelt before him and slowly stood up with her arms over her head. But words will never describe the process completely. It took her about twelve minutes to get all the way up. At the fourth minute the crowd began to realize that her body was trembling. It wasn't a wriggle or a shimmy, or anything as crude as that. It was a steady, apparently uncontrollable shiver. At about the eighth minute the audience began to realize it was controlled, and just how completely controlled it was. It was hypnotic, incredible. At the final crescendo she was on her tiptoes with her arms stretched high, and when the music stopped she made no flourish; she simply relaxed and stood still, smiling at Jud. Even from where I stood I could see the moisture on Jud's face.

A big man standing beside me grunted, a tight, painful sound. I turned to him; it was Clinton. Tension crawled through his jaw-muscles like a rat under a rug. I put my hand on his arm. It was rocky. "Clint."

"Wh—oh. Hi."

"Thirsty?"

"No," he said. He turned back to the dance floor, searched it with his eyes, found Flower.

"Yes, you are, son," I said. "Come on."

"Why don't you go and—" He got hold of himself. "You're right. I am thirsty."

We went to the almost deserted Card Room and dispensed ourselves some methyl-caffeine. I didn't say anything until we'd found a table. He sat stiffly looking at his drink without seeing it. Then he said, "Thanks."

"For what?"

"I was about to be real uncivilized in there."

I just waited.

He said truculently, "Well, damn it, she's free to do what she wants, isn't she? She likes to dance—good. Why shouldn't she? Damn it, what is there to get excited about?"

"Who's excited?"

"It's that Judson. What's he have to be crawling around her all the time for? She hasn't done a damn thing about getting her certificate since he got here." He drank his liquor down at a gulp. It had no apparent effect, which meant something.

"What had she done before he got here?" I asked quietly. When he didn't answer I said, "Jud's Outbound, Clint. I wouldn't worry. I can guarantee Flower won't be with him when he goes, and that will be real soon. Hold on and wait."

"Wait?" His lip curled. "I've been ready to go for weeks. I used to think of . . . of Flower and me working together, helping each other. I used to make plans for a celebration the day we got certified. I used to look at the stars and think about the net we'd help throw around them, pull 'em down, pack 'em in a basket. Flower and me, back on Earth after six thousand years, watching humanity come into its own, knowing we'd done something to help. I've been waiting, and you say wait some more."

"This," I said, "is what you call an unstable situation. It can't stay the way it is and it won't. Wait, I tell you: wait. There's got to be a blow-off."

There was.

In my office the chime sounded. Moira and Bill. Certificates denied to Hester, Elizabeth, Jenks, Mella. Hester back to earth. Hallowell and Letitia, marriage recorded. Certificates granted to Aaron, Musette, n'Guchi, Mancinelli, Judson.

Judson took the news quietly, glowing. I hadn't seen much of him recently. Flower took up a lot of his time, and training the rest. After he was certified and I'd gone with him to test the hand-scanner by the gate and give him his final briefing, he cut out on the double, I guess to give Flower the great news. I remember wondering how he'd like her reaction.

When I got back to my office Tween was there. She rose from the foyer couch as I wheezed in off the ramp. I took one look at her and said, "Come inside." She followed me through the inner door. I waved my hand over the infrared plate and it closed. Then I put out my arms.

She bleated like a new-born lamb and flew to me. Her tears were scalding, and I don't think human muscles are built for the wrenching those agonized sobs gave her. People should cry more. They ought to learn how to do it easily, like laughing or sweating. Crying piles up. In people like Tween, who do nothing if they can't smile and make a habit-pattern of it, it really piles up. With a reservoir like that, and no developed outlet, things get torn when the pressure builds too high.

I just held her tight so she wouldn't explode. The only

thing I said to her was "sh-h-h" once when she tried to talk while she wept. One thing at a time.

It took a while, but when she was finished she was finished. She didn't taper off. She was weak from all that punishment, but calm. She talked.

"He isn't a real thing at all," she said bleakly. "He's something I made up out of starshine, out of wanting as much to be a part of something as big as this project. I never felt I had anything big about me except that. I wanted to join it with something bigger than I was, and, together, we'd build something so big it would be worthy of Curbstone.

"I thought it was Wold. I *made* it be Wold. Oh, none of this is his fault. I could have seen what he was, and I just wouldn't. What I did with him, what I felt for him, was just as crazy as if I'd convinced myself he had wings and then hated him because he wouldn't fly. He isn't anything but a h-hero. He struts to the newcomers and the rejected ones pretending he's a man who will one day give himself to humanity and the stars. He . . . probably believes that about himself. But he won't complete his training, and he . . . now I know, now I can see it—he tried everything he could think of to stop me from being certified. I was no use to him with a certificate. He couldn't treat me as his pretty slightly stupid little girl, once I was certified. And he couldn't get his own certificate because if he did he'd have to go Out, one of these days, and that's something he can't face.

"He—*wants* me to leave him. If I will, if it's my decision, he can wear my memory like a black band on his arm, and delude himself for the rest of his life that his succession of women is just a search for something to replace me. Then he'll always have an excuse; he'll never have to risk his neck. He'll be the shattered hero, and women as stupid as I will try to heal the wounds he's arranged for me to give him."

"You don't hate him?" I asked her quietly.

"No. Oh, no, *no!* I told you, it wasn't his fault. I—loved *something*. A man lived in my heart, lived there for years. He had no name and no face. I gave him Wold's name and Wold's face and just wouldn't believe it wasn't Wold. I did it. Wold didn't. I don't hate him. I don't like him. I just don't . . . *anything*."

I patted her shoulder. "Good. You're cured. If you hated him, he'd still be important. What are you going to do?"

"What shall I do?"

"I'd never tell you what to do about a thing like this, Tween. You know that. You've got to figure out your own answers. I can advise you to use those new-opened eyes of yours carefully, though. And don't think that that man who lives in your heart doesn't exist anywhere else. He does. Right here on this station, maybe. You just haven't been able to see him before."

"Who?"

"God, girl, don't ask me that! Ask Tween next time you see her; no one will ever know for sure but Tween."

"You're so wise. . . ."

"Nah. I'm old enough to have made more mistakes than most people, that's all, and I have a good memory."

She rose shakily. I put out a hand and helped her. "You're played out, Tween. Look—don't go back yet. Hide out for a few days and get some rest and do some thinking. There's a suite on this level. No one will bother you, and you'll find everything there you need, including silence and privacy."

"That would be good," she said softly. "Thank you."

"All right . . . listen. Mind if I send someone in to talk to you?"

"Talk? Who?"

"Let me play it as it comes."

The ruby eyes sent a warm wave to me, and she smiled. I thought, I wish I was as confident of myself as she is of me. "It's 412," I said, "the third door to your left. Stay there as long as you want to. Come back when you feel like it."

She came close to me and tried to say something. I thought for a second she was going to kiss me on the mouth. She didn't; she kissed my hand. "I'll swat your bottom!" I roared, flustered. "Git, now, dammit!" She laughed . . . she always had a bit of laughter tucked away in her, no matter what, bless her cotton head. . . .

As soon as she was gone, I turned to the annunciator and sent out a call for Judson. *Hell,* I thought, *you can try, can't you?* Waiting, I thought about Judson's hungry upward look, and that hole in his head . . . that quality of reachableness, and what happened when he was reached by the wrong thing. Lord, responsive people certainly make the worst damn fools of all!

He was there in minutes, looking flushed, excited, happy, and worried all at once. "Was on my way here when your call went out," he said.

"Sit down, Jud. I have a small project in mind. Maybe you could help."

He sat. I looked for just the right words to use. I couldn't say anything about Flower. She had her hooks into him; if I said anything about her, he'd defend her. And one of the oldest phenomena in human relations is that we come to be very fond of the thing we find ourselves defending, even if we didn't like it before. I thought again of the hunger that lived in Jud, and what Tween might see of it with her newly opened eyes.

"Jud—"

"I'm married," he blurted.

I sat very still. I don't think my face did anything at all.

"It was the right thing for me to do," he said, almost angrily. "Don't you see? You know what my problem is—it was you who found it for me. I was looking for something that should belong to me . . . or something to belong to."

"Flower," I said.

"Of course. Who else? Listen, that girl's got trouble, too. What do you suppose blocks her from taking her certificate? She doesn't think she's *worthy* of it."

My, I said. Fortunately, I said it to myself.

Jud said, "No matter what happens, I've done the right thing. If I can help her get her certificate, we'll go Out together, and that's what we're here for. If I can't help her do that, but find that she fills that place in me that's been so empty for so long, well and good—that's what *I'm* here for. We can go back to Earth and be happy."

"You're quite sure of all this."

"Sure I'm sure! Do you think I'd have gone ahead with the marriage if I weren't sure?"

Sure you would, I thought. I said, "Congratulations, then. You know I wish you the best."

He stood up uncertainly, started to say something, and apparently couldn't find it. He went to the door, turned back. "Will you come for dinner tonight?" I hesitated. He said, "Please. I'd appreciate it."

I cocked an eyebrow. "Answer me straight, Jud. Is dinner your idea or Flower's?"

He laughed embarrassedly. "Damn it, you always see too much. Mine . . . sort of . . . I mean, it isn't that she dislikes you, but . . . well, hell, I want the two of you to be friends, and I think you'd understand her and me too, a lot better if you made the effort."

I could think of things I'd much rather do than have dinner with Flower. A short swim in boiling oil, for example. I looked up at his anxious face. Oh, hell. "I'd love to," I said. "Around eight?"

"Fine! Gee," he said, like a school kid. "Gee, thanks." He shuffled, not knowing whether to go right away or not. "Hey," he said suddenly. "You sent out a call for me. What's this project you wanted me for?"

"Nothing, Jud," I said tiredly. "I've . . . changed my mind. See you later, son."

The dinner was something special. Steaks. Jud had broiled them himself. I got the idea that he'd selected them, too, and set the table. It was Flower, though, who got me something to sit on. She looked me over, slowly and without concealing it, went to the table, pulled the light formed-aluminum chair away, and dragged over a massive relaxer. She then smiled straight at me. A little unnecessary, I thought; I'm bulky, but those aluminum chairs have always held up under me so far.

I won't give it to you round by round. The meal passed with Flower either in a sullen silence or manufacturing small brittle whips of conversation. When she was quiet, Jud tried to goad her into talking. When she talked, he tried to turn the conversation away from me. The occasion, I think, was a complete success—for Flower. For Jud it must have been hell. For me—well, it was interesting.

Item: Flower poked and prodded at her steak, and when she got a lull in the labored talk Jud and I were squeezing out, she began to cut me meticulously around the edges of the steak. "If there is anything I can't stand the sight or the smell of," she said clearly, "it's fat."

Item: She said, "Oh, Lord" this and "Lord sakes" that in a drawl that made it come out "Lard" every time.

Item: I sneezed once. She whipped a tissue over to me swiftly and politely enough, and then said "Render unto sneezers . . ." which stood as a cute quip until she nudged her husband and said, *"Render!"* at which point things got real hushed.

Item: When she had finished, she leaned back and sighed. "If I ate like that all the time, I'd be as big as—" She looked straight at me and stopped. Jud, flushing miserably, tried to kick her under the table; I know, because it was me he kicked. Flower finished, "—as big as a lifeboat." But she kept looking at me, easily and insultingly.

Item—You get the idea. All I can say for myself is that I got through it all. I wouldn't give her the satisfaction of driving me out until I'd had all she could give me. I wouldn't be overtly angry, because if I did, she'd present me to Jud ever after as the man who hated her. If Jud ever had wit enough, this evening could be remembered as the time she was insufferably insulting, and that was all I wanted.

It was over at last, and I made my excuses as late as I possibly could without staying overnight. As I left, she took Jud's arm and held it tight until I was out of sight, thereby removing the one chance he had to come along a little way and apologize to me.

He didn't get close enough to speak to me for four days, and when he did, I had the impression that he had lied to be there, that Flower thought he was somewhere else. He said rapidly, "About the other night, you mustn't think that—"

And I cut him off as gently and firmly as I could: "I understand it perfectly, Jud. Think a minute and you'll know that."

"Look, Flower was just out of sorts. I'll work on her. Next time you come there'll be a real difference. You'll see."

"I'm sure I will, Jud. But drop it, will you? There's no harm done." And I thought, next time I come will be six months after the Outbounders get back. That gives me sixty centuries or so to get case-hardened.

About a week after Jud's wedding, I was in the Upper Central corridor where it ramps into the Gate passageway. Now whether it was some sixth sense, or whether I actually did smell something, I don't know. I got a powerful, sourceless impression of methyl-caffeine in the air, and at the same time I looked down the passage and saw the Gate just closing.

I got down there altogether too fast to do my leaky valves any good. I palmed the doors open and sprinted across the court. When anything my size and shape gets to sprinting, it's harder to stop it than let it keep going. One of the ship ports was open and I was heading for it. It started to swing closed. I lost all thought of trying to slow down and put what little energy I could find into pumping my old legs faster.

With a horrible slow-motion feeling of disaster, I felt one toe tip my other heel, and my center of gravity began to move forward faster than I was traveling. I was in mid-air for an age—long enough to chew and swallow a tongue—and then I hit on my stomach, rocked forward on my receding chest and two of my chins, and slid. I had my hands out in front of me. My left hit the bulkhead and buckled. My right shot through what was left of the opening of the door, which crunched shut on my forearm. Then my forehead hit the sill and I blacked out.

When the lights dimmed on again, I was spread out on a ship's bunk, apparently alone. My left arm hurt more than I could bear, and my right arm hurt worse, and both of them together couldn't match what was going on in my head.

A man appeared from the service cubicle when I let out a groan. He had a bowl of warm water and the ship's B first-aid kit in his hands. He crossed quickly to me, and began to stanch the blood from between some of my chins. It wasn't until then that my blurring sight made out who he was.

"Clinton, you hub-forted son of a bastich!" I roared at him. "Leave the chin alone and get some plexicaine into those arms!"

He had the gall to laugh at me. "One thing at a time, old man. You are bleeding. Let's try to be a patient, not an impatient."

"Impatient, out-patient," I yelped, "get that plex into me! I am just not the strong, silent type!"

"Okay, okay." He got the needle out of the kit, squirted it upward, and plunged it deftly into my arms. A good boy. He hit the biceps on one, the forearm on the other, and got just the right ganglia. The pain vanished. That left my head, but he fed me an analgesic and that cataclysmic ache began to recede.

"I'm afraid the left is broken," he said. "As for the right—well, if I hadn't seen that hand come crawling in over the sill like a pet puppy, and reversed the door control, I'd have cut your fingernails off clear up to the elbow. What in time did you think you were doing?"

"I can't remember; maybe I've got a concussion. For some reason or other it seemed I had to look inside the ship. Can you splint this arm?"

"Let's call the medic."

"You can do just as well."

He went for the C kit and got a traction splint out. He whipped the prepared cushioning around the swelling arm, clamped the ends of the splint at wrist and elbow, and played an infra-red lamp on it. In a few seconds the splint began to lengthen. When the broken forearm was a few millimeters longer than the other, he shut off the heat and the thermoplastic splint automatically set and snugged into the cushioning. Clinton threw off the clamps. "That's good enough for now. All right, are you ready to tell me what made you get in my way?"

"No."

"Stop trying to look like an innocent babe! Your stubble gives you away. You knew I was going to solo, didn't you?"

"No one said anything to me."

"No one ever has to," he said in irritation, and then chuckled. "Man, I wish I could stay mad at you. All right— what next?"

"You're not going to take off?"

"With you in here? Don't be foolish. That station'd lose too much and I wouldn't be gaining a thing. Damn you! I'd worked up the most glamorous drunk on methyl-caffeine, and you had to get me all anxious and drive away the fumes. . . . Well, go ahead. I'll play it your way. What do we do?"

"Stop trying to make a Machiavelli out of me," I growled. "Give me a hand back to my quarters and I'll let you go do whatever you want."

"It's never that simple with you," he half-grinned. "Okay. Let's go."

When I got to my feet—with more of his help than I like to admit—my heart began to pound. He must have felt it, because he said nothing while we stood there and waited for it to behave itself. Clinton was a good lad.

We negotiated the court and the Gate all right, but slowly. When we got to the foot of my ramp, I shook my head. "Not that," I wheezed. "Couldn't make it. Down this way."

We went down the lateral corridor to 112. The door slid back for me.

"Hi!" I called. "Company."

"What? Who is it?" came the crystal voice. Tween appeared. "Oh—oh! I didn't want to see anyone just—why, what's happened?"

My eyelids flickered. I moaned. Clinton said, "I think we better get him spread out. He's not doing so well."

Tween ran to us and took my arm gently above the splint. They got me to a couch and I collapsed on it.

"Damn him," said Clinton good-humoredly. "He seems to be working full time to keep me from going Out."

There was such a long silence that I opened one eye to look at them. Tween was staring at him as if she had never seen him before—as, actually, she hadn't, with her eyes so full of Wold.

"Do you really want to go Out?" she asked softly.

"More than. . . ." He looked at her hair, her lovely face. "I don't think I've seen you around much. You're—Tween, aren't you?"

She nodded and they stopped talking. I snapped my eyes shut because they were sure to look at me just for something to do.

"Is he all right?" she asked.

"I think he's—yes, he's asleep. Don't wonder. He's been through a lot."

"Let's go in the other room where we can talk together without disturbing him."

They closed the door. I could barely hear them. It went on for a long time, with occasional silences. Finally I heard what I'd been listening for: "If it hadn't been for him, I'd be gone now. I was just about to solo."

"No! Oh, I'm glad. . . . I'm glad you didn't."

One of those silences. Then, "So am I, Tween. Tween. . . ." in a whisper of astonishment.

I got up off the couch and silently let myself out. I went back to my quarters, even managing to climb the ramp. I felt real fine.

I heard an ugly rumor.

I'd seen a lot and I'd done a lot, and I regarded myself

as pretty shockproof, but this one jolted me to the core. I took refuge in the old ointment, "It can't be, it just can't be," but in my heart I knew it could.

I got hold of Judson. He was hollow-eyed and much quieter than usual. I asked him what he was doing these days, though I knew.

"Boning up on the fine points of astrogation," he told me. "I've never hit anything so fascinating. It's one thing to have the stuff shoveled into your head when you're asleep, and something else again to experience it all, note by note, like music."

"But you're spending an awful lot of time in the archives, son."

"It takes a lot of time."

"Can't you study at home?"

I think he only just then realized what I was driving at. "Look," he said quietly, "I have my troubles. I have things wrong with me. But I'm not blind. I'm not stupid. You wouldn't tell me to my face that I couldn't handle problems that are strictly my own, would you?"

"I would if I were sure," I said. "Dam it, I'm not. And I'm not going to pry for details."

"I'm glad of that," he said soberly. "Now we don't have to talk about it at all, do we?"

In spite of myself, I laughed aloud.

"What's funny?"

"I am, Jud, boy. I been—handled."

He saw the point, and smiled a little with me. "Hell, I know what you've been hinting at. But you're not close enough to the situation to know all the angles. I am. When the time comes, I'll take care of it. Until then, it's no one's problem but my own."

He picked up his star-chart reels and I knew that one single word more would be one too many. I squeezed his arm and let him go.

Five people, I thought: Wold, Judson, Tween, Clinton, Flower. Take away two and that leaves three. Three's a crowd—in this case, a very explosive kind of crowd.

Nothing, *nothing* justifies infidelity in a modern marriage. But the ugly rumors kept trickling in.

"I want my certificate," Wold said.

I looked up at him and a bushel of conjecture flipped through my mind. So you want your certificate? Why? And why just now, of all times? What can a man do with a certificate that he can't do without one—aside from going Out? Because, damn you, you'll never go Out. Not of your own accord, you won't.

All this, but none of it slipped out. I said, "All right. That's what I'm here for, Wold." And we got to work.

He worked hard, and smoothly and easily, the way he talked, the way he moved. I am constantly astonished at how small accomplished people can make themselves at times.

He was certified easy as breathing. And can you believe it, I worked with him, saw how hard he was working, helped him through, and never realized what it was he was after?

After going through the routines of certification for him, I wasn't happy. There was something wrong somewhere . . . something missing. This was a puzzle that ought to fall together easily, and it wouldn't. I wish—Lord, how I wish I could have thought a little faster.

I let a day go by after Wold was certified. I couldn't sleep, and I couldn't eat, and I couldn't analyze what it was that was bothering me. So I began to cruise, to see if I could find out.

I went to the archives. "Where's Judson?"

The girl told me he hadn't been there for forty-eight hours.

I looked in the Recreation Sector, in the libraries, in the stereo and observation rooms. Some kind of rock-bottom good sense kept me from sending out a general call for him. But it began to be obvious that he just wasn't around. Of course, there were hundreds of rooms and corridors in Curbstone that were unused—they wouldn't be used until the interplanetary project was completed and the matter transmitters started working. But Jud wasn't the kind to hide from anything.

I squared my shoulders and realized that I was doing a lot of speculation to delay looking in the obvious place. I think, more than anything else, I was afraid that he would *not* be there. . . .

I passed my hand over the door announcer. In a moment she answered; she had apparently come in from the sun-field and hadn't bothered to see who it was. She was warm brown from head to toe, all spring-steel and velvet. Her long eyes were sleepy and her mouth was pouty. But when she recognized me, she stood squarely in the doorway.

I think that in the back of every human mind is a machine that works out all the answers and never makes mistakes. I think mine had had enough data to figure out what was happening, what was going to happen, for a long while now. Only I hadn't been able to read the answer until now. Seeing Flower, in that split second, opened more than one door for me. . . .

"*You* want something?" she asked. The emphasis was hard and very insulting.

I went in. It was completely up to her whether she moved aside or was walked down. She moved aside. The door swung shut.

"Where's Jud?"

"I don't know."

I looked into those long secret eyes and raised my hand. I think I was going to hit her. Instead I put my hand on her chest and shoved. She fell, unhurt but terrified, across a relaxer. "What do you th—"

"You won't see him again," I said, and my voice bounced harshly off the acoust-absorbing walls. "He's gone. *They're* gone."

"They?" Her face went pasty under the deep tan.

"You ought to be killed," I said. "But I think it's better if you live with it. You couldn't hold either of them, or anyone else."

I went out.

My head was buzzing and my knitting arm throbbed. I moved with utter certainty; never once did it occur to me to ask myself: "Why did I say that?" All the ugly pieces made sense.

I found Wold in the Recreation Sector. He was tanked. I decided against speaking to him, went straight to the launching court and tried the row of ship ports. There was no one there, no one in any of them. My eye must have photographed something in the third ship, because I felt compelled to go back there and look again.

I stared hard at the deep-flocked floor. The soft pile of it looked right and yet not-right. I went to the control panel and untracked an emergency torch, turned it to needle-focus and put it, lit, on the floor. A horizontal beam will tell you things no other light knows about.

I turned the light on the door and slowly swung the sharp

streak across the carpet. The monotone, amorphous surface took on streaks and ridges, shadows and shadings. A curved scuff inside. Two parallel ones, long, where something had been dragged. A blurred sector where something heavy had lain long enough to press the springy fibers down for a while, over by the left-hand bunk.

I looked at the bunk. It was unruffled, which meant nothing; the resilient surface was meant to leave no impressions. But at the edge was a single rubbed spot, as if something had spilled there and been wiped hard.

I went to the service cubicle. Everything seemed in order, except one of the cabinet doors, which wouldn't quite close. I looked inside.

It was a food locker. The food was there all right, each container socketed in place in the prepared shelves. But on, between, and among them were micro-reels for the book projector.

I frowned and looked further. Reels were packed into the disposal lock, the towel dispenser, the spare-parts chest for the air exchanger.

Something was where the book-reels belonged, and the reels had been hidden by someone who could not leave them in sight or carry them off.

And where did the reels belong?

I went back to the central chamber and the left-hand bunk. I touched the stud that should have rolled the bunk outward, opening the top, so that the storage space under it could be reached. The bunk didn't move.

I examined the stud. It was coated over with quick-setting leak-sealer. The stuff was tough but resilient. I got a steel rod and a hammer from the tool-rack and, placing the rod against the stud, hit it once. The leak-sealer cracked off. The bed rolled forward and opened.

It was useless to move him or touch him, or, for that matter, to say anything. Judson was dead, his head twisted almost all the way around. His face was bluish and his eyes stared. He was pushed, jammed, wedged into the small space.

I hit the stud again and the bunk rolled back. Moving without any volition that I could analyze, feeling nothing but a great angry numbness, I cleaned up. I put the rod and the hammer away and fluffed up the piling of the carpeting by the bunk. Then I went and stood in the service cubicle and began to wait.

Wait. Not just stay—wait. I knew he'd be back, just as I suddenly and belatedly understood what it was that every factor in five people had made inevitable. I was coldly hating myself for not having known it sooner.

The great, the admirable, the adventurous in modern civilization were Outbounders. To one who wanted and needed personal power, there would be an ultimate goal, greater even than being an Outbounder. And that would be to stand between an Outbounder and his destiny.

For months Flower had blocked Clinton. When she saw she must ultimately lose him to the stars, she went hunting. She saw Judson—reachable, restless Jud—and she heard my assurance that he would soon go Out. Then and there Judson was doomed.

Wold needed admiration the way Flower needed power. To be an Outbounder and wait for poor struggling Tween suited him perfectly. Tween's certification gave him no alternative but to get rid of her; he couldn't bring himself to go Out.

Once I had taken care of Tween for him, there remained one person on the entire project who could keep him from going Out—and she was married to Jud. Having married, Jud would stay married. Wold did what he could to smash that marriage. When Jud still hung on, wanting to help Flower, wanting to show me that he had made the right choice, there remained one alternative for Wold. Evidence of that lay cramped and staring under the bunk.

But Wold wasn't finished. He wouldn't be finished while Jud's body remained on Curbstone. In Wold's emotional state, he would have to go somewhere and drink to figure out the next step. There was no way of sending a ship Out without riding it. So—I waited.

He came back all right. I was cramped, then, and one foot was asleep. I curled and uncurled the toes frantically when I saw the door begin to move, and tried to flatten my big bulk back down out of sight.

He was breathing hard. He put his lips together and blew like a winded horse, wiped his lips on his forearm. He seemed to have difficulty in focusing his eyes. I wondered how much liquor he had poured into that empty place where most men keep their courage.

He took a fine coil of single-strand plastic cord out of his belt-pouch. Fumbling for the end, he found it and dropped the coil. With the exaggerated care of a drunk, he threw a bowline and drew the loop tight, pulled the bight through the loop so he had a running noose. He made this fast to a triangular bracket over the control panel, led it along the edge of the chart-rack and down to the launching control lever. He bent two half-hitches in the cord, slipped it over the end of the lever and drew it tight. The cord now bound the lever in the up—"off"—position.

From the bulkhead he unfastened the clamps which held the heavy-duty fire extinguisher and lifted it down. It weighed half as much as he did. He set it on the floor in front of the control panel, brought the dangling end of the cord through the U-shaped clamp gudgeons on the extinguisher, took a loose half-hitch around the bight, and, lifting the extinguisher between his free arm and his body, pulled the knot tight. Another half-hitch secured it.

Now the heavy extinguisher dangled in mid-air under the control panel. The cord which supported it ran up to the handle of the launching lever and from there, bending over the edge of the chart-rack, to the bracket.

Panting, Wold took out a cigarette and shook it alight. He drew on it hungrily, and then put it on the chart-rack, resting it against the plastic cord.

When the cigarette burned down to the cord, the thermo-plastic would melt through with great enthusiasm. The cord would break, the extinguisher would fall, dragging the lever down. And Out would go all the evidence, to be hidden forever, as far as Wold was concerned, and 6,000 years from anyone else.

Wold stepped back to survey his work just as I stepped forward out of the service cubicle. I brought up my broken arm and swung it with all my weight—and that is really weight—against the side of his head. The cast, though not heavy, was hard, and it must have hit him like a crowbar.

He went down like an elevator, hitched to his knees, and for a second seemed about to topple. His head sagged. He shook it, slowly looked up, and saw me.

"I could use one of those needle-guns," I said. "Or I could kick you cold and let Coördination handle you. There are regulations for things like you. But I'd rather do it this way. Get up."

"I never. . . ."

"Get up!" I bellowed, and kicked at him.

He threw his arms around my leg and rolled. As I started down, I pulled the leg in close and whipped it out again. We both hit with a crash on opposite sides of the room. The bunk broke my fall; he was not so lucky. He rose groggily, sliding his back up the door. I lumbered across, deliberately crashed into him, and heard ribs crack as the wind gushed out of his lungs.

I stood back a little as he began to sag. I hit him savagely in the face, and his face came back and hit my hand again as his head bounced off the door. I let him fall, then knelt beside him.

There are things you can do to a human body if you know enough physiology—pressures on this and that nerve center which paralyze and cramp and immobilize whole motor-trunk systems. I did these things, and got up, finally, leaving him twisted, sweating in agony. I wheezed over to the control bank and looked critically at the smoldering cigarette. Less than a minute.

"I know you can hear me," I whispered with what breath I could find. "I'd . . . like you to know . . . that you'll be a hero. Your name will . . . be on the Great Roll of the . . . Outbounders. You always . . . wanted that without any . . . effort on your part . . . now you've got it."

I went out. I stopped and leaned back against the wall beside the door. In a few seconds it swung silently shut. I forced back the waves of gray that wanted to engulf me, turned and peered into the port. It showed only blackness.

Jud . . . Jud, boy . . . you always wanted it, too. You almost got cheated out of it. You'll be all right now, son. . . .

I tottered across the court and out the gate. There was someone standing there. She flew to me, pounded my chest with small hard hands. "Did he go? Did he really go?"

I brushed her off as if she had been a midge, and closed one eye so I could get a single image. It was Flower, without her come-on tunic. Her hair was disarrayed and her eyes were bloodshot.

"*They* left," I croaked. "I told you they would. Jud and Wold . . . you couldn't stop them."

"Together? They left *together*?"

"That's what Wold got certified for." I looked bluntly up

and down her supple body. "Like everybody else who goes Out together, they had *some*thing in common."

I pushed past her and went back to my office. Lights were blazing over the desk. Judson and Wold. Ship replaced. Quarters cleaned. Palm-key removed and filed. I sat and looked blindly until they were all lit and the board blanked out.

I thought, this pump of mine won't last much longer under this kind of treatment.

I thought, I keep convincing myself that I handle things impartially and fairly, without getting involved.

I felt bad. Bad.

I thought, this is a job without authority, without any real power. I certify 'em, send 'em along, check 'em out. A clerk's job. And because of that I have to be God. I have to make up my own justice, and execute it myself. Wold was no threat to me or to Curbstone, yet it was in me to give oblivion to him and purgatory to Flower.

I felt frightened and disgusted and puny.

Someone came in, and I looked up blindly. For a moment I could make out nothing but a silver-haloed figure and a muted, wordless murmuring. I forced my eyes to focus, and I had to close them again, as if I had looked into the sun.

Her hair was unbound beneath a diamond ring that circled her brows. The silver silk cascaded about her, brushing the floor behind her, mantling her warm-toned shoulders, capturing small threads of light and weaving them in and about the gleaming light that was her hair. Her deep pigeon's-blood eyes shone and her lips trembled.

"Tween. . . ."

The soft murmuring became words, laughter that wept with happiness, small shaking syllables of rapture. "He's waiting. He wanted to say good-by to you, too . . . but he asked me to do it for him. He said you'd like that better."

I could only nod.

She came close to the desk. "I love him. I love him more than I thought anyone could. Somehow, loving him that much, I can . . . love you, too."

She bent over the desk and kissed my mouth. Her lips were cool. She—blurred then. Or maybe it was my eyes. When I could see again, she was gone.

The chime, and the lights, one after another.

Marriage recorded. . . .

Suddenly I relaxed and I knew I could live with the viciousness of what I had done to Wold and to Flower. It had been my will that Judson go Out, and that Tween be happy, and I had been crossed, and I had taken vengeance. And that was small, and decidedly human—not godlike at all.

So, I thought every day I find something out about people. And, today, I'm people. I felt the pudgy lips that Tween had kissed. I'm old and I'm fat, I thought, and by the Lord, I'm people.

When they call me Charon, they forget what it must be like to be denied both worlds instead of only one.

And they forget the other thing—the little-known fragment of the Charon legend. To the Etruscans, he was more than a ferryman.

He was an executioner.

OCCAM'S
SCALPEL

Who was the richest man in the world in 1971, while I was writing this? And what came creeping into my typewriter to suggest that any particular rich man would die under inexplicably mysterious circumstances?

I am unabashedly proud of some of the things I have done and can do with a typewriter. I've gone through a lot of grinding and tumbling and polishing to learn to do it.

But there's something else that happens once in a while, something I'm unaware of at the time, which doesn't manifest itself to me until after I've written a passage and reread it. I see then some hundreds or thousands of words written outside any learned idiom, written, as it were, in a different "voice," and containing, sometimes, factual material which I did not and could not have known at the time, and (rather more often) emotional reactions and attitudes which I know I have not experienced. This phenomenon is quite beyond my control; that is, I know of no way to command or evoke it. I just have to wait for it to happen, which it seldom does. When it does, it keeps me humble; when I'm complimented on it, I feel guilty.

I

Joe Trilling had a funny way of making a living. It was a good living, but of course he didn't make anything like the bundle he could have in the city. On the other hand he lived in the mountains a half mile away from a picturesque village in clean air and piney-birchy woods along with lots of mountain laurel and he was his own boss. There wasn't much competition for what he did; he had his wife and kids around all the time and more orders than he could fill. He was one of the night people and after the family had gone to bed he could work quietly and uninterruptedly. He was happy as a clam.

One night—very early morning, really—he was interrupted. *Bup-pup, bup, bup.* Knock at the window, two shorts, two longs. He froze, he whirled, for he knew that knock. He hadn't heard it for years but it had been a part of his life since he was born. He saw the face outside and filled his lungs for a whoop that would have roused them at the fire station on the village green, but then he saw the finger on the lips and let the air out. The finger beckoned and Joe Trilling whirled again, turned down a flame, read a gauge, made a note, threw a switch and joyfully but silently dove for the outside door. He slid out, closed it carefully, peered out into the dark.

"Karl?"

"Shh."

There he was, edge of the woods. Joe Trilling went there and, whispering because Karl had asked for it, they hit each other, cursed, called each other the filthiest possible names. It would not be easy to explain this to an extra-terrestrial; it isn't necessarily a human thing to do. It's a cultural thing. It means, I want to touch you, it means I love you; but they were men and brothers, so they hit each others arms and shoulders and swore despicable oaths and insults, until at last even those words wouldn't do and they stood in the shadows, holding each others biceps and grinning and drilling into each other with eyes. Then Karl Trilling moved his head sidewards toward the road and they walked away from the house.

"I don't want Hazel to hear us talking," Karl said. "I don't want her or anyone to know I was here. How is she?"

'Beautiful. Aren't you going to see her at all—or the kids?"

"Yes but not this trip. There's the car. We can talk there. I really am afraid of that bastard."

"Ah," said Joe. "How is the great man?"

"Po'ly," said Karl. "But we're talking about two different bastards. The great man is only the richest man in the world, but I'm not afraid of him, especially now. I'm talking about Cleveland Wheeler."

"Who's Cleveland Wheeler?"

They got into the car. "It's a rental," said Karl. "Matter of fact, it's the second rental. I got out of the executive jet and took a company car and rented another—and then this. Reasonably sure it's not bugged. That's one kind of answer to your question, who's Cleve Wheeler. Other answers would be the man behind the throne. Next in line. Multi-faceted genius. Killer shark."

"Next in line," said Joe, responding to the only clause that made any sense. "The old man is sinking?"

"Officially—and an official secret—his hemoglobin reading is four. That mean anything to you, Doctor?"

"Sure does, Doctor. Malnutritive anemia, if other rumors I hear are true. Richest man in the world—dying of starvation."

"And old age—and stubbornness—and obsession. You want to hear about Wheeler?"

"Tell me."

"Mister lucky. Born with everything. Greek coin profile. Michaelangelo muscles. Discovered early by a bright-eyed elementary school principal, sent to a private school, used to go straight to the teachers' lounge in the morning and say what he'd been reading or thinking about. Then they'd tell off a teacher to work with him or go out with him or whatever. High school at twelve, varsity track, basketball, football and high-diving—three letters for each—yes, he graduated in three years, *summa cum*. Read all the text-books at the beginning of each term, never cracked them again. More than anything else he had the habit of success.

"College, the same thing: turned sixteen in his first semester, just ate everything up. Very popular. Graduated at the top again, of course."

Joe Trilling, who had slogged through college and medical school like a hodcarrier, grunted enviously. "I've seen one or two like that. Everybody marvels, nobody sees how easy it was for them."

Karl shook his head. "Wasn't quite like that with Cleve Wheeler. If anything was easy for him it was because of the nature of his equipment. He was like a four-hundred horse-power car moving in sixty-horsepower traffic. When his muscles were called on he used them, I mean really put it down to the floor. A very willing guy. Well—he had his choice of jobs—hell, choice of careers. He went into an architectural firm that could use his math, administrative ability, public presence, knowledge of materials, art. Gravitated right to the top, got a partnership. Picked up a doctorate on the side while he was doing it. Married extremely well.

"Mister Lucky," Joe said.

"Mister Lucky, yeah. Listen. Wheeler became a partner and he did his work and he knew his stuff—everything he could learn or understand. Learning and understanding are not enough to cope with some things like greed or unexpected stupidity or accident or sheer bad breaks. Two of the other partners got into a deal I won't bother you with— a high-rise apartment complex in the wrong place for the wrong residents and land acquired the wrong way. Wheeler saw it coming, called them in and talked it over. They said yes-yes and went right ahead and did what they wanted anyway—something that Wheeler never in the world expected. The one thing high capability and straight morals and a good education doesn't give you is the end of innocence. Cleve Wheeler was an innocent.

"Well, it happened, the disaster that Cleve had predicted, but it happened far worse. Things like that, when they surface, have a way of exposing a lot of other concealed rot. The firm collapsed. Cleve Wheeler had never failed at anything in his whole life. It was the one thing he had no practice in dealing with. Anyone with the most rudimentary intelligence would have seen that this was the time to walk away—lie down, even. Cut his losses. But I don't think these things even occurred to him."

Karl Trilling laughed suddenly. "In one of Philip Wylie's novels is a tremendous description of a forest fire and how the animals run away from it, the foxes and the rabbits running shoulder to shoulder, the owls flying in the daytime to get ahead of the flames. Then there's this beetle, lumbering along on the ground. The beetle comes to a burned patch, the edge of twenty acres of hell. It stops, it wiggles its feelers, it turns to the side and begins to walk around the fire—" He laughed again. "That's the special thing Cleveland Wheeler has, you see, under all that muscle and brain and brilliance. If he had to—and were a beetle—he wouldn't turn back and he wouldn't quit. If all he could do was walk around it, he'd start walking."

"What happened?" asked Joe.

"He hung on. He used everything he had. He used his brains and his personality and his reputation and all his worldly goods. He also borrowed and promised—and he worked. Oh, he worked. Well, he kept the firm. He cleaned out the rot and built it all up again from the inside, strong and straight this time. But it cost.

"It cost him time—all the hours of every day but the four or so he used for sleeping. And just about when he had it leveled off and starting up, it cost him his wife."

"You said he'd married well."

"He'd married what you marry when you're a young block-buster on top of everything and going higher. She was a nice enough girl, I suppose, and maybe you can't blame her, but she was no more used to failure than he was. Only he could walk around it. He could rent a room and ride the bus. She just didn't know how—and of course with women like that there's always the discarded swain somewhere in the wings."

"How did he take that?"

"Hard. He'd married the way he played ball or took examinations—with everything he had. It did something to him. All this did things to him, I suppose, but that was the biggest chunk of it.

"He didn't let it stop him. He didn't let anything stop him. He went on until all the bills were paid—every cent.

All the interest. He kept at it until the net worth was exactly what it had been before his ex-partners had begun to eat out the core. Then he gave it away. Gave it away! Sold all right and title to his interest for a dollar."

"Finally cracked, hm?"

Karl Trilling looked at his brother scornfully. "Cracked. Matter of definition, isn't it? Cleve Wheeler's goal was zero —can you understand that? What is success anyhow? Isn't it making up your mind what you're going to do and then doing it, all the way?"

"In that case," said his brother quietly, "suicide is success."

Karl gave him a long penetrating look. "Right," he said, and thought about it a moment.

"Anyhow," Joe asked, "why zero?"

"I did a lot of research on Cleve Wheeler, but I couldn't get inside his head. I don't know. But I can guess. He meant to owe no man anything. I don't know how he felt about the company he saved, but I can imagine. The man he became—was becoming—wouldn't want to owe it one damned thing. I'd say he just wanted out—but on his own terms, which included leaving nothing behind to work on him."

"Okay," said Joe.

Karl Trilling thought, *The nice thing about old Joe is that he'll wait. All these years apart with hardly any communication beyond birthday cards—and not always that— and here he is, just as if we were still together every day. I wouldn't be here if it weren't important; I wouldn't be telling him all this unless he needed to know; he wouldn't need any of it unless he was going to help. All that unsaid—I don't have to ask him a damn thing. What am I interrupting in his life? What am I going to interrupt? I won't have to worry about that. He'll take care of it.*

He said, "I'm glad I came here, Joe."

Joe said, "That's all right," which meant all the things Karl had been thinking. Karl grinned and hit him on the shoulder and went on talking.

"Wheeler dropped out. It's not easy to map his trail for that period. It pops up all over. He lived in at least three communes—maybe more, but those three were a mess when he came and a model when he left. He started businesses—all things that had never happened before, like a supermarket with no shelves, no canned music, no games or stamps, just neat stacks of open cases, where the customer took what he wanted and marked it according to the card posted by the case, with a marker hanging on a string. Eggs and frozen meat and fish and the like, and local produce were priced a flat two percent over wholesale. People were honest because they could never be sure the checkout counter didn't know the prices of everything—besides, to cheat on the prices listed would have been just too embarrassing. With nothing but a big empty warehouse for overhead and no employees spending thousands of man hours marking individual items, the prices beat any discount house that ever lived. He sold that one, too, and moved on. He started a line of organic baby foods without preservatives, franchised it and moved on again. He developed a plastic container that would burn without polluting and patented it and sold the patent."

"I've heard of that one. Haven't seen it around, though."

"Maybe you will," Karl said in a guarded tone. "Maybe you will. Anyway, he had a CPA in Pasadena handling details, and just did his thing all over. I never heard of a failure in anything he tried."

"Sounds like a junior edition of the great man himself, your honored boss."

"You're not the only one who realized that. The boss may be a ding-a-ling in many ways, but nobody ever faulted his business sense. He has always had his tentacles out for wandering pieces of very special manpower. For all I know he had drawn a bead on Cleveland Wheeler years back. I wouldn't doubt that he'd made offers from time to time, only during that period Cleve Wheeler wasn't about to go to work for anyone that big. His whole pattern is to run things his way, and you don't do that in an established empire."

"Heir apparent," said Joe, reminding him of something he had said earlier.

"Right," nodded Karl. "I knew you'd begin to get the idea before I was finished."

"But finish," said Joe.

"Right. Now what I'm going to tell you, I just want you to know, I don't expect you to understand it or what it means or what it has all done to Cleve Wheeler. I need your help, and you can't really help me unless you know the whole story."

"Shoot."

Karl Trilling shot: "Wheeler found a girl. Her name was Clara Prieta and her folks came from Sonora. She was bright as hell—in her way, I suppose, as bright as Cleve, though with a tenth of his schooling—and pretty as well, and it was Cleve she wanted, not what he might get for her. She fell for him when he had nothing—when he really wanted nothing. They were a daily, hourly joy to each other. I guess that was about the time he started building this business and that, making something again. He bought a little house and a car. He bought two cars, one for her. I don't think she wanted it, but he couldn't do enough—he was always looking for more things to do for her. They went out for an evening to some friend's house, she from shopping, he from whatever it was he was working on then, so they had both cars. He followed her on the way home and had to watch her lose control and spin out. She died in his arms."

"Oh, Jesus."

"Mister Lucky. Listen: a week later he turned a corner downtown and found himself looking at a bank robbery. He caught a stray bullet—grazed the back of his neck. He had seven months to lie still and think about things. When he got out he was told his business manager had embezzled everything and headed south with his secretary. Everything."

"What did he do?"

"Went to work and paid his hospital bill."

They sat in the car in the dark for a long time, until Joe said, "Was he paralyzed, there in the hospital?"

"For nearly five months."

"Wonder what he thought about."

Karl Trilling said, "I can imagine what he thought about. What I can't imagine is what he decided. What he concluded. What he determined to be. Damn it, there are no accurate words for it. We all do the best we can with what we've got, or try to. Or should. He *did*—and with the best possible material to start out with. He played it straight; he worked hard; he was honest and lawful and fair; he was fit; he was bright. He came out of the hospital with those last two qualities intact. God alone knows what's happened to the rest of it."

"So he went to work for the old man."

"He did—and somehow that frightens me. It was as if all his qualifications were not enough to suit both of them until these things happened to him—until they made him become what he is."

"And what is that?"

"There isn't a short answer to that, Joe. The old man has become a modern myth. Nobody ever sees him. Nobody can predict what he's going to do or why. Cleveland Wheeler stepped into his shadow and disappeared almost as completely as the boss. There are very few things you can say for certain. The boss has always been a recluse and in the ten years Cleve Wheeler has been with him he has become more so. It's been business as usual with him, of course—which means the constantly unusual—long periods of quiet, and then these spectacular unexpected wheelings and dealings. You assume that the old man dreams these things up and some high-powered genius on his staff gets them done. But it could be the genius that instigates the moves—who can know? Only the people closest to him—Wheeler, Epstein, me. And I don't know."

"But Epstein died."

Karl Trilling nodded in the dark. "Epstein died. Which leaves only Wheeler to watch the store. I'm the old man's personal physician, not Wheeler's, and there's no guarantee that I ever will be Wheeler's."

Joe Trilling recrossed his legs and leaned back, looking out into the whispering dark. "It begins to take shape," he murmured. "The old man's on the way out, you very well might be and there's nobody to take over but this Wheeler."

"Yes, and I don't know what he is or what he'll do. I do know he will command more power than any single human being on Earth. He'll have so much that he'll be above any kind of cupidity that you or I could imagine—you or I can't think in that order of magnitude. But you see, he's a man who, you might say, has had it proved to him that being good and smart and strong and honest doesn't particularly pay off. Where will he go with all this? And hypothesizing that he's been making more and more of the decisions lately, and extrapolating from that—where is he going? All you can be sure of is that he will succeed in anything he tries. That is his habit."

"What does he want? Isn't that what you're trying to figure out? What would a man like that want, if he knew he could get it?"

"I knew I'd come to the right place," said Karl almost happily. "That's it exactly. As for me, I have all I need now and there are plenty of other places I could go. I wish Epstein were still around, but he's dead and cremated."

"Cremated?"

"That's right—you wouldn't know about that. Old man's instructions, I handled it myself. You've heard of the hot and cold private swimming pools—but I bet you never heard of a man with his own private crematorium in the second sub-basement."

Joe threw up his hands. "I guess if you reach into your pocket and pull out two billion real dollars, you can have anything you want. By the way—was that legal?"

"Like you said—if you have two billion. Actually, the county medical examiner was present and signed the papers. And he'll be there when the old man pushes off too—it's all in the final instructions. Hey—wait, I don't want to cast any aspersions on the M.E. He wasn't bought. He did a very competent examination on Epstein."

"Okay—we know what to expect when the time comes. It's afterward you're worried about."

"Right. What has the old man—I'm speaking of the corporate old man now—what has he been doing all along? What has he been doing in the last ten years, since he got Wheeler—and is it any different from what he was doing before? How much of this difference, if any, is more Wheeler than boss? That's all we have to go on, Joe, and from it we have to extrapolate what Wheeler's going to do with the biggest private economic force this world has ever known."

"Let's talk about that," said Joe, beginning to smile.

Karl Trilling knew the signs, so he began to smile a little, too. They talked about it.

II

The crematorium in the second sub-basement was purely functional, as if all concessions to sentiment and ritual had been made elsewhere, or canceled. The latter most accurately described what had happened when at last, at long long last, the old man died. Everything was done precisely according to his instructions, immediately after he was certifiably dead and before any public announcements were made—right up to and including the moment when the square mouth of the furnace opened with a startling clang, a blare of heat, a flare of light—the hue the old-time blacksmiths called straw color. The simple coffin slid rapidly in, small flames exploding into being on its corners, and the door banged shut. It took a moment for the eyes to adjust to the bare room, the empty greased track, the closed door. It took the same moment for the conditioners to whisk away the sudden smell of scorched soft pine.

The medical examiner leaned over the small table and signed his name twice. Karl Trilling and Cleveland Wheeler did the same. The M.E. tore off copies and folded them and put them away in his breast pocket. He looked at the closed square iron door, opened his mouth, closed it again and shrugged. He held out his hand.

"Good night, Doctor."

"Good night, Doctor. Rugosi's outside—he'll show you out."

The M.E. shook hands wordlessly with Cleveland Wheeler and left.

"I know just what he's feeling," Karl said. "Something ought to be said. Something memorable—end of an era. Like 'One small step for man—' "

Cleveland Wheeler smiled the bright smile of the college hero, fifteen years after—a little less wide, a little less even, a great deal less in the eyes. He said in the voice that commanded, whatever he said, "If you think you're quoting the first words from an astronaut on the moon, you're not. What he said was from the ladder, when he poked his boot down. He said, 'It's some kind of soft stuff. I can kick it around with my foot.' I've always liked that much better. It was real, it wasn't rehearsed or memorized or thought out and it had to do with that moment and the next. The M.E. said good night and you told him the chauffeur was waiting outside. I like that better than anything anyone could say. I think he would, too." Wheeler added, barely gesturing, with a very strong slightly cleft chin, toward the hot black door.

"But he wasn't exactly human."

"So they say." Wheeler half smiled and, even as he turned away, Karl could sense himself tuned out, the room itself become of secondary importance—the next thing Wheeler was to do, and the next and the one after, becoming more real than the here and now.

Karl put a fast end to that.

He said levelly, "I meant what I just said, Wheeler."

It couldn't have been the words, which by themselves might have elicited another half-smile and a forgetting. It was the tone, and perhaps the "Wheeler." There is a ritual about these things. To those few on his own level, and those on the level below, he was Cleve. Below that he was mister to his face and Wheeler behind his back. No one of his peers would call him mister unless it was meant as the herald of an insult; no one of his peers or immediate underlings would call him Wheeler at all, ever. Whatever the component, it removed Cleveland Wheeler's hand from the knob and turned him. His face was completely alert and interested. "You'd best tell me what you mean, Doctor."

Karl said, "I'll do better than that. Come." Without gestures, suggestions or explanations he walked to the left rear of the room, leaving it up to Wheeler to decide whether or not to follow. Wheeler followed.

In the corner Karl rounded on him. "If you ever say anything about this to anyone—even me—when we leave here, I'll just deny it. If you ever get in here again, you won't find anything to back up your story." He took a complex four-inch blade of machined stainless steel from his belt and slid it between the big masonry blocks. Silently, massively, the course of blocks in the corner began to move upward. Looking up at them in the dim light from the narrow corridor they revealed, anyone could see that they were real blocks and that to get through them without that key and the precise knowledge of where to put it would be a long-term project.

Again Karl proceeded without looking around, leaving go, no-go as a matter for Wheeler to decide. Wheeler followed. Karl heard his footsteps behind him and noticed with pleasure and something like admiration that when the heavy blocks whooshed down and seated themselves solidly behind them, Wheeler may have looked over his shoulder but did not pause.

"You've noticed we're alongside the furnace," Karl said, like a guided-tour bus driver. "And now, behind it."

He stood aside to let Wheeler pass him and see the small room.

It was just large enough for the tracks which protruded from the back of the furnace and a little standing space on each side. On the far side was a small table with a black suitcase standing on it. On the track stood the coffin, its corners carboned, its top and sides wet and slightly steaming.

"Sorry to have to close that stone gate that way," Karl said matter-of-factly. "I don't expect anyone down here at all, but I wouldn't want to explain any of this to persons other than yourself."

Wheeler was staring at the coffin. He seemed perfectly composed, but it was a seeming. Karl was quite aware of what it was costing him.

Wheeler said, "I wish you'd explain it to *me*." And he laughed. It was the first time Karl had ever seen this man do anything badly.

"I will. I am." He clicked open the suitcase and laid it open and flat on the little table. There was a glisten of chrome and steel and small vials in little pockets. The first tool he removed was a screwdriver. "No need to use screws when you're cremating 'em," he said cheerfully and placed the tip under one corner of the lid. He struck the handle smartly with the heel of one hand and the lid popped loose. "Stand this up against the wall behind you, will you?"

Silently Cleveland Wheeler did as he was told. It gave him something to do with his muscles; it gave him the chance to turn his head away for a moment; it gave him a chance to think—and it gave Karl the opportunity for a quick glance at his steady countenance.

He's a mensch, Karl thought. *He really is . . .*

Wheeler set up the lid neatly and carefully and they stood, one on each side, looking down into the coffin.

"He—got a lot older," Wheeler said at last.

"You haven't seen him recently."

"Here and in there," said the executive. "I've spent more time in the same room with him during the past month than I have in the last eight, nine years. Still, it was a matter of minutes, each time."

Karl nodded understandingly. "I'd heard that. Phone calls, any time of the day or night, and then those long silences two days, three, not calling out, not having anyone in—"

"Are you going to tell me about the phony oven?"

"Oven? Furnace? It's not a phony at all. When we've finished here it'll do the job, all right."

"Then why the theatricals?"

"That was for the M.E. Those papers he signed are in sort of a never-never country just now. When we slide this back in and turn on the heat they'll become as legal as he thinks they are."

"Then why—"

"Because there are some things you have to know."

Karl reached into the coffin and unfolded the gnarled hands. They came apart reluctantly and he pressed them down at the sides of the body. He unbuttoned the jacket, laid it back, unbuttoned the shirt, unzipped the trousers. When he had finished with this, he looked up and found Wheeler's sharp gaze, not on the old man's corpse, but on him.

"I have the feeling," said Cleveland Wheeler, "that I have never seen you before."

Silently Karl Trilling responded: *But you do now.* And, *Thanks, Joey. You were dead right.* Joe had known the answer to that one plaguing question, *How should I act?*

Talk just the way he talks, Joe had said. *Be what he is, the whole time . . .*

Be what he is. A man without illusions (they don't work) and without hope (who needs it?) who has the unbreakable habit of succeeding. And who can say it's a nice day in such a way that everyone around snaps to attention and says: *Yes, SIR!*

"You've been busy," Karl responded shortly. He took off his jacket, folded it and put it on the table beside the kit. He put on surgeon's gloves and slipped the sterile sleeve off a new scalpel. "Some people scream and faint the first time they watch a dissection."

Wheeler smiled thinly. "I don't scream and faint." But it was not lost on Karl Trilling that only then, at the last possible moment, did Wheeler actually view the old man's body. When he did he neither screamed nor fainted; he uttered an astonished grunt.

"Thought that would surprise you," Karl said easily. "In case you were wondering, though, he really was a male. The species seems to be oviparous. Mammals too, but it has to be oviparous. I'd sure like a look at a female. That isn't a vagina. It's a cloaca."

"Until this moment," said Wheeler in a hypnotized voice, "I thought that 'not human' remark of yours was a figure of speech."

"No, you didn't," Karl responded shortly.

Leaving the words to hang in the air, as words will if a speaker has the wit to isolate them with wedges of silence, he deftly slit the corpse from the sternum to the pubic symphysis. For the first-time viewer this was always the difficult moment. It's hard not to realize viscerally that the cadaver does not feel anything and will not protest. Nerve-alive to Wheeler, Karl looked for a gasp or a shudder; Wheeler merely held his breath.

"We could spend hours—weeks I imagine, going into the details," Karl said, deftly making a transverse incision in the ensiform area, almost around to the trapezoid on each side, "but this is the thing I wanted you to see." Grasping the flesh at the juncture of the cross he had cut, on the left side, he pulled upward and to the left. The cutaneous layers came away easily, with the fat under them. They were not pinkish, but an off-white lavender shade. Now the muscular striations over the ribs were in view. "If you'd palpated the old man's chest," he said, demonstrating on the right side, "you'd have felt what seemed to be normal human ribs. But look at this."

With a few deft strokes he separated the muscle fibers from the bone on a mid-costal area about four inches square, and scraped. A rib emerged and, as he widened the area and scraped between it and the next one, it became clear that the ribs were joined by a thin flexible layer of bone or chitin.

"It's like baleen—whalebone," said Karl. "See this?" He sectioned out a piece, flexed it.

"My God."

III

"Now look at this." Karl took surgical shears from the kit, snapped through the sternum right up to the clavicle and then across the lower margin of the ribs. Slipping his fingers under them, he pulled upward. With a dull snap the entire ribcage opened like a door, exposing the lung.

The lung was not pink, nor the liverish-brownish-black of a smoker, but yellow—the clear bright yellow of pure sulfur.

"His metabolism," Karl said, straightening up at last and flexing the tension out of his shoulders, "is fantastic. Or was. He lived on oxygen, same as us, but he broke it out of carbon monoxide, sulfur dioxide and trioxide and carbon dioxide mostly. I'm not saying he could—I mean he had to. When he was forced to breathe what we call clean air, he could take just so much of it and then had to duck out and find a few breaths of his own atmosphere. When he was younger he could take it for hours at a time, but as the years went by he had to spend more and more time in the kind of smog he could breathe. Those long disappearances of his, and that reclusiveness—they weren't as kinky as people supposed."

Wheeler made a gesture toward the corpse. "But—what is he? Where—"

"I can't tell you. Except for a good deal of medical and biochemical details, you now know as much as I do. Somehow, somewhere, he arrived. He came, he saw, he began to make his moves. Look at this."

He opened the other side of the chest and then broke the sternum up and away. He pointed. The lung tissue was not in two discreet parts, but extended across the median line. "One lung, all the way across, though it has these two lobes. The kidneys and gonads show the same right-left fusion."

"I'll take your word for it," said Wheeler a little hoarsely. "Damn it, what *is* it?"

"A featherless biped, as Plato once described homo sap. *I* don't know what it is. I just know *that* it is—and I thought you ought to know. That's all."

"But you've seen one before. That's obvious."

"Sure. Epstein."

"Epstein?"

"Sure. The old man had to have a go-between—someone who could, without suspicion, spend long hours with him and hours away. The old man could do a lot over the phone, but not everything. Epstein was, you might say, a right arm that could hold its breath a little longer than he could. It got to him in the end, though, and he died of it."

"Why didn't you say something long before this?"

"First of all, I value my own skin. I could say reputation, but skin is the word. I signed a contract as his personal physician because he needed a personal physician—another bit of window-dressing. But I did precious little doctoring —except over the phone—and nine-tenths of that was, I realized quite recently, purely diversionary. Even a doctor, I suppose, can be a trusting soul. One or the other would call and give a set of symptoms and I'd cautiously suggest and prescribe. Then I'd get another call that the patient was improving and that was that. Why, I even got specimens—blood, urine, stools—and did the pathology on them and never realized that they were from the same source as what the medical examiner checked out and signed for."

"What do you mean, same source?"

Karl shrugged. "He could get anything he wanted—anything."

"Then—what the M.E. examined wasn't—" he waved a hand at the casket.

"Of course not. That's why the crematorium has a back door. There's a little pocket sleight-of-hand trick you can buy for fifty cents that operates the same way. This body here was inside the furnace. The ringer—a look-alike that came from God knows where; I swear to you I don't—was lying out there waiting for the M.E. When the button was pushed the fires started up and that coffin slid in—pushing this one out and at the same time drenching it with water as it came through. While we've been in here, the human body is turning to ashes. My personal private secret instructions, both for Epstein and for the boss, were to wait until I was certain I was alone and then come in here after an hour and push the second button, which would slide this one back into the fire. I was to do no investigations, ask no questions, make no reports. It came through as logical but not reasonable, like so many of his orders." He laughed suddenly. "Do you know why the old man—and Epstein too, for that matter, in case you never noticed—wouldn't shake hands with anyone?"

"I presumed it was because he had an obsession with germs."

"It was because his normal body temperature was a hundred and seven."

Wheeler touched one of his own hands with the other and said nothing.

When Karl felt that the wedge of silence was thick enough he asked lightly, "Well, boss, where do we go from here?"

Cleveland Wheeler turned away from the corpse and to Karl slowly, as if diverting his mind with an effort.

"What did you call me?"

"Figure of speech," said Karl and smiled. "Actually, I'm working for the company—and that's you. I'm under orders, which have been finally and completely discharged when I push that button—I have no others. So it really is up to you."

Wheeler's eyes fell again to the corpse. "You mean about him? This? What we should do?"

"That, yes. Whether to burn it up and forget it—or call in top management and an echelon of scientists. Or scare the living hell out of everyone on Earth by phoning the papers. Sure, that has to be decided, but I was thinking on a much wider spectrum than that."

"Such as—"

Karl gestured toward the box with his head. "What was he doing here, anyway? What has he done? What was he trying to do?"

"You'd better go on," said Wheeler; and for the very first time said something in a way that suggested diffidence. "You've had a while to think about all this. I—" and almost helplessly, he spread his hands.

"I can understand that," Karl said gently. "Up to now I've been coming on like a hired lecturer and I know it. I'm not going to embarrass you with personalities except to say that you've absorbed all this with less buckling of the knees than anyone in the world I could think of."

"I'll buckle when I have time for it. Just now I'm looking for a way to think this out."

"Right. Well, there's a simple technique you learn in elementary algebra. It has to do with the construction of graphs. You place a dot on the graph where known data put it. You get more data, you put down another dot and then a third. With just three dots—of course, the more the better, but it can be done with three—you can connect them and establish a curve. This curve has certain characteristics and it's fair to extend the curve a little farther with the assumption that later data will bear you out."

"Extrapolation."

"Extrapolation. X axis, the fortunes of our late boss. Y axis, time. The curve is his fortunes—that is to say, his influence."

"Pretty tall graph."

"Over thirty years."

"Still pretty tall."

"All right," said Karl. "Now, over the same thirty years, another curve: change in the environment." He held up a hand. "I'm not going to read you a treatise on ecology. Let's be more objective than that. Let's just say changes. Okay: a measurable rise in the mean temperature because of CO_2 and the greenhouse effect. Draw the curve. Incidence of heavy metals, mercury and lithium, in organic tissue. Draw a curve. Likewise chlorinated hydrocarbons, hypertrophy of algae due to phosphates, incidence of coronaries . . . All right, let's superimpose all these curves on the same graph."

"I see what you're getting at. But you have to be careful with that kind of statistics game. Like, the increase of traffic fatalities coincides with the increased use of aluminum cans and plastic-tipped baby pins."

"Right. I don't think I'm falling into that trap. I just want to find reasonable answers to a couple of otherwise unreasonable situations. One is this: if the changes occurring in our planet are the result of mere carelessness—a more or less random thing, carelessness—then how come nobody is being careless in a way that benefits the environment? Strike that. I promised, no ecology lessons. Rephrase: how come all these carelessnesses promote a change and not a preservation?

"Next question: What is the direction of the change? You've seen speculative writing about 'terraforming'— altering other planets to make them habitable by humans. Suppose an effort were being made to change this planet to suit someone else? Suppose they wanted more water and were willing to melt the polar caps by the greenhouse effect? Increase the oxides of sulfur, eliminate certain marine forms from plankton to whales? Reduce the population by increases in lung cancer, emphysema, heart attacks and even war?"

Both men found themselves looking down at the sleeping face in the coffin. Karl said softly. "Look what he was into—petrochemicals, fossil fuels, food processing, advertising, all the things that made the changes or helped the changers—"

"You're not blaming him for all of it."

"Certainly not. He found willing helpers by the million."

"You don't think he was trying to change a whole planet just so he could be comfortable in it."

"No, I don't think so—and that's the central point I have to make. I don't know if there are any more around like him and Epstein, but I can suppose this: if the changes now going on keep on—and accelerate—then we can expect them."

Wheeler said, "So what would you like to do? Mobilize the world against the invader?"

"Nothing like that. I think I'd slowly and quietly reverse the changes. If this planet is normally unsuitable to them, then I'd keep it so. I don't think they'd have to be driven back. I think they just wouldn't come."

"Or they'd try some other way."

"I don't think so," said Karl. "Because they tried this one. If they thought they could do it with fleets of spaceships and super-zap guns, they'd be doing it. No—this is their way and if it doesn't work, they can try somewhere else."

Wheeler began pulling thoughtfully at his lip. Karl said softly, "All it would take is someone who knew what he was doing, who could command enough clout and who had the wit to make it pay. They might even arrange a man's life—to get the kind of man they need."

And before Wheeler could answer, Karl took up his scalpel.

"I want you to do something for me," he said sharply in a new, commanding tone—actually Wheeler's own. "I want you to do it because I've done it and I'll be damned if I want to be the only man in the world who has."

Leaning over the head of the casket, he made an incision along the hairline from temple to temple. Then, bracing his elbows against the edge of the box and steadying one hand with the other, he drew the scalpel straight down the center of the forehead and down on to the nose, splitting it exactly in two. Down he went through the upper lip and then the lower, around the point of the chin and under it to the throat. Then he stood up.

"Put your hands on his cheeks," he ordered. Wheeler frowned briefly (how long had it been since anyone had spoken to him that way?), hesitated, then did as he was told.

"Now press your hands together and down."

The incision widened slightly under the pressure, then abruptly the flesh gave and the entire skin of the face slipped off. The unexpected lack of resistance brought Wheeler's hands to the bottom of the coffin and he found himself face to face, inches away, with the corpse.

Like the lungs and kidneys, the eyes—eye?—passed the median, very slightly reduced at the center. The pupil was oval, its long axis transverse. The skin was pale lavender with yellow vessels and in place of a nose was a thread-fringed hole. The mouth was circular, the teeth not quite radially placed; there was little chin.

Without moving, Wheeler closed his eyes, held them shut for one second, two, and then courageously opened them again. Karl whipped around the end of the coffin and got an arm around Wheeler's chest. Wheeler leaned on it heavily for a moment, then stood up quickly and brushed the arm away.

"You didn't have to do that."

"Yes, I did," said Karl. "Would you want to be the only man in the world who'd gone through that—with nobody to tell it to?"

And after all, Wheeler could laugh. When he had finished he said, "Push that button."

"Hand me that cover."

Most obediently Cleveland Wheeler brought the coffin lid and they placed it.

Karl pushed the button and they watched the coffin slide into the square of flame. Then they left.

Joe Trilling had a funny way of making a living. It was a good living, but of course he didn't make anything like the bundle he could have made in the city. On the other hand, he lived in the mountains a half-mile away from a picturesque village, in clean air and piney-birchy woods along with lots of mountain laurel and he was his own boss. There wasn't much competition for what he did.

What he did was to make simulacra of medical specimens, mostly for the armed forces, although he had plenty of orders from medical schools, film producers and an occasional individual, no questions asked. He could make a model of anything inside, affixed to or penetrating a body or any part of it. He could make models to be looked at, models to be felt, smelled and palpated. He could give you gangrene that stunk or dewy thyroids with real dew on them. He could make one-of-a-kind or he could set up a production line. Dr. Joe Trilling was, to put it briefly, the best there was at what he did.

"The clincher," Karl told him (in much more relaxed circumstances than their previous ones; daytime now, with beer), "the real clincher was the face bit. God, Joe, that was a beautiful piece of work."

"Just nuts and bolts. The beautiful part was your idea—his hands on it."

"How do you mean?"

"I've been thinking back to that," Joe said. "I don't think you yourself realize how brilliant a stroke that was. It's all very well to set up a show for the guy, but to make him put his hands as well as his eyes and brains on it—that was the stroke of genius. It's like—well, I can remember when I was a kid coming home from school and putting my hand on a fence rail and somebody had spat on it." He displayed his hand, shook it. "All these years I can remember how that felt. All these years couldn't wear it away, all those scrubbings couldn't wash it away. It's more than a cerebral or psychic thing, Karl—more than the memory of an episode. I think there's a kind of memory mechanism in the cells themselves, especially on the hands, that can be invoked. What I'm getting to is that no matter how long he lives, Cleve Wheeler is going to feel that skin slip under his palms and that is going to bring him nose to nose with that face. No, you're the genius, not me."

"Na. You knew what you were doing. I didn't."

"Hell you didn't." Joe leaned far back in his lawn chaise —so far he could hold up his beer and look at the sun through it from the underside. Watching the receding bubbles defy perspective (because they swell as they rise), he murmured, "Karl?"

"Yuh."

"Ever hear of Occam's Razor?"

"Um. Long time back. Philosophical principle. Or logic or something. Let's see. Given an effect and a choice of possible causes, the simplest cause is always the one most likely to be true. Is that it?"

"Not too close, but close enough," said Joe Trilling lazily. "Hm. You're the one who used to proclaim that logic is sufficient unto itself and need have nothing to do with truth."

"I still proclaim it."

"Okay. Now, you and I know that human greed and carelessness are quite enough all by themselves to wreck this planet. We didn't think that was enough for the likes of Cleve Wheeler, who can really do something about it, so we constructed him a smog-breathing extra-terrestrial. I mean, he hadn't done anything about saving the world for our reasons, so we gave him a whizzer of a reason of his own. Right out of our heads."

"Dictated by all available factors. Yes. What are you getting at, Joe?"

"Oh—just that our complicated hoax is simple, really, in the sense that it brought everything down to a single cause. Occam's Razor slices things down to simplest causes. Single causes have a fair chance of being right."

Karl put down his beer with a bump. "I never thought of that. I've been too busy to think of that. *Suppose we were right?*"

They looked at each other, shaken.

At last Karl said, "What do we look for now, Joe— space ships?"

DAZED

What a strange little story this is! As people keep asking me: "Where do you get your crazy ideas?"

Harlan Ellison claims he gets his from a little old lady in Schenectady, who sends them in a plain brown wrapper. I don't know her. I think that what I do is to make some sort of sense out of the world and its population, an activity that repeatedly drives me into fantasy as the only area in which logic seems to have any consistency.

Of one thing I can assure you: virtually no character in my bibliography stands out as clearly in my mind as this dazed man. I don't think he shows up in a particularly sharp focus to the reader, but he does to me—every gesture, every intonation. And unlike most of my characters, he isn't modeled on anyone I know. He's uniquely himself, this dazed man.

Strange. Very strange.

I

I work for a stockbroker on the twenty-first floor. Things have not been good for stockbrokers recently, what with tight money and hysterical reaction to the news and all that. When business gets really bad for a brokerage it often doesn't fail—it merges. This has something to do with the public image. The company I work for is going through the agony. For the lower echelons—me—that means detail you wouldn't believe, with a reduced staff. In other words, night work. Last night I worked without looking up until my whole body was the shape of the chair and there was a blue haze around the edges of everything I could see. I finished a stack and peered at the row of stacks still to be done and tried to get up. It took three tries before my hips and knees would straighten enough to let me totter into the hall and down to the men's room. It never occurred to me to close the office door and I guess the confusion, all the strange faces coming and going for the past few days, extending to the security man downstairs. However it happened, there was a dazed man in my office when I came back a moment later.

He was well dressed—I guess that, too, helped him pass the guards—in a brown sharkskin suit with funny lapels, what you might call up-to-the-minute camp. He wore an orange knitted tie the like of which you only see in a new boutique or an old movie. I'd say he was in his twenties—not yet twenty-five. And dazed.

When I walked in and stopped dead he gave me a lost look and said, "This is my office."

I said the only thing I could think of. "Oh?"

He pivoted slowly all the way around, looking at the desk, the shelves, the files.

When he came around to face me again he said, "This isn't my office."

He had to be with the big five-name brokerage house that was gobbling up my company in its time of need. I asked him.

"No," he said, "I work for *Fortune.*"

"Look," I said, "you're not only in the wrong office, you're in the wrong building. Time-Life is on Sixth Avenue—been there since nineteen fifty-two."

"Fifty-*two*—" He looked around the room again. "But I—but it's—"

He sat down on the settle. I had the idea he'd have collapsed on the floor if the settle hadn't been there. He asked me what day it was. I think I misunderstood.

"Thursday," I said. I looked at my watch. "Well, it's now Friday."

"I mean, what's the date?"

I pointed to the desk calendar right beside him. He looked at it twice, each one a long careful look. I never saw a man turn the color he turned. He covered his eyes. Even his lips went white.

"Oh my God."

"You all right?" I asked—a very stupid question.

"Tell me something," he said after a while. "Has there been a war?"

"You have to be kidding."

He took his hand down and looked at me, so lost, so frightened. Not frightened. There has to be a word. Anguished. He needed answers—needed them. Not questions, not now.

I said, "It's been going on a long time."

"A lot of young guys killed?"

"Upwards of fifty thousand." Something made me add: "Americans. The other side, five, six times that."

"Oh, my God," he said again. Then: "It's my fault."

Now I have to tell you up front that it never occurred to me for one second that this guy was on any kind of a drug trip. Not that I'm an expert, but there are times when you just know. Whatever was bothering him was genuine— at least genuine to him. Besides, there was something about him I had to like. Not the clothes, not the face, just the guy, the kind of guy he was.

I said, "Hey, you look like hell and I'm sick and tired

of what I'm doing. Let's take a break and go to the Automat for coffee."

He gave me that lost look again. "Is the lid off on sex? I mean, young kids—"

"Like rabbits," I said. "Also your friendly neighborhood movie—I don't know what they're going to do for an encore." I had to ask him, "Where've you been?"

He shook his head and said candidly, "I don't know where it was. Are people leaving their jobs—and school—going off to live on the land?"

"Some," I said. "Come on."

I switched off the overhead light, leaving my desk lamp lit. He got to his feet as if he were wired to the switch, but then just stood looking at the calendar.

"Are there bombings?"

"Three yesterday, in Newark. Come on."

"Oh, my God," he said and came. I locked the door and we went down the corridor to the elevators. Air wheezed in the shaft as the elevator rose. "It always whistles like that late at night," he said. I had never noticed that but knew he was right as soon as he said it. He also said weakly, "You don't feel like walking down?"

"Twenty-one flights?"

The doors slid open. The guy didn't want to get in. But I mean, he *really* didn't. I stood on the crack while he screwed up his courage. It didn't take long but I could see it was a mighty battle. He won it and came in, turned around and leaned against the back wall. I pushed the button and we started down. He looked pretty bad. I said something to him but he put up a hand, waved my words away before they were out. He didn't move again until the doors opened and then he looked into the lobby as if he didn't know what to expect. But it was just the lobby, with the oval information desk we called the fishbowl and the shiny floor and the portable wooden desk, like a lectern, where you signed in and out after hours and where the guard was supposed to be. We breezed by it and out into Rockefeller Center. He took a deep breath and immediately coughed.

"What's that smell?"

I'd been about to say something trivial about the one good thing about working late—you could breathe the air, but I didn't say it.

"The smog, I guess."

"Smog. Oh yes, smoke and fog. I remember." Then he seemed to remember something else, something that brought his predicament, whatever it was, back with a hammer blow. "Well of course," he said as if to himself. "Has to be."

On Sixth Avenue (New Yorkers still won't call it Avenue of the Americas) we passed two laughing couples. One of the girls was wearing a see-through top made of plastic chainmail. The other had on a very maxi coat swinging open over hotpants. My companion was appreciative but not astonished. I think what he said was, "That too—" nodding his head. He watched every automobile that passed and his eyes flicked over the places where they used to sell books and back-date periodicals, every single one of them now given over to peepshows and beaver magazines. He had the same nod of his head for this.

We reached the Automat and it occurred to me that an uncharacteristic touch of genius had made me suggest it. I had first seen the Automat when I had ridden in on my mother's hip more years ago than I'll mention—and many times since—and very little has changed—except, of course, the numbers on the little off-white cards that tell you how many nickels you have to put in the slot to claim your food. After a few years' absence one tends to yelp at the sight of them. I always do and the strange young man with me did, too. Aside from that, there is a timeless quality about the place, especially in the small hours of the morning. The overage, over-painted woman furtively eating catsup is there as she, or someone just like her, has been for fifty years; and the young couple, homely to you but beautiful to each other, full of sleepiness and discovery; and the working stiff in the case-hardened slideway of his life, grabbing a bite on the way from bed to work and not yet awake—no need to be—and his counterpart headed in the other direction; no need for him to be awake either. And all around: the same marble change counter with the deep worn pits in it from countless millions of coins dropped and scooped; behind it the same weary automaton; and around you the same nickel (not chrome) framing for the hundreds of little glass-fronted doors through which the food always looks so much better than it is. All in all, it's a fine place for the reorientation of time-travelers.

"Are you a time-traveler?" I asked, following my own whimsy and hoping to make him smile.

He didn't smile. "No," he said. "Yes, I—well—" flickering panic showed in his eyes—"I don't really know."

We bought our coffee straight out of the lion's mouth and carried it to a corner table. I think that when we were settled there he really looked at me for the first time.

He said, "You've been very kind."

"Well," I said, "I was glad of the break."

"Look, I'm going to tell you what happened. I guess I don't expect you to believe me. I wouldn't in your place."

"Try me," I offered. "And anyway—what difference does it make whether I believe you?"

" 'Belief or nonbelief has no power over objective truth.' " I could tell by his voice he was quoting somebody. The smile I had been looking for almost came and he said, "You're right. I'll tell you what happened because—well, because I want to. Have to."

I said fine and told him to shoot. He shot.

I work in Circulation Promotion [he began]. Or maybe I should say I *worked*—I guess I should. You'll have to pardon me, I'm a little confused. There's so much—

Maybe I should start over. It didn't begin in Rockefeller Center. It started, oh, I don't know how long ago, with me wondering about things. Not that I'm anything special— I'm not saying I am—but it seems nobody else wonders about the same things I do. I mean, people are so close to what happens that they don't seem to know what's going on.

Wait, I don't want to confuse you, too. One of us is enough. Let me give you an example.

World War II was starting up when I was a kid and one day a bunch of us sat around, trying to figure out who would be fighting who. Us and the British and French on one side, sure—the Germans and Austrians and Italians on the other—that was clear enough. And the Japanese. But beyond that?

It's all history and hindsight now and there's no special reason to think about it, but at the time it was totally impossible for anyone to predict the lineup that actually came about. Go back in the files of newspaper editorials—*Harper*'s or *Reader's Digest* or any other—and you'll see what I mean. Nobody predicted that up to the very end of the war our best and strongest friends would be at peace with our worst and deadliest enemy. I mean, if you put it on personal terms—if you and I are friends and there's somebody out to kill me and I find out that you and he are buddies— could we even so much as speak to each other again? Yet here was the Soviet Union, fighting shoulder to shoulder with us against the Nazis, while for nearly five years they were at peace with Japan!

And about Japan: there were hundreds of thousands of Chinese who had been fighting a life-and-death war against the Japanese for ten years—ten years, man!—and along with them, Koreans. So we spent billions getting ourselves together to mount air strikes against Japan from thousands of miles away—New Guinea, the Solomons, Saipan, Tinian. Do you know how far it is from the Chinese mainland to Tokyo, across the Sea of Japan? Six hundred miles. Do you know how far it is from Pusan, Korea to Hiroshima? A hundred and thirty!

I'm sorry. I get excited like that to this day when I think of it. But damn it—why didn't we negotiate to move in and set up airstrips on the mainland and Korea? Do you think the natives would have turned us down? Or is it that we just don't like chop suey? Oh, sure—there are a lot of arguments like backing up Chiang against the Communists and I even read somewhere that it was not our policy to interfere in Southeast Asia. (Did I say something funny?) But you know Chiang and the Communists had a truce—and kept it too—to fight the common enemy.

Well—all right. All that seems a long way from what happened to me, I suppose, but it's the kind of thing I've spent my life wondering about. It's not just wars that bring out the thing I'm talking about, though God knows they make it plainer to see. Italy and Germany sharpening their newest weapons and strategies in the Spanish civil war, for example, or Mussolini's invasion of Ethiopia—hell, the more sophisticated people got the less they could see what was in front of them. Any kid in a kindergarten knows a bully when he sees one and has sense enough at least to be afraid. Any sixth-grader knows how to organize a pressure group against a bad guy. Wars, you see, are really life-and-death situations, where what's possible, practical—logical— has a right to emerge. When it doesn't—you have to wonder. French peasants taxed till they bled to build the Maginot Line all through the thirties, carefully preparing against the kind of war they fought in nineteen fourteen.

But let's look some place else. Gonorrhea could be absolutely stamped out in six months, syphilis maybe in a year. I picked up a pamphlet last month—hey, I have to watch that "last month," "nowadays," things like that—anyway, the pamphlet drew a correlation between smoking cigarettes and a rising curve of lung cancer, said scientific tests prove that something in cigarettes can cause cancer in mice. Now I bet if the government came out with an official statement about that, people would read it and get scared—and go on smoking cigarettes. You're smiling again. That's funny?

"It isn't funny," I told the dazed man. "Here—let me bring some more coffee."

"On me this time." He spilled coins on the table. "But you were smiling, all the same."

"It wasn't that kind of a smile, like for a funny," I told him. "The Surgeon General came out with a report years ago, Cigarette advertising is finally banned from TV, but how much difference does it make? Look around you."

While he was looking around him I was looking at his coins. Silver quarters. Silver dimes. Nickels: 1948, 1950, 1945. I began to feel very strange about this dude. Correction: my feel-strange went up another notch.

He said, "A lot of the people who aren't smoking are coughing, too."

We sat there together, looking around. Again he had shown me something I had always seen, never known. How many people cough.

I went for more coffee.

II

He went on.

Every four weeks I get—got?—got a makeready. A makeready is a copy of a magazine with all the proofing done and the type set, your last look before the presses roll. I have to admit it gives me—used to give me—a sense of importance to get it free (it's an expensive magazine) even before the "men high in government, industry, com-

merce and the professions" (as it says in the circulation promotion letters I write) had a chance to read it and move
and shake, for they are the movers and shakers.

Anyway, there's this article in the new—not current;
really new—issue called *The Silent Generation*. It's all
about this year's graduating class, the young men who in
June would go into the world and begin to fit their hands to
the reins. This is nineteen-fifty I'm talking about, you understand, in the spring. And it was frightening. I mean, it
spooked me while I read it and it spooked me more and
more as I thought about it—the stupidity of it, the unbelievable blindness of people—not necessarily people as a
whole, but these people in the article—*The Class of 1950*—
young and bright and informed. They had their formal education behind them and you assumed it was fresh in their
minds—not only what they had learned, but the other
thing college is really for: learning how to learn.

And yet what do you suppose they were concerned
about? What was it they talked about until three o'clock in
the morning? What kind of plans were they making for
themselves—and for all the rest of us (for they were going
to be the ones who run things)? Democracy? Ultimate purpose? The relationship of man to his planet—or of modern
man to history? Hell, no.

According to this article, they worried about fringe benefits. Retirement income, for God's sake! Speed of promotion in specialized versus diversified industry! Did they
spend their last few collegiate weeks in sharpening their
new tools or in beering it up—or even in one last panty
raid? Uh-uh. They spent them moving from office to office
of the campus recruiters for big electronic and chemical
and finance companies, working out the deal that would
get them the steadiest, surest income and the biggest scam
on the side and the softest place to lie down at the end of it.

The Silent Generation, the guy who wrote the article
called them. He himself graduated in the late 'thirties and
he had a lot to say about *his* generation. There was a lot
wrong about them and they did some pretty crazy things.
They argued a lot with each other and with their elders and
betters and they joined things like the Young Socialist
League—not so much because they were really lefties, but
because those groups seemed the only ones around that
gave a damn about the state the world was in. Most of all,

you knew they were there. They were a noisy generation. They had that mixture of curiosity and rebellion that let you know they were alive.

The writer looked at the Class of '50 with a kind of despair—and something like terror, too. Because if they came to run things, experience wouldn't merely modify them and steady them. It would harden them like an old man's arteries. It would mean more-of-the-same until they'd be living in a completely unreal world of their own with no real way of communicating with the rest of us. Growing and changing and trying new ways would only frighten them. They'd have the power, and what they'd use it for would be to suppress growth and change, not knowing that societies need growth and change to live, just like trees or babies or art or science. So all he could see ahead was a solid, silent, prosperous standstill—and then some sudden and total collapse, like a tree gone to dry rot.

Well I don't know what you think of all this—or if you understand how hard it hit me. But I've tried to explain to you how all my life I've been plagued by these—well, I call them wonderments—how, when something makes no sense, it kind of hurts. When I was a toddler I couldn't sleep for wanting someone to tell me why a wet towel is darker than a dry one when water has no color. In grade school nobody could tell me why the sound of a falling bomb gets lower and lower in pitch as it approaches the ground, when by all the laws of physics it ought to rise. And in high school I wouldn't buy the idea about a limitation on the velocity of light. (And I still don't.) About things like these I've never lost faith that somebody, some day, would come up with an answer that would satisfy me—and sure enough, from time to time somebody does. But when I was old enough to wonder why smart people do dumb things that kind of faith could only last so long. And I began to feel that there was some other factor, or force, at work.

Do you remember *Gulliver's Travels?* When he was in Lilliput there was a war between the Lilliputians and an-other nation of little people—I forget what they called themselves—and Gulliver intervened and ended the war. Anyway, he researched the two countries and found they had once been one. And he tried to find out what caused so many years of bitter enmity between them after they split. He found that there had been two factions in that original kingdom—the Big Endians and the Little Endians. And do you know where that started? Far back in their history, at breakfast one morning, one of the king's courtiers opened his boiled egg at the big end and another told him that was wrong, it should be opened at the small end! The point Dean Swift was making is that from such insignificant causes grow conflicts that can last centuries and kill thousands. Well, he was near the thing that's plagued me all my life, but he was content to say it happened that way. What blowtorches me is—*why*. *Why* are human beings capable of hating each other over such trifles? Why, when an ancient triviality is proved to be the cause of trouble, don't people just stop fighting?

But I'm off on wars again—I guess because when you're talking about stupidity, wars give you too many good examples. So tell me—why, when someone's sure to die of an incurable disease and needs something for pain—why don't they give him heroin instead of morphine? Is it because heroin's habit-forming? What difference could that possibly make? And besides, morphine is, too. I'll tell you why—it's because heroin makes you feel wonderful and morphine makes you feel numb and gray. In other words, heroin's fun (mind you, I'm talking about terminal cases, dying in agony, not normally healthy people) and morphine is not—and if it's fun, there must be something evil or wrong about it. A dying man is not supposed to be made to feel good. And laws that keep venereal disease from being recognized and treated; and laws against abortion; and all the obscenity statutes—right down at the root these are all anti-pleasure laws. Would you like the job of explaining that to a man from Mars, who hadn't been brought up with them? He couldn't follow reasoning like that any more than he could understand why we have never designed a heat engine—which is essentially what an internal combustion engine is—that can run without a cooling system—a system designed to dissipate heat!

And lots more.

So maybe you see what happened to me when I read the article about the Class of 'fifty. The article peaked a tall pyramid inside me, brought everything to a sharp point.

"Have you a pencil?" said the young man. All this time and he hadn't yet lost the dazed look. I guess it was hard to blame him. "Pens are no good on paper napkins," he said.

I handed him my felt-tip. "Try this."

He tried it. "Hey, this is great. This is really keen." A felt-tip does fine on paper napkins. He studied it as if he had never seen such a thing before. "Really keen," he said again. Then he drew this:

"Yinyang," I said. "Right?"

He nodded. "One of the oldest symbols on Earth. Then you know what it means."

"Well, some anyway. All opposites—life and death, light and dark, male and female, heavy and light—anything that has an opposite."

"That's it," he said. "Well, let me show you something." Using another napkin, folded in two, as a straightedge, he lay it across the symbol.

"You see, if you were to travel in a straight line across a diameter—any diameter—you'd have to go on both black and white somewhere along the way. You can't go all the way on just one color without bending the line or going a short way, less than the diameter.

"Now let's say this circle is the board on which the game of human affairs is played. The straight line can be any human course—a life, a marriage, a philosophy, a business. The optimum course is a full diameter, and that's what most people naturally strive for; a few might travel short chords or bent ones—sick ones. Most people can and do travel the diameter. For each person, life, marriage, whatever, there's a different starting point and a different arrival point, but if they travel the one straight line that goes through the center, they will travel black country exactly as much as white, ying as much as yang. The balance is perfect, no matter which way you go. Got it?"

"I see what you mean," I said. "Your coffee's cold."

"So's yours. Now look: suppose some force came along and shifted one of these colors away from the center point, like this—" And he drew again.

We studied his drawing. He drew well and quickly.

He said, "You see, if the shift were gradual, then from the very second it began there would be some people—some lives, philosophies—who would no longer have that perfect balance between black and white, between ying and yang. Nothing wrong with the course they traveled—they still aim for the very center and pass on through.

"And if the shift continued to where I've drawn it, you can see that some people might travel all the way on the white only.

"And *that's* what has happened to us. *That's* the answer to what seems to be human stupidity. There's nothing wrong with people! Far and away most of them want to travel that one straight line, and they do. It isn't their fault that the rules have been changed and that the only way to the old balance for anyone is to travel a course that is sick or twisted or short.

"The coffee *is* cold. Oh, God, I've been running off at the mouth. You'll want to get back to the office."

"No, I won't," I said. "The hell with it. You go on." For somewhere along the line he had filled me with a deep, strange excitement. The things that he said had plagued him all his life—or things like them—had plagued me, too. How often had I stood in a voting booth, trying to decide between Tweedle-Dee and Tweedle-Dum, the Big Endians versus the Little Endians? Why can't you tell someone, "Honesty is the best policy—" or "do as you would be done by—" and straighten his whole life out, even when it might make the difference between life and death? Why do people go on smoking cigarettes? Why is a woman's breast—which for thousands of artists has been the source of beauty and for millions of children the source of life—regarded as obscene? Why do we manipulate to increase the cost of this road or that school so we can "bring in Federal money" as if the Federal money weren't coming from our own pockets? And since most people try to be decent and honest and kind—why do they do the stupid things they do?

What in the name of God put us into Viet Nam? What are ghettoes all about? Why can't the honest sincere liberals just shut up and quietly move into the ghettoes any time they can guarantee that someone from the ghetto can take their place in the old neighborhood—and keep right on doing it until there are no more ghettoes? Why can't they establish a country called Suez out of territory on both sides of the canal—and populate it from Israel and all the Arab countries and all the refugees and finance it with canal tolls and put in atomic power plants to de-salt seawater and make the desert bloom, and forbid weapons and this-or-that "quarters" and hatred? In other words, why are simple solutions always impossible? Why is any solution that does not involve killing people unacceptable? What makes us undercopulate and overbreed when the perfect balance is available to everybody?

And at this weary time of a quiet morning in the Automat, I was pinioned by the slender bright shard of hope that my dazed friend had answers.

Go back to the office? Really, the hell with it.

"You go ahead," I said, and he did.

III

Well, okay [he went on], I read that article about the class of '50—the Silent Generation—and I began to get mad-scared, and it grew and grew until I felt I had to do something about it. If the class of '50 ever got to run things, they'd have the money, they'd have the power. In a very real sense they'd have the guns. It would be the beginning of a long period—maybe forever—of more-of-the-sameness. There didn't seem any way to stop it.

Now I'd worked out this yingyang theory when I was a college sophomore, because it was the only theory that would fit all the facts. Given that some force had shifted the center, good people, traveling straight the way they should, had to do bad things because they could never, never achieve that balance. There was only one thing I didn't know.

What force had moved the center?

I sat in the office, dithering and ignoring my work, and tried to put myself together. *Courage, mon camarade, le diable est mort,* is what I said to myself. That mean anything to you?

No?

Okay—when I was a kid I read a book called *The Cloister and the Hearth,* by Charles Reade. It was about a kid raised in a monastery who went into the world—an eighteenth-century kind of world, or earlier, I forget now. Anyway, one of the people he meets is a crazy Frenchman, always kicking up his heels and cheering people up and at the worst of times that's what he'd say: *Courage, buddy— the devil is dead.* It stuck with me and I used to say it when everything fell apart and there seemed nowhere to turn and nothing to grab hold of. I said it now, and you know, it was like a flash bulb going off between my ears.

Mind you, it was real things I was fretting about, not myths or fantasies or religious principles. It was overpopulation and laws against fun and the Dust Bowl (remember that? Well, look it up some time) and nowhere to put the garbage, and greed and killing and cruelty and apathy.

I took a pad of paper and drew these same diagrams and sat looking at them. I was very excited. I felt I was very near an answer.

Ying and Yang. Good and evil—sure—but nobody who understands it would ever assign good to one color and bad to the other. The whole point is, they both have to be there and in perfect balance. Light and dark, male and female, closed and open, life and death, that-which-is-outgoing and that-which-comes-together—all of it, everything—opposition, balance.

Well now, for a long time the devil had a bad name. Say a bad press. And why not? Just for the sake of argument, say it is the yang country he used to rule and that is the one that was forced aside. Anyone living and thinking in a straight line could spend his whole life and career and all his thinking in ying country. He'd have to know that yang was there, but he'd never encounter it, never experience it. More than likely he'd be afraid of it because that's what ignorance does to people, even good people.

And the ones who did have some experience of yang, the devil's country, would find much more of the other as they went along, because the balance would be gone. And the more the shift went on, the more innocent, well-meaning, thoughtful people ran the course of their lives and thoughts, the worse they would think of the devil's country and the worse they would talk about it and him. It would get so you couldn't trust the books; they'd all been written from the one point of view, the majority side of imbalance. It would begin to look as if the yang part of the universe were a blot which had to be stamped out to make a nice clean all-ying universe—and you have your John Knox types and your Cotton Mathers: just good people traveling straight and strong and acting from evidence that was all wrong by reason that couldn't be rational.

And I thought, *That's it!*

The devil is dead!

I have to do something about it.

But what?

Tell somebody, that's what. Tell everybody, but let's be practical. There must be somebody, somewhere, who knows what to do about it—or at least how to explain about the yinyang and how it's gone wrong, so that everybody could rethink what we've done, what we've been.

Then I remembered the *Saturday Review*. The *Saturday Review* has a personal column in it that's read by all sorts of people—judging by the messages. But I mean *all* kinds of people. If I could write the right ad, word it just the right way.

I felt like a damn fool. Year of Our Lord 1950, turning all my skills as a professional copywriter to telling the world that the devil was dead, but it was an obsession, you see, and I had to do something, even something insane. I had to start somewhere.

So I wrote the ad.

> THE TROUBLE IS the light-bearer's torch is out and we're all on the same end of the seesaw. Help or we'll die of it. Whoever knows the answer call DU6-1212 Extension 2103.

I'm not going to tell you how many drafts I wrote or all the reasons why, copywise, that was best, mixed metaphors and all. I knew that whoever could help would know what I was asking.

Now comes the hard part. For you, I mean, not me. Me, I did what I had to. You're going to have to believe it.

Well, maybe you don't have to. Just—well, just suspend disbelief until you hear me out, okay?

All right. I wrote up the copy and addressed an envelope. I put on a stamp and a special delivery. I put in the copy and a check. I sealed it and crossed the hall—you know where the mail chute is—right across from my door. Your door. It was late by then, everyone had gone home and my footsteps echoed and I coud hear that funny whistle under the elevator doors. I slid the envelope into the slot and let go, and my phone rang.

I'd never heard it ring quite like that before. I can say that, yet I can't tell you how it was different.

I sprinted into the office and sat down and picked up the phone. I'm glad I sat down first.

There was this Voice . . .

I have a hell of an ear, you know that? I've thought a lot about that Voice and recalled it to myself and I can tell you what it was made of—a tone, its octave and the fifth harmonic. I mean if you can imagine a voice made of three notes, two an octave apart and the third reinforcing, but not really three notes at all, because they sounded absolutely together like one. Then, they weren't pure notes, but voice-tones, with all the overtones that means. And none of that tells you anything either, any more than if I described the physical characteristics of a vibrating string and the sound it produced—when the string happened to be on a cello played by Pablo Casals. You know how it is in a room full of people when you suddenly become aware of a single voice that commands attention because of what it is, not what it says. When a voice like that has, in addition, something to say—well, you listen.

I listened. The first thing I heard—I didn't even have a chance to say hello—was: "You're right. You're absolutely right."

I said, "Who is this?" and the Voice sighed a little and waited.

Then it said, "Let's not go into that. It would be best if you figured it out by yourself."

As things turned out, that was a hundred percent on target. I think if the Voice hadn't taken that tack I'd have hung up, or anyway wasted a lot of time in being convinced.

The Voice said. "What matters is your ad in the *Saturday Review.*"

"I just mailed it!"

"I just read it," the Voice said, then explained: "Time isn't quite the same here." At least I think that's what it said. It said, "How far are you willing to go to make everything right again?"

I didn't know what to say. I remember holding the phone

away from my face and looking at it as if it could tell me something. Then I listened again. The Voice told me everything I was going through, carefully, not bored exactly but the way you explain to a child that you know what's bothering him.

The Voice said, "You know who I am but you won't think the words. You don't want to believe any part of this but you have to and you know you will. You're so pleased with yourself for being right that you cannot think straight —which is only one of the reasons you can't think straight. Now pull yourself together and answer my question."

I couldn't remember the question, so I had to be asked once more—how far was I willing to go to make everything right again?

You have to understand that this Voice meant what it said. If you'd heard it, you'd have believed it—anybody would. I know I was being asked to make a commitment and that was pretty scary, but over and above that I knew I was being told that everything could be made right again —that the crazy tilt that had been plaguing mankind for hundreds, maybe thousands of years could be fixed. And I might be the guy to do it—me, for God's sake.

If I had any doubts, any this-can't-be kind of feelings— they disappeared. How far would I go?

I said, "All the way."

The Voice said, "Good. If this works you can take the credit. If it doesn't you take the blame—and you'll have to live with the idea that you might have done it and you failed. I won't be able to help you with that."

I said, anyway I'd know I'd tried.

The Voice said, "Even if you succeed you may not like what has to be done."

I said, "Suppose I don't do it—what will happen?"

The Voice said, "You ever read *1984*?"

I said I had.

The Voice said, "Like that, only more so and sooner. There isn't any other way it can go now."

That's what I'd been thinking—that's what had upset me when I read the article.

"I'll do it," is all I said.

The voice said that was fine.

It said "I'm going to send you to see somebody. You

have to persuade him. He won't talk to me and he's the only one who can do anything."

I began to have cold feet. "But who is he? Where? What do I say?"

"You know what to say. Or I wouldn't be talking to you."

I asked, "What do I have to do?"

And all I was told was to take the elevator. Then the line went dead.

So I turned out the lights and went to the door—and then I remembered and went back for my drawings of the yinyang, one as it ought to be and the other showing it out of balance. I held them like you'd hold an airline ticket on a first flight. I went to the elevators.

How am I going to make you believe this?

Well, you're right—it doesn't matter if you do or not. Okay, here's what happened.

I pushed the call button and the door opened instantly, the way it does once in a while. I stepped into the elevator and turned around—and there I was.

The door hadn't closed, the car hadn't moved. It all happened when I was turning around. The door was open, but not in the hallway on the twenty-first floor. The scene was gray. Hard gray outdoor ground and gray mist. I stood a while looking out and my heart was thumping like someone was pounding me on the back with fists. But nothing happened, so I stepped out.

I was scared.

Nothing happened. The gray fog was neither still nor blowing. Sometimes there seemed to be shapes out there somewhere—trees, rocks, buildings—but then there was nothing and maybe it was all a vast plain. It had an outdoors feel to it—that's all I can say for sure.

The elevator door was solidly behind me, which was reassuring. I took one step away from it—a little one, I'll have you know—and called out. It took three tries before my voice would work.

"Lucifer!"

A voice answered me. Somehow it wasn't as—well, as grand as the one I'd heard over the phone, but in other ways it was bigger.

It said, "Who is that? What do you want?"

It was cranky. It was the voice of someone interrupted,

someone who felt damn capable of handling the interruption, too. And this time there really was something looming closer through the fog.

I clapped my hands over my face. I felt my knees hit the gray dirt. I didn't kneel down, you understand. The knees just buckled as if they didn't belong to me any more. But hell, the wings. Bat's wings, leathery, and a tail with a point on it like a big arrowhead. That face, eyes. And thirty feet tall, man!

He touched my shoulder and I would have screamed like a schoolgirl if I'd had the breath for it.

"Come on now." It was a different voice altogether—he'd changed it—but it was his all the same. He said, "I don't look like that. That came out of your head. Here—look at me."

I looked. I guess it was funny, me kind of peeping up quickly so in case it was more than I could take I could hide my face again—as if that would do any good. But I'd had more than I could handle.

What I saw was a middle-aged guy in a buff corduroy jacket and brown slacks. He had graying hair and a smooth suntanned forehead and the brightest blue eyes I have ever seen. He helped me to my feet.

He said, "I don't look like this either, but—" he shrugged and smiled.

I said, "Well, thanks anyway—" and felt stupid. I looked around at the fog. "Where is this?"

He kind of waved his hand. "I can't really say. Where would you want it to be?"

How do you answer a question like that? I couldn't.

He could. He put the back of his hand against my cheek and gently turned my face toward him and bent close. He did something I can only describe as what you do when you pick up a magazine and run your thumb across the edge of the pages and flip it open somewhere. Only he did it inside my head somehow. Anyway there was a blaze of golden light that made me blink.

When I got my eyes adjusted to it the gray was gone. When I was a kid I worked one year on a farm in Vermont. I used to go for the cows in the late afternoon. The day pasture was huge, with a stand of pine at the upper end and the whole thing was steep as a roof, with granite outcroppings all over, gray, and white limestone. That's where we were, the very smell of it, the little lake with the dirt road around the end of it far down at the bottom and the wind hissing through the pine trees up there and a woodchuck ducking out of sight on the skyline. I could even see three of the Holsteins, standing level on the sidehill in that miraculous way they have as if they had two short legs and two long ones. I never did figure out how they do it.

And I got a flash of panic, too, because my elevator door was gone—but he seemed to know and just waved his hand casually over to my left. And there it was, a Rockefeller Center elevator door in the middle of a Vermont pasture. Funny. When I was fourteen that door in the pasture would have scared the hell out of me. Now I was scared without it. I looked around me and smelled the late August early evening and marveled.

"It's so real," is what I said.

"Seems real."

"But I was here—right here—when I was a kid."

"Seemed real then, too, didn't it?"

I think he was trying to make me rethink all along the line—not so much to doubt things, but to wipe everything clean and start over.

"Belief or nonbelief has no power over objective truth," is what he told me. He said that if two people believe the same thing from the same evidence, it means that they believe the same thing, nothing more.

While I was chewing on that he took the sketches out of my hand—the same ones I just did for you. I had quite forgotten I was holding them. He looked at them and grunted. "It's like that, is it?"

I took back the sketches and began to make my speech. I said, "You see, it's like this. Here the balance is—" and he kind of laughed a little and said wait, wait, we don't have to go through all that.

I think he meant, words. I mean he touched the side of my face again and made me face him and did that thing with his eyes inside my head. Only this time it was like taking both your thumbs and pulling open the pages of a book that are sort of stuck together. I wouldn't say it hurt but I wouldn't want much more of it either. I remember a single flash of shame that things I'd read, studied, things I'd thought out, I'd been careless with or had forgotten. And all the while—a very short while—he was digging in my head he was curing the shame, too. I began to understand that what he could get from me wasn't just what I'd learned and understood—it was everything, *everything* that had ever passed through my pipeline. And all in a moment.

Then he stepped back and said, "Bastard!"

I thought, what have I done?

He laughed at me. "Not you. *Him.*"

I thought, oh. The Voice on the phone. The one who sent me.

He looked at me with those sixty-thousand candle power eyes and laughed again and wagged his head.

"I swore I'd have nothing to do with him any more," he said, "and now look—he's thrown me a hook."

I guess I looked mixed-up, because I was. He began to talk to me kindly, trying to make me feel better.

He said, "It's not easy to explain. You've learned so much that just ain't so and you've learned it from people who also didn't understand. Couldn't. It goes back a long time. I mean, for you it does. For me—well, time is different here."

He thought a bit and said, "Calling me Lucifer was real bright of you, you know that? Lucifer means 'bringer of light.' If you're going to stick with the yinyang symbol— and it's a good one—you'll see that there's a center for the dark part and a center for the light—sometimes they're drawn in, a little dot on each part right where a pollywog's eye would be. I am that dot and the Voice you heard is the other one. Lucifer I may be, but I'm not the devil. I'm just the other. It takes two of us to make the whole. What I just might have overlooked is that it takes two of us to keep the whole. Really, I had no idea—" and he leaned forward and got another quick look inside my head—" no idea at all that things would get into such a mess so quickly. Maybe I shouldn't have left."

I had to ask him. "Why did you?"

He said, "I got mad. I had a crazy notion one day and wanted to try something and he didn't want me to do it. But I did it anyway and then when it got me into trouble he wouldn't pull me out of it. I had to play it all the way through. It hurt." He laughed a funny laugh. I understood that "it hurt" was a gigantic understatement. "So I got mad and cut out and came here. He's been yelling and sending messages and all, ever since, but I paid him no mind until you."

"Why me?"

"Yes," he said, "why you?" He thought it over. "Tell me something—have you got anything to keep you where you are? I mean a wife or a career or kids or something that would get hurt if you suddenly disappeared?"

"Nothing like that, no. Some friends—but no wife, no folks. And my job's just a job."

"Thought so," he said. Talking to himself, he said, "Bastard. Built this one from the ground up, he did. Knew damn well I'd get a jolt when I saw what a rotten mess this was." Then he said very warmly, "Don't take that personally. You can't help it."

I couldn't help it. I couldn't help taking it a little personally either.

Maybe I was a little sharp when I said, "Well—are you going to come back or not?"

He gave it right back to me.

"I really don't know," he said. "Why don't I leave it to you? You decide."

"Me?"

"Why not? You got yourself into this."

"Did I?"

"No matter how carefully he set you up for it, friend, he had to get your permission first. Right?"

I remembered that Voice. *How far are you willing to go?*

The one I had called Lucifer fixed me with the blazing eyes. "I am going to lay it right on you. I will do what you say. If you tell me to stay here, to stay out of it, it's going to be like Orwell said: 'To visualize the future you must visualize a boot stamping eternally on a human face.' But if I come back it's going to be almost as bad. Things are really out of hand, so much that it can't be straightened out overnight. It would take years. People aren't made to take the truth on sight and act on it. They have to be prodded and pushed—usually by being made so miserable in so many ways that they get mad. When enough of them get mad enough they'll find the way."

"Well, good then."

He mimicked me. I think he was a little sore and just maybe he didn't want to go back to work.

" 'Well, good, then,' " he mocked me. "We'll have to shovel stupidity on them. We'll have to get them into long meaningless wars. We'll make them live under laws that absolutely make no sense and keep passing more of them. We'll lay taxes on them until they can't have luxuries and comforts without getting into trouble and we'll lay on more until it hurts to buy enough just to live."

I said, "That's the same thing as the boot!"

He said, "No it isn't. Let the class of '50 take over and you'll have that. Orwell said *eternally* and he was right. No conflict, no dissent, no division, no balance. If I come back, there'll be plenty of all that. People will die—lots of them. And hurt—plenty."

"There's no other way?"

"Look," he said, "you can't give people what they want. They have to earn it or take it. When they start doing that there'll be bombings and riots and people—especially young people—will do what they want to and what works for them, not what they're told. They'll find their own ways— and it won't be anything like what grandpa said."

I thought about all that and then about the class of '50 and the stamping boot.

"Come back," I said.

He sighed and said, "Oh, God."

I don't know what he meant. But I think he was glad.

Suddenly—well, it seemed sudden—there was more light outside the Automat than inside. I felt as dazed as my friend looked.

I said, "And what have you been doing since nineteen fifty?"

He said, "Don't you understand? All this happened last night! Last night was nineteen fifty! I got back into the elevator and walked into my—your—the office and there you were!"

"And the dev—Lucif—whoever it was, he's back, too?"

"Time is different for him. He came back right away. You've already told me enough about what's been happening since then. He's back. He's been back. Things are moving toward the center again. It's hard to do, but it's happening."

I stuck my spoon into my cold old coffee and swirled it around and thought of the purposeless crime and the useless deaths and the really decent people who didn't know they were greedy, and a deep joy began to kindle inside me.

"Then maybe it's not all useless."

"Oh, God, it better not be," he whispered. "Because all of it is my fault."

"No it isn't. Things are going to be all right." As I said that I was sure of it. I looked at him, so lost and dazed and I thought, *I am going to help this guy. I am going to help him help me to understand better, to work out how we can bring it all into balance again.* I wondered if he knew he was a messiah, that he had saved the world. I don't think he did.

Sudden thought: "Hey," I said, "did he tell you why he dropped out mad like that? What was it—he did something the other one didn't want him to do?"

"Didn't I mention that? Sorry," said the dazed man. "He got tired of being a—a force. Whatever you call it. Spirit. He wanted to be a man for a while, to see what it was like. He could do it—but he couldn't get out of it again without the other's help. So he walked around for a while as a man."

"And?"

"And got crucified."

Dell Bestsellers

- [ ] **SHARKY'S MACHINE** by William Diehl $2.50 (18292-1)
- [ ] **EVERGREEN** by Belva Plain $2.75 (13294-0)
- [ ] **WHISTLE** by James Jones $2.75 (19262-5)
- [ ] **A STRANGER IS WATCHING**
  by Mary Higgins Clark $2.50 (18125-9)
- [ ] **SUMMER'S END** by Danielle Steel $2.50 (18418-5)
- [ ] **MORTAL FRIENDS** by James Carroll $2.75 (15789-7)
- [ ] **THE BLACK MARBLE**
  by Joseph Wambaugh $2.50 (10647-8)
- [ ] **MY MOTHER/MY SELF** by Nancy Friday $2.50 (15663-7)
- [ ] **SEASON OF PASSION** by Danielle Steel $2.25 (17703-0)
- [ ] **BAD BLOOD** by Barbara Petty $2.25 (10438-6)
- [ ] **THE SEDUCTION OF JOE TYNAN**
  by Richard Cohen $2.25 (17610-7)
- [ ] **GREEN ICE** by Gerald A. Browne $2.50 (13224-X)
- [ ] **THE TRITON ULTIMATUM**
  by Laurence Delaney $2.25 (18744-3)
- [ ] **AIR FORCE ONE** by Edwin Corley $2.50 (10063-1)
- [ ] **BEYOND THE POSEIDON ADVENTURE**
  by Paul Gallico $2.50 (10497-1)
- [ ] **THE TAMING** by Aleen Malcolm $2.50 (18510-6)
- [ ] **AFTER THE WIND** by Eileen Lottman $2.50 (18138-0)
- [ ] **THE ROUNDTREE WOMEN: BOOK I**
  by Margaret Lewerth $2.50 (17594-1)
- [ ] **TRIPLE PLATINUM** by Stephen Holden $2.50 (18650-1)
- [ ] **THE MEMORY OF EVA RYKER**
  by Donald A. Stanwood $2.50 (15550-9)
- [ ] **BLIZZARD** by George Stone $2.25 (11080-7)
- [ ] **THE DARK HORSEMAN**
  by Marianne Harvey $2.50 (11758-5)

At your local bookstore or use this handy coupon for ordering:

Dell **DELL BOOKS**
P.O. BOX 1000, PINEBROOK, N.J. 07058

Please send me the books I have checked above. I am enclosing $_____
(please add 75¢ per copy to cover postage and handling). Send check or money order—no cash or C.O.D.'s. Please allow up to 8 weeks for shipment.

Mr/Mrs/Miss_____

Address_____

City_____State/Zip_____

DREAM SNAKE

Vonda N. McIntyre

"Rich in character, background and incident—unusually absorbing and moving."

Publishers Weekly

"This is an exciting future-dream with real characters, a believable mythos and, what's more important, an excellent readable story."

Frank Herbert

The *"haunting, rich and tender novel"** of a unique healer and her strange ordeal.

** Robert Silverberg*

A Dell Book $2.25   (11729-1)